home truths

Susan Lewis is the bestselling author of over forty books across the genres of family drama, thriller, suspense and crime. She is also the author of *Just One More Day* and *One Day at a Time*, the moving memoirs of her childhood in Bristol during the 1960s. Following periods of living in Los Angeles and the South of France, she currently lives in Gloucestershire with her husband, James, stepsons, Michael and Luke, and mischievous dogs, Coco and Lulu.

To find out more about Susan Lewis:

www.susanlewis.com
www.facebook.com/SusanLewisBooks
@susanlewisbooks

Also by Susan Lewis

Fiction

A Class Apart
Dance While You Can
Stolen Beginnings
Darkest Longings
Obsession
Vengeance
Summer Madness
Last Resort
Wildfire
Cruel Venus
Strange Allure
The Mill House
A French Affair
Missing
Out of the Shadows
Lost Innocence
The Choice
Forgotten
Stolen
No Turning Back
Losing You
The Truth About You
Never Say Goodbye
Too Close to Home
No Place to Hide
The Secret Keeper
One Minute Later

Books that run in sequence

Chasing Dreams
Taking Chances

No Child of Mine
Don't Let Me Go
You Said Forever

Featuring Detective Andee Lawrence

Behind Closed Doors
The Girl Who Came Back
The Moment She Left
Hiding in Plain Sight
Believe in Me

Featuring Laurie Forbes and Elliott Russell

Silent Truths
Wicked Beauty
Intimate Strangers
The Hornbeam Tree

Memoirs

Just One More Day
One Day at a Time

Susan
LEWIS

home truths

HarperCollins*Publishers*

HarperCollins*Publishers* Ltd
The News Building
1 London Bridge Street
London SE1 9GF

www.harpercollins.co.uk

Published by HarperCollins*Publishers* 2019
1

A catalogue record for this book
is available from the British Library

ISBN HB: 978-0-00-828678-1
ISBN TPB: 978-0-00-828679-8

Typeset in Sabon LT Std by Palimpsest Book Production Ltd,
Falkirk, Stirlingshire

Printed and bound in Great Britain by CPI Group (UK) Ltd,
Croydon CR0 4YY

MIX
Paper from
responsible sources
FSC™ C007454

This book is produced from independently certified FSC™ paper
to ensure responsible forest management.
For more information visit: www.harpercollins.co.uk/green

To Rachel Parfitt
and to everyone who gives
so selflessly of their time and expertise
to help those in need

'Don't go! Please... Oh God, no, please don't...'

'I can't take any more, Angie. I swear... If you'd seen what I just have...'

'Whatever it is...'

'Our five-year-old son had a syringe in his hand,' he raged, almost choking on the words.

'Oh my God. Oh Steve...'

'I need to find Liam, and when I do I'm turning him in to the police along with every other one of those lowlife bastards...'

'No! *No!*'

He could still hear his wife screaming down the phone, begging him to stop as he tossed his mobile on to the passenger seat and steered the van, almost on two wheels, out of the street.

He'd had enough. He didn't care about the danger he was putting himself in, or what might happen after, he was too enraged for that. *You bastard! How dare you… He's a child, for God's sake…* The words circled endlessly through his head.

It took a while to get across town. He barely even saw the traffic, or the red lights that tried to delay him, as though giving him some time to think. He didn't want it. He was past thinking, past caring about anything other than the need to make this stop.

When he reached the hellish streets, the sore at the heart of the sprawling estate, he screeched to a halt on the infamous Colemead Lane and leapt out. He was so pumped with fury that his fists were already clenched, his muscles tensed for attack. His rationale had fled, along with his temper and sense of self-preservation.

He looked around, his eyes fierce. The mostly destitute houses with boarded-up windows and padlocked doors were as silent as graves. The tower blocks at the end with graffitied walls and urine-soaked stairwells rose drearily towards a patched grey sky. Even the pub looked deserted, its sign dangling from one hinge, its barred windows telling their own story.

'I know you're here,' he roared at the top of his lungs. 'Liam Watts! Get out here now!'

His rage echoed around the silence like useless gunshot scattering over a ghost town.

'*Liam Watts!* Show your face.'

Everything remained still.

Seconds ticked by as though the world was holding its breath, waiting to see what would happen next. He sensed he wasn't alone, that he was being watched, that this was a charged hiatus before the storm broke.

He was ready for it. His whole body was primed to take it.

There was a scuffling behind him, sharp yet muffled, and he spun round, heart thudding thickly with fury and fear, eyes blazing.

'Go home,' a wretched young woman hissed from a nearby doorway. She was thin, shaking, her eyes seeming to bleed in their sockets. She waved feebly in no particular direction before stumbling into a side alley and disappearing.

He didn't see them coming at first, he only heard them: faint, deliberate footsteps crunching, pounding, almost military in their pace. He peered around, trying to get a sense of where they were. How many they were.

'*Liam Watts!*' he roared again.

The sun slipped its cover of cloud, dazzling him, throwing a rich golden glow over the street, as though to paint this purgatory into something glorious.

He listened, hearing his heartbeat, hectic, scared; the sound of a dog barking, a scream cut suddenly short.

Then he saw them emerging from the shadows like ghouls, closing on him from each end of the street, slowly, purposefully, faces wrapped in black balaclavas, baseball bats and iron bars slapping into palms, chains rattling through brutal fingers.

As his survival instinct kicked in he turned to run. He couldn't take on this many. He'd be a fool to try. 'Liam,' he shouted, more panicked than angry now.

He reached the van, tore open the door, but it was too late. A flying brick hit his back, sending him sprawling into the dust.

He tried to scramble up.

A crippling blow to the backs of his knees buckled his legs under him.

'Liam,' he cried raggedly as he hit the ground.

A steel toe-capped boot slammed into his head.

He rolled on to his back, dazed, blood in his eyes. He could make out the faces gathered over him in a blur, laughing, as blind to his humanity as to their own.

He crossed his arms over his head to protect it. He tried in the chaos to spot Liam, to beg him to put a stop to this.

Time, reality, slipped to another dimension as his hearing faded and vicious blows continued pummelling his body. He thought of his other children, Grace and Zac, as more blood swilled around his eyes and his teeth were crunched from their roots.

He thought of his wife, his beautiful wife whom he loved with all his heart.

The thudding of boots and weapons grew worse, more frenzied, unstoppable; pain exploded through his body with a thousand jagged edges as bloodied vomit choked from his mouth. Darkness loomed, shrank away then tried to swallow him again. Dimly he heard screaming, a distant siren, and somewhere inside the mayhem he was murmuring his son's name, 'Liam, Liam,' until he could murmur no more.

CHAPTER ONE

'Come along in, no need to be shy.' Angie's smile was encouraging and jolly, and reflected all the natural kindness in her big, soft heart. She was a petite woman in her early forties with a fiery mop of disorderly curls, sky-blue eyes, a naturally pink mouth and freckles all over her creamy round cheeks. It was impossible to look at her without seeing sunshine and colour and all sorts of good things, even on the greyest of days.

Everyone loved Angie, and she loved them right back. Or most of them anyway; there were always exceptions.

Today's newcomer was Mark Fields, a wiry man in his late twenties with buckets of attitude (she'd been warned) and not much hair. He was apparently showing his timid side now, since his demeanour was quite guarded, and the little flecks of paper blotting up the shaving nicks in his cheeks made him seem vulnerable, or clumsy, probably both. In Angie's view it was easy to love beautiful people who washed regularly, ate healthily and lived under proper roofs with smart windows and secure front doors. It took an extra effort to empathize with those on the other side of the divide.

'Everyone!' she announced to the room at large. It was a big square kitchen that boasted a series of old-fashioned melamine units, a five-ring gas stove, a tall steamy casement window currently speckled with raindrops and old paint, and a grungy sitting area off to one side with a monster TV and a four-bar gas fire. For all its shabbiness and lack of feminine touch it was actually very cosy, she'd always thought. 'This is Mark,' she said, indicating the man she'd brought in with her, 'he's going to be taking over Austin's place here at Hill Lodge. Can we have a lovely welcome for him, please?'

The three men seated at a central Formica table, two in their twenties, the other past sixty, rose to their feet, stainless steel chair legs scraping over the lino floor. Their card game had been abandoned as soon as Angie had entered, for she was always the most welcome of visitors, notwithstanding that she was the only one. The eldest resident, Hamish, was showing the kind of smile that was rare for a man in his position, in that it was almost white with no missing teeth. He reached for Mark's scarred and bony hand, eager to welcome the stranger and get him off on the right foot. Hamish was the unofficial head of house, partly due to age, but mostly because of his avuncular manner and the fact that his chronic lung condition had earned him permanent residency.

His greeting, along with that of the two younger residents, Lennie and Alexei, both in their late twenties, was everything Angie could have hoped for, and indeed what she'd expected. This little family of misfits was nothing if not generous of spirit (when they weren't fighting for the remote control or whose turn it was in the bathroom), and she couldn't have felt prouder of them today if she were their mum. Given her age, she accepted that her maternal feelings were slightly off-kilter, but everything about this place was out of whack one way or another, so she wasn't going to waste any time worrying about the tenderness she felt for people who didn't get much of it elsewhere.

Hamish plonked the new housemate down at the table, asking if he played poker, and offering him a pile of the ring pulls they used for currency.

Lennie said, 'I'll put the kettle on.' Lennie had recently been taken on as an apprentice to a car mechanic and had been so thrilled by this that he'd hardly stopped grinning for a week. He'd tried to give Angie credit for finding him the job, his first in over five years with the best part of them spent on the streets, but she was having none of it. He'd gone through the proper channels at the jobcentre and won it on his own merits. And that, she'd told him, was how he was going to keep it.

Alexei, whose pugnacious face and lispy stammer were touchingly at odds with each other, had recently found employment too. He'd been taken on by John Lewis as a delivery driver, and he was so proud of being selected by such an upmarket store that Angie had to laugh at the little touch of snobbery from someone who'd not so long ago been sleeping in a bus shelter most nights of the week.

Fingers crossed he'd make a success of it, and never forget to take the medication intended to control his psychotic episodes. Thank God for the individuals and companies who gave second chances to those who were trying to turn their lives around. This little family all bore the scars of misfortune, whether drug addiction, alcohol abuse, homelessness, redundancy, marriage break-up, mental burnout, or prison, but they wouldn't have been at Hill Lodge if they hadn't already undergone a period of rehabilitation. Even so, they were at risk of falling back into old habits, as many did if they felt unable to cope with life or their new responsibilities, or became scared of people too ready to judge them harshly.

The fifth resident of Hill Lodge was young Craig, a slender, almost skeletal lad of twenty-three, with a riot of inky dark curls that tumbled around his beautiful face in a way that, in another existence, might have made him a male model, or even the pop star he longed to be. He was standing in front of the large kitchen fireplace – empty apart from an overflowing waste-paper basket and a well-worn trainer – watching proceedings with curious, hazel eyes. Angie smiled to beckon him forward. His gaze remained on the newcomer, studying him with frank intensity. It was hard for Angie to look at him without feeling an extra wave of affection, or a tug back into her past that was never welcome.

Cups of tea were soon being handed around, no sugar for Angie, two for everyone else, no biscuits – who half-inched the last digestives? Alexei, you toerag – when Craig finally stepped forward and went to stand in front of Mark. His expression was solemn, his stance stiff and awkward as he looked the older man up and down.

Clearly thrown by this scrutiny, Mark glanced at Angie, but before she could make the introduction Craig said, abruptly, '*You* are welcome here.'

Mark blinked and the others grinned.

Craig's eyes remained on Mark as he rose hesitantly to his feet, holding out a hand to shake. 'Thanks mate,' he mumbled.

Craig took a step back and watched in alarm as one of Mark's shaving papers floated like a petal down to the table.

'Don't take offence,' Hamish advised. 'It's just his way. Isn't it, Craig?'

Seeming not to hear, Craig turned around and reached for the guitar propped against the fireplace. After a few introductory chords that filled the kitchen with reasonably tuned sound he began to sing, 'Welcome to Wherever You Are'.

'Bon Jovi,' Lennie mouthed to Angie, in case she didn't recognize the number. Craig's renditions didn't always bear close resemblance to the originals; nevertheless, it was astonishing and touching the way he could come up with a song for most occasions.

When he finished, mid-chorus, mid-word even, he put the guitar down, bowed to his applauding audience and took the cuppa Lennie had poured for him. 'I'm getting together with some people later,' he informed everyone. 'We're going to form a band and make some videos.'

Angie glanced at Hamish, whose expression was saying, *I've no idea if it's real or imagined, but I'll plump for the latter.*

Craig said, 'One of them reckons he can get us some gigs at a pub on Moorside.'

It would be good to know that Craig was making friends provided she could be certain they were genuine, and not out to steal his guitar, or rough him up just for the fun of it.

Finishing her tea, Angie picked up her bag and rose to her feet. 'OK, I have to be going, guys, but tell me first, Alexei, are you remembering to take your medication?' He'd told her himself that he'd served four years for grievous bodily harm, and she'd been warned that he'd present a danger to society, and to himself, if he forgot, or decided to stop taking his drugs.

'Definitely,' he assured her, tapping a finger to his forehead in an odd sort of salute.

Hamish nodded confirmation, letting her know that he was keeping a close eye on it.

Hamish was a hero in the way he looked out for the residents as if they really were his family, watching them come and go, succeed and fail, struggle with everything from computers to cravings to job searches and even personal hygiene, always ready to lend a hand. She knew he was ex-forces and had served in the first Iraq war, but it was a time of his life he never wanted to discuss, although he had once admitted that he'd come back in a terrible state and had been turfed out by his wife. These days he'd probably be diagnosed as suffering with PTSD, she realized, although it still wasn't certain how much help he'd receive. He was as gently spoken and courteous as he was smartly turned out – always in a collar and tie when he left the house, frayed though it might be, shoes shining and trousers neatly pressed. And he was so grateful to have been made a permanent resident that he not only took care of this house and its small garden, but also the one next door that Angie's sister, Emma, managed for their organisation Bridging the Gap.

It was Angie and Emma's job to help the residents progress from all the difficulties they'd fought to overcome on the streets, in prison, in various shelters or rehab centres, back into a society where they could function as worthy and hard-working individuals.

As usual a barrage of questions followed her to the door as she left, mixed in with some teasing, and the merry tune of her mobile ringing. Seeing it was a resident from Hope House, presumably unable to get hold of Emma, she let it go to messages. She needed to get a move on now or a parking warden would start salivating over her little van like he'd just found a tasty sandwich still in its wrapper, and didn't want be late for her afternoon stint at the food bank.

As she closed the front door behind her, satisfied that all was well inside for now, she started along the front path and with each step she felt herself becoming aware of her thoughts moving ahead of her across the street, and over the rooftops to a terraced house on the avenue behind. It was where she and Steve had lived when they'd first come to Kesterly, almost fourteen years ago, in a cramped and draughty second-floor flat that Steve, with his wonderful enthusiasm and decorator's skills, had transformed into a warm and welcoming home.

She could hear Liam, aged five, calling out for his dad to come and read him a story. 'Daddy! Giraffe, monkey, pelly,' and minutes later Steve would be rolling up laughing at his favourite Roald Dahl story. Liam always chose it because of how much it made his daddy laugh, and Angie would stand outside the door listening, loving them with all her heart and wishing Liam was able to read it himself.

'He'll get there,' Steve's mother always assured them, 'he's just a late learner, that's all. You wait, before you know it he'll be streets ahead of everyone else and you won't be able to keep up with him.'

Due to her role as a teaching assistant at the local school, Angie was able to monitor his progress, and it definitely wasn't happening at the same rate as other kids his age. On the other hand he was always so happy and eager to try new things, and even when he was teased or left out of a game he never seemed to get upset. He'd just laugh along with the others, not caring that he was the butt of the joke, and if anyone ever appeared sad he'd quickly invite them home to play trains or do some colouring with him and his dad.

'He's a special boy,' Hari Shalik, Steve's boss, would often say, ruffling Liam's hair and smiling down at the small upturned face in a grandfatherly way.

'Can I come and work for you when I'm grown up?' Liam would sometimes ask.

Hari's chuckle rang with notes of surprise and delight. 'Of course, if it's what you still want when the time comes, but you might have other ideas by then.'

'He's going to fly to the moon, aren't you, Liam?' Steve would prompt.

Liam's nod was earnest and slow until he broke into a grin and wrapped his arms around his daddy's legs. 'Only if you come with me,' he whispered.

'Well, I wouldn't let you go on your own.'

'Can we take Mummy?'

'I think we should.'

To Hari Liam said, 'Mummy's going to have a baby.'

Hari's golden-brown eyes widened with interest. 'So you'll have a brother or a sister? Will you take them to the moon as well?'

Liam thought about it. 'They might be too small, so they'll have to stay with Granny Watts until we come back.'

'Good idea, and don't forget to let me know when you're going so I can come and give you a good send-off.'

Recalling that conversation now as she drove away from Hill Lodge, Angie was smiling at how precious and pure those memories were, like long hot summer days before autumn came to shadow the sunlight, and rain began falling like tears from gathering clouds.

CHAPTER TWO

Emma was Angie's younger sister by a year and several months. She was also plumper and louder, happily divorced and a hard-working mother of two small boys. She had a similar abundance of fiery red hair to Angie's, and the same arresting blue eyes that changed shade according to her mood.

The two of them had taken over at Bridging the Gap about a year ago after Angie had lost her job as a teaching assistant (cuts to the education budget), and Emma had no longer been required as a receptionist at a local dentist's after it was absorbed into the Kesterly Health Centre. It was pure luck that the husband-and-wife team who'd been running Bridging the Gap since its inception had decided to retire at that time, and Ivan, the parish manager of St Mary's, the local church, had decided to give the sisters a chance.

'Why not?' he'd agreed, in the slow, doleful tones that had unnerved Angie and Emma at first. 'You've excellent references, the pair of you, and we could do with some younger and livelier input around here. Yes, you'll suit us very well, and I hope we'll suit you too. Just make sure there's no dossing in the church, or anywhere else on the site.'

'Don't worry, we promise to go home at night,' Emma had assured him with mock sincerity.

Ivan blinked, taking a moment to understand, but he didn't seem to find it funny. 'I was referring to the men you'll be taking care of,' he explained. 'Or, more accurately, to their associates from the streets. There are shelters for them to go to at night and this church isn't one of them. Nor are the residences we are fortunate to have use of.'

Both of Bridging the Gap's properties belonged to an octogenarian recluse, Carlene Masters, who had apparently handed the rundown Victorian villas to St Mary's to use as the vicar and parish committee saw fit while she went to live in Spain. All she required in return was a small rental income. Angie and Emma had never met her, but they did know that she'd waived the rent for two months during the introduction of universal credit. Since housing allowances were what paid the rent and contributed to BtG's running costs, the change of system could have proved disastrous for the organization and residents alike when payments had dried up for weeks on end.

Now, as Angie went to update the whiteboard that dominated one wall of the shed-like office she and Emma worked from, she spotted a couple of parish outreach workers crossing the small courtyard outside and gave them a wave. From the large plastic sacks the two women were carrying it was clear they were on their way to the storeroom next door, where charity-shop rejects were kept before being sent to those in need overseas. They were the only people Angie and Emma ever saw at this end of the rambling church complex, apart from Ivan who occasionally dropped by to make sure everything was running as it should.

Their little enclave was tucked in behind the church hall and sheltered by a magnificent copper beech tree, and contained only their bunker of an office with its en suite loo, tiny kitchenette and semi-efficient heating, and the adjacent storeroom. Their window looked out over the courtyard where a sealed-up wishing-well served as a bird table and a high, thorny hedge separated them from the main road beyond. To get to the church they had to follow a stone pathway through a wilderness of old fruit trees and long-forgotten shrubs to connect up with the car park next to St Mary's offices, where the vicar's wife and parish manager carried out God's admin work.

The rectory was the other side of the centuries-old church, looking out over a sprawl of suburban rooftops that ended way off in the distance where the sea could be glimpsed sparkling away like a feast of temptation on crystal clear days. The old graveyard meandered gently down the south-facing hillside for at least a quarter of a mile to the busy residential street below. This was where Hill Lodge and Hope House were situated, in amongst a number of similar formerly grand villas, most of which had now been converted to flats. Angie and Emma never took the route through the tombstones and neglected shrines; no one did, it was too creepy and far too overgrown. Whoever needed burying these days was ferried to the newer, more desirable cemetery in the nearby semi-rural suburb of Morton Leigh.

'So what's your new bloke like?' Emma asked as Angie added Mark Fields's name to the Hill Lodge section of the whiteboard.

Raising her eyebrows as a fierce gust of wind whistled around their red-tiled roof Angie said, 'He seems OK. Early days though. If he doesn't settle in, Hamish will be sure to let us know.'

'What's his story?'

Spotting the outreach ladies leaving, heads down as they battled the wind, Angie said, 'Apparently he broke up with his wife after he was laid off work, and ended up with nowhere to stay when she got the house. Booze played a part in it somewhere, but Shawn, who referred him from the rehab clinic, says he's been a regular at AA for over six months and is ready to start again.'

'No history of violence?'

'Not that I'm aware of.'

Emma looked both dubious and cautious. 'He knows he'll be out on his ear if he starts drinking again?' she pressed.

'He does, but let's assume that he won't. Did Douglas get hold of you?'

'Douglas from Hope House? Yes, he did. Apparently he's lost weight so his belt's too big and his trousers are falling down. He wants to know how to make a new hole.'

Angie's eyes danced with amusement. 'So what did you tell him?' she asked, able to gauge from Emma's expression that some sort of irreverence was afoot.

'I said that if he took himself to Timpson's in town someone there would be able to help him. He, of course, wanted to do it himself with a hammer and nail, but I reminded him that the last time he'd had those objects in his hands someone had ended up attached to the wall.'

Angie had to laugh. It wasn't funny really, but the way Emma told it made it sound like a comedy sketch rather than a crime that had ended with his victim in hospital and him behind bars. 'Do you think the belt story was real?' she probed.

'No idea, but it might be worth asking Hamish to pop in later to make sure there's no live art hanging over the fireplace.'

Choking on another laugh, Angie checked her mobile as it rang. Seeing it was Tamsin, a support worker from the main homeless shelter in town, she clicked on. 'Hi Tams,' she said, returning to her desk, 'If you've got any referrals I'm afraid we're all booked up at the moment.'

'I wish it were so simple,' Tamsin responded with a sigh. 'I'm hoping you or Emma could collect my kids from school when you go for your own.'

Angie said, 'It's OK, I'll take them back to mine.'

'You're an angel.'

'So they keep telling me. What I say is, you just haven't met my demons yet.' The instant the words were out she wanted to take them back, return them to the dark and awful place they'd come from, but it was too late. They'd already spilled along the connection, doing their damnedest, and as she looked at her sister she could imagine only too well what both Emma and Tamsin were thinking. *Oh, but we have, Angie, we know what you did to your own son, but we won't talk about it, and we won't mention what happened to his father either.*

CHAPTER THREE

'I hope you're not peeping,' Steve warned, glancing at Angie who was next to him in the car, hands over her eyes, as instructed. 'Or you,' he added, checking six-year-old Liam in the rear-view mirror.

'Can't see anything,' Liam promised.

Satisfied they weren't cheating, Steve signalled to turn into a cul-de-sac of twenty mock-Tudor new builds, each with leaded windows and its own small plot of land, front and back. He drew up outside number fourteen, just behind a skip and a few plaster-caked wheelbarrows – though the work was at an end the clearing up was still under way.

Opposite the smart detached residences with their red brick façades and artfully placed wooden beams was a freshly laid green with a stony brook babbling along on the far side sheltered by a couple of magnificent weeping willows and an ironwork footbridge that linked this street to the next.

'Can we look yet?' Liam urged from the back. His auburn

curls were still damp from a quick swim in the sea and his round cheeks were flushed with excitement. Liam loved surprises, especially when they were a secret from his mother as well.

Steve grinned as Angie parted her fingers, pretending to take a peek. 'OK, you can look now,' he announced.

As Angie lowered her hands she gazed around the street of brand spanking new houses, not quite understanding.

'Oh Dad! There's a bridge,' Liam exclaimed in awe, and as though his father had just given him the best thing ever he leapt out of the back to go and investigate.

As they watched him, Angie said, 'Are we on the Fairweather estate?'

'We are,' Steve confirmed.

'And you,' she continued to guess, 'worked on these houses so you've brought us to see them before their new owners move in?'

'Kind of,' he smiled, and getting out of the compact Peugeot they'd bought for her a couple of years back, he came round to open her door.

'Dad! Dad! Look at me,' Liam cried from the bridge, and making certain Steve was watching he raced across it and back again, looking so pleased with himself that Steve wanted to go and swing him up so high he'd scream with delight. He still wasn't learning as quickly as other children, but it didn't make him stupid, it was simply that his progress was happening at a different speed. In every other way he was an adorable, playful, and happy young boy who wanted no more than to be everyone's friend.

Steve and Angie sometimes wondered if Liam's shortcomings were what made him even more special. Certainly they brought out his father's protective instincts in a way nothing else ever had. However, they were careful not to smother or overindulge him. They just wanted him to feel like any other child of his age and to know that even when the new baby came, which would be any day now, he would still be their number one.

After almost six years and four heart-breaking miscarriages, Liam was at last going to have a little sister.

'OK, I give up, what are we supposed to be looking at?' Angie demanded as Steve tugged her out of the car.

'It's the bridge,' Liam insisted as he ran back to join them.

'Not quite,' Steve replied, 'although it's a part of it,' and stooping so Liam could jump on his back, he turned towards the double-fronted house in front of them. 'This, my darling,' he said to Angie, feeling so much pride and happiness welling up in him it was hard to keep his voice steady, 'is our new home.'

Angie blinked, looked at it and then at him. 'But we can't afford anything like this,' she protested.

It was true, they couldn't, although Steve certainly earned well. His skills as a painter and decorator and all-round Mr Fix-It were always in high demand, but he was so keen for them all to have everything they wanted – her car, Liam's extra classes, his own sports gear, great holidays – that they'd never managed to save very much. However, now their family was growing they needed somewhere bigger than the small flat they'd been squashed into for the past couple of years. 'We don't have to buy it,' he explained. 'Hari is going to let us rent it from him at a price we can afford.'

Angie's mouth fell open as her eyes lit with disbelief and the first hint of excitement.

Apart from being Steve's boss, Hari Shalik had become like a father figure to them since they'd arrived in Kesterly. In fact, he was the reason they'd moved to this coastal town in the first place. Someone had told him about the high quality of

Steve's work, so Hari had tried him out on a six-month contract and after three months he'd offered to put Steve in charge of all his development projects if he would agree to move his family to the area. So Steve and Angie had come here with Liam and although Steve effectively remained his own boss, meaning he was free to take on other jobs when Hari had no need of him, most of his work came either from, or through his mentor. Hari was a good man, wise and patient, always fair, and he made it plain that if they ever hit any difficulties they must always come to him. Since Steve's father had died when he was very young, this had meant a lot to him.

'So let me get this straight,' Angie said, 'after building all these beautiful houses…'

'Hari didn't build them,' Steve came in, 'he invested in the project and gave me the job of painting, decorating and finishing off the ones he'd earmarked for himself. There are two on this street – he's already sold the other, no doubt at an enormous profit – and half a dozen semis just over the bridge. He's going to be renting them out too, so I've already put Emma and Ben forward as prospective tenants.'

Angie was still staring at him in amazement.

Knowing she was absorbing the idea of having her beloved sister nearby, Steve marked himself up another point and said with a grin, 'I've got the keys.'

'But…' Words were still clearly failing her, until she broke into helpless laughter. 'Why on earth would Hari give us something like this*?' she cried.*

'He told me it's his way of saying thanks for all the deadlines I've helped him keep, and holes I've dug him out of.'

'But an entire house…'

'We're renting it,' he reminded her, 'and he's promised it'll always be at a price we can afford.'

'Does Roland know about it?' she asked, referring to Hari's

son who was a few years older than Steve, and openly resentful of Steve's closeness to his father.

'I've no idea,' Steve replied. 'Now, come on, let's go inside and take a look.'

It was a dream home for them, with more space than they were able to imagine filling, and it exuded such a welcoming air that it seemed to embrace them the minute they walked in. To the right of the hall with its wide wooden staircase and built-in cupboards was a huge family-cum-play-room that went all the way from the front to the back of the house, where floor-to-ceiling French doors – still criss-crossed with manufacturers' tape – opened on to a newly laid patio.

'I thought I could put my piano here,' Steve indicated a dusty space just inside the doors, 'that way you can hear me playing when you're outside drinking wine in the garden.' The piano had been in storage since his mother's death three years ago because they'd had nowhere to put it, and he missed it more than he'd expected to.

'You can have the piano wherever you like,' Angie told him, looking misty-eyed, 'just as long as you promise to sing Nat King Cole songs whenever I ask.'

'It's a deal,' he laughed, pressing a kiss to her forehead. 'Now what's going on with you up there?' he asked Liam, who was still riding on his father's back. 'You've gone very quiet.'

In a worried voice Liam said, 'Will I be moving in too?'

Swinging him round into his arms, Steve said, 'We'd never go anywhere without you, my boy. This is going to be your home from now on, and because you're the oldest you get to choose your room first.'

Lighting up at that, Liam said, 'Can I have this one?'

'For playing and entertaining,' Steve promised, 'but you need a bedroom, so why don't you run upstairs and decide which one you want?'

As Liam zoomed off Steve put an arm round Angie and led her across the hall to the sitting room that felt as though it was waiting for them. He explained how he envisaged fitting in two large sofas and an armchair, a good-sized TV and an eight-seater dining table and chairs at the far end for when they had guests. Next came the kitchen, not huge, but at least four times the size of the one they had now, with pale oak veneer cabinets, a double sink, and mock-granite worktops. There was space for a small table and chairs, also for one of the big American-style fridge-freezers they'd always promised themselves they'd get one day. There was even a separate alcove for the washing machine and tumble dryer.

'Obviously everything's brand new,' Steve announced like a salesman, 'from the heating, to the electrics, to the plumbing, all the kitchen units... We've even got a dishwasher.'

As he laughed, Angie slid her arms around him. 'You might have to pinch me,' she said, 'because I'm still trying to take it in.'

Holding her face between his hands, he said, 'Just tell me you think we can be happy here.'

'Of course we can,' she murmured. 'I can be happy anywhere as long as I'm with you.'

Although it was the answer he'd expected, it still made his heart soar to the stars. He loved his wife a thousand times more than he'd ever be able to put into words. 'I'm getting carried away with everything,' he said, 'but you know all the decisions will be yours. All I want is a small space for the piano.'

'And a barbecue built into the terrace,' she teased, 'and swings, slides, sandpits for the children, and a shed somewhere to keep your surfing gear.'

Smiling at the way she read him so easily, he kissed her tenderly, hoping to feel the baby fluttering against him, but she – Grace they were going to call her – was so close to arriving now that there wasn't much room for her to move.

'Found it!' Liam yelled from the top of the stairs. 'Can I have a bed like an aeroplane? Preston Andrews has got one and it's really cool.'

'Do you feel up to climbing the stairs?' Steve asked.

Angie shook her head. 'Not right at this moment, but tell me what's up there.'

'Not three, but four bedrooms,' he declared as if even he was still trying to believe it, 'the master has room for an en suite if we want one, but there's a really big bathroom with a walk-in shower that I know you're going to love. I did it myself, using the tiles you picked out when I told you Hari was trying to make up his mind which way to go.'

Eyebrows raised, she said, 'So how long have you known he was going to let us rent this place?'

'Only a couple of days. When I worked on it I had no idea.'

Turning at the sound of Liam thundering down the stairs, Steve shouted, 'We're through here.'

Finding them, Liam cried, 'I can't wait to bring all my friends here. They're going to love it.'

'And they'll all be very welcome,' Steve assured him, knowing how much it meant to his son to have friends, even those who didn't always treat him well.

CHAPTER FOUR

It was early on Sunday morning. Angie was in the bathroom staring through specks of water on the mirror's surface at her tired blue eyes as they assessed her reflection. It was as though it belonged to someone else, someone who looked vaguely like her; a kind of clone living another life over there in an alternative world.

Angie through the looking glass.

Maybe, in that elusive back-to-front place, things were actually as they should be, continuing unassumingly, happily, along the path she'd been on since she and Steve had moved to Kesterly fourteen years ago. OK, she'd understood that the odd curve ball could be lobbed in from out of the blue now and again, meaning tears had to be dried and hurdles overcome. Sometimes, Liam was picked on at school, and three miscarriages had followed Grace's birth, making a total of seven altogether. In spite of the challenges they'd loved being parents right from the start; holding Liam in their arms knowing he belonged to them, that he was them, had made them feel as though they'd found the right way in the world. They were meant to create a family full of love and laughter, understanding and adventure, and for the most part that was how it had been. Now their youngest, Zac, was soon to be seven, making six years between each of the children, though somehow it had never seemed to matter – until one day they'd realized that it did.

The first time Liam had been brought home by the police he was only eleven – *eleven*. His PE teacher had found a stash of drugs in his school bag and instead of contacting them he'd reported it. It was all a big mistake, of course, Liam didn't even know what drugs were, much less how to get hold of them – or so they'd believed at the time. It was only later that they'd discovered how wrong they were, how life had already started slow-rolling the worst curve ball of all.

In the weeks and months that followed, the problems increased in ways they'd never have imagined possible for their sweet-natured little boy who'd always been desperate to be noticed, to feel he belonged, to impress those he considered friends. They seemed to lose all connection with him as he was sucked deeper and deeper into the worst kind of crowd. He all but stopped going to school, and began spending his days hanging around street corners and municipal parks with kids from the notorious Temple Fields estate, thinking he was as cool and smart as them when he was anything but. They used him, abused him, had fun at his expense and he never saw them as anything but heroes. When he was expelled from school he wore his disgrace like a badge of honour and reviled his parents for trying to punish him. He began disappearing for days on end, and after the first few occasions the police simply told them that he'd come back when he was ready. His known involvement with the Satan Squad, as the biggest gang on the estate had ingloriously named itself, made him of far less interest to the overstretched authorities than any normal child of his age would be.

No one had ever told his parents about the county line gangs that infiltrated small communities, priming local gangs to prey on vulnerable children and turning them into couriers or addicts, or both. They'd had no idea until it was already too late just how cruelly Liam was being exploited, manipulated and brainwashed by forces so evil that neither Angie nor Steve knew how to combat them. Even the police seemed to struggle. By the time he was fourteen they'd lost all contact with the sweet, innocent boy he'd been. He behaved as though he despised them.

Steve became gaunt with worry, so stressed and fearful that it began affecting his health. Each time the police knocked at the door they expected the worst, that Liam had been stabbed, or he'd overdosed, he was in prison or he'd killed someone. Usually the police came because he was thought to be a witness to a crime, but they never found him at home.

It was the day Steve spotted five-year-old Zac with an old syringe, making to jab it into his arm, that he'd finally lost it.

Angie hadn't been at home; if she had maybe she could have stopped him. As it was she'd been at the end of the phone when he'd said, 'I've had enough, Ange. He's no longer a son of mine.'

'Don't say that, Steve. Just tell me what's happened. Where is he?'

'I don't know, but I'm going to find him and when I do…'

'Steve,' she cried in a panic. "Don't go! *Please…* Oh God, no, please don't…'

'I can't take any more, Angie. I swear… If you'd seen what I just have…'

'Whatever it is…'

'Our five-year-old son had a syringe in his hand.'

She'd all but choked on the horror. 'Oh my God. Oh Steve…'

'I've got to go,' he told her. 'I need to find Liam, and when I do I'm turning him in to the police along with every other one of those lowlife bastards…'

'No! *No!*' but the line had already gone dead.

She'd arrived home fifteen minutes later to find the house with its front door wide open, and no sign of Steve or his van. She tried telling herself that he wouldn't actually go to that terrible estate, that he'd turn off and stop somewhere to calm down. But he wasn't answering his phone and a sickening, terrifying intuition was taking hold of her.

It was around five in the evening when a female detective came to tell her what had happened on the estate. Angie would never forget the earth-shattering moment when her world had spun out of control. They'd beaten Steve to death. With iron bars, clubs, chains and heavy boots they'd laid into him with so much savagery that they hadn't been able to stop, this was how a lawyer later described it in court.

Five of the attackers were arrested and charged the same day; Liam had also been taken in, but Angie received a call twenty-four hours later to tell her he'd been released on police bail.

'Where is he now?' she asked the officer who'd rung to let her know, her throat raw and tight with grief, her head gripped in a throbbing vice. Grace sat with her, holding her hand, dabbing away their tears, while Emma took charge of Zac and her own two boys. Angie felt almost as horrified by the thought of Liam coming home as she did by the fact that Steve never would.

It turned out no one knew where Liam had gone. He didn't show up that day, or the next. Apparently he'd been present during the attack on his father. He'd told the police that he'd tried to stop it, and realizing he wasn't the entire full shilling, as one insensitive officer had described him, they'd held back on charges for the time being.

He came home eventually, three days after his release, so foul-smelling and spaced out that he could barely speak. Angie didn't even let him in the door.

'Get out!' she'd yelled into his stupefied face. 'Get out of this house and don't ever come back. You're dead to me, do you hear that? *Dead, dead, dead.*'

What she hadn't spared a thought for that day, or many days after, was what it must have been like for Liam to watch his father die in such a horrific attack. How had he felt when he'd realized he had no power to stop it, for she didn't want to believe he'd been a part of it. No! No matter what else he was capable of, he surely to God didn't have it in him to murder the father he'd once loved so much. Afterwards, he just hadn't been able to cope with what had happened, and then his mother had lost her mind and told him he was dead to her.

During the months following Steve's funeral, Angie had thought so much about Hari, their dear friend and landlord who she knew would have done anything to help her had he not lost his battle with leukaemia the year before. Having no other stabilizing or fatherly influence to guide her she'd acted alone, doing everything she could to find Liam, even venturing into the dreaded zone of Temple Fields when everyone had warned her to stay away. The streets, tower blocks, shops, pubs, were not so very different to any other housing estate on that side of town, at least on the outside. On the inside… things were different. Every other window was boarded up, burned-out cars lurked like decaying teeth between shinier new ones, the stench of urine, cooking and vomit soured stairwells, and a chilling sense of menace filled the air. The families and fellow gang members of those in custody for Steve's murder were all in this area, and she was sure she could feel them watching her. No one wanted to talk to her; a pub landlord told her to go home if she knew what was good for her, and aware of the hostility and resentment her intrusion had triggered, she remembered her other children and took his advice.

The police hadn't been interested when she'd tried to report Liam missing. Given his age and who he'd hung out with they didn't even bother filing a report. As far as they were concerned the London gang that controlled him had reeled him in and no doubt set him loose on some other undeserving community a long way from here. Though Angie knew how likely that was, she'd still tried the homeless shelters, rehab centres, helplines, missing person charities, Salvation Army and even the government's prisoners location services in her efforts to find him. If she'd had the money she'd have hired a private detective, but with Steve's income gone and her own barely covering the rent that she now paid to Roland Shalik, Hari's son, she'd already had to apply for benefits to help keep her reduced family going. Then, due to cutbacks in the local education budget, she'd lost her job as a teaching assistant. It had been the last straw. Grace had come home that day to find her mother scratching herself frenziedly, tearing her clothes, sobbing and begging God to tell her what to do.

Summoned by Grace, Emma had rushed straight over, rung the doctor, and eventually, between them they'd managed to calm Angie down. The sedative knocked her out until the following morning, and when she'd woken she'd been too groggy to remember much of what had happened. It had come back to her during the day and realizing how much she'd frightened her daughter, and her sister, she'd vowed to herself and to them that it would never happen again. She needed to get herself back in control, and to find another job before someone turned up from social services to take her children into care.

Two weeks later, after a soul-crushing interview at the jobcentre, Emma had called, all excitement, to tell her about the opening at Bridging the Gap.

Exactly why their predecessors had decided to recommend her and Emma as their replacements to run the organization's two transition houses, Angie had no idea. What she did know was that it had been a lifesaver for her in so many ways, not least of all because it allowed her to focus on those in a far more vulnerable state than she was, and to take heart from their courage. It was as though helping them back to a better world was helping her too, and though she'd never admitted this to anyone, Craig at Hill Lodge had soon come to represent Liam. They even looked vaguely alike for her, with the same ragged mop of curly hair and lazy gait. Craig was older, but his learning difficulties made him seem younger, and Angie had it fixed in her head that as long as she took care of this boy, someone else somewhere would take care of Liam.

Liam was turning nineteen today and she still had no idea where he was.

He could be dead.

This was her biggest fear, the one that kept her awake at nights, that tore at her conscience so savagely that she wanted to scream as though noise could somehow drown the pain and madness of it all. Even after everything that had happened, the mother in her continued to see past all the horror and heartache to the small boy who'd never even thought about harming anyone. He hadn't had it in him before the gangs had got hold of him, and she'd asked herself many times why they'd picked on him, what – or who – had really been behind the grooming and corruption of her and Steve's innocent boy.

Steve. Oh God, Steve.

She missed him more than she could ever have imagined possible, and it wasn't getting any easier. If anything it was becoming worse.

'Mum?'

Angie was still at the bathroom mirror rigidly trapped in the worst time of her life, but as her eyes moved to the other face reflected behind hers, a smaller, younger image of her own, and yet like her father too, she felt her limbs start to relax.

'Grace,' she said, and bringing up a smile she was aware of her anxiety retreating into a small, contained ball, as love for her thirteen-year-old daughter eclipsed it. 'What are you doing up so early?'

Grace's normally bright eyes were circled with shadows of worry, and grief – Angie must never forget that the children were suffering too. Two years had passed, and she wasn't sure any of them were close to getting over what had happened to Steve. Grace and Zac had loved their father every bit as much as she had, and the last thing they needed was to feel afraid that she couldn't cope. It was how she often felt, but she must never let it be true.

Except it was already true.

'I could ask you the same question,' Grace responded. 'It's Sunday. I thought we were having a lie-in.'

Relieved that Grace hadn't come into the bathroom to find her mother filling the luxury shampoo bottle with the same colour washing-up liquid, a regular occurrence, Angie said, 'And so we are. Come on, let's go and snuggle up under the blankets.'

It was still only seven o'clock; the heating was due to kick in at eight – always later at weekends, even if they had to get up early for one reason or another. Every little saving helped, or it was supposed to anyway. She wasn't sure that the smart meter she'd had installed was really onside, for it wasn't making anything less expensive, it just kept going round and round like a horror ride at the fairground, showing her how much it was all costing.

She wouldn't have minded a cup of tea, something warm to help soothe her gently into the day, but it took electricity to heat the kettle and they were going to need what was left on her key card for showers in a while. She just hoped the remaining credit would be enough to cover all bases, since the post office was closed on Sundays and so were the nearest PayPoints.

She should have sorted it out yesterday while everything was open, and she would have had she not needed to put petrol in Steve's van, now hers – five pounds' worth instead of ten, so there was enough left over to give Grace some spending money for bus fare and a coffee in town with her friends. The other twenty in her purse had gone to Lidl, so at least there was food in the cupboard – for now.

It was the roll-out of universal credit fourteen months ago that had tipped her from the precarious edge of just about managing into the terrifying downward spiral she was now caught in. Nine entire weeks had passed without any benefits at all, so she'd simply been unable to pay her bills. True, she'd still had her widow's pension – something they hadn't taken into the universal system for some reason – but thirty-four pounds a week was an impossible sum for a single person to live on, never mind a family. The only way she'd managed to survive was by running up her credit cards, going overdrawn at the bank and selling her car. Her rent, council tax and utility bills had gone into arrears and that was how they remained, with the outstanding amounts getting bigger all the time. She could no longer bear to open the envelopes when they dropped ominously through the letterbox like voices with only doom to deliver.

She was receiving her benefits again now, but she was two hundred crucial pounds a month worse off than before, over three hundred if she counted the loss of her widow's pension. That was only paid for the first year following a death so it had run out eleven months ago, and she supposed she had to feel thankful that Steve had been forty-five by the time he died, any younger and she'd have got nothing.

Her head began hurting as she ran through everything she had to pay out this coming week. By the time she'd topped up her electricity key, retrieved Grace's boots from the repairer's, put a fiver aside for Zac's upcoming birthday party, paid a token amount towards the water bill and covered their school lunches, there might be enough left over to pay a little bit more than the interest on her credit card.

There would be nothing at all for the rent, or the council tax.

The breath was so tight in her chest that it felt like a solid mass of fear. She didn't want to admit it, even to herself, but things were moving out of her reach so fast that she was terrified of where they were heading.

A cuddle with Grace might help to relieve some tension and even somehow set her up for the day.

Feeling her teenager's slender body folding into hers, those smooth, gangly limbs and the sleepy morning smell of her opened Angie's heart to how blessed she was to have her. She was a beautiful girl, full of life and fun, but thoughtful and patient with an understanding of situations and people that sometimes made her seem twice her age. She worked hard at school, was a favourite amongst the teachers and other students, and possessed not a mean bone in her body. She was, in fact, just like her father, always seeing the positive side of a situation; the first to help in a time of need, and able to summon a sense of humour when the rest of the world was losing theirs.

Angie guessed Grace didn't find it so funny losing her beloved Lush cruelty-free cosmetics, Boux Avenue undies and weekly pop magazines – or the subs she had to pay to belong to the Fairweather Players. Her great passion was acting, and she was good at it. She'd been cast in many parts for the local am dram society since the age of eight and always received great reviews. She sang too, and danced, but for the time being she'd had to give up those lessons along with her Players membership – although her best friend Lois had bought her three months' worth of dance classes for Christmas. What a blessing that had been, and how guilty it had made Angie feel knowing she was unable to do it herself.

'It's all right, Mum,' Grace had whispered when she'd realized this. 'I know things are difficult now, but it'll all come good in the end. Promise.'

How like her father she'd sounded, and for one heady moment Angie had felt as though Steve was trying to communicate through their daughter. Whether he was or wasn't hardly mattered now, for the debts were still piling up and only two weeks after Christmas she'd been forced to sell Steve's beloved piano. She'd cried as hard that day as she had on the day they'd cremated him, for it had felt as though a special and intrinsic part of their marriage had been carried out of the door by strangers, who'd given her fifty quid less than she'd asked for it.

'You and the children matter way more than a dumb old piano,' she'd heard Steve telling her, and of course he was right, but it hadn't made her feel any better. If only he were here now to tell her how to handle Roland Shalik, who'd taken over his father's businesses when Hari died, and had, if the rumours were true, incorporated them into various far shadier dealings of his own. He liked to portray himself as a tough guy, someone of influence, not to be messed with, and on the whole he succeeded, though Steve had never really been taken in by his bluster. In fact Steve had mostly kept out of his way and for the most part they'd seen or heard little of him, probably because they'd never been short of money to pay the rent then, nor had they complained when Roland had increased it. He'd only done it once, and not by a huge amount, but since Steve had gone and Angie had fallen into arrears things had changed. Roland had none of his father's softly spoken, courteous manner, nor, it turned out, did he feel any sense of loyalty or duty of care to the many tenants around Kesterly who'd been fortunate enough to have Hari for a landlord.

'Mum, you're squeezing too tight,' Grace murmured in protest.

Realizing she was, Angie slackened her hold and stroked her daughter's tangled red hair, careful not to catch any knots. She felt a glow of love, remembering how proud Steve had been of his precious girl.

Hearing a thud in the next room, followed by the hurried patter of feet and needless cry of 'I'm awake,' she felt rather than heard Grace laugh, and broke into a smile of her own. She wasn't going to think any more this morning about what had gone before, or how desperately she still missed Steve, or how much she hated herself for throwing Liam out. She was going to give all her time and attention to the two children who'd never caused her a moment's concern, apart from how to keep a roof over their heads, food in their mouths, clothes on their backs, vital gadgets in their pockets and ears... She could go on, and on, but her boisterous, fearless, head-first-into-the-bed six-year-old had just landed, and simply had to be tucked in tightly with them, or tickled.

It turned into a tickle, which she ran away from when they decided she was next. She loved them so much she could eat them, but they always won at tickling so she needed a refuge. Too bad the bolt inside the bathroom door was hanging off, she'd have got away if she'd remembered to fix it, but she wasn't sure how to – and no sooner had she shut herself in than they were there with her, putting their arms around her, telling her not to be scared.

'Scared!' she cried. 'Who's scared?' and putting on her most ferocious monster growl she ran after them.

Who needed heating when there were two children to play with?

OK, they did when the excitement was over and they finally settled down to breakfast, but a few minutes later the radiators clicked and rumbled into action and by the time the Lidl cornflakes had been devoured and Grace had finished her porridge the water was hot enough for showers. It might be Sunday, but they had a busy day ahead, and any minute now Angie would remember what they were supposed to be doing. For the moment her mind was filling up with figures that she couldn't make add up anywhere close to where they needed to be.

Don't stress. Just don't. It'll be all right. You'll find a way out of this.

Her own breakfast was the mouthful of porridge Grace left. Never mind that she was hungry enough to down half an elephant, a cup of instant coffee should deal with the pangs, and to save on hot water she'd treat herself to a damned good wash instead of a shower. They'd be OK at the end of the month when her salary was due to be paid into the one bank account she had that wasn't overdrawn. Well, not OK, exactly, but better than today, for her quick calculations were already warning her that by the end of tomorrow she'd have no more than sixteen pounds fifty in her account at Santander. The account at HSBC was already overdrawn by six hundred pounds with monstrous interest accruing by the day, so she couldn't go there for anything at all.

What utter fools she and Steve had been not to take out life insurance. They'd meant to, had even sent for some forms, but they'd never quite got round to filling them in. Angie had found them days after the funeral, exactly where she'd put them when they'd arrived, in a tray on Steve's desk with a prepaid and ready-addressed envelope attached. She'd stared at them, dumb with misery, rigid with the worst kind of understanding. She was holding a lifeline with nothing and no one attached to the other end, a limp rope in the water, an illusion of safety that would disappear in the cold light of day. She could do nothing to save herself or her family; these papers meant they were going to drown.

She'd told herself right away that she wouldn't let it happen. As though using up fierce and determined last gasps of air, she'd silently promised herself that Grace and Zac would never, for a single moment, feel any less special than they had while their father was alive. She'd quickly let it be known amongst her friends and neighbours that she could fill in people's shifts if they needed cover, whether cleaning, waitressing, delivering, babysitting: whatever was in her gift she would give it to make sure her children didn't go without.

She'd been in no doubt then that she could make everything work, and right up until she'd been made to wait for universal credit, she'd somehow managed to keep their heads above water. Now, in spite of still taking on all the extra jobs she could, it was impossible to make ends meet.

Grace, because she was Grace, had lately begun challenging her mother and brother to find the best bargains online or in charity shops, and they'd had some stunning successes: a pair of brand-new Nikes at Oxfam for Zac, price tag still taped to the bottom and half a size too big so he could grow into them, how perfect was that? A last-season white Zara blazer for Grace that would have cost fifty quid in the shop, and was just two pounds at Blue Cross (only a button missing, which was easily fixed). They'd even found a padded winter coat for Angie and wrapped it up for her birthday – what a memorable moment it had been when she'd opened it – it fitted, and they'd told her it had only cost a tenner (five quid contributed by Auntie Em). They'd jumped up and down with triumph, thinking themselves the smartest (in every sense) people alive, and how stupid was everyone else to pay full price?

It had also been Grace's idea to try and sell their old toys and clothes on eBay or Depop, while Angie began visiting a pawnshop in the old town, a place she hadn't even known existed while Steve was alive. By now she'd forfeited the white-gold watch he'd given her for her thirtieth; an emerald-studded bracelet he'd once accepted from an old lady in lieu of payment for decorating her kitchen; a pair of binoculars that had belonged to his father; his paintbrushes, best toolkit and protective gear; the rocking horse he'd carved for Liam; his surfboards; just about everything she could raise a few pounds for, right down to the electric heaters for when it was especially cold. Each time she went she felt as though she was giving away more pieces of her heart. All she had left to pawn now was her wedding ring, and the nine-carat gold locket Steve's mother had worn on her wedding day, and Angie had so proudly worn on hers.

She wasn't going to think any more about all that now, though. Instead, she was going to try to make herself believe that all would come good, maybe even by this time tomorrow. God only knew how, unless she caved in and took out one of those lethal payday loans… The fact that she was actually considering it made her feel sick inside, but what choice did she have when Roland Shalik had already begun the eviction process?

CHAPTER FIVE

An hour later, with Zac down at the beach flying kites with his friends, and Grace watching the Fairweather Players rehearsing at the community centre – there was no part for her this year, on account of being unable to pay her membership fees – Angie spent a moment imagining how wonderful it would be to waltz into the centre and slip Grace enough cash to rejoin the company. The thought of it felt so good that she was almost annoyed when her mobile jolted her back to reality with a text. It was Emma letting her know that there was an offer at the Seafront Café today, provided they got there before twelve. Two coffees for the price of one. *Boys with their father this morning (he didn't forget today) so how about it? I'll drive.*

Angie didn't hesitate. She might have a ton of chores on her plate, but they'd still be waiting when she got back, so why not indulge in this little treat? *Pick me up in fifteen,* she messaged back.

Though Emma and her husband Ben had moved into one of Hari's semis, just over the footbridge, around the same time as Angie and Steve had moved into 14 Willow Close, Ben had taken off just over five years ago. He'd found someone else, an older uglier version of Emma was how Steve had described the new woman, and he hadn't been far wrong. Ben now had two other children with his second wife, and had been promoted to manager at a Tesco Express over in the old town, so he was reasonably reliable with the maintenance for his and Emma's boys. Certainly the rent was always paid, and so far Roland Shalik hadn't attempted to increase it.

Trying not to think about bacon, sausages and eggs – her usual breakfast at the Seafront when she was feeling flush – Angie fixated on a lovely creamy latte instead. Later she'd have a proper meal, as they always did on Sundays, when she and Emma took it in turns to cook a delicious roast for them all with a surprise pudding to follow. It was at her place this week, so she'd bought everything in Lidl yesterday, and had even added a tub of ice cream for a pound to go with the apple pie. The kids would like that, and so would she, although she and Emma would probably have preferred a bottle of Pinot Grigio to help it all down.

Wine was a luxury they really couldn't afford these days.

Glancing at her mobile as it jingled with another text, she saw it was from Hamish at Hill Lodge with a photo attached showing a close-up of what looked like… She wasn't sure what it was. Then she realized he must have tracked down some more original tiles to continue his restoration of the cracked Victorian flooring in the hallway of the Lodge.

She texted back right away: *Genius. Going to end up on Grand Designs.* ☺

He sent her a happy smiley back with the words, *Craig didn't come home last night.*

Since none of them knew where Craig spent the nights he didn't return to the residence she replied, *Let me know when he shows up.*

He would show up, she felt sure of that because he always did, eventually, and if she rang him right now he'd probably answer his phone. She didn't put it to the test because Emma had just tooted her car horn, and with the prospect of a latte at the Seafront Café pulling her like a magnet towards town, she pocketed her phone and all but ran out of the house.

'You're looking lovely,' she told Emma as she got into the passenger seat. 'Must be all that wonderful sex you're not getting.'

'I see it's working wonders for you too,' Emma quipped, checking the rear-view mirror as she pulled away from the kerb. She was wearing a purple wool coat they'd found at a new boutique in town before Christmas, very stylish, by a designer they'd never heard of, and a dusky pink scarf that Grace had knitted to go with it. In her black padded parka and equally black scarf Angie couldn't help feeling drab next to those lovely colours, but that was OK, the brightness of her red hair kind of made up for it.

'Who was that bloke rubbernecking the van?' Emma asked, as they headed out of the cul-de-sac. 'Please don't tell me you're selling it? You can't. You'd never manage without it.'

The mere thought of letting Steve's van go was enough to make Angie's heart lurch with dread. Selling the piano had been bad enough, beyond terrible in fact, but there had been no practical justification for keeping it. The van was her only means of transport, and God knew how painful it had been having his business insignia removed from the sides and back doors.

'No I'm not selling it, and I didn't see anyone,' Angie said, trying to hide her anxiety. It could have been a bailiff nosing around, carrying out a quick assessment for someone she owed money to. Emma didn't know how bad things really were so she wouldn't have guessed at that. 'Are you sure it was my van he was looking at?' she asked.

Emma shrugged. 'Hard to say for certain. Sorry, didn't mean to worry you.' She glanced at Angie and said, 'It's his birthday today.'

Angie's heart twisted as she nodded.

'I know you haven't heard anything, because you'd have told me. That wasn't him, by the way, who I saw scoping the van.'

'No, I guessed not.'

After a while Emma said, 'Does it make you feel afraid, when you think he might be around?'

Angie swallowed the concern that tightened her throat. Emma had never asked that before, so was it her way of saying that she was afraid? It hurt Angie deeply to think of her sister being fearful of her son, but she couldn't deny that on some levels she was too. Or she was scared of the people he could still be hanging out with. She pushed a hand through her hair and caught a whiff of the soap she'd used under her arms. It wasn't good enough because it didn't manage to cover the faint trace of body odour she'd been trying to wash away. Why was that? She was clean, for heaven's sake, so it didn't seem right that she couldn't make herself smell good, or at least have no smell at all.

She'd never smelled bad in her entire life.

'Angie?' Emma said gently, her tone questioning and concerned.

'There's something about me that smells,' Angie stated loudly. 'I'm obviously using the wrong deodorant.'

Emma looked at her sideways. 'What sort of an answer is that?' she demanded.

Angie started to smile. 'It's my way of saying I'd rather think about that than Liam, or birthdays or…' She could have said *how fast I seem to be going under,* but instead she said, 'or anything else that might come between us and our lattes.'

Half an hour later they were seated at a corner table in their favourite café, close to the window and next to a rowdy group of teens apparently just back from a ski trip. As the youngsters relived seemingly every minute of their amazing time away they kept exploding with hilarity, and their laughter was so infectious it was making Angie and Emma laugh too. Others were becoming tetchy and disapproving, but the skiers seemed not to notice; they were in a world full of nothing but black runs, snowboards and *vin chaud*, and why not when it was clearly a great place to be?

'I don't suppose they live on the Temple Fields estate,' Emma remarked drily as the group finally piled out of the door, leaving a very generous twenty-quid tip on the table.

'They probably don't even know where it is,' Angie smiled, hardly able to tear her eyes from the cash or her thoughts from what she could do with it. 'I've seen one of the girls before. She used to be in Grace's class in primary, but she went on to private school somewhere in Somerset.'

'You must let me help to send Grace to private school,' Hari had said a year before he died. 'After your experiences with Liam, I think it would be wise to find her somewhere safer, even out of the area.'

Angie and Steve had discussed it, and decided they were in favour of it even if it meant she'd have to board during the week. Steve had foreseen a great future for their daughter among the kind of people he and Angie only worked for and occasionally mixed with. He'd made Angie laugh so much putting on a posh accent – the same accent he affected, without quite realizing it, when he took her to openings of hotels or restaurants he'd decorated – that she'd ended up hitting him to make him stop.

He wouldn't. 'Oh dahling, can't you imagine how proud one will be to see our girl doing so well?'

'Let's talk some more with Hari first, find out exactly how much help he's comfortable giving. We can't expect him to pay for it all.'

Before they'd had a chance to do that Hari's illness had taken hold, and the subject was quietly forgotten.

'What's that look about?' Emma asked curiously.

Realizing she'd drifted, Angie said, 'Sorry, where were we?'

Emma grimaced. 'Actually, I'm just getting to the point where I have a favour to ask. Is there any chance you could lend me twenty quid until the end of the week?'

Angie groaned in dismay. 'I'm really sorry. You know I would if I could.'

Emma sighed sadly, because of course she knew that. She didn't wonder aloud how she and Angie had got to this place in their lives where they were almost always broke, because they knew only too well how it had happened. They'd never been high earners, even before they'd turned into single mothers through no fault of their own, nor would they ever be. At least in her case she got something from her ex; for Angie there was no Child Maintenance Service to help squeeze blood out of a slippery stone.

'Actually,' Emma said, suddenly brightening, 'I've had a brilliant idea that should get us both sorted out.'

Angie was all ears.

Emma said, 'We're two intelligent, attractive women…'

'In our forties, with more bags under our eyes…'

'Listen to what I'm saying. We're good people. We do the right thing, we've never been in trouble with the law – don't let's include Liam in this – we're terrific mothers…'

'Do you want to come to the point?'

'What I'm saying is...' She broke off as Fliss, the café's owner, came to collect their mugs.

'Two more, ladies?' she offered.

As Angie's longing flared up, Emma said, 'We've already used our voucher, Fliss, but thanks anyway.'

Fliss looked surprised. 'Oh, I think we forgot to put it through,' she declared, 'so we'll treat the next ones as though they're your first.'

Angie could have kissed her, although realizing that Fliss had guessed at their straitened circumstances made her feel she was paying with a small piece of her pride.

With a wink Fliss scooped up the twenty-pound note the youngsters had left, and instructed a baffled-looking server to clean the table ready for a couple of newcomers to sit down.

'Bugger, I was going to pocket that,' Emma muttered.

'Not if I'd beaten you to it,' Angie retorted, knowing that neither of them were serious. Or not very, anyway. Stealing from Fliss, a good friend for many years, would never be an option, no matter how desperate they were. 'So,' she said wryly, 'I'm guessing your brilliant idea is to do away with good reputations, such as they are, and rob a bank?'

Emma's jaw dropped in amazement. 'Oh my God, you read my mind. So, do you think we could do it?'

'No. So what's next?'

Emma broke into one of her more mischievous grins. 'You are so going to love it,' she announced. 'I've thought it all through and I reckon we can pull it off, no problem at all.'

Angie said, 'Are we still talking about the bank?'

'No, no. I'm talking about finding ourselves a couple of rich blokes whose lives would be complete with someone like us. Don't get me wrong, I think we should carry on working, it's important what we do, but you've got to admit we're never going to meet anyone with more than a couple of halfpennies to scratch their bits with the way we're going now. So, we've got to get with the dating programme. As you know, it all happens on the Internet these days. People twice our age are going on dates. They're even having sex – OK, don't go there – but they're finding new lives, even getting married again, so if they can do it, why can't we?'

Knowing she was nowhere near to wanting a relationship with anyone who wasn't Steve, Angie said, 'Don't you have to pay to be a member of those websites?'

Emma grimaced. 'Probably, if you find someone you want to meet, but initially you can just go on and have a look, see if there's anyone suitable. Of course they're all going to say they're rich, and half of them are probably psychos, but what do we have to lose?'

Angie's expression was one of pure irony.

Emma laughed. 'OK, I get that it could all go horribly wrong, but there's a chance it won't...'

'What if you end up with some creep who pretends to like kids, but doesn't?' Angie interrupted. 'Or does, but in the wrong way? No, I'm sorry, you're on your own with this one. I'll come along as back-up if you go on a date... What is it?' she asked, following Emma's gaze to the window.

'Not what, who?' Emma responded curiously. 'Isn't that Craig over there? Your Craig, from Hill Lodge?'

Spotting him on the opposite corner, holding tightly to his guitar as a couple of youths in hoodies and combat gear crowded him up against a wall, Angie's heart sank. 'Yes, that's him. Oh God, please don't let them be trying to recruit him. I'm going over there,' she declared, getting to her feet.

Emma's hand shot out to stop her. 'Don't mess with them, Angie. You of all people know what they're capable of, and you have two kids to think about.'

Angie desperately wanted to argue, but knowing her sister was right, she watched with growing dismay as Craig took something from the hoodies, put it into an inside pocket and walked away – with his guitar.

The best she could hope for was that he was delivering, not selling or using. Whatever, he needed to be much more careful than this, because the last thing he'd want was to find himself back in prison after the hellish experience he'd had there before. The other inmates had bullied and abused him so badly that the poor lad lived in mortal terror of the police and his probation officer now, certain their only purpose in life was to send him back inside.

Her phone rang, and concern for Craig vanished as a stranger's voice said, 'Am I speaking to Mrs Watts?'

She was immediately tense. It was someone after money. Or maybe someone had found Liam and with a wave of sadness she realised that hope was no longer first to her mind. 'Yes,' she replied cautiously, looking at Emma who was raising her eyebrows. 'Who's this please?'

'It's DC Leo Johnson, from Kesterly CID. We'd like to talk to you, Mrs Watts. Could you come to the station today?'

Today? Sunday? Her head was suddenly spinning, her heart thudding thickly. 'What's it about?' she asked, trying to stay calm.

'We can discuss it when you get here,' came the reply. 'Shall we say in an hour?'

'Yes. No! Wait. Is it about my son, Liam? Have you found him?'

'It would help if you could bring something of his when you come,' the detective told her, and before she could say any more he'd rung off.

CHAPTER SIX

'It'll be about DNA,' Emma said decisively, as they drove along the seafront heading back to the house. 'I can't think why else they'd want something of his.'

Knowing that had to be true, Angie tried desperately not to connect with what it could mean. 'But they already have it from when… From when he was arrested. Don't they automatically take it these days?'

'But he wasn't charged, so I think by law they have to delete it.'

Angie's nails were digging into her palms as she gazed out at the heaving grey mass of waves in the bay. They were doing what they always did, swelling and dipping, hurling on to rocks and drowning the beach. Why did they seem so ominous?

Was Steve watching? Did he know what was going on?

When they got home she waited in the kitchen while Emma went up to Liam's room. It wasn't that Angie never went in there, if anything she spent far too much time sitting amongst his things trying to work out what more she could do to find him, even trying telepathically to reach him. It was simply that Emma had decided she ought to be the one to go up there today.

She came back with a light-blue Donald Duck toothbrush that made Angie want to cry. All his life he'd had the same one, changing it every few months for a newer model of the same. Right up until he died Steve had also owned a Donald Duck toothbrush to match Liam's, in spite of using an electric one for the actual job.

Angie took it, doing her best not to engage with the role it was about to play, and after insisting she was all right to drive, she left Emma in the house trying to find someone to be there for the kids when they got back so she could follow Angie to the police station.

By the time Angie was left to wait in a room that was soulless and smelled of sweat and cheap polish she was somehow managing to breathe normally, though only just. So many terrible and terrifying scenarios had been racing through her mind this past hour that she'd lost sight of any good that might be about to unfold. Did anything good ever unfold in this awful space with no windows, just a roof vent that seemed clogged by leaves and a small, thick glass panel in the door?

'Mrs Watts?'

She looked up from the table where her hands were clasped tightly together and her eyes, until then, had been on the ring stains that formed random patterns over the chipped surface.

'Leo Johnson.' A young, red-haired man with boyish freckles and a skewed sky-blue tie introduced himself with a friendly smile.

Angie started to get up, but Johnson insisted she stay seated. 'Has someone offered you tea or coffee?' he asked, taking a chair opposite her at the table.

She shook her head. 'I'm fine, thank you,' she told him hoarsely. 'I'd just like to know what this is about.'

'Of course.' He glanced at his watch and seemed relieved when the door opened again and a middle-aged woman with a pale complexion and deep frown lines between her close-set eyes came in. 'Sorry to have kept you,' she said to Angie, seeming to mean it. 'I'm Detective Sergeant Anthea Ellis. Please call me Anthea, and may I call you Angela?'

'Angie. Everyone calls me Angie.' *Why were they being so friendly? The only reason she could think of was that they were about to break bad news.*

Anthea Ellis smiled, her plain features softening into a less stressed expression that did little to put Angie at ease. 'Thanks very much for coming,' the detective said. 'I'm sorry to drag you in here on a Sunday, but we've been contacted by our Avon and Somerset colleagues who are investigating a murder that took place in Bristol the day before yesterday.'

Angie's heart stopped beating. She could feel her breath shortening, her mind racing with the horror of what this could mean. *They think it's him. It's why they want his DNA. He's dead and they're trying to identify him. Oh God, oh God, oh God, how was she going to handle this?*

Anthea Ellis was saying, '... the girl's body was found beside a canal. She's been identified as...'

'What?' Angie interrupted, not understanding. 'A girl... Who...? Why are you...?'

Leo Johnson said, 'We're told that the main suspects in the case are individuals who might be known to your son. Have you heard from him at all lately?'

Still trying to get a handle on things, Angie said, 'No. Not since his father...' She stopped; they'd know what she meant.

With an understanding expression Anthea Ellis said, 'Do you have any idea where he might be?'

Angie shook her head. 'I've tried to find him, but I've never got anywhere. Who are these people, the ones they think killed the girl?'

'I guess we can assume,' Ellis replied, 'that they're members of the gang Liam was – or still is – involved with. As you know, only five members are behind bars.'

Angie searched around for what she wanted to say, or needed to know. It was like trying to catch something invisible and turn it into something real. 'Where – where did they find the girl?' she finally managed. 'You said a canal...'

'It's in the Lawrence Hill area of Bristol,' Johnson told her. 'Is that anywhere you know? Somewhere your son might have visited?'

Angie shook her head. 'I've never been there, but I'm not sure about Liam. Please tell me you don't think he did this. You know he's not like other boys his age; he has difficulties... If he did do it they'll have put him up to it.'

'Let's not jump to conclusions,' Ellis said kindly.

'But why else would they want his DNA?'

Johnson said, 'They're checking on everyone known to have had some involvement with this particular gang, either directly or indirectly.'

Wild-eyed now, Angie's voice shook as she said, 'You know what those thugs do to people who turn them in, don't you? I've seen a programme about it, they call them snitches and if they're found they're stabbed to death. So you have to stop looking for Liam. Please. Because even if he doesn't tell you anything, if someone's arrested they'll think he talked and blame him.'

Quietly, almost regretfully, Ellis said, 'Did you bring something of his with you?'

Angie stiffened and would have denied it if she could. She reached into her bag and handed over the ludicrous toothbrush.

As Johnson took it he regarded it with something that seemed like sadness.

'Thank you for coming,' Anthea Ellis said again. As she got up to leave, Angie suddenly cried, 'Is that it? Aren't you at least going to say that you'll let me know when you find out that this has nothing to do with my son?'

'Of course,' Ellis assured her. 'We have your number. As soon as there's any news, one way or the other, DC Johnson will be in touch.'

Getting to her feet, Angie said angrily, 'So now he's a suspect in a murder case you'll go out of your way to find him. You didn't want to know when I came in here almost two years ago. Maybe if you'd listened to me then that girl would still be…' She stopped abruptly, horrified by what she'd been about to say.

'I made it sound as though I think he's as guilty as they do,' she ranted to Emma when she got back. 'How could I have said that? What the hell is the matter with me? I know he didn't do it…' She choked on a sob. 'He'd never kill anyone. He just wouldn't – unless someone put him up to it. They might have forced him to do it.'

'They don't know yet if it was him,' Emma reminded her softly.

Angie nodded, seizing the doubt to try and still herself. 'So does this mean he's in Bristol?' she asked. 'I know there are connections between the gangs here and there.'

Once again Emma said, 'They don't know yet if it's him.'

Angie turned to look out of the kitchen window, seeing shadowy figures over a girl next to a canal, knives, fists, blood… She couldn't make out any faces, but surely none belonged to Liam.

Her hand tightened around a mug of tea as she focused on

Zac in the garden with Emma's boys, Harry aged almost seven and Jack aged nine. They were crawling over the climbing ropes Steve had hung between the shed and an end post for the washing line. Once they reached the top they tumbled over on to the trampoline below, roaring like warriors, fearless and mighty. Liam had loved to play on those ropes when he was small, shouting out for his dad to watch as he threw himself on to the deadly enemy below.

'How many have you slain so far?' Steve would cry out, waving his plastic sword with a madman's intent.

'Millions,' Liam would reply. 'Look out! There's one behind you.'

Steve whipped round, saw off an invisible attacker and shouted, 'Thanks Liam, you saved me there.'

'That's all right Dad. You're safe now.'

Grace came into the kitchen, her laptop held open in both hands. 'Nightmare,' she declared. 'I've found some stories about the murdered girl and they're not good.'

There had been no point trying to hide anything from her daughter when she'd come back from the station; Grace had been there and had known right away that something was wrong. Lying, or trying to skirt the issue was never the way to go with Grace. She'd somehow get to the truth in the end, and would be hurt and disappointed in her mother for not trusting her.

As she put the computer down in front of Emma, Angie saw how pale she was, and wondered whether she already believed her brother was a killer, or if she was trying to give him the benefit of the doubt. What was it going to mean to her future if it turned out he'd killed that girl? She'd always be the sister of a murderer, the daughter of a man who'd been beaten to death in a frenzy of gang violence; someone whose family wasn't like other families, whose bad luck might be contagious. That was how the world viewed people who'd had dealings with the very worst elements of society, even through no fault of their own; the stigma, the shame, rubbed off on the innocent.

'She's called Khrystyna Kolisnyk,' Grace was saying. 'She was twenty-four and came from Ukraine, but she'd been in the St Paul's area of Bristol flat-sharing with other girls for the past couple of years. No one reported her missing. The police only knew about her when a jogger nearly fell over her body while he was out for a morning run. Apparently the police want to speak to her boyfriend, Darren Milligan, and others.' She looked up. 'The main thing is there's no mention of Liam.'

Hating the fact that Grace even knew about anything like this, Angie went to close the laptop down. 'That's enough for now,' she said quietly. 'I'll put the chicken in the oven and start peeling the potatoes before we get a bunch of hangry boys on our hands.'

Later, after they'd eaten every last mouthful of the roast, followed by a golden crust apple pie and vanilla ice cream, they settled down to play their usual game of Monopoly. It was a Sunday evening tradition, dating back to happier times when Steve and Liam had played too – always loudly, and Angie was sure they'd both cheated for they never seemed to spend any time in jail. These past few months it had returned to being a noisy and highly competitive couple of hours at the close of the weekend and this evening's were no exception, with whoops of triumph over big property purchases, followed by groans of outrage at extortionate rents, and shouts of protest when someone was declared bankrupt. Angie was aware of Grace's eyes flicking to her from time to time, wanting to be sure that her mother was genuinely enjoying herself and not secretly worrying herself into a state of panic.

Angie wasn't, at least not tonight. She was doing her best to think only of how blessed she was to be sitting here with her family, warmth coming from the fire, a solid roof to keep them dry, food to eat and no illnesses to scare them. There would be time enough later to think about Liam, when she knew for certain whether or not he was a person of real interest to the police. And as for everything else... There was no point thinking about that tonight either, so she winked at Grace to make her smile, the way Steve always used to, and was relieved when Grace winked back.

Later, Grace was in her room that her dad had made look like an actor's dressing room, with famous theatre and movie posters in an artful montage all over the walls, a mirror with big globe lights around it, a little seating area of bean bags and coffee table for when she had visitors, and there was even an old-fashioned modesty screen that he'd bought at an antiques fair and restored for her. It was draped with various movie props and costumes that they'd tracked down on eBay; she even had a pair of dancing shoes that had been worn by one of the stars of a Broadway show. He'd made her fancy bed frame with a canopy overhead smothered in muslins and lace that cascaded all the way down to the floor.

She no longer had the computer desk he'd refashioned from an old *escritoire* for her to work at; after she'd uploaded photos of it to Depop it had sold right away for fifty pounds. The small collection of perfume bottles that her mum had started her off with when she was six had sold for eighty-five pounds, and the vintage-style doll's pram Granny Watts had given her when she was four had sold for thirty-two pounds. It was amazing what people would buy, for most of her jewellery had gone – not the silver christening bangle, or her nine-carat-gold watch or the tiny diamond chip set in a signet ring that was supposed to be a family heirloom, her mum would have had a meltdown if she tried to sell any of that. It was the ordinary stuff from Zara and Next and Topshop that had gone, along with at least half of her old dolls and teddies, most of her books, her play shop, her Micro Sprite scooter and the bike she'd long since outgrown but had been planning to keep along with the vintage pram, in case she had a little girl one day who might like them.

Now, as she uploaded yet more photos of clothes that had hardly been worn and even still fitted, along with a well-thumbed set of Winnie the Pooh books Auntie Em had bought her one Christmas, she was thinking about the way her mum had winked at her earlier, and how much it had reminded her of her dad. She loved it when her mum did that, but at the same time it seemed to dig right down in her chest to remind her of how much she missed him. Sometimes, to get herself past the worst parts of it, she'd talk to him, inside her head, as if he was still there and able to answer. She asked him to tell her what to do to help Mum, or if he was upset that she'd sold the desk, or what she should upload next; she even asked if he knew where Liam was.

Do you blame Liam, Dad? Can you see him now? What is he doing? Do you want us to find him?

She didn't always hear him as well as she'd like to, and even when she did she thought she might be making it up, but occasionally she found herself slipping back in time to one of the chats they'd had when she was small, some that she actually remembered, others that she didn't, but they'd made him laugh so much when he'd told her about them later that she'd wanted to hear about them again and again, just because he seemed to love them – and her – so much.

'Daddy?' she said.

'Mmm?' he replied.

She gave a small sigh to let him know that she required his full attention.

Getting the message, he put down the screwdriver he was using to assemble her new wardrobe and turned to sit cross-legged on the floor facing her.

'You know I'm five tomorrow?' she said earnestly.

'I do,' he replied, matching her tone.

'Well, when I have my party on Saturday, I hope you're going to behave yourself. Only you don't always, do you?'

He crumpled in shame. 'I promise I'll do my best,' he said.

She frowned, not certain that was good enough. 'I know,' she declared, hitting on the answer. 'I'll ask Mummy to keep an eye on you.'

His mouth twitched like he was going to laugh, but he sounded serious as he said, 'I think that's a very good idea.'

She continued to sit where she was, hands folded together in her lap as she worked herself up to what else she needed to say. To her surprise he started to turn back to what he was doing. 'I haven't finished, Daddy,' she told him bossily.

'Oh, sorry. What else is it?'

'Will Liam be coming to the party?' she asked worriedly.

The light in his eyes seemed to dull as he sighed and pushed a hand through his dusty hair. 'I don't know, sweetheart,' he replied. 'Do you want him to?'

She didn't want to say no, but she didn't want to say yes either. 'He might not be here,' she said hopefully. 'He goes out with his friends all the time.'

Grimly, Steve said, 'I wouldn't call them friends, exactly, but you're right, he does go out a lot.'

'Where does he go?'

With another sigh he gathered her on to his lap and wrapped his arms around her. 'Things are a bit difficult for Liam at the moment,' he said softly, 'so we have to try and be patient and find ways to help him.'

'Will it help him to come to my party?'

Squeezing her, he said, 'I'm not sure, honey. It's hard to know what to do, but we'll find a way to make everything all right, don't you worry.'

He wasn't here to make things right any more, and it was horrible, so bad sometimes that she felt she was drowning in the need for him to pick her up in his strong arms and tell her it was all a bad dream. But he wasn't going to do that, so she must try her best to help her mum the way she knew he'd want her to. The trouble was she would soon run out of things to sell online, so she needed to find another way to earn some money.

Any ideas yet? she messaged to her best friend Lois, who was helping her to find out what kind of jobs were possible for girls of thirteen. She was already doing some of her fellow students' homework for two pounds a time, but apart from the fact that she was helping them to cheat, it wasn't nearly enough to make a difference for her mum.

Lois's reply came quickly. *Still working on it, but will have info to share by tomorrow. #SAVINGGRACE.*

CHAPTER SEVEN

Angie was sitting in the driver's seat of her van, hands clutching the steering wheel, eyes fixed on the frosty green across the street where, back when they were a normal family, the children had played cricket against the adults in summer and roasted chestnuts and marshmallows over bonfires in winter.

She should start the engine, head off into the day, but she was having trouble making herself go through even the most familiar of motions this morning.

Grace and Zac had already left for school; Emma had taken them, and she, Angie, needed to get to work. She had to clean a restaurant in town for one of her neighbours first – she must text to say that she needed the cash asap – and then she had a meeting with one of Bridging the Gap's main sponsors. Later she was planning to carry out a job search for a couple of the residents – any success she achieved on their behalf always gave her a lift, so she was actually looking forward to that. Then she'd go to the office to answer emails and make phone calls. All this would happen as it should if she could make herself go any further from the house than this.

It was the email she'd opened only minutes ago that was holding her in a paralysis of dread. It had been sent yesterday, but she hadn't read it until after the children had left this morning, with Zac's chirpy voice telling her he wanted a unicorn cake for his birthday.

Came by the house earlier today. Your van was there, but reckon you slipped out while I was looking for you round the back.

Mr Shalik wants to help you, Angie, so call me tomorrow.

It was from Agi, the thug, goon, muscle, whatever anyone wanted to call him that Roland Shalik used as his right-hand man.

A tap on the van window made her jump, breaking her so abruptly from the turmoil in her head that she almost gasped. She looked up at the face staring in, trying to process the reality of it. For a moment fear tricked her eyes into seeing a stranger, until she realized it was her neighbour, Melvin, who lived two doors down with his wife, Mandy, and their twin girls who were Zac's age. He was clearly concerned, perplexed, as he circled a finger for her to lower the window.

She did so and as cold morning air swept into the van her lungs grasped it as though she'd been suffocating them. 'Sorry,' she said, 'I was miles away.' Melvin and his family hadn't lived in Willow Close for long, and hadn't gone out of their way to be friendly, just nodding good morning when they came out with the bins, or to get in the car. She understood that some people preferred to keep themselves to themselves, but she'd been surprised when they hadn't joined in the carol-singing party that Grace and her friends had organized at the community centre before Christmas. Everyone else had taken part, bringing flasks of hot chocolate, mince pies and handmade ornaments to decorate the tree. Bob, from across the street, had asked Angie if she'd mind him being Santa this year, a role Steve had always played, and she'd told him she thought it was a lovely idea.

Steve would have wanted her to say that, and Bob would hopefully never know that it had almost broken her to go and watch someone else in her husband's place.

'Are you OK?' Melvin asked. He looked awkward, apparently not wanting to get involved if there was a problem, but here he was anyway. 'You've been sitting there for a while,' he explained. 'Are you having engine trouble? I'm about to go into town so I can give you a lift...?'

'No, I'm fine, thanks,' she assured him. 'I was just... I...' Her hand tightened around her phone. 'I was waiting for someone to call, and didn't want to drive...' She stopped, the fear of a call silencing her. It hadn't happened yet, but she knew it would, just as she knew she'd have to take it.

Melvin was watching her through the thick lenses of his dark-rimmed glasses, seeming to see past her excuse, all the way to... To what? Even she didn't know the real reason she was sitting here like someone who had no idea how to drive, so there was no way he could.

'OK, if you're sure...' He gestured behind him to his own car.

'Sure,' she insisted. She hadn't realized until now that he was quite good-looking. She and Emma often likened men to movie stars, and she guessed Melvin-from-down-the-street could qualify, on a dark night at a good distance, as a bit of a Matt Damon. Smaller, thinner, kind of gaunt, but still managing to be attractive. He was more Emma's type than hers.

'I should be going,' she said, starting the engine. 'Hope you have a good day.'

As she drove away she glanced in the rear-view mirror and saw that he was walking back down the street. She wondered what his story was, why he and his family were so aloof, although he'd seemed fairly neighbourly just then.

By the time she'd cleaned the restaurant, and met with the sponsor who'd willingly committed for another year, she'd forgotten all about Melvin, had even managed to push Liam out of her mind for the time being. Now, having completed an hour at the office, she was picking her way through the ruts and puddles of a building site on the outer edge of town, heading for the portacabins tucked in against the hillside like metal mushrooms.

She hadn't received the dreaded phone call yet, nor had she responded to Agi's email, although she was ready to admit that she couldn't go on avoiding him. The trouble was she still didn't know how to deal with the mess she was in, what her next step should be to avoid sinking her and her family completely.

A burning prickle of fear coasted down her spine.

As she approached the first portacabin a tall, muscular man in a hard hat and hi-vis jacket came out in a hurry, and almost collided with her at the foot of the steps.

'Christ, I'm sorry,' he apologized, reaching out to steady her. 'I didn't see you. Are you OK?'

'I'm fine,' she assured him, dimly aware that this was the second time today that she'd had this start to a conversation. He really did look concerned, and then his frown deepened as he peered at her more closely.

'Do I know you?' he asked. 'You look familiar.'

She shook her head, certain their paths hadn't crossed, but it wasn't rare for people to think they recognized her, since her face had been all over the press at the time of Steve's death. Anyway, this man was a bit of a Daniel Craig, so she'd surely remember if they'd met.

Two handsome men, and it wasn't even noon. Maybe the day wasn't going to be so bad after all.

'I know,' he suddenly cried, 'you're Wattie's wife. Steve Watts, the decorator?'

As the pain of hearing her husband's name tightened her heart, Angie said, 'That's right.' It wasn't a surprise that this man had known Steve, for just about everyone who worked on the buildings in this town had. 'Don't tell me, he did some work for you?' she ventured. As everything about Daniel Craig – he wasn't so much like him really, maybe better – suggested he was some sort of boss, it was a reasonable guess that he'd employed Steve at some stage.

The man smiled. 'When we could get him,' he replied. Then his eyes softened in an almost tender way as he said, 'I'm so sorry about what happened. It must have been very difficult for you and your family.'

Angie didn't deny it, why would she, but she didn't want to get into it, so using words to cut off the swell of emotion she said, 'I'm here to find out if you'd be willing to give a second chance to one or more of my residents. My sister and I run Bridging the Gap, you might have heard of it. Well, you might not have, but we help people, men mostly, to find their way back from difficult times.'

'Actually, I have heard of it,' he told her, going with the change of subject, though she could tell he was still thinking about Steve and no doubt remembering now the full detail of just how terrible his death had been, 'but it's not me you need to speak to, it's Cliff, the site manager.' He turned back up the steps. 'He's inside,' he said over his shoulder, 'I'll introduce you and make sure he understands that this is a construction company that believes in second chances.'

Appreciating his readiness to help, she stepped through the door he was holding open for her and felt the welcoming warmth of the interior embrace her. As expected, the place was a dumping ground for everything: boots, jackets, paperwork, plans, hard hats and every other kind of builder paraphernalia. Seated at an enormous desk in one corner was a gruff-looking man in his fifties with flattened grey hair, no doubt from the wearing of a hat, a bulbous nose, flinty eyes and a ragged white beard.

No chance of making it a hat trick of handsome blokes with this one, she couldn't help reflecting wryly to herself.

'Cliff, this is Steve Watts's wife,' Daniel Craig said. 'Mrs Watts…'

'Angie,' she interjected.

'Angie,' he repeated with a smile that made her smile too, 'wants to talk to you about taking on a couple of her residents. They're blokes who haven't had the easiest of times and need someone to give them a bit of a leg-up. I said we'd be happy to do that.'

Cliff's whiskery eyebrows rose in a way that told her he might not be quite as ready to throw out lifelines, were the decision his. Apparently it wasn't, since he didn't argue, simply said, 'What skills do your residents have, Mrs Watts?'

Prepared for the question, Angie said, 'Most of them don't have a skill, but they could be labourers, or maybe apprentices to some of the tradesmen…'

'The tradesmen take on their own people,' he interrupted. 'That's nothing to do with us.'

'But you can put in a word,' the man who was apparently his boss interrupted. 'And you were telling me only minutes ago that you're short of a gofer.' He smiled roguishly in Angie's direction, and checking his watch said, 'Sorry, I have to go, but Cliff will take your details and sort something out for you.' As pleasantly as it was said, it was clearly an instruction, but before Angie could thank him he'd gone.

She looked at the older man, and tried to tease out a smile with one of her own.

It didn't work. 'Write everything down,' he said brusquely,

and pushing a tea-stained A4 pad towards her he tossed a pen after it. 'If you haven't heard from me in a couple of days, you can give me a call, but don't expect miracles.'

Sensing this was the best she could hope for from this curmudgeon she wrote down her details, followed by the reminder of why she was there, and pushed the pad back to him.

'Incidentally,' she said, turning round as she reached the door, 'I'd like to thank the man who brought me in here, but I don't know his name or how to get hold of him.'

The site manager smirked in a way that made her hackles rise. She stared at him hard. Surely he didn't think she was trying to make a move on his boss, for that was what his manner seemed to suggest. The very idea made her want to slap the grin right off his smug face. Instead, she opened the door and stepped back into the hectic cacophony of the site.

It was at the bottom of the steps where she'd almost collided with the boss and now paused to let a transit van pass that she saw the words Stone Construction emblazoned on the side, and could have kicked herself.

Of course she'd known the name of the company before coming, but she'd been too distracted to make the connection. Now, as she did, it felt strangely as though sunbeams were breaking free of the dull grey sky to carry her back to when she'd first met the owner of Stone Construction.

Steve was laughing in that annoyingly teasing way of his that made her laugh too when she really didn't want to.

'You should have seen your face when I introduced you,' he told her, eyes twinkling wickedly. 'I don't think I've ever seen you blush like that before.'

'I did not blush,' she protested.

'Oh but you did. So come on, admit it, you fancied him.'

'You're delusional, and may I remind you we were at his father's funeral, so you need to show more respect.'

Suitably chastened, he tugged off his tie and threw his suit jacket over the end of the bed as he said, 'Everyone's going to miss Dougie Stone. He was the best mayor this town's ever had, and a great businessman. Now what everyone wants to know is whether or not his son, who's apparently going to inherit everything, the construction company, the properties, all the other businesses, will keep it all going.'

'What was his name again?' Angie asked casually, stepping out of her formal grey dress and reaching for a hanger. Wasn't it just typical of her husband to notice when she found another man attractive? She couldn't get anything past him.

Steve was grinning. 'Martin,' he replied, and coming up behind her he drew her against him. 'They say he's minted in his own right,' he murmured against her neck, 'even before he cleans up from his father.'

'Oh well, in that case,' she said, turning in his arms, 'perhaps I did fancy him.'

Laughing, he touched his mouth to hers.

'Are you jealous?' she teased.

'Madly,' he declared, not sounding it at all. 'Now get the rest of that kit off, woman, and let me have my way with you before Coronation Street *starts.'*

Coronation Street, she was smiling to herself as she returned to the van. He'd never watched an episode in his life. However he had worked for Martin Stone a few times since Martin had taken over the company, but today was the only other time she'd met the man. She felt pleased that he'd remembered Steve so fondly, and touched by his willingness to help her small charity – and sorry that she hadn't made more of an effort with her appearance this morning, as if he'd have noticed, which of course he wouldn't have.

It would be quite something though to attract someone like him, a real boost to her spirits and her confidence, to her outlook on everything, so she might play with the fantasy for a while. Better that than make an immediate return to the grimness of her actual life.

Half an hour later, Angie was leaving Hill Lodge, and focussing on her next meeting, which was with an independent-living agency for those with mental health issues. They didn't have any apartments free at the moment, but it did no harm to keep in touch with these people, to make sure Bridging the Gap's residents weren't forgotten when something did come up.

On reaching the front gate of the Lodge she looked up and had to fight the sudden impulse to run back inside. A man was slouching against her van, clearly waiting for her, and she knew exactly who he was.

Suddenly damned if she was going to let him see her fear, she raised her chin as she approached him, eyes blazing contempt, hands clenched in fists in her pockets.

'Hello, Angie,' he drawled, straightening up in an absurdly awkward way, as if he were pulling up his trousers, or shaking them out to dry. He was short and bald-headed with a prize-fighter's physique, multiple piercings in his ears and nose and a smile that, in spite of his attempts to appear friendly, made him look like an untrained pit bull.

This was Agi, the charmer Roland Shalik sent to carry out his dirty work.

'Get out of my way,' she said tightly.

'Angie, Angie,' he drawled, putting his hands together as though in prayer. 'You know you have to pay your rent. It's the law, and yet you don't pay yours. So how can you expect to stay where you are?'

She regarded him fiercely, teeth gritted, sweat prickling the back of her neck as her heart thudded with dread.

'Mr Shalik has asked me to inform you,' he said smoothly,

'of the steps he has taken to remove you from the house. Do you know of them? Are you opening your mail?'

Temper flashed in her eyes. 'Yes, I know, and you can tell him from me...' She broke off as he closed the short distance between them.

'If you need help,' he said quietly, 'Mr Shalik is still willing to arrange a loan...'

She stepped back, shaking her head in disgust. Taking a loan from that shark would end her up in ten times more debt than she was in already, more even, and she wasn't going to do it. Not even to save her home. There would be no point, for she'd end up losing it anyway.

Agi's smile was one of sad understanding, even benevolence, as he murmured, 'Of course there are other possibilities...'

She stared at him, not sure she wanted to know where this was going.

His eyes took on a mocking gleam. 'You have a very beautiful daughter,' he reminded her, 'it would be...' He broke off as her hand slammed across his face.

'Don't you bring my daughter into this,' she hissed at him. 'Do you hear me? If you try it again I'll have the immigration people on you so fast your feet won't hit the ground as they throw you back to the sewer you came from,' and pushing past him she ran to get in the van.

As she drove away she heard him call after her. 'Don't forget you have choices, Angie. We always have choices,' and for one blinding moment she almost turned the van around to drive straight at him.

'How dare he threaten me like that?' Angie raged, pacing up and down the office in a frenzy of fury that was likely to erupt at any moment into an explosion of panic. The door was tightly closed so no chance passer-by could hear if she swore, and Emma had switched the phones to voicemail as soon as she'd seen Angie coming in the door.

'Why the hell are you only telling me about him now?' Emma demanded angrily. 'How many times has he threatened you before?'

'Once, twice, I don't know. It doesn't matter. Shalik knows very well there's no way I can get the money, so what's he going to do, send more heavies round to scare it out of me? Well, good luck with that.'

'There are laws to protect people in your position,' Emma reminded her fiercely. 'He has to give proper notice and he knows it.'

'He already has. It's going through the courts as we speak.'

Emma regarded her aghast. 'For God's sake, Angie. How could you have kept this from me? I mean, I knew it was bad, but…' Words failed her as she tried to grasp the enormity of Angie's plight. 'We have to get a lawyer,' she stated. 'We know plenty, thanks to what we do here…'

'They're not going to do it for free,' Angie interrupted, 'and there's just no way I can pay them. I can't even afford a bloody birthday cake for Zac next week. Christ, what am I saying? We'll be lucky to have a damned kitchen next week the way things are going, never mind a cake.' She stared at Emma, so horrified by this possibility that she felt herself starting to shake. 'I need to speak to Roland Shalik,' she declared, grabbing her phone. 'I know he won't take my call, snivelling coward that he is, hiding behind his ludicrous army of thugs and bullies, but I have to try.'

Emma watched uneasily as Angie connected to the number. 'What are you going to say?' she asked.

Angie put up a hand as a female voice answered with the name of Shalik's company. 'Put me through to Mr Shalik,' she said abruptly.

'Who's calling please?'

'Angela Watts from Willow Close.' Immediately the words were out she realized her mistake.

'You need to speak to the tenancy manager,' she was told. 'I'll give you the number…'

'Thanks, I have it,' and she cut the call dead.

Her eyes went to Emma, and she saw a reflection of her own outrage and helplessness. She knew her sister would do anything in her power to help if she could, but her finances weren't in a healthy state either – the only reason she wasn't being hounded out of her house was because she had an ex-husband to pay the rent.

Emma said, 'Whatever happens, he won't get away with throwing you out. You're a single mother with two children…'

Angie regarded her incredulously. 'Are you serious? You know very well that's no insurance. Women are losing their homes all the time, and in some cases their kids end up in care.' The chance of that nightmare scenario struck her another horrific blow; it was one she simply couldn't let happen.

'No one's going to take Grace and Zac away,' Emma said forcefully, 'and you've got to stop telling yourself they will. We need to fight this rationally, make a plan…'

'Don't you think I've been trying to come up with one? I've got no idea how to get the money, unless I take one of their crooked doorstep loans so I'll be in hock to them for evermore. Well, that's not going to happen. I'd rather be on the streets than let Roland Shalik control my life any more than he does already.' She faltered for a moment, knowing she didn't mean that about the streets – or did she?

'I know, why don't I try to get a loan?' Emma suggested. 'I mean a legit one, from the bank. You can pay me back…'

'No, I can't let you do that, and besides they'd never lend you as much as I need.'

Emma's anxiety visibly grew. 'So how much rent do you owe?' she asked carefully.

Angie looked away, unable to speak the figure even to her sister.

'Five, six thousand?' Emma ventured.

Angie shook her head. 'Try doubling it,' she said, thinking of the council tax and how much more that was adding to it, along with the utilities, credit cards, overdraft...

Emma said gravely, 'Well, if the worst comes to the worst you'll come and stay with me. It'll be tight with all of us, but we'll...'

'You know that won't work,' Angie reminded her despairingly. 'Remember how hard Shalik came down on you for overcrowding when you let Cherie Burrows and her kids stay after they lost their flat? He threatened to evict you and he could have done it, because your house is a single-family residence.' They were both afraid that he might seek to get rid of Emma anyway, although for the moment he'd made no move to.

'He'd never have known about Cherie if it weren't for Amy effing Cutler,' Emma snarled, referring to her next-door neighbour who'd once made a move on Steve and had been firmly rebuffed. She'd detested them all ever since, as if they were responsible for her knickerless attempt to straddle the man under her kitchen sink trying to clear the U-bend.

'She'll go to Shalik again,' Angie warned, 'and think about how bad you felt when you had to make Cherie and her kids leave; it'll be a hundred times worse if you have to do it to me.'

Having to accept that was true, Emma slapped a hand on the desk. 'That's why we have to get a lawyer,' she insisted. 'If we can find someone who'll give us the first hour for free, it might be all we need.'

This time Angie didn't argue; however, an hour later, having called every solicitor on their contact list, they still weren't able to get an appointment before the middle of next week.

Angie forced back tears and picked up the tea Emma had put in front of her. She felt sick, terrified, unable to think straight as everything seemed to close in on her. 'Oh God, how has this become my life?' she cried wretchedly. 'What did I do to make it happen? Isn't it enough that I've lost my husband and son, do I really have to lose my home as well?'

Without explaining anything, Emma picked up Angie's mobile and made a call. When it was answered, she said, 'Hello, I have Miles Granger on the line for Mr Shalik.' Granger was their local MP.

Angie's eyes widened in surprise, and she almost managed a smile as she caught on to Emma's ruse.

'What's it *about*?' Emma cried, indignantly echoing the voice at the other end of the line. 'I've just told you, it's Miles Granger calling. He'll discuss his business with Mr Shalik, when you put us through.' She glanced at Angie and winked. A moment later, she said, 'Mr Shalik? Thank you, I'll put Mr Granger on.'

As she held out the receiver Angie stared at it, so thrown she couldn't get a single thought through the chaos in her head. A brief reminder of her children, a birthday cake, the threat of eviction brought her to her senses, and taking the phone she said, quickly, 'Mr Shalik, it's Angie Watts. I'm sure you know that your father…'

'Mrs Watts,' came the dark, drawling tones of her landlord, 'I don't appreciate being tricked into taking phone calls. I believe Agi offered you a loan to help with your difficulties…'

'You know very well I can't take it.'

'That's your choice. My position is clear. I wish to sell that house and you presumably know by now that you have until the end of this month to make alternative arrangements.'

Angie was so unprepared for his last words that she thought for a moment she'd imagined them. But she hadn't, he really had said the end of this month, which must mean things had progressed through the courts even faster than she'd realized.

CHAPTER EIGHT

It was a free period after lunch, and Grace and her best friend Lois were in an empty art room getting down to business. #SAVINGGRACE.

Lois, with her short brown hair and big tawny eyes, was bright, loyal and shared Grace's passion for film and theatre. Unlike Grace, who longed to act, her ambition was to direct or produce, so it wasn't unusual for her to select monologues or songs, sometimes dances, for Grace to perform and her to assess before they uploaded them to YouTube and shared them with their friends on social media. They'd been doing a lot more of that since Grace had been relegated to the wings of the Fairweather Players, but they kind of enjoyed being their own little production company with a slowly growing band of followers.

Today, however, their artistic endeavours weren't receiving their usual attention. They were concerned with more pressing matters such as how Grace could earn some money.

'OK,' Lois said, glancing up from her phone as Grace worked on her laptop, 'before we get on to jobs for you, here's an app I found that you can download for your mum. It checks what she's spending in the supermarket as she shops. Very useful, I'd say, stroke of genius on my part in finding it.'

Grace glanced at it, not sure how much use it was going to be, but maybe she could suggest it.

Lois continued, 'Have you worked out yet what you're going to do about your phone? I mean, you can't not have a phone.'

Grace looked crestfallen. The contract was due to end in just over a month and Lois was right, she couldn't not have a phone. 'Mum's getting me a sim so I'll still be able to make calls and send texts,' she said dolefully.

Lois regarded her with heartfelt sympathy. 'Well, we're almost always together,' she said brightly, 'so you can use my phone if you need to for Instagram and stuff.'

With a small but grateful smile, Grace pressed send on the latest homework assignment she'd carried out for a boy in her environmental studies class – an essay on the purpose of zoos in the twenty-first century – for which she'd already been paid two pounds, with two more to come after it had been read and approved by him.

'You need to charge more,' Lois told her sagely.

'No one our age can afford it. So, tell me what you found out about me being able to get a job.'

Clicking through to the results of a Google search, Lois read from her phone. 'OK, by law you can't work during school hours, obvs, or before 7 a.m. or after 7 p.m., or for more than four hours without taking a break.'

'Which leaves like no time at all. Does it say what kind of jobs I can do?'

Lois pulled a face as she scrolled on down. 'You could clear tables at a café or restaurant after school, provided you can fit it in around all the other stuff we've got going on. Or you could wash up in the same sort of places, same hours, or you could help out with old people – actually that might be voluntary. Yes, it is.' She looked defeated, but only for a moment. 'I nearly forgot,' she cried excitedly, 'you could design websites. There's no age restriction on that.'

'Yeah, if I knew how.'

'All right. So invent a video game…'

'Lois!'

'OK, OK! Let's check to see how many views you've had for the video we posted on YouTube last night.'

'I did, just now, and it's still only twelve – I told you, not everyone gets Shakespeare – and I don't see how it's going to make us any money even if we got a thousand views.' Grace sighed and picked up the 'Glass is Greener' water bottle Lois had given her for Christmas along with the dance classes. She drank, put the bottle down and watched Lois changing the screen on her phone. 'What are you doing?' she asked.

'It's time,' Lois replied confidently, 'to ask our Instagram and Facebook followers for any bright ideas on how to earn decent money at our age.'

Grace looked worried. This was something she knew neither of her parents would approve of, for it was too random, too likely to attract the wrong sort of suggestions. However, her dad was never going to know and nor would her mum, provided no one told her and it all worked out. So maybe Lois was right, they should cast the net wider, see if someone out there could come up with something brilliant that they hadn't thought of. And if any creepy or gross responses came back, all they had to do was delete them.

Angie was in the office alone when she received an unexpected email from Martin Stone.

Hope Cliff was able to help this morning. Let me know if any problems, or anything more we can do. Martin.

In spite of being touched by the kindness Angie almost laughed to think of all the help she needed, and of how shocked he'd be if she sent him a list. Of course she never would, not only because she still had some pride in spite of not being able to afford it, but because he wasn't actually offering to help *her*.

She messaged back: *That's really kind of you. A couple of residents have been in touch with Cliff, and were told he'll get back to them in a couple of days. Angie. PS: I'll let you know how it goes.*

Wondering if her subconscious had added the last words in order to keep the door open for her to contact him again, she didn't bother to try and analyse it further. She simply put it, and the pleasing lift his message had brought, out of her mind. She had far more serious and pressing issues to deal with right now than being in touch with a man who'd be even more embarrassed than she was if he thought she was in any way interested in him.

She wasn't. All that mattered to her was how she was going to protect herself and her children from what was coming their way.

She'd opened the court letters now, having popped home an hour ago, so she knew that Roland Shalik hadn't been making an idle threat. Notice had been served for her to be out of the house in less than four weeks. It wouldn't even matter if she could pay the arrears, he wanted the house back and he wasn't prepared to waste any more time in getting it.

Somewhere deep in her gut she felt nauseous, twisted up with anxiety, burning with a need to scream, but above it all, in a weirdly subdued sort of state, she was stunned and ashamed and so lost for answers that she wasn't even capable of feeling a need to act. How could she, when she had no idea at this moment what to do?

She jumped at the sound of a thud in the next door store-room, and relaxed again when she remembered Emma was in there sorting through a recent delivery of second-hand clothes to see if there was anything suitable for their residents. It was surplus from one of the charity shops on the seafront, brought here before the refugee crisis team came to scoop it up in the morning.

Angie dropped her head into her hands. She'd been worse than a fool – completely insane would be putting it mildly – to ignore the official-looking mail when it had come, but for the last few weeks she simply hadn't been able to face any more bad news. There was no escaping it now, and as she pictured the children's bedrooms, Liam's zoo with all sorts of wild animals on the walls, Grace's artiste's dressing room, Zac's soccer changing room, and all the treasured possessions they hadn't yet sold, she had to fight back a bitter onslaught of tears. There was so much packing to be done, all kinds of painful decisions to make...

Taking a quick breath she forced herself back into the moment, and focused on what they were going to eat this evening. Thanks to the booty of freshly baked loaves from one of the resident's overnight shift at the bakery they weren't short of bread, and she was sure there were three cans of beans in the cupboard and two eggs in the fridge. There was more than that, such as a bottle of sunflower oil, a bag of flour, a jar of tomato purée, all kinds of things she couldn't do much with unless she was able to combine them with ingredients they didn't have.

A quick check at the ATM had told her that she still had six pounds in her account, so if she gave the children egg on toast tonight, they could have jacket potatoes and beans tomorrow. She'd have just toast. However, she might get the cash from the cleaning shift she'd covered at the restaurant this morning. They could have something far more wholesome then, maybe a big leafy salad with avocado dressing, one of Grace's favourites, or chicken burgers and sweet potato mash, always a hit with Zac.

Her mouth watered almost painfully as she sent another text to her neighbour reminding her that she needed to be paid. The trouble was, Kirsty probably wouldn't be able to manage it until she'd been paid herself.

Sending a silent message of thanks for the bread, she set about updating her files following the day's meetings. The irony of having spent time trying to sort out long-term accommodation for her residents when she was about to lose her own home wasn't lost on her, but what else could she do? Just because she was in trouble didn't make their needs any the less, and she'd be certifiably crazy if she didn't focus on her job. Without it she'd never exist on her reduced benefits, unless some miracle position with double the salary and the same semi-flexible hours cropped up, and she wasn't holding her breath for that. Maybe she could talk to Ivan, see if he could arrange a loan from the church funds, but no sooner had the thought entered her head than she dismissed it. The amount she needed was too large, and anyway he'd just channel the vicar and start spouting passages from the Bible, as if holy words were some sort of universal panacea that held the answer to everything. In her experience they had the answer to just about nothing, but maybe she simply wasn't clever enough to understand the clues.

'Are you OK?' Emma asked as she came into the office with a coat and two pairs of boots.

Angie sighed and would have said no, of course not, but that wasn't going to help either of them, so she simply shrugged and tried for a smile.

'I thought this might fit Douglas,' Emma said, holding up the coat. 'If it's too big he can always use his belt to keep it together. It'll make him look a bit of a dick, of course, but as I don't think he ever looks in the mirror that shouldn't be too much of a problem.'

Angie had to laugh.

'Oh, wow,' Emma murmured, glancing at her computer screen. 'I've got a wave,' and dropping the coat and boots on the floor she sat down, reaching for her mouse.

'A what?' Angie asked, frowning.

Emma's eyes remained fixed on the screen. 'A wave, from an admirer,' she explained. A moment later she let go of the mouse and turned guilty eyes to Angie. 'Sorry, bad timing, I…'

Angie shook her head. 'Don't be sorry. There's no reason for your life to go on hold just because mine is falling apart.'

Emma flushed unhappily.

'That came out badly,' Angie sighed. 'Why don't you go ahead and check him out?'

Emma watched her sister as Angie made a pretence of carrying on with some work.

Though Angie could feel the scrutiny she didn't acknowledge it, for she wasn't yet ready to admit that she'd opened the court letters. She realized this meant she was in some form of denial, but better there for the moment than in the clutch of terrifying reality.

They couldn't leave Willow Close, they just couldn't. It was their home where Grace and Zac had always lived, where all their memories had been made, where Steve's spirit still kept them going.

'Angie,' Emma probed gently.

Angie bit her lip and tried to smile. 'So tell me about this dating site,' she encouraged. 'What's he like, the guy who gave you a wave?'

Emma pulled a face. 'A bit of a jerk,' she admitted. She let a few moments pass and said chattily, 'What if there's someone out there who's right for you, but he doesn't know any other way to meet you?'

Angie's eyes widened with as much surprise as annoyance as she said, 'I'm hardly what you'd call a good catch right now, and anyway, don't you find it a bit galling, or maybe demeaning, to think that a man has to be the answer to everything?'

Emma bristled. 'That's not what I think. Not even close, but what's wrong with someone who makes you laugh, who thinks about you and how to make you happy?'

'You've been watching too many rom-coms.'

Ignoring the put-down, Emma said, 'Do you really think Steve would want you to carry on like this?'

Wishing with all her heart that Emma hadn't mentioned Steve, Angie forced herself to remain silent as a ravaging, desperate grief rose up to swamp her.

'What if,' Emma persisted, 'the answer to all your…'

'Em, stop,' Angie broke in raggedly. 'Even if I wanted to meet someone, which I don't, and even if he happens to be on that website, which I doubt, you have to admit that now really isn't the time. So you go ahead and wave, use your bloody knickers if you want to, just please get off my case.'

Emma fell silent, so did Angie, but as the minutes ticked by Angie's struggle to hold back her emotions started to fail. She was afraid to take a breath in case it turned into a sob, could barely move, aching with dread, guilt, grief, and despair.

Emma got up from her desk, but realizing her sister was about to hug her, Angie put up a hand to stop her. She couldn't handle sympathy or tenderness right now; it would be the end of her. 'I'm fine,' she managed to say, and to try and prove it she quickly typed a search into Google. When the results came up she clicked a profile on the home page and turned the screen so Emma could see it. 'How about him?' she said recklessly.

Emma blinked first in surprise, then in confusion.

'It's Martin Stone,' Angie told her. 'I ran into him this morning at the retirement village building site. He knew Steve.'

'Well he would, being who he is,' Emma said carefully. 'So why are you…? What are you saying?'

'Nothing.' Angie shrugged, feeling stupid now. 'It's possible we can get Dougie and Mark Fields a job on the site,' she explained. 'We're waiting to hear.'

'That's good.' Emma still seemed puzzled. 'His dad's name was Dougie,' she stated, making an absurd connection. 'Remember he was the mayor who did so much for this town like revamping the old cinema, and bringing in one-pound bus fares for every journey. He got the planning department to…'

Angie closed the screen down.

Emma frowned. 'Why did you do that?'

Angie shook her head. 'I don't know. I'm sorry.' She pressed her hands to her face. 'I'm all over the place at the moment,' she confessed. 'I can't seem to get my head straight.'

Realizing it was time to let the subject of Martin Stone go, Emma returned to her desk and another silence fell as they got on with their work.

Half an hour later, as she and Emma locked up and started through to the car park, Angie noticed the misty rain settling over her sister's hair turning the stray strands into a sparkling cobwebby net. It reminded her of when they were young, walking to school in winter, or making dens at the end of the garden. She thought of how much they'd meant to their mother, how safe they'd always felt with her, and how she'd done her best to take care of Emma after their mother had gone. She loved Emma so much, and was so glad, *relieved* to have her it was close to making her cry, for without her she'd be totally alone. She just didn't want to be a burden on her, making her worry about things she couldn't change, or feel she had somehow to come up with the answers that were beyond them both.

'I wonder if he's married,' Emma said as she unlocked her car.

Knowing exactly who she was talking about, Angie's eyes flashed, but she had to laugh. 'Of course he is,' she replied, 'and anyway, the way my luck's going right now the only match I'm likely to get in the next few days is Liam's DNA to that murder in Bristol.' Even as she said it, she felt herself spinning off into a realm of madness. How could she even begin to joke about something like that; how could she even think of it without completely falling apart?

Twenty quid for topless shot. #SAVINGGRACE

Fifty quid to get your kit off. #SAVINGGRACE

You're mad asking for suggestions. Look what you're getting. #SAVINGGRACE

Run away and join circus. #SAVINGGRACE

They're looking for dancers in Vegas. You'd be brilliant. #SAVINGGRACE

How many creeps does it take to change a lightbulb? Let us know when they've screwed you. #SAVING GRACE

'That's not even a joke,' Lois muttered angrily.

'But what we're doing is,' Grace responded. 'We need to take it down.'

Lois nodded glumly, but as Grace started to delete all the nonsense suggestions, she said, 'Tell you what, once you've got rid of all that crap let's add something to our message like, *Idiots and perverts don't bother wasting our time.*'

'That'll really put them off,' Grace said wryly.

Lois laughed. 'OK, but let's give it a couple more days. You never know who might get in touch, and we don't want to miss out if the best opportunity of all hasn't quite got to us yet, do we?'

CHAPTER NINE

Two days later, having fitted in a lunchtime shift at the Bear Street chippie, Angie was at the food bank on Wesley Street, two roads back from the Promenade, in what used to be a betting shop. Balloons and bunting were pinned around the door to try and make people feel welcome, and tea and biscuits were in plentiful supply for those who'd been referred from doctors, the local authority, and various churches.

At her reception table just inside the entrance, one of eight spread out around the wood-panelled room, Angie had spent the last two hours listening sympathetically, fearfully and even in shared anger to the stories of why today's hungry and largely blameless were there. In most of their stressed and often embarrassed faces, she kept seeing herself in the near future. She imagined coming here in some ludicrous disguise as some of them did, hoping no one would recognize her. How crazy was that when all the volunteers knew her and she could already see the shock on their faces when they realized her predicament, and feel their eagerness to help her in any way they could.

'You're only two pay cheques away from the streets,' one of them would undoubtedly comment soulfully, using a phrase – a truism – that was often heard in this place. It obviously wasn't a certainty for all, but it was for those who came here. They weren't homeless – an address was required for a referral to the food bank – but many were known as the working poor, for they had jobs, in some cases more than one. Their earnings were so low and outgoings so high, however, that they were no longer able to put food on the table. So, as one dear old soul had put it in a husky, tearful voice today, they had to come here and beg.

'You're not begging,' Angie had told him softly. 'You're just accepting a little help to get yourself through this difficult time. There's nothing wrong with that.'

The old man was in his eighties, well dressed, hair neatly combed, he even smelled of aftershave. He'd clearly gone to some effort to make himself presentable today, probably hoping no one would think the worst of him. He was even wearing his service medals; a reminder to others that he'd mattered once. Those medals had made Angie's heart ache. Apparently his wife had died a few months ago. She'd always been in charge of the money; she sorted their pensions, did the shopping, paid all the bills and since her passing he'd fallen into a depression. They had no family, just each other and a kind neighbour who popped in now and again to check up on him. He might be lonely and crushed by sadness, but at least he had money, it just needed to be sorted out so he could access it. (Why did banks make these things so difficult?) In the meantime his doctor had referred him here to make sure he had enough food in his cupboard to see him through the coming week.

There were so many stories, tragedies, involving people of all ages and backgrounds, some with mental health issues, and those who were so riddled with shame to be in this position that they couldn't look anyone in the eye. Then there were the druggies and alcoholics who'd all but stopped caring about themselves so they were missing teeth, had sores on their faces and piercings that were going septic. Each time she came in for a shift Angie could feel the web of hardship tightening around them all. Their needs, their sadness, anger and bewilderment, combined with the unfairness, even hostility of a system that relied on food banks and charities to provide for vulnerable citizens were becoming increasingly hard to take. She wanted to help them, she really did, and she would, it was why she was here, but today she couldn't help feeling a tiny bit sorrier for herself than she did for them.

After making sure that a middle-aged, disabled woman with speech difficulties and a sad, sallow face was being taken care of by one of the helpers who filled the grocery bags in the back room, Angie quickly checked her phone.

No messages.

Her heart contracted with a painful stab of panic. She was waiting for so many callbacks, mostly from job agencies for some night shifts or anything else she could add to her hours at BtG, but apparently nothing had come up yet for which she was suitable.

'Angie? Hello? Are you with us?'

Angie looked up into the kindly grey eyes of Brenda Crompton, a fellow volunteer. The ex-Salvation Army major was regarding her curiously, seeming to sense something was amiss and trying to decide whether or not to ask. Apparently concluding she should, she settled herself into the chair that the disabled woman had just vacated.

Angie smiled at her. She saw that there were only a couple

of clients left at the other tables, and noticing the time she realized no more were likely to come now.

Brenda signalled to someone in the kitchenette and a moment later Bill, an elderly man with a cheery demeanour, put a fresh cup of tea in front of Angie. At the same time Brenda pushed a half-empty plate of biscuits towards her.

Angie's mouth watered almost as stingingly as it had earlier in the afternoon when the snacks had first come out. But the jammy dodgers and Hobnobs, donated by Brenda and her husband, were for the clients, not those who were supposed to be helping them.

Brenda winked and taking a biscuit herself she bit into it, cupping a hand beneath her chin to catch the crumbs.

Though Angie understood this was Brenda's way of telling her it was all right to have a little treat, she still couldn't allow herself to take one. If she did she might never be able to stop and she couldn't bear anyone to know just how hungry she was. 'Watching my waistline,' she joked, and suddenly, out of nowhere, she felt her spirits lift a little, for she'd been paid cash in hand at the chippie. This meant she should be able to dish up a decent meal tonight.

Brenda watched fondly as Angie's conscience allowed her to crunch into a Hobnob. It appeared she was about to say something, but there was a sudden crash in the back room so she got up to go and investigate. 'I'll be back,' she promised Angie, and added with a nod at the plate, 'why not finish them off before they go stale?'

Wondering how Brenda had realized she was so hungry, Angie watched the older woman go, hips swaying like a saucy tambourine, and felt grateful and embarrassed and so ready for another biscuit that she crammed a whole one in her mouth at once just as her mobile started to vibrate.

She should have let the call go to messages instead of blowing crumbs on to the table and down her front as she tried to say hello, but she didn't.

'Mrs Watts?' Luckily the caller didn't wait for her to confirm it. 'It's DC Leo Johnson here from Kesterly CID. I have some news regarding Liam's DNA.'

Angie stopped chewing, every crumb turning to dust in her mouth as her heart dropped to a dull, heavy beat of dread. Realizing she was unable to swallow, she grabbed a tissue and emptied the half-chewed biscuit into it.

'Are you there, Mrs Watts?'

'Yes,' she replied thinly. 'I'm here.' *Oh God, please don't let this be*… She couldn't even put her fear into words, it was too awful.

Leo Johnson was saying, '… so I thought you'd like to know that Liam's DNA wasn't a match to the DNA taken from the victim…'

Angie didn't hear what else he was telling her. She could hardly bring her own voice past her throat as she said, 'Did you say that it *wasn't* a match?'

'That's right,' he confirmed. 'They got the results back this morning. I called as soon as we heard. I thought you'd want to know.'

'Yes, yes,' she mumbled, feeling oddly light-headed and something else she couldn't understand, for it was too far out of reach. 'Do they still want to talk to him?' she asked dully.

'Given that his name's on a list linked to the main suspect, that's likely. On the other hand, if there's nothing to say he's in the area, or still in touch with his former cronies they'll probably let it go.'

Did that make him safer? It should if no one was going to try and force him to talk, but it still didn't mean he was no longer being controlled by the London gangs. He could be anywhere, in any city, working for them in any capacity…

Or maybe he'd managed to break with them.

Whichever way, it still didn't tell her where or how he was.

What she did know though, was that he was no longer a suspected killer.

An hour later, with her chip-shop earnings in her purse, Angie was in Asda searching out as many two-for-one and half-price deals as she could find up to twenty-five pounds – the most she could allow herself to spend. Pizzas, chicken nuggets, three lasagnes for six quid, a bag of white potatoes, a day-old French loaf, a round lettuce for forty p… Grace preferred fresh food and if it could be kind of vegan that would be good, because she loved animals and fish and she didn't want plants to die for her either, but she understood that she had to live. (She also understood that more often than not it was easier – cheaper – if she could just go with the flow and if that meant eating eggs, cheese, and a portion of chicken with her Sunday roast, she'd do it.)

In a rush of recklessness Angie added a bottle of Chilean Sauvignon to her trolley – special offer, reduced from seven quid to three ninety-nine – and realized how utterly insane it was to be celebrating the fact that her absent son was no longer a suspected killer.

In her world, today, given what she was going through, that had to be worth celebrating, though.

After making sure she had all the ingredients for Zac's unicorn cake she wheeled her trolley to the checkout to wait in line. Grace was determined to bake the cake for her brother, and knowing it was her daughter's way of trying to cut down on costs made Angie's heart ache. It was true, novelty cakes at the bakery were far too expensive for them to afford, but Grace shouldn't have to be worrying about things like that. She shouldn't have to be giving up her smartphone either, when the contract ran out in the next few weeks, but Angie was afraid it was inevitable. Zac's gym club membership would now have to go the way of his rowing club and archery fees. The SkySports package Steve had signed them up for when Zac was four – a birthday treat for their sports-mad youngest – had already been cancelled. Zac didn't know that yet, for it didn't run out until the end of the month, nor was he aware that the Adidas X16.1 football boots he had his heart set on for his birthday would have to be downgraded to a cheaper pair, probably second-hand from Depop. He wasn't going to like it, Angie was certain of that, in fact he would probably have a serious rant about it, until Grace took him aside to explain why he had to understand that things were different now.

Though their finances had held together for a while after Steve had gone, everything was collapsing so fast now that Angie couldn't even see what might fall next.

They were going to lose the house at the end of the month.

It wasn't until after she'd paid the bill that she realized with a pang of shame that she couldn't possibly justify a bottle of wine for herself and Emma when she was depriving Grace and Zac of so much. So, wheeling her trolley from the checkout, she joined a queue at the information desk in the hope of receiving a cash credit for her crazy idea of a celebration. She eyed her trolley for more items she ought to put back, and realized she'd been rash, unthinking, acting as though the twenty-five quid she'd earned at the chippie was going to magically replace itself like some fairy-tale egg...

Deciding to ask for credit on her entire trolley so she could start again, she fought back a wave of misery and frustration and after inching forward a few feet she found herself tuning into a conversation behind her.

'Oh, that's really generous of you, that is. Really generous.'

Angie turned and saw an elderly lady watching an obviously well-off woman of around forty emptying a full bag of groceries into a foodbank box.

Since this was where the donations started Angie decided to take more notice of the generous woman, and came to the conclusion that not only was she a caring citizen, but she was really quite beautiful in a very classy way. Her hair was a mass of thick dark curls styled in a loose bob, her skin was creamy and shone with health, and the effortless elegance of her movements made Angie wonder if she was a dancer.

'Look at all that,' the older lady chuntered on admiringly. 'You're a very kind person is all I can say. Makes me wonder what this bloody country's coming to that we have to do things like this. Shame on them is what I say. Bloody shame on them.'

The dark-haired woman's eyes sparkled with humour but Angie couldn't hear what she said, could only tell that she wasn't trying to brush the old lady off.

'There ain't many would do what you just did,' the old lady declared, picking up a large box of Kellogg's cornflakes and looking as though she'd like to make off with it.

'Well,' the dark-haired woman replied, 'if the day comes when I need this sort of help, perhaps someone will fill up the box for me.'

As Angie watched her walk away, upright and slender, the very epitome of someone who'd never need a food bank, she felt an odd sort of longing stirring inside her. She'd love to be that woman, or like her; or maybe she just wanted to know her. It was people like that who made the world feel like a good place to be, which was a very weird assessment of someone she'd only seen for a few minutes and would probably never see again.

Nevertheless, as though the woman had sprinkled some sort of hope over her, Angie turned her trolley to the door and headed out into the car park. She'd take this lot home, have her little celebration – or drown her sorrows – then she'd work things out.

As she approached her van a Mercedes saloon reversed out of the space next to it, and she didn't feel surprised to see the dark-haired woman at the wheel. Their eyes didn't meet, Angie was certain the woman hadn't clocked her at all, nevertheless she continued to feel affected by her as she watched the car drive away. She wondered what life was like for her, and where she lived. What kind of job did she have, if she even had one? Her husband was probably loaded, judging by the car, and her kids, if she had any, were no doubt at private schools and completely brilliant at everything they did.

With a small, wry smile to herself Angie finished stacking her groceries into the van and got into the driver's seat. If her work with people who'd hit hard times had taught her anything at all, it was never to assume something about a person based on the way things looked. Even rich people had bad experiences; they bled, they hurt, they lost their money and they even lost their homes. Some of them had sons who went off the rails, and husbands who died when their children were still small and before they'd taken out any life insurance.

No one was immune to the vagaries of fate, any more than they were incapable of making mistakes. Everyone, no matter who they were, or how dire their straits, had to find a way of dealing with the worst-case scenarios life threw at them. She wasn't alone in that, plenty of people were struggling and many were in even worse situations than her. True, she couldn't think of anyone right now, but she knew they existed, and she knew too that somehow she'd get herself and her children through these dark times. She was someone who coped, who rose to challenges and overcame them, and one way or another she was going to keep them together as a family with a roof over their heads and hope in their hearts.

CHAPTER TEN

Just when Angie thought she didn't have a single laugh left in her, that even if she did it'd never make it past all the stress and anxiety corked up in her soul, it erupted in a great choking guffaw. It wasn't supposed to be funny, it really wasn't. In fact, it was the biggest disaster to come out of Angie's oven since the day Steve had set fire to his mother's boots while trying to dry them.

Grace's unicorn cake was… Well, it was different, that was for sure, unique even, and so explicitly something it wasn't supposed to be that even she gave a snort of laughter when she realized why her mother and aunt were beside themselves.

Zac had been boasting to his mates for days that he was going to have the biggest, most amazing unicorn cake ever, and that was certainly true.

'It's definitely got the biggest, most amazing…' Emma gestured to the horn as she gasped and dabbed her eyes with a party napkin. 'I've never seen one like it. Were those cake balls part of the recipe, or did you… was it…?'

Falling against her mother as they all exploded again, Grace managed to say, 'There were supposed to be three of them – there *were* three, I swear it, I just don't know how it's come out as two.'

'Well, I'm sorry, my darling,' Emma said, putting an arm around her niece. 'It might be the best cake we've ever tasted, but no way can we serve it like that. It's… It's…'

'Obscene, I know,' Grace declared, and transporting it to the table she waited for her mother and aunt to pull themselves together, saying, 'Stop. He'll be in any minute.'

Angie glanced down the hall towards the front door. Since it was closed it wasn't possible to see beyond it, but they could hear the shouts of Zac and his friends playing footie over on the green. They'd already stuffed themselves with jelly and egg sandwiches since coming in from school, and now they were working up an appetite for the cake while Grace iced it.

This wasn't going well.

'We've got to do something,' Grace hissed, searching for ideas. 'I know! Shall I drop it?'

Emma burst into more hilarity, while Angie, still choking with mirth, decided that before they did anything at all they needed a photograph.

In the end, after crushing the two cake balls into one spongy mess that they then coated in lashings of crimson buttermilk icing, and remoulding the horn into a suitably slimmer and less excited version of its former self, Grace added a pair of spidery eyes in a place that seemed to work and carried the unique creation to the bomb site of a dining table.

Angie could only look on as Zac and his cousins came tumbling back through the front door, with four equally muddy friends on their heels, kicking off their boots first and then descending on the 'most awesome cake ever'.

'That's what I love about boys,' Emma murmured in her ear, 'so easy to please.'

This was certainly true of Zac. Most other boys his age had birthday parties at Pizza Express or a Game Wagon Video event or even a ride in a hot-air balloon, all so way beyond her means that she hadn't even bothered Googling for ideas. One day, though, when she was back on her feet, he was going to have the best birthday party money could buy.

'No, I'm not going to make one for you,' Grace told Harry, Emma's youngest, who was soon due to be seven himself. 'No, not for you either,' she said to several other boys who were waving grubby hands in the air, because their mouths were too full to shout. 'This is a one-off, I mean, like real art, so make the most of it.'

'Mum, did you see what Freddie gave me for my birthday?' Zac shouted, 'It's only a Liverpool training shirt. Liverpool's my favourite team,' he informed his friend Freddie, as if Freddie had pulled off a mega mind-reading trick.

'When Zac comes to our house,' Jack piped up, 'we watch football in our room so we don't get on Mum's nerves with all our shouting. We get on Mum's nerves quite a lot, but she doesn't mind really.'

'I do, I do,' Emma assured him, knocking back another mouthful of tepid lemonade.

'It's only you who gets on her nerves,' Harry told his brother, and reached for more cake before the last bit went.

'Auntie Angie,' Harry said as she smoothed his hair, feeling the mix of mud and cream under her palm, 'can me and Jack sleep here tonight?'

'You've got school in the morning,' Emma reminded

him. 'You can stay at the weekend – while I go out and have a good time.' Her glance at Angie was full of mischief and meaning.

Catching on, Angie's eyes widened as she said, 'So that's me babysitting then, is it?'

'Where are you going?' Grace wanted to know.

Emma winked. 'That's for me to know and you to find out.'

Grace turned to her mother. 'Is she allowed to have secrets?'

'Not from us,' Angie replied.

'Or from us,' Harry put in excitedly. 'Me and Zac and Jack know lots of secrets and we never tell anyone, do we? My best secret is that Zac's got a girlfriend called Olivia…'

Zac clapped a hand over his cousin's mouth, but as the other boys began ribbing him he jumped up on a chair and declared himself a babe magnet.

Angie and Emma burst out laughing.

'So who's Olivia?' Grace wanted to know.

'She's in my class,' Zac told her, 'and actually she's not my girlfriend, I just snog her when she's not looking.'

Deciding not to pursue that, Angie refilled the glasses and noticing one of the boys – Edward, whose family lived opposite Emma – had wandered across the sitting room to look out of the front window, she paused a moment to watch him. He seemed to be peering round the curtains as if trying to spot someone or something outside.

'Edward?' she called out. 'Is everything all right?'

The other boys swung round to look his way, and suddenly they all flooded across the room to kneel down in front of the window, only their eyes showing above the sill.

'Is he there?' Zac whispered.

'I don't think so,' Edward whispered back.

'I bet he's behind the tree,' Jack warned gravely.

'Who are you talking about?' Angie asked, foreboding

darkening the light-heartedness of the day. Surely to God Agi wasn't out there stalking her, or some other lowlife debt collector.

'Mum! Get down,' Zac hissed. 'He might have a gun.'

Angie and Emma exchanged glances, not entirely sure if this was a game. Certainly small boys loved creating terrifying adventures about spies and monsters and kidnappers...

Angie peered across the green to where the bare trees and winter-torn grasses were masking the brook. The only people she could see were Terry Forrest from number thirty walking his dog, and a couple of teenage girls from The Beeches wandering over the footbridge towards Willow Close. Apart from that the street seemed empty.

'He's really creepy,' Zac whispered to her.

'Who is?'

'We don't know his name, but he comes around sometimes and watches us play on the green.'

Not liking the sound of that one bit, Angie looked at Emma and saw she was just as perturbed.

'Does he ever speak to you?' Emma asked.

The boys shook their heads.

'So what does he do?' Angie asked.

'He just watches us,' Zac replied. 'It's really weird.'

Swallowing uneasily, Angie slipped an arm round Grace as she came to join them. 'Have you ever seen him?' she asked her.

Grace shook her head.

Thinking of drug dealers, recruiters for the county lines as well as perverts, Angie looked at Emma and mouthed, 'Police?'

Emma nodded.

Leaving her and Grace to shepherd the boys back to the table, Angie went into the kitchen to make the call. After explaining what she thought might be happening, she was told that a patrol car would be directed to the estate within the next hour or two.

Knowing this was the best they could hope for given that no crime had been committed, Angie clicked off and almost immediately her mobile rang. At first she thought it was the police calling her back, but then she recognized the number and her insides twisted with anger and unease.

She let the call go to messages. She had nothing to say to Agi that he'd want to hear, and she definitely didn't want to know what he had to say to her.

Her phone rang again, and realizing it would probably keep on ringing until she answered, she made herself click on. 'Why don't you leave me alone?' she hissed. 'I'm trying to sort things out. If you call again I'll report you for harassment.'

There was a moment's silence, before a familiar voice said, 'Angie, I'm… Is everything all right? It doesn't sound as though it is.'

'Oh, Hamish, I'm sorry. I thought… I thought you were someone else. Please ignore what I said. What is it? Is everything OK?'

'Yes, yes, of course.'

She could tell by his tone that it wasn't, and he wouldn't have rung unless he had good reason.

'Tell me what it is,' she insisted.

Sounding hesitant, he said, 'I know it's your boy's birthday… It can wait till tomorrow.'

She wished he would ring off, while knowing if he did she'd only ring him back to press him harder.

In the end he said, 'OK, it's Craig. He's got himself into a bit of a state. He's marching about the place like he doesn't even know where he is. He won't sit down, or eat, or listen to anyone… He just keeps saying that he didn't do it. I asked what he didn't do, but he won't tell me. It's like someone's got inside his head and all he can say is, "I didn't do it. It's not my fault." And then he said, "Please tell Angie I didn't do it." That was when I thought I should ring...'

As Angie drove across town to Hill Lodge, windscreen wipers swiping at the rain as she tried to keep to the speed limit, she was aware of how wildly out of control her thoughts were becoming. She had no idea what could have upset Craig, or why Agi had tried to call, or who had been lurking about the green watching the boys, she only knew that she kept flashing on Liam as though he was nearby too. She saw his face in a desperate grimace of pain; she could hear him calling her, pleading with her to help him.

Taking deep breaths she tried to rein herself in, calm herself down. An anxiety attack now wasn't going to help anyone, least of all her. She needed to stay in the moment, focus on one thing at a time and stop mixing everything up in her head. The children weren't going to be evicted in the next hour while she was at Hill Lodge, the police were sending someone to check out the creep hanging about the green, and she was on her way to sort out Craig. Tomorrow she'd ring around the shelters and hotels in Bristol to see if anyone there knew Liam.

Tears suddenly burned her eyes. Everyone who was supposed to get back to her, potential employers, the housing department, the bank, even the payday loan company she'd called earlier today hadn't contacted her yet. She was in a constant state of waiting, dreading, imagining the worst, while all the time she was somehow making herself believe that it would be all right. She would keep the house, her debts would be paid off and Liam would come home.

Suddenly dazzled by oncoming headlights she slammed on the brakes and just managed to avoid hitting a car. It was a Mercedes which, fleetingly, made her think of the woman she'd seen at the supermarket a few days ago, and who would probably never bang her hand on the horn so aggressively as this person was doing.

Waving an apology to the man who was glaring at her as if he'd like to punch her, she drove on, and tried soothing her nerves with more thoughts of the dark-haired woman, as if she were some sort of spiritual force that could send out invisible waves of rationale and calm. She tried imagining what the woman might be doing now, who she was with. It was easy for Angie to picture an idyllic life for her, since it was what she seemed to exude and deserve. But didn't everyone deserve a good life in their own way? After all, what had she, Angie, done to cause the violence and heartache that had devastated her life two years ago? Or the terror of debt and homelessness that was stalking her every minute of the day?

By the time she reached Hill Lodge she'd managed to channel her thoughts into what might await, while wondering if Emma had already alerted their neighbourhood watch volunteers to the sighting of a suspicious character hanging about the children's play areas. They'd probably be even more effective at seeing him off than the police, given their greater numbers – and ferocity.

If it turned out to be Agi then let him deal with the volunteers, if he could, she thought grimly as she closed the van door. Let him explain that he wasn't a paedo in search of new victims; that he was only there to intimidate and bully a single mother who'd fallen on hard times and couldn't find a way out of them.

Letting herself in through the grand blue front door, she listened out for voices as she closed it behind her. All was quiet, and when she went along the hall into the open-plan kitchen area there was no sign of anyone. She called out for Hamish, and receiving no response was about to go to the bottom of the stairs to try again when Mark Fields came into the kitchen behind her.

'You startled me,' she told him, stepping back and trying not to show her unease. What was it about this man that was so… unsettling? For someone who was neither tall, nor particularly well built, he had a peculiarly oppressive air about him that made him seem as though he was standing far closer than he actually was. Still, at least he had his shirt on today; she wanted no more sightings of that pale, hairy chest, nor a repeat of the unedifying experience of seeing how her discomfort with his semi-nudity had seemed to please him. In fact, this evening he didn't seem to be paying her much attention at all. His eyes were on his phone, and he was wearing a navy blue suit, slightly grubby and shiny, with a yellow tie that looked new and his hair was slickly combed.

'Hamish is around here somewhere,' he told her, still checking his phone. 'The crazy kid was flipping out, so I think he took him up to his room.'

Angie nodded. 'You're looking very smart,' she said, trying to sound friendly. 'Off somewhere nice?'

He looked up and broke into a smile that was somewhere between delighted and boyishly bashful, and might have been endearing were it not for the unwholesome gleam in his eye. 'Got myself a date,' he admitted. 'She's a bit of a looker. A delivery driver for a builder's supplier. I met her when I went for the interview at the retirement village site last Friday.'

Interested to know more, Angie said, 'Did you get the job?'

'They're checking references, apparently, but my hopes are high.' His eyes suddenly fixed on hers, so intently that she almost took another step back. 'Don't suppose you'd be interested in going out with me?' he asked in a kind of growl. 'I mean once I get a place of my own…'

'You should probably be going if you don't want to be

late,' Angie interrupted, needing to shut that down before it got rooted in his head as anything approaching a possibility. She wanted to add a caution for him not to drink too much, but Alexei came down the stairs at that moment and did it for her.

'Getting pissed is a right turn-off for a woman,' he warned Mark in his gravelly Polish accent, while towel-drying his hair. 'Unless she wants to get pissed with you, of course, but if she does, then she's not the right one for you. Not if you want Angie and Emma to keep you on here.'

'Thanks for the lecture,' Fields retorted, already starting for the front door. 'Don't wait up.'

'And don't bring her back here,' Alexei called after him. 'You know the rules.'

As the door slammed behind him, Alexei turned to Angie and broke into a smile. 'I h-have a surprise for you,' he stammered. 'Today I take a parcel to a farm about ten miles from here, and they g-give me wonderful tip. I get it.'

As he went to open a cupboard, Angie said, 'How's Craig? Do you know what was wrong with him?'

Alexei shrugged, and tapped a finger to his head. 'Not quite right, as you know. Poor lad.'

'But why was he upset?'

'Angie.'

Angie turned as Hamish came into the kitchen with Craig close behind him. Craig's eyes were huge bright circles of worry, his face was pale and pinched, and she could see from the stains on his shirt that he'd either thrown up, or spilled something down himself. 'It wasn't my fault,' he told her brokenly. 'I didn't tell them.' He clutched his hands to his head as though to ward off any more accusations or feelings of guilt.

Taking his hands and lowering them gently into her own, she led him to the sofa as she said, 'Didn't tell who what, Craig?'

'I didn't tell them,' he insisted, gazing so earnestly into her eyes that it was as if he truly believed she knew what he was talking about.

'You have to explain it to me,' she told him kindly. 'What has happened?'

'They took her. She didn't want to go but they made her.'

Puzzled, she said, 'Who are you talking about?'

'Sasha.'

'She's the friend you've been protecting?'

He nodded.

'So what happened to her?'

'They took her. It wasn't my fault. I didn't tell anyone where to find her.'

Glancing at Hamish in the hope he might have got further by now, she saw from his expression that he hadn't, so she tightened her hold on Craig's hands. Only then did she register that he hadn't snatched himself free, the way he usually did when someone touched him. He was frightened, she realized, and clinging to her because he thought she could save him.

But save him from what?

'Craig,' she said gently, 'I want you to tell me who Sasha is.'

'She is my friend.'

'How long have you known her?'

He blinked confusedly.

'Where does she live?'

'With me. She lives with me.'

'But you live here...'

'She lives with me,' he insisted.

Wondering now if they were discussing an imaginary friend, Angie glanced at Hamish again. Neither of them was qualified to deal with someone like Craig, who suffered hallucinations thanks to the drugs he'd been force-fed as a child, but those who could help him professionally would claim to have far more serious cases on their hands. So all they could do was try to comfort him and make him feel safe.

'Is Sasha all right now?' Angie decided to venture.

Craig's eyes filled with tears. 'I don't know,' he replied. 'They took her away.'

She frowned. 'Who's they?'

'Men. They took her in a van.'

Slightly thrown by this, Angie said, 'What men? The police?'

'No! Not the police. I don't know their names. I didn't tell them where she was. It wasn't my fault.'

She looked at Hamish again. 'Do you know where he was today?' she asked.

Hamish shook his head.

'I was singing to her,' Craig said earnestly. 'She likes it when I sing. She sings with me.'

Having no idea of what to say or do next, Angie looked at Alexei, who was hovering in the kitchen holding a box of eggs in both hands.

'This was my t-tip,' he told her, clearly glad to be noticed, 'and I want to share with you.'

'He came back with two dozen, not so fresh,' Hamish explained under his breath.

Craig was again looking at her with beseeching eyes that seemed to need something from Angie, if she only knew what.

'I didn't tell them,' he said softly.

Her smile became tender and sorrowful as she finally realized what he was waiting to hear. 'I know you didn't, Craig. It wasn't your fault. You didn't do anything wrong.'

And that was all it took for him to let go of her hands and reach for his guitar.

By the time she left the house, a few minutes later, he was singing 'I Am the Eggman', and seeming free, for the moment at least, of whatever demons had been troubling him.

Glancing at her mobile as it jingled with a text, she saw it was from Emma and clicked on. *Mystery of perve in park solved. One of neighbourhood watch guys keeping an eye on things, making sure no one creepy about!!! Like really???? Nearly said someone needs to keep an eye on him, but fortunately managed to zip it, cos apparently have been a couple of weirdos around lately. Not anywhere near us, but he thought it best to be on safe side by making his presence felt. Hope everything OK your end.*

Caught somewhere between relief, amusement and exhaustion, Angie texted back *On way home. All good here.*

As she put her phone down on the passenger seat she was thinking of the girl Craig had talked about, Sasha, wondering if she was real, if there actually had been some men who'd come to take her away in a van. Maybe something like that had once happened to his mother...

She thought of Mark Fields's interview at the building-site village, and her mind went straight to Martin Stone, but it was too early to thank him for anything yet. She would though, as soon as she could, and hopefully he'd send a message back that might only be a smiley face, or *Glad to have been of help*, but whatever it was she knew it would make her feel good when it came. And so little did these days.

Then she was thinking of herself and the children and all the online forms she'd filled in for the local housing office over the past couple of days. They didn't make it easy, that was for sure, but she'd already known that, thanks to her work at BtG. She'd received confirmation now that they didn't consider her case to be urgent, and it would only become so when her eviction was about to happen. In the meantime, she had to wait her turn. She had a case number, her situation was going forward for assessment and someone would be in touch within the next seven to ten days to discuss things further.

She felt a burning need to be more proactive, to do something, anything, to prove to herself and the children that she was capable of sorting out the terrible mess she'd got them into. But what the hell was she supposed to do when everyone was barricaded behind computers these days, or kept her hanging on the phone for so long that she had to ring off just to remain sane?

CHAPTER ELEVEN

Grace was in Lois's loft-conversion bedroom, using her friend's Macbook Air to check and complete other students' homework while Lois sorted a problem on her mother's computer downstairs. Although Grace had more or less finished her latest task – a short essay demonstrating understanding of the present perfect tense – she just had to message the girl who requested it and let her know that as soon as she handed over her two quid in the morning she'd receive the assignment.

That done, she began searching her social media pages for any more suggestions on how she could make some decent money. There weren't as many stupid and disgusting ones now, but the more obvious suggestions had finally started to turn up. She'd known they would, but there was nothing in the world that would tempt her to start selling drugs. She hadn't needed a warning from the police when they'd come to the school a few months ago to describe the dangers of county-line gangs and how they operated; she'd already learned the hard way what getting involved with them could do to a family. Yes, it was big money, hundreds, even thousands, one of the messages had promised, but she only had to think of Liam to know that no matter how desperate they were she'd never risk it. She wanted to help her mother, not break her heart the way Liam had, even though Grace knew that he hadn't really meant to. He just hadn't been able to help it.

She'd asked him about it once when she was eleven and he was seventeen. She'd said, 'Liam? Why do you take drugs?'

He hadn't got angry, the way she'd expected him to. That day, one of the rare days he was at home, he'd been calmer than usual, but still screwed up inside himself like he was in pain and didn't want anyone to help him.

'It's called addiction,' he told her, sniffing and dabbing his watery eyes. 'Once you start it's impossible to stop.' He growled like a dog and coughed, bringing up phlegm and swallowing it again. 'They won't let you stop.' He turned to her, his eyes blazing and yellow, and caught her by the arm. 'You have to promise me that you'll never start. You're not weak up here, like me,' he jabbed a finger to his head, 'so you have to promise me *now*.'

His grip hurt and his emphasis on *now* had made her jump. 'I promise,' she whispered.

His head went down, showing her his lank, greasy hair, as he let her go and went back to the jigsaw puzzle spread out on the desk in his room – he'd always liked puzzles, ones with big pieces so he didn't have to struggle too hard to find the right ones. Today his hand was shaking so much he was even struggling to pick anything up.

She asked her next question with her heart in her mouth. 'Why do you hate Mum and Dad so much?'

He didn't look up, only held his jigsaw piece suspended in

mid-air and she thought a tear dropped on to the forming picture. 'I don't hate them,' he rasped.

'But you act like you do. They're really worried about you.'

A sob got caught in his throat, making him sound like an animal in distress.

She was scared, but she didn't want to leave him. 'Liam?' she said.

He let the piece drop and pressed his fists to his face. Suddenly he turned to her again and cried, 'I'm not a bad person, Grace, I swear it, please don't think I'm a bad person.'

'I don't,' she lied, but even if he was bad he was still her brother, and sometimes, like now, she felt she was older than him.

'If I stop,' he choked, 'bad things will happen to you and Zac and I don't want bad things to happen to you.'

Terrified by that, she said, 'What sort of bad things?'

'It doesn't matter, because I'm going to keep you safe.'

She stared at him and wondered how this ghastly spectre, trembling, weeping, snuffling and grinding his teeth, could keep anyone safe. He wasn't strong enough, he never had been, he was like a child trapped inside a body that wasn't his, with stubble sprouting from his chin and a voice that was gravelly and deep. She tried to see in him the open-hearted, carefree older brother she'd always loved. The one who'd taught her to surf when she was four; who had a passion for colouring books and puzzles, who used to carry her on his back in piggyback races with Mum and Dad, who built sandcastles so big they came up to her waist. He laughed all the time, especially with Dad, everything was always an adventure for him and he'd made it the same for her – until the gangs had got hold of him and ruined him.

She wanted to protect him, to bring him back to them so he could be the real Liam again, but she didn't know how.

'You have to tell Mum and Dad about the bad things,' she urged him.

He shook his head. 'Dad will try to do something about it...'

'He'll keep you safe.'

'He can't. He thinks he can solve everything...'

'Because he can.'

'No, he can't. I used to think the same, but you don't know these people, Grace. If you mess with them you pay. I've seen what they do.'

'Liam, please...'

His bony hands gripped her shoulders again. 'Grace, listen to me, please. I can't tell Dad and nor can you. If anyone tries to get me away from them they'll come after my family. It's how they operate. They've told me that and I know they mean it. So please, don't tell Dad what I've just told you. Just know you're safe as long as I keep working for them and he doesn't try to mess with them.'

But her dad had tried to mess with them, not because Grace had broken her promise and told him that Liam was trying to protect them, but because Zac had found a syringe and played at injecting himself. She still didn't know how involved Liam had been in their dad's death, but when she finally broke her promise, after her mum had sent Liam away, her mum had said that even if Dad had known that Liam was trying to save them it wouldn't have changed what happened that day.

'What we need to do now, Grace,' she'd said, 'is keep trying to think the best of him and do what we can to find him.'

But they still hadn't found him and he hadn't tried to contact them either.

If he was here now Grace felt sure he'd want to help Mum through this difficult time, although there was no way she'd take money that had come from drugs. She'd like to know he was safe though, which was why Grace often posted messages asking if anyone had seen him. *If you know where my brother is please tell me, or tell him to come home. #LIAMWATTSISMISSING*

That brought replies from sickos too, but she had to do something.

'Hey, have you finished?' Lois asked, popping her head up through the ladder hatch.

'All done,' Grace replied, going to pick up the tray that Lois had slid on to the floor as she climbed into the loft. Hot chocolate and fig cookies. She wondered if her mum and Zac were having the same and knew they probably weren't.

'So, any good suggestions for making money turned up yet?' Lois asked, going to sit on the bed. 'I mean apart from the usual stupid stuff?'

'Nothing new,' Grace confirmed.

Biting into a biscuit, Lois said, 'Do you still have the WhatsApp from the woman who's supposed to be an old friend of your dad's?'

Calling it up, Grace reached for a mug, took a sip of chocolate and said, 'Yep, still here.'

'Mm, read it to me again.

'*Hi Grace, we haven't met but I used to know your dad really well. He was a lovely man. Everyone liked him. I see from your post that you're trying to find a way to make some money. Does that mean things aren't going too well for you and your family since he died? I'm really sorry if that's true, but if it is I think I can help. If you're interested to know more, just message me back. Anya.*'

Lois swallowed her mouthful and said, 'Did you ever mention it to your mum?'

Grace almost laughed. 'She'd go nuts if she thought I was even trying to earn some money, never mind going online to ask for suggestions on how to do it.'

Clearly understanding that, Lois said, 'So, do you know anyone called Anya?'

'I don't think so.'

After finishing a biscuit Lois said, 'It's the best offer we've had so far, so what would be the harm in going back to ask how she can help? I mean, it's not like you're agreeing to meet some weirdo or something. This is a woman, and looking at her picture she's kind of cool. Reminds me a bit of Lady Gaga, but older?'

Grace studied the image on her phone. It was true, she did look a bit like Lady Gaga when the singer's hair was platinum blonde. 'I wonder how my dad knew her?' she said. An image of her mother looking sad and tired flashed in her mind, and at the same time the longing for her father became horribly intense. He would definitely want her to help, and if this Anya was a friend of his...

'If I do answer her,' she said, 'what should I say?'

Lois gave it some thought. 'Well, I think we should start by finding out how she thinks she can help. If she's got some sort of loan in mind it's a non-starter, because we'll never be able to pay it back.'

'Do you think that's it?' Grace responded worriedly.

'I'm just guessing,' Lois reminded her, 'we won't know anything unless you ask, so it's up to you. Do you want to message back?'

Grace was torn. It might not even be a woman; it could be anyone. 'Would you, if you were me?'

Lois nodded. 'Definitely,' she confirmed. 'You don't have anything to lose, and unless we ask we'll never know if there's something to be gained.'

CHAPTER TWELVE

Steve's smell had seemed to linger in this room for a long time after he'd gone, dusty paint mingled with a tang of sweat and the maleness that was uniquely him. Angie used to sit here at his desk at the front end of the playroom just to breathe him in, her eyes closed as she imagined him coming in and sliding his arms around her. Sometimes she could hear him singing as he played the piano, 'Unforgettable' for her, 'Fly Me to the Moon' for Liam, a Justin Bieber song for Grace, 'The Teddy Bear's Picnic' for Zac. It could seem so real that she felt sure if she turned around he'd be there, and even when he wasn't she still sensed him as though he was watching over them. It warmed her heart to think that he was, and she'd smile or scowl in case he could see her.

This evening, she was in here to try and get a sense of what she should do next, but instead of the calming connection to her husband that she'd needed and hoped for, the room seemed full of her fear.

She'd spent over an hour on the phone to the CLA today – Civil Legal Advice – but they'd only ended up telling her what she already knew. It was the same as the lawyer had told her – another hour spent clutching at straws that fell apart at the first touch. Her landlord had done everything by the book. Every *i* was dotted and *t* crossed, all legal requirements had been met; he even had her signature on a recorded delivery informing her that he was taking his case to court. Of course there was no record of Agi's intimidation over these past months, any more than there was evidence of what had happened earlier today at Roland Shalik's office when she'd gone to beg for more time.

She hadn't forced herself in exactly, but she had managed to get as far as his secretary's office on the third floor of the building before she'd been stopped. After that she'd planted herself in the lift lobby, refusing to move until he agreed to see her. She'd known he was in there because she'd watched from a Costa across the street as a dark blue Range Rover had pulled up outside the glass-fronted block and the driver had held open a rear door for his boss to get out.

Everything appeared so upscale and respectable, the swanky offices, a chauffeur, an expensive suit, not a sign of the small band of thugs who carried out all his dirty work behind the scenes. She doubted they even came here; their territory would be far less exalted, tucked away in the heart of the region's most run-down estates where no decent human being should ever have to tread. Shalik wouldn't want his henchmen in this place, tainting his image as a respectable businessman. Perhaps some of his dealings were legal, but the expansion of his father's property portfolio into areas Hari would never have touched unless to help in some way was well known for the atrocity it was.

When he'd finally let her into his hallowed inner sanctum,

sighing sadly as he pointed her to a faux leather button-back wing chair across the wide expanse of his desk, Shalik had listened quietly as she'd made her case. There had been two others in the room, both men, lounging on sofas in a corner, apparently engaged in their phones and laptops. Shalik's long head with tight curls on each side and none on the top tilted to an angle as if he were interested to hear of her plight, curious even as to how so much misfortune had come her way. There was nothing hostile in his manner, or even vaguely impatient or derisive as she reminded him yet again that his father would never have wanted her and her family to be in this position.

When he finally responded, in a voice that sounded convincingly regretful, he said, 'You're right, of course, about my father; he would never have wanted this for you.'

Angie waited for more, daring to hope that she might finally be getting through to him.

'But time has moved on, Angie,' he said mournfully. 'Things are different now, and my dear father…' He waved a ringed hand in a circular motion, almost as if Hari had somehow spiralled off into thin air. He gave an unconvincing smile and brought them back to the point. 'Can I remind you that we have other houses that could accommodate you,' he said, 'and at a rent you are more able to afford. I hope we've made that clear to you…'

'I know the houses you mean,' she gritted out angrily, 'and you know very well I can't accept one. I have two children, for God's sake.'

He nodded, as though accepting her reasoning. 'Plenty of children live on the Temple Meads estate,' he said mildly, 'and some do very well…'

'Not the children who live in your hovels,' she cut in fiercely. 'I know what goes on in them, the drugs, the prostitution and trafficking. The only decent properties you own are on the Fairweather estate…'

'Which you can't afford,' he came in quietly. 'We've established that, but I think one of the houses on Colemead Lane would suit you very well.'

Angie baulked in shock – Colemead Lane was where Steve had been beaten to death. How could he even think it, never mind say it out loud?

As a consuming rage took hold of her she leapt to her feet. 'What kind of man are you?' she cried savagely. 'Your father would be so ashamed of you he'd disown you if he knew how you were treating me.'

Shalik's eyebrows rose. 'You have a very romantic view of my father,' he informed her, 'but that is understandable. He was a charismatic man with a social conscience, especially where you and your husband were concerned. But he knew what he was doing when he passed his affairs over to me. He could see the way things were going so he decided to leave the difficult work to his only son. And it is difficult, Angie, you know this, because I have tried to explain it to you before. Our biggest problem is that you don't want to listen. You are here today to beg for more time, and you cannot deny that I have given you this often in the past. I am even offering you another house so that you will continue to have a roof over your heads, but you won't accept it. I've also made it clear that we're willing to arrange a loan to help meet your financial obligations, but you won't take that either. And still I am prepared to help you. If you – and perhaps your daughter – come to work for me your debts could be paid off in less than a few months; we might even see our way to letting you stay on in Willow Close if you are acceptable to our terms of…'

Angie would have grabbed him by the throat if his desk hadn't been so wide. She could hardly see through the red mist of rage that blinded her, the hate and disgust. '*You* are not your father's son,' she hissed at him savagely. 'You are an abomination that can't even call itself human.' She leaned in closer. 'Go anywhere near my daughter, and you will *die*, I swear...'

She got no further as big arms suddenly heaved her away, manhandled her across the office and out of the door – and even in the heated, horrific moments of it, she'd wondered how she'd got to this terrible place in her life, who she even was any more.

Now, as she sat at Steve's desk, cringing at the memory of the day, she stared down at the eviction notice that was on the top of a pile of red-reminders and other threatening letters. There was nothing she could do to make any of it go away, or to change the date on the notice. Their time in this house would come to an end in fifteen days, at which point court enforcers – bailiffs – would arrive to ensure she left. Of course, she could go earlier and avoid the shame of having them knock on the door, the horror of even seeing them... Or she could stay and fight, knowing that the law wasn't on her side, and that she had neither the right nor the physical strength to prevent them from carrying out their job.

If it were just her without the children she might be able to work things out more easily, she wouldn't have to worry about schools, friends, what people would say... She might even consider one of Shalik's other houses for a while, but Grace and Zac would always come first and she'd already lost one child to the lawless streets of that appalling estate; nothing in the world would persuade her to risk losing another.

Rubbing her hands over her face, she turned out the light and left the room. She must try to make herself accept the fact that they were going to have to leave this house. There was simply no way to avoid it now, but before she broke it to the children and got them to start packing up all the things that mattered most to them, she needed to be able to tell them where they were going.

By the end of the day tomorrow she should be able to do that.

'Anything from the Anya woman?' Lois yawned, as she and Grace woke up in their separate beds each side of the sloping ceiling of Lois's loft. 'Yes, alive and breathing,' she shouted as her mother called out to make sure they were awake and getting ready for school.

Still bleary-eyed Grace picked up her phone, switched it on and opened WhatsApp. 'Nothing,' she replied, and clicking through to Facebook she came fully awake when she saw there was a reply to her latest attempt to find Liam.

If you want to know where he is meet me at the corner of Fisher Road and the playing fields at six o'clock. #LIAMWATTSISMISSING

Her heart sank, for even without checking she knew it would be from one of the Northsider gang at school, and as if to confirm it there was a PM from Ryan Gibbs, the only decent one amongst them.

Don't fall for it Grace. You know what they're after and you don't need it. No one knows where he is. I promise if they did I'd tell you.

Not a great start to the day, but at least she was due to collect eight quid from homework assignments when she got to school – enough to pay for her and Lois's snacks after dance class later, something Lois always did – and with any luck Anya would have got back to her by then with some brilliant way of fixing everything.

The number printed on a flimsy ticket in Angie's hand was 59. This meant there were fifteen people ahead of her in the queue, and with only six pods open the wait was likely to be long.

It was rare she came to this soulless block of offices behind the town hall; those with housing issues were strongly discouraged from making their cases in person, so she didn't even come for the residents. It was all done online, provided you had a computer, and if you didn't you had to hope you knew someone who did.

She looked around at the worried and stressed expressions of her fellow claimants. Some seemed angry, frustrated, and talked in loud voices about how badly they were being treated by 'the system', what a disgrace it was and how no one was even interested in helping. She found herself trying to offer small smiles of reassurance whenever she caught someone's eye – it was second nature for her to do that in spite of how wretched she was feeling, a few times her smile was returned.

Time ticked slowly on.

She managed to keep herself calm with the reminder of what she'd read online many times these past several days. *The council has a duty to rehouse you if you have children who rely on you financially and they need somewhere to live.* If there was nowhere to put them as a family, it was possible the council would call in a social worker to take the children and leave her to fend for herself.

Don't be ridiculous, Emma will take them, she reminded herself forcefully.

Finally her number came up on the digital display, and she went to the pod where a thin, sallow man was indicating the chair in front of him. There was no friendly smile, and no hello as he tapped his keyboard with quick, bony fingers and kept looking at his screen as though it were annoying him. Or perhaps he was deliberately extending her wait.

'Name?' he suddenly asked.

She gave it, and because she knew the procedure she added her current address; her date of birth, the fact she was female, no, she hadn't made a claim for housing before, only housing benefit, and yes she had a case number from her online application, which she read out.

'So how can I help?' he asked in a tone that suggested he'd like to do anything but.

She explained as succinctly as she could about the eviction, putting the notice on the desk between them so he could examine it for himself. He gave it a quick glance, added something to whatever window he had open on his screen, and said, 'Children?'

She swallowed dryly. 'Three. Two living at home.'

'Ages?'

'Thirteen and seven.'

For some reason he took a while to upload these details, leaving her heart to race with anxiety as she was cast in the role of involuntary eavesdropper on the case in the next pod. The woman had apparently already had her children taken into care; she was here to beg for a bigger place so she could have them back.

The next fifteen minutes felt interminable, and punishing, as she was grilled about everything from her finances to her employment status, to whether she or her children had a history of antisocial behaviour. He wanted to know more about the rent arrears and all other debts; whether she had a husband and which schools the children attended. He asked if the place they were living in was insanitary or overcrowded; was she pregnant, did anyone in the family suffer from mental illness, did she have any family living nearby. There were so many questions, so much detail required that she'd already provided in her online application, but apparently it had to be gone through again.

Eventually, after watching something happen on his screen, he got up and disappeared through a door at the back of the hall marked Staff Only.

As more minutes ticked by panic started building inside her, and suddenly fearful that he was sending someone to the school to seize her children, she found herself running across the hall to bang on the door. 'You can't do this to people,' she shouted furiously. 'It's inhuman making us wait, playing with our lives…'

'You're causing a disturbance,' a security guard informed her. 'Please sit down or we'll have to ask you to leave.'

Turning abruptly away, she said, 'It isn't *your* money so why do you treat people like this?'

Ignoring her question, he watched her return to the pod before going back to his station.

Her eviction notice was still next to the clerk's computer. She wanted to beg someone to make this stop, but all she could do was suffer the humiliation and wait.

In the end the thin man came back, and still failing to look her in the eye he said, 'I'm afraid we can't help you…'

'What are you talking about?' she cried in shock. 'I've got children…'

'… at this time. Your tenancy is not yet at an end so your case is not urgent. You also have family in the area. You could arrange to stay with them.'

'If I do that my sister will be thrown out for overcrowding. For God's sake, is it your intention to put families on the streets? You have an obligation…'

His hand went up to stop her. 'If you'll let me finish. The records are showing that we should have a two-bedroomed house available six weeks from now…'

'You've seen the date on that notice. That'll leave us with nowhere to go for over three weeks.'

'Perhaps you can make arrangements with your sister and her landlord to allow the children to stay with her.'

'And what about me?' she cried shrilly. 'What do you suggest *I* do?'

As though she hadn't spoken, he said, 'If it turns out that your sister is unable to accommodate the children you will need to come back so we can refer the matter to children's services.' He sorted out a leaflet from the racks next to his desk. 'There's a lot of helpful information here,' he told her, unfolding it, 'this is the number to call to make an appointment concerning your children.'

She wanted to yell at him, even punch him, tell him he couldn't treat her like this, but the prospect of children's services had silenced her.

'You already have a case number,' he reminded her. 'I will add details of our meeting today to the file and put a notice on the property I mentioned to signify your interest. I'm afraid I can't guarantee that someone with a more urgent need won't supersede you in the queue.'

Snatching the leaflet, she stuffed it in her bag and turned away. A sea of faces blurred and swayed in front of her as she left, people in their own dire straits watching her with sympathy and dismay, who knew better than to make a scene the way she had because it would get them precisely nowhere.

Never having felt so powerless, she walked out of the building and across the road to the car park where she'd left the van. It had cost her almost five pounds in parking to have it confirmed that she was just a case number with notes being added to a file.

As she got into the driver's seat she had no clear idea of what she was going to do next. For the moment she couldn't think, couldn't make herself function at all, until finally she was able to remind herself that falling apart wasn't an option when she had two children who needed her.

CHAPTER THIRTEEN

Feeling as though the visit to the housing department had just about crushed her, Angie sorely needed the cuppa Emma was making to help restore some life to her soul.

'What I have to sort out now,' she said as Emma passed her a steaming mug of builder's brew, 'is how I'm going to break this to the children.' Tears stung harshly at her eyes. 'I've gone about this in totally the wrong way,' she said shakily. 'I should have asked for help as soon as I missed the first month's rent, and I should have been honest with Grace and Zac from the start. I mean, they know things are tight, but once they realize how bad it's become… It's going to be almost as awful for them as losing their father, in a way it might even be worse, and I'm completely to blame.'

'Don't be so hard on yourself,' Emma soothed. 'It's not your fault you were left without any money for all that time when they changed over to universal credit, and how could either of us have known that it would lead to this?'

Registering the paleness of her sister's face, and the angst in her eyes, Angie felt even worse for bringing all this worry into their lives. 'I have to find more work,' she said hoarsely. 'I need to be more open-minded, take anything I can get...' She turned to her computer and opened up Google. 'I heard there might be some night shifts going at the online packing depot out on the ring road,' she said, 'but it'll mean you having the children...'

'You know I will, but is working nights a good idea? You need to sleep sometime and you're already covering shifts for half the neighbourhood...'

'Which is hardly going to help pay off my debts.'

'A night shift won't either, but let's not discuss it now. We need to stay focused on today and whether you want me to be there when you tell the children about the house.'

As a sickening jolt brought her back to reality Angie took a breath, trying to weigh it up.

'I think I should be,' Emma told her. 'I can reassure them that we're going to tackle this as a family.'

Angie smiled and nodded, knowing that of course Emma would be there for them all, she'd never doubt it, but she couldn't depend on her completely. She needed to take more action herself, and if she was going to get one of the night shifts she must respond quickly.

Once her application was in she switched screens ready to get on with BtG work, for the last thing she needed was to lose the one regular job she had. 'Have we heard anything from Dougie or Mark Fields about whether they got the jobs at the building site?' she asked, thinking of Martin Stone and wondering what he might be doing today.

'Actually, we have,' Emma confirmed. 'I got a call from someone called Cliff Mercer. Right charmer, he was. He said he's willing to take on a couple of our losers – yes, he actually called them that, prick – so I've let Dougie and Mark Fields know that they're in.'

'That's good,' Angie murmured, feeling glad to have a chance to thank Martin for making this happen. 'I'm sure they'll be pleased. I should find out how Craig got on with his interview at the care home.'

'Hamish rang earlier. Apparently they quite liked him and they're going to be in touch.'

Emma watched Angie drop her head into her hands, and understanding how overwhelmed she was feeling she said softly, 'Why don't you go home? I can cope here and when I'm done I'll come and give you a hand with... things.'

Realizing Emma was referring to the packing that needed to be started, Angie felt herself recoiling from the horror of it. She couldn't even think of how to begin, much less where she was going to put everything or how she was going to pay for storage while they waited for their new place to come free.

Maybe something else would come up between now and then that they could move into straight away.

Her eyes closed against the resistance that was building to a pitch inside her. She didn't want to leave Willow Close. She just couldn't give up the home she loved so much.

Before Angie left, Emma said, 'Let's all have tea at mine later. We can pop round the corner to pick up some fish and chips, the kids always like that, and I don't know when you last ate, but I'll bet it wasn't any time this week.'

Angie forced a smile. 'It's not quite that bad,' she assured her, but it was bad enough, for in truth she couldn't actually remember when she'd last eaten, or even when she'd last had an appetite.

When Angie got to the van she decided to send a brief email to Martin before going anywhere else. *Thanks very much for stepping in to help my residents. I shall warn them they'll have me to deal with if they let you down. Angie Watts.*

She didn't expect a reply straight away, nor did she get one.

Instead of driving home she parked the van in a side street not far from the church and caught a bus to Temple Fields, the district, not the estate. With fares to anywhere in town being only a pound she'd save some money on petrol by making the journey to the pawnshop this way.

As she passed through the labyrinth of terraced houses that spread down over the hill towards the seafront, she was recalling how her mother had once tried to explain to her and Emma that bad things could happen to good people. The subject had come up because of something on the news that day – Angie was sure it was about Nelson Mandela being released from prison. She and Emma were aged around eight and nine at the time, and were bewildered by why someone so important and who everyone said was a hero had ever been locked up in the first place. The memory of how her mother had tried to explain apartheid had gone, but later, when she'd succumbed to cancer the words had come back to Angie.

Bad things – and cancer was one of the worst – *can happen to good people.*

For no rational reason her thoughts moved to the woman with dark hair whom she'd seen at Asda filling the foodbank box.

She doubted very much that the woman had ever been inside a pawnshop, but how could she know that for sure? If she had, Angie suspected it would probably have been to buy something that had caught her eye, a collectable, or something precious that had belonged to her cleaner, or a luckless friend who'd just confessed some kind of hardship. She only wished that she had someone to come along after to her to buy back her wedding ring and the treasured locket that had belonged to Steve's mother which she was about to sell. They were her last possessions of any real value, and handing them over left her feeling so bereft that it was as though she'd parted with her very soul.

When she re-emerged from the shop ten minutes later with less than a hundred pounds in her purse, she was so upset by the exploitation of her misery that it was hard to look calm as she crossed the busy street to the bus stop. Still, at least she could pay for the fish and chips tonight. She could also put some petrol in the van, and just to buoy her a little further, when she checked her phone she found she'd had a reply from Martin.

Hope it works out for them. Are you really terrifying? Do I need to be worried? M

Laughing, she typed a quick message back, *Completely terrifying. Ask anyone* and she added four smiley faces.

She was still feeling good as she boarded the bus, but it wasn't long before she began focusing on what else she needed to do with her ninety-four pounds. To begin with she should drive into town to buy Zac the school shoes he needed. And then she wondered if she should give them to him before, or after, she dropped the bombshell that would shatter his young life all over again.

Zac stared at his mother in confusion. His small, freckled face, with his father's deep blue eyes and his mother's permanently rosy cheeks, was showing his struggle to understand what she'd just told him.

'We have to leave this house,' she'd said softly. 'I know you won't want to, but I need you to be brave and to start thinking about what you'd like to take with you.'

There was nothing in any parental guidebook she'd ever seen to advise on the best way to do this, nothing that had gone before in her life to warn her that one day this was where she would be.

She wondered where Zac's thoughts were going now, how fractured they might be, how frenziedly they were darting between his special bedroom, his toys, gadgets, video games and collection of football magazines. Maybe they were in the chill-out shed his dad had built in the garden so the children had somewhere to take their friends on rainy days for sandwiches and cartoons on the specially installed TV. Maybe they were across the street on the green where he played football and rounders; sang carols at Christmas and fished for sticklebacks in the stream most summers. There were so many things he wouldn't be able to take with him, so much of his past that was here and had shaped him as a boy, shaped them all as a family.

She glanced at Emma and received a small smile of encouragement.

Zac said shakily, 'Will I still go to the same school?'

Angie nodded and smoothed a hand over his messy hair. 'Probably,' she replied. 'I hope so. We'll definitely stay in Kesterly so we can always be near Auntie Em and the boys.'

'You can stay with us any time you like,' Emma told him. 'You know how much you enjoy sleepovers in Jack's room.'

Zac's troubled eyes went back to his mother. 'Jack's got Minecraft on his computer,' he said, his words tripping on an awkward breath telling her how hard he was finding it to process this. 'He lets us play it sometimes.'

Aching for the way he was trying to salvage small pieces of the world that was crumbling around him, Angie said, 'He told me you're good at it.'

Zac's eyes moved to the front window, and following them Angie saw Grace coming across the footbridge towards the house. Her heart turned over in dread. She'd expected to be past the shock stage with Zac before talking to Grace, had hoped he might be upstairs with Emma by now, starting the big sort-out of what he wanted to take with him, but he was still right here on the sofa and Grace was putting her key in the lock.

Angie watched her daughter come into the sitting room unwinding the blue knitted scarf she'd made herself. She seemed to be in a good mood, until registering the way she was being watched by her mother, her aunt and her brother, she came to a stop. Angie wondered why she was only noticing now how lifeless and endy her daughter's beautiful hair had become; how it had almost changed colour to a faded, straw-like version of its natural honey tones. Was it the washing-up liquid they'd had to use instead of shampoo over the last months; the poor diet, though Angie tried hard to make sure the children had the right nutrients, the fact they couldn't afford a proper hairdresser, or was it simply a lack of summer sun? It would be all of the above. Her clothes were faintly shabby too, a second-hand puffer jacket that didn't quite fit her any more, and fake Ugg boots scuffed at the toe. With a heart-wrenching clarity she realized how hardship was blurring them all, taking away their colour, their verve, the very essence of who they really were.

'What is it?' Grace asked, staring wide-eyed at her mother.

Before Angie could tell her to sit down, Zac said, 'We have to leave this house,' and running to her he circled his arms tightly around her waist.

Angie watched Grace's face, the way her complexion paled and her mouth tightened as she registered her brother's words. Her eyes became dark and accusing as she glared at her mother.

Angie started to speak, but to her dismay no words came. Using a thumb to rub the place where her wedding ring had been, as though seeking strength from Steve, she tried again, but Grace was tilting Zac away from her and looking down at him.

'It's OK. I'll always be here for you,' she told him in a tone that was more harsh than comforting.

Angie felt the words like a slap in the face, and knew she'd been meant to. Her chest heaved with guilt-filled pain, and so much love and shame that she had no idea what to do or say.

Emma said, 'We'll pull together as a family, sweetie. All of us need support right now, especially your mum, because she's the one…'

'… who got us into this,' Angie finished. 'I'm sorry, Grace. I didn't mean… I thought… Grace!' she cried as Grace turned into the hall, taking Zac with her.

Emma put out a hand to stop Angie going after them. 'She needs to feel angry and afraid, and she probably needs to hurt you too. But you know what she's like, she'll come round. She always does.'

Angie didn't argue; she was so knotted up in this terrible nightmare that she'd lost all sense of what must come next. She could feel a terrifying distance creeping between her and her children, as if a gulf were opening up in their world with them on one side and her on the other.

'I can't lose them,' she whispered to Emma.

'You won't,' Emma said softly. 'We'll make sure of that.'

'Grace is right to blame me. I should go and speak to her.'

'Give her some time. Let her talk to Zac first. It's what they both seem to need.'

Angie swallowed hard and looked around the room. She felt sick and panicked, as everything that was left of what she and Steve had brought to this home, the things that hadn't been sold or pawned, seemed to look back at her in sadness and with a need not to be thrown out or left behind. She knew it was crazy to see her furniture, the remaining photograph frames, the coffee table, bookcase and books as part of the family, but it was how they felt. They'd been specially chosen because they were wanted and admired and loved, and were still here, she had to admit, because they had no value to anyone else.

Knowing she couldn't allow herself to break down, that she had to stay strong for the children, and even for herself, she took Emma's hand and held it between her own. 'I need to decide what to do about the furniture,' she said hoarsely. 'We've got nowhere to store it, but we'll need at least some of it when we get somewhere else.'

'You can leave it here,' Emma told her. 'They won't be able to sell it to cover your arrears, and the law says they have to keep it for a reasonable time. I don't know exactly how long, but at least it'll be safe for a while.'

'He'll charge me for storage,' Angie said. She took a breath and brought Emma's hand to her cheek. 'I still have Steve's and Liam's things upstairs. I've never had the heart to…'

'I know,' Emma whispered, stroking her hair, 'but one step at a time. You still have a couple of weeks, and if you'd like me to I'll take care of it.' She stopped at the sound of footsteps on the stairs.

A moment later Grace and Zac appeared in the doorway wearing their coats and with a large holdall each over their shoulders.

Looking at her aunt, Grace said, 'Can we come and stay with you tonight please?'

As Angie's heart turned over, Zac said, 'We've already packed.'

Emma tightened her hold on Angie's hand as she said, 'Of course you can, but there'll be more packing to do before you leave. Mum and I will need your help…'

Grace turned around and opened the front door. 'Come on, Zac,' she said stiffly, edging him ahead of her, 'this isn't our home any more.'

'Oh no, that's terrible,' Lois cried when Grace rang to tell her what was happening. 'I didn't realize it was so bad. What the hell are we going to do?'

'I don't know. I'm completely terrified.'

'I would be too in your shoes.'

Grace was thinking of the nude photos the boys at school had offered lots of money for, and wondered if she could do it. She really didn't want to, it made her feel sick even to think of it, but maybe, if she could be certain they'd never get shared, she'd have to.

'But you can't *ever* be certain,' Lois protested when Grace made the suggestion. 'They're bound to pass them around and you'll get called names; every time you see someone watching you you'll know that they've seen you with no clothes on. No Grace, I won't let you do it.'

'Then come up with something else,' Grace shouted in despair.

'OK, I will, I promise. First though, I think you should message this Anya again. Tell her what's happened and if she's a friend of your dad's, she's bound to want to help.'

CHAPTER FOURTEEN

The following day Angie went online to see if she could find some details of the house she might be given, hoping to God it wasn't on the Temple Fields estate. It turned out to be on Stanley Road, in Feltree, which still wasn't a great area – some parts were half derelict, she recalled – and it was seven or eight miles from Emma and the Fairweather estate, but at least it was on a bus route that would ferry the children directly to and from school.

She considered driving over to take a look at it from the outside, but with no guarantee they'd actually get it she needed to watch every penny – and every drop of petrol. Not that this small saving was going to help much with the payment of the one-thousand-pound fine she'd just received by recorded delivery for non-payment of the TV licence.

There was a time when that would have terrified her; now she just added it to the file to deal with when she could.

It was around four o'clock the next day when she learned

that she might as well forget about the house in Feltree, for it had been allocated to another family. She immediately tried getting through to the emergency number she'd been given to find out if there was somewhere else for her and the children, but she was told to call back nearer the time of her eviction. They clearly weren't into offering any sense of security, or hope that everything would fall into place when it was supposed to, they simply wanted to kick her over to the sidelines while they dealt with the issues of today.

She needed to do the same, deal with today, and the most pressing issue for her at the moment was Grace.

I understand how upset and worried you are, but please answer my messages. You know how much I love you and how sorry I am that this is happening, but we need to pull together, Grace. Don't shut me out. Mum x

Grace read her mother's latest text with mounting guilt – and an almost crippling need to shout at her again, or to be able to tell her that at least *she* had found a way to make things better.

I'm fine, she texted back shortly. *Stop worrying about me.*

She meant it, she didn't want her mum to worry, it only made her feel worse, if that could even be possible, and as far as she was concerned it couldn't.

Still, at least there was some small glimmer on the horizon.

She'd received a reply from Anya this morning. It wasn't as much as she'd hoped for: she wasn't even sure what that was apart from her dad coming back, Liam letting them know he was OK, and being able to stay in their house. Anya was hardly going to be able to pull off any one of those impossible feats. However, the kindly-looking woman had responded straight away when Grace had told her about losing the house, and her words, her promise, were definitely giving Grace something to hang on to.

Oh Grace, I am so sad to hear what is happening to you and your family. This isn't what you deserve at all. I'm out of the country at the moment on business, but don't worry, I shall be back in a week or so and by then I promise to have worked something out to help you. If my plans come good I think you'll be pleased. Anya ☺ PS. Stay strong, you know it's what your dad would want.

Over the next two weeks Grace and Zac continued to stay with Emma, and when Angie wasn't packing, or racing between a crazy schedule of temporary jobs and ad hoc shifts, she was doing her best to focus on BtG. It seemed to help, putting her mind elsewhere for a while, knowing that she was doing some good for those who were worse off than she was. In many ways they seemed better off, for at least the residents had some certainty in their lives, no fear of finding themselves homeless again, unless they messed up in some way.

As the days passed and she was repeatedly told that no other properties were available at this time, she kept reminding herself that the children would be fine with Emma. She didn't think about herself too much, just tried to stay focused on practicalities such as continuing the packing and redirecting her mail to the office. She'd never imagined how destabilizing it would be to separate her name from 14 Willow Close. It felt, absurdly, as though she was leaving Steve, and when she wasn't seeing it that way she saw it as cutting adrift from a safe harbour, with nothing but eddies and riptides ahead of her.

She contacted the schools to explain that the children were probably going to be staying with their aunt for a while, and why. They were sympathetic, of course, and assured her they would keep a close eye on things, but after ending the calls Angie sat with her head in her hands, unable to do any more that day, for even breathing was starting to feel hard. She wasn't coping well, she realized that, although she scarcely knew what coping well meant anymore.

And Grace was still barely communicating with her.

However, at least she was talking to Emma, so Angie knew she was eating, going to school and spending most nights at Lois's.

'We need to formulate a plan for Friday,' Emma said gently two days before the dreaded bailiffs were due – and there was still nowhere for them to go as a family. 'Have you organized yourself somewhere to stay yet?' she asked, looking so worried that Angie had to turn away from her.

'No, but I will,' Angie replied. 'What matters is making sure the children are OK. I know they will be with you, but when Grace gets back from school on Thursday, I want you to send her home to me. I need to speak to her. Zac too, of course, but I need to see her first.'

Hello Grace, I'm finally back in the country and I want you to know that my plans to help you are starting to come good. I'll be in touch again as soon as the details are finalized. It's all very exciting. For now, I just want you to be sure that I haven't forgotten you. A ☺

Grace looked up from the message and turned to Lois, who'd read it over her shoulder. 'Whatever it is,' she said, 'it's obviously not going to help us stay in the house. Not that I thought it would, it's just…' She shrugged, unsure what else she'd thought.

'I wonder what she means by exciting,' Lois frowned. 'I mean, it has to be good or she wouldn't put it like that, so maybe she's sorting out somewhere else for you to live and wants it to be a surprise.'

Liking the sound of that – staying where they were would

be much better of course – Grace checked her phone again as a text arrived from Auntie Em.

Mum wants to see you after school, sweetheart. Please go. She needs your support right now, and believe it or not you need hers.

An hour later Grace was staring hard at her mother, her mouth tight, her normally creamy, freckled skin flushed crimson with resentment. Angie could tell she'd done a lot of crying these past two weeks, and could hardly bear that she'd been unable to comfort her. She knew Emma had tried, and no doubt Lois and her mother, Becky, had too, but carrying so much anger and fear in her heart would be hard for Grace when those negative emotions were usually alien to her.

'Thanks for coming,' Angie said gently. 'Would you like something to drink?'

Grace's voice shook as she said, 'Me and Zac have lived here all our lives, we have our own special bedrooms that Dad made for us and now we have to leave because *you* didn't pay the rent. It's not our fault. I don't see why we have to leave too.'

Angie said carefully, 'I'm sorry, sweetheart. I'm sorrier than you'll ever know, and I wish with all my heart that it wasn't happening…'

'Then make it stop!' Grace cried angrily. 'Get the money and pay what you owe.'

'You know I would if I could, but right now I can't see a way…'

'Get a loan,' Grace shouted in frustration. 'That's what other people do when they can't afford things.'

'The banks won't give me one, and if I resort to a payday loan it'll only make things worse in the long run.' She raised a hand as Grace started to shout again. 'I never dreamt we'd end up like this,' she said softly. 'I've done my best to try and stay on top of it all, but there are some things I can't control. You and Zac are growing fast. You need shoes and coats, new shirts, money for your drama club, dance classes...'

'Stop blaming us. We're not the ones who thought it was all right to stop paying the rent...'

'I never thought it was all right and I'm not blaming you. I know I'm responsible, and I'd give anything, *anything* for none of this to be happening; to be able to turn back the clock so Daddy and Liam were still with us, or at least to a time when I could cope, but I can't. I've screwed up so badly I hardly know what to do any more, but I'll work it out, Grace. I promise you, I'll find a way through this for us...'

'How? Tell me how you're going to do that when you don't stand a single chance of ever being able to buy a house, of getting us a proper home that's ours and that we don't feel afraid of losing.'

'Even people who own their homes can end up losing them,' Angie pointed out. 'There are no safeguards against things changing in your life... Grace, please don't walk away.'

Grace turned back, mascara running down her cheeks as grief and fear twisted her mouth. 'Have you thought about how Liam's going to find us once we leave here?' she demanded. 'He won't know where to look. He'll think we've gone off without him and that we couldn't care less about him.'

Angie's heart was so tight that every beat hurt. 'If he does come back,' she said softly, 'and obviously we're never going to give up hope that he will...'

'Why aren't you out there looking for him?'

'You know I've tried, and not a month goes by that Auntie Em and I don't call shelters and hostels, police stations and even prisons all over the country in the hope of some news. And you put your messages on social media. I know the answers aren't always helpful, but it's good that you keep posting them, because if he sees them he'll know we still care and want to see him.'

Grace's face remained pinched.

Angie went towards her, but as she tried to embrace her Grace pushed her away. 'You ruined his life,' she sobbed, 'and now you're ruining mine,' and before Angie could stop her she tore open the door and dashed across to the street towards Emma's.

Ten minutes later Emma came in with Zac. The instant he saw his mother, on her knees in the middle of the floor surrounded by half-filled boxes and plastic bags, he ran straight to her. Angie had no idea if he realized how hard she'd been crying, or how wonderful it was to feel his sturdy little body in her arms, she only knew that she would cherish the relief and love in this moment for ever.

'I don't want to leave, Mum,' he wailed. 'I want us to stay here forever.'

'I know, I know,' she murmured, pressing her lips to his tousled hair. 'I wish we could, Zac. I'd do anything to make it happen, I…' As her words were choked away by tears, Emma said, 'Where's Grace?'

Registering the question, Angie felt herself tensing. 'Didn't she come to yours?' Realizing Zac was pulling away to look at her, she wrapped him in her arms again as she said, 'She must have gone to Lois's.'

'Was she all right when she left?' Emma asked.

Angie gave a small shake of her head.

Taking out her phone Emma scrolled to Grace's number and went through to the kitchen to make the call.

Holding Zac's dear little face between her hands, Angie gazed into his teary eyes and attempted a smile. 'I'm nearly done here, and I expect you're hungry.'

He nodded and sobbed as he said, 'Can I sleep here in your bed with you tonight?'

'Of course you can.' It would be the last time they'd sleep in this house. She smoothed back his hair and planted a kiss on his forehead. 'You're my special boy, you know that, don't you?' she murmured tenderly.

Ducking back into her arms, he held on tight as he said, 'I forgot to take my dinosaurs to Auntie Em's. And my kite that Dad made.'

Angie swallowed hard as she wondered how much else he'd hung on to that his dad had given him, and not just material things. Had she talked to him enough about Steve? If she hadn't, now wasn't the time to try and correct it.

'I left a message,' Emma said, coming back into the room.

Understanding that Grace was deliberately ignoring them, Angie snuggled in closer with Zac as she said, 'Where are Harry and Jack?'

'At home on their own,' Emma replied, 'so I'd better get back. I've put a casserole in the oven for tea. There's enough for all of us. I thought we could have a game of Twister after to cheer us all up.'

Remembering the hilarity of past games, especially when Steve was playing, Angie managed a smile, and wished there was more she could do to thank Emma besides giving her just about everything she earned while the children were with her. She wasn't going to need much for herself, and the last thing she wanted was Emma finding herself out of pocket or depriving her boys in some way because she was trying to help.

Angie and Emma were in Emma's kitchen. It was after nine by now and Grace still wasn't answering her phone.

I know you're angry with me, Angie texted, *but please think of Zac. He needs to hear from you, if only to know you're all right.*

'I was sure she'd be with Lois,' she said, putting the phone down, but when she'd called a while ago Lois had claimed not to know where she was.

She was becoming more agitated by the minute and hardly engaged with Emma's words as she said, 'Should I call the police? She went out over four hours ago and it's dark out there. They'll see her as vulnerable…' She started as her phone jingled with a text.

There were two, one straight after the other. One from Hamish at Hill Lodge, the other from Grace.

She clicked on to Grace's first, leaving Emma to pick up Hamish's on her own phone. *Tell Zac I'll see him at Auntie Em's tomorrow. Staying with Lois tonight.*

Angie sent a text back. *Are you sure that's where you are?*

Sure. I'll send a photo if you don't believe me.

OK, I won't tell Lois's mum that you girls lied to me when I rang half an hour ago, but I can do without this right now, Grace. We need to pull together, and frightening me doesn't help either of us.

She pressed send and showed it to Emma. 'Too harsh?' she asked when she saw Emma grimace.

'Deserved,' Emma replied decisively. 'And now you'd better take a look at the one from Hamish.'

Hamish's text read: *Are you all right, Angie? Craig says he just saw you in the cemetery.*

As Angie looked up from the text in dismay, Emma said, 'You've got enough to do. I'll call him back.'

'It's OK,' Angie interrupted and scrolled to Hamish's number. She didn't blame him for troubling her at this time, he had no idea what was happening to her, and she had to admit she felt almost relieved to have something outside her own troubles to deal with tonight. 'What's happening over there?' she asked when Hamish answered, putting the call on speaker so Emma could hear.

He sighed wearily. 'I asked him to take out some rubbish and the next thing I knew he was running back into the kitchen saying you were in the cemetery and we should go and get you.'

Angie said, 'Where is he now?'

'Sitting right here, listening on speakerphone.'

To Craig she said, 'Are you satisfied now that I'm at home?'

'Why were you in the cemetery?' he asked.

Opting for distraction as a means of coping, she said, 'I hear you got the job at the care home.'

'He did,' Hamish confirmed, 'isn't that grand? We're about to find a few Elvis songs for him to try out on his first day.'

'I'm going to get my guitar,' Craig informed them.

After listening to Craig strum out a few indecipherable numbers Angie and Emma rang off and sat staring at one another, not sure what to say next, until, without even realizing it was going to happen, Angie let out a guffaw of laughter. Had that phone call really just happened? Had they actually sat there listening to the worst jamming session in history when the world was falling apart around them?

Picking up on the weirdness of it all Emma started laughing too, and soon they were unable to stop. They clutched their hands to their faces and grasped their sides, and realizing they were moving in sync made them laugh even harder. The hilarity began bordering on hysteria and still they couldn't stop in spite of knowing it was going to end in tears. It didn't matter; it felt so good to laugh, never mind the madness, because for these few crazy moments at least it was as though the demons had stopped winning.

In the end Angie noticed Zac standing in the doorway and reached out a hand to him.

'What's so funny?' he asked, going to her.

Drying her cheeks and still panting, Angie looked to Emma, hoping she might have a sensible answer.

'We're just being silly,' Emma told him, dabbing her face. 'Have you finished your game?'

Zac nodded and climbed into his mother's lap. 'Can we make a snowman?' he asked.

Remembering that a few flurries had been forecast for tonight, Angie turned to the window and saw a handful of flakes wafting lazily about in the darkness. 'I don't think it'll pitch,' she told him, and started as the back door suddenly opened wide.

To everyone's surprise Grace came in, bringing an icy gust with her.

Far more relieved to see her than she felt was wise to show, Angie said, 'I thought you were staying at Lois's.'

Grace shrugged and avoided looking at her mother as she tugged off her beanie, scarf and gloves. Her eyes were red and swollen, her mouth as pale as her cheeks.

Emma said, 'Grace, sweetie, lovely as it is to see you, you shouldn't be out after dark on your own.'

'I can always go if I'm not wanted,' Grace told her snappishly.

'That's not what I'm saying. You never know who might be hanging about…'

'I brought you something,' Grace said to her mother, and digging into her pocket she pulled out a brightly coloured card.

'Oh cool,' Zac cried, reaching for it.

'It's for Mum,' Grace cried, snatching it back.

Seeing it was a scratch card with a star prize of fifty thousand pounds Angie's throat tightened with emotion.

'I reckon it's a winner,' Grace told Zac.

'I bet it is,' he agreed confidently. 'And if it is, will that mean we can stay in our house, Mum?'

Knowing she had to avoid the question, Angie said, 'Go and get Harry and Jack and we'll take it in turns to scratch a square.'

Zac whizzed into the sitting room shouting for the others, and moments later three small, excited faces were ready to begin.

Angie looked at Grace. 'Would you like to go first?' she offered.

Grace shook her head.

'I will! I will!' the boys cried.

It took only minutes to reveal the numbers, but in that time Angie felt the ludicrous, impossible dream of an eleventh-hour miracle rooting into her heart, as it was in everyone else's. Of course they'd tried scratch cards before, and EuroMillions, and Thunderball, she'd even signed them up for a month of Postcode Lottery, but this time, tonight, it felt different. It was just one card, bought by Grace, and given as a final desperate hope that they could stay in their home. Angie looked at her daughter and couldn't stop herself from thinking that maybe, just maybe, serendipity had put the card into her hand for just that purpose.

CHAPTER FIFTEEN

The court enforcers were due at three o'clock.

Apparently they weren't obliged to give a time, but that was what it said on the notice so Angie was working on the assumption that they'd keep to it.

Persuading the children to go to school hadn't been easy. Emma had come for them at eight thirty and had fought her own tears as she'd prised them away from their mother before loading them into her car. Grace's sweet and crazily hopeful effort to rescue them from the nightmare hadn't worked. The scratch card had been torn to pieces after the last reveal had turned their hopes to dust, and they'd vowed never to buy one again.

They would, of course, when they had an odd pound or two to spare; it was the only way Angie could see of them ever getting back on their feet.

The three of them had slept in her bed last night, their last at 14 Willow Close, snug and warm in the one room that was heated. The others were cold and dark, full of memories, some that would come with them, others that would stay, and crammed with boxes ready to be stacked in the family room before being taken over to Emma's to store in the attic.

After changing into their pyjamas and quickly cleaning their teeth in an icy bathroom, Grace had decided she wanted to French-plait her mother's hair. It had seemed strange to do something so normal given the situation they were in, but Angie had sat down in front of the dressing table with its near-empty and faintly dusty surface while Grace went gently about her task. She found it soothing to feel her daughter's fingers entwining her hair while Zac sat up in bed reading to them from *The Giraffe and the Pelly and Me*. He was a good reader, top of his class, and listening to him, Angie couldn't have felt more torn up inside. He wasn't to know that he'd chosen Liam's favourite book from when he was the same age. She remembered how Steve used to crack up laughing every time he read it. They'd always said that the only reason Liam kept asking for it was because of how much it made his father laugh.

Eventually they turned out the light and snuggled up under the duvet with Angie on her back so both children's heads could rest on her shoulders. As she listened to them breathing and felt their love and trust in her binding them even more tightly together she thought of the text she'd had from Roland Shalik before leaving Emma's.

Don't forget, Angie, you have options.

She'd texted back: *If I take a loan from you can we stay in the house?*

His reply wasn't long in coming. *I'm afraid that is not possible.*

Of course she'd known what he was really offering, and feeling as desperate as she did now she wondered if working for him was the answer. She felt her skin crawl as she tried imagining herself with men she didn't know, the kinds of things she'd have to do, and where they might happen. Would she be expected to work in a club, or just wait in a room somewhere for them to come to her? Would she be subjected to violence; would she ever be allowed to say no? Her mouth opened in a silent scream as she imagined Steve watching her from afar, or Martin Stone finding out… Why did he even matter? She had no idea, he'd just come into her mind, and the horror if it all sickened and overwhelmed her. It would be for the children, she reminded herself, she'd just have to blot out everything and everyone else and think of them, but even if she could do it, and she couldn't, she knew it wasn't really her Shalik was after.

It was Grace, and she would kill him with her bare hands if he ever went anywhere near her daughter.

Now, this morning, she forced herself to focus on what needed to be done over the next few hours and walked through to the sitting room. The furniture seemed oddly mournful, stripped as it was of the magazines, discarded clothes and cushions that had always given it life. There were only half a dozen boxes in here, most containing files and books that she was going to leave in the corner until everything could be moved to their new home.

Their new home – as if it were a place that actually existed.

After today they would have no home.

She returned to the kitchen, made herself some tea and forgot about it while she was upstairs checking she had everything she needed from her wardrobe, the airing cupboard, and bathroom. Emma had already packed up Steve's clothes and gone through Liam's room to sort out what should or shouldn't be kept. Grateful for that, she closed her bedroom door and stood on the landing where they used to keep the wooden rocking horse that Steve had carved for Liam before he'd even come into the world. All three children had taken their turns on it. They'd loved it as if it were a real pet and now it was gone, sold on eBay for seventy pounds.

At midday she called Roland Shalik's number, but rang off before the connection was made. She couldn't bear to speak to him, so instead she sent an email asking if this was really what he wanted, to make an innocent family homeless?

A reply came back half an hour later confirming that options were still on the table, and the decisions were hers.

She messaged back. *Is there another kind of job you can offer?*

What are you suggesting?

Something clerical? Cleaning? Driving?

There are no vacancies for those positions.

Accepting she'd never get anywhere with him, she rang the housing department and was put on hold for twenty minutes before being told to call back tomorrow.

'But we're being evicted today,' she cried angrily. 'I have *children…*'

'You have relatives in the area,' she was reminded.

She rang off abruptly and would have thrown her phone at the wall in frustration if she weren't so dependent on it. Thankfully BtG covered her contract, so there was no danger at this point of the service being cut off.

She knew that sometime in the future, when she looked back on this day it would seem that it had flown by, but that wasn't how it felt now. Each minute was more like an hour, as though deliberately and cruelly drawing out the agony.

At two o'clock she found herself in the back garden, looking around at the winter-torn beds and empty chill-out shed. The barbecue, sandpit, climbing frame, and tree swing were still there, and somewhere close by she could hear Steve playing 'Those Lazy Hazy Crazy Days of Summer'… She could see them dancing to the music, surrounded by friends, laughing, drinking too much wine… There they were puffing air into inflatables to take to the beach, wrestling tents out of bags to set up for the kids' camp on the green, planting new flowers each spring to mark the anniversary of being in the house. She felt Steve's arm going round her as he slid a hand over her pregnant belly (Zac), and watched six-year-old Grace reach up to do the same. Her beautiful children who'd lived here for ever…

Her elder boy who'd arrived in Willow Close when he was six, so excited and joyful and innocent of what life had in store. Where was he now?

She turned her face to the sky, with memories still swirling around her mind as unstoppably as the clouds passing overhead. She didn't hear her mobile jingle with a text, but she felt the vibration and checked it. As she read the words her heart stopped beating.

Saw your daughter's post online. Thought you'd like to know Liam is safe.

She read it again and again, certain she'd imagined it.

There was no name, no number. It was signed *A friend.*

Who could have sent it? And why now?

Her mind spun crazily to Steve, as if it had been him understanding that she'd needed something today. She thought of guardian angels, the police, even Martin Stone. Who could have known how desperately she wanted to hear this? What had made them choose today of all days to send it?

She felt herself falling with nowhere to land. She tried to take a breath and found that she couldn't. She wasn't aware of her knees buckling, or of sinking on to the wet grass. She didn't even hear herself sobbing; she only knew it was happening when arms went around her and tried to lift her. For a bewildering moment she thought it was Steve and couldn't work out if she'd died, or if he'd come back to her.

Then her vision cleared and she realized it was Melvin from down the street.

'Did you send me a text?' she asked him.

He looked baffled. 'Come on, let's get you inside,' he said.

Her body was still shaking with sobs as she allowed him to lead her into the kitchen; her legs were wet, her hands and feet were like ice. Dully she wondered what time it was and if he was one of the bailiffs here to evict her.

Thought you'd like to know Liam is safe.

'I'll make you some tea,' Melvin said, sitting her down at the table. 'Do you take sugar?'

She shook her head and pushed a hand through her dishevelled plait, catching strands between her fingers and leaving them to coil and stick to her face.

'I saw the front door wide open,' he explained, 'and your van half parked on the kerb... I thought I ought to check everything was OK.'

He must have noticed the near-empty cupboards by now and boxes all over the place, but he didn't remark on it. He simply put a mug of tea in front of her and turned to the fridge.

'There isn't any milk,' she told him. 'We used the last at breakfast this morning.'

Accepting this with no more than a nod he came to sit across from her, no tea for him – there was only one mug left unpacked – and bunched his hands on the table. As he stared down at them she wanted to ask again if he'd texted her, but she knew it couldn't have been him. He probably didn't even know Liam existed.

'It's none of my business...' he said.

'We're being evicted, today,' she told him, and heard her voice rising in a shredded echo from the misery inside her. She wondered if he already knew; maybe everyone did. If that were true then no one had mentioned it, or offered to help in some way, if only to store or carry something, or simply to say how sorry they were. They couldn't know, her neighbours wouldn't be that cruel. 'The bailiffs are due here at three,' she said.

His eyes were green and gentle, but barely disguised his shock as he said, 'I'm sorry. This is obviously a very distressing time for you. I didn't mean to intrude...'

She expected him to get up and leave, but he didn't. He continued sitting where he was, as though sensing she didn't want to be alone, and because she had no idea what else to say she sipped her tea and wondered where Emma was. She'd promised to be here by half two so Angie wouldn't have to go through the final steps alone. If she hadn't been moving one of the Hope House residents into an independent apartment this morning, she'd have come straight back after dropping the children at school.

'Do you have anywhere to go?' Melvin asked quietly.

'My sister's,' she said. She swallowed more tea and framed the words to thank him and tell him she was fine now so he could go. Instead she began talking to him about the day Steve had first brought her here, and about Liam helping his dad to build things in the garden, and paint the walls in his bedroom. She told him about Steve and Liam's excursions to the beach searching for crabs and mussels and limpets, and how they'd bring home horrid things like sea worms and snails to make her shiver and shriek.

Liam used to laugh delightedly when she shrieked, so she'd do it again and again until they were all wrapped up in so much laughter they might have dissolved in it.

By the time Emma ran in, full of apologies for being late and coming to an abrupt halt on seeing a stranger at the table, Angie had described what had happened to Steve, and that she had no idea where Liam was now. She hadn't got round to the text yet, but she was holding it close to her heart, thinking of it as a star fallen from the heavens to give her the strength to get through this dreadful day.

'Emma, this is Melvin who lives two doors down,' she said, introducing them. 'He came in to make sure I was all right.'

Though Emma appeared baffled and faintly suspicious as she watched Melvin get to his feet holding out a hand to shake, Angie didn't miss the quick flicker of interest. Emma could never hide anything from her.

'I was passing,' he explained, keeping his eyes on Emma's, 'and I saw the door open. I was afraid there might be burglars.' He turned to Angie. 'I should go...'

'No, please don't,' Emma said quickly, surprising both him and Angie. To Angie she said, 'Have you told him what's happening today?'

Angie nodded.

'Then I think we should ask him to stay in case... In case someone turns ugly.'

Angie's eyes widened in protest.

'I don't mind,' Melvin assured them.

Emma glanced at him gratefully, and apparently came to another quick decision. 'Actually,' she said, 'if you're sure about it I think I should take Angie to my place before anyone comes. Do you mind handing over the keys and making sure no one takes anything?'

Before Melvin could respond, Angie cried, 'No, Emma, that's too much to ask.'

Melvin said, 'I don't have to be at my next appointment until five...'

'If I leave now,' Angie said, 'it'll feel as though I'm abandoning the place, that I don't care about it...'

'That's nonsense,' Emma exclaimed in despair. Then, softening her tone, 'Look, I know how much this house means to you... Angie, stop! Where are you going?'

Angie paused at the bottom of the stairs, unsure how to answer, only knowing that she didn't want to argue, that she wanted to wake up now and find this was all a terrible dream.

Melvin said, 'Have you made arrangements to move your furniture?'

'We're leaving it here for now,' Emma replied. 'Storage is so expensive, and we can't sell it because Angie will need it, or at least some of it, when she gets a new place. Apparently the landlord can't take anything in lieu of rent. If he does he can be fined.'

Melvin nodded. 'So have you made an inventory of everything?'

Angie's stomach dipped as she realized they hadn't, and should have done.

Equally appalled by the oversight, Emma said, 'We need to do it right now. We don't have long.'

'We can take a room each,' Melvin said, pulling out his phone to start taking photos. 'If you do the kitchen, I'll sort out the sitting room and maybe you, Angie, could make a start upstairs?'

Understanding that she had to act fast Angie took out her own phone and ran up to her bedroom, grateful for the urgency since it allowed little time to think of anything else. Even the backdrop of the walls Steve had specially decorated for the children didn't throw her off track; she simply forced herself to focus on making sure that all moveable items were included.

Was Liam really safe, or was it a cruel joke?

It was just after three-fifteen when the bailiffs finally arrived, pulling up outside in a black 4×4 and looking, to Angie's mind, exactly what they were. Both were heavily built, and both wore dark padded jackets, jeans and boots; one carried a clipboard, the other had a tablet that he used to take a shot of the front of the house.

Angie went to the door, sick to her stomach, but managing to look them in the eye.

'Mrs Watts?' one of them asked. His voice was rough, but his manner wasn't hostile, only enquiring.

She stood aside for them to come in. Part of her had expected Agi to be with them, checking to make sure everything went to plan, but there was no sign of him.

'Can we see your ID please?' Melvin asked, as they entered the sitting room.

Apparently unperturbed, both men complied, and at the same time introduced themselves. Nigel Hastings and Bruno Gesh. As they looked around, Hastings said, 'You received notice to vacate the premises today, Mrs Watts, that includes your furniture...'

'We don't have anywhere to put it,' Emma snapped at him.

Hastings glanced at his partner as Gesh put a hand on his arm and nodded towards the window.

Angie turned to see a small red van with gold lettering on its panels pulling up behind the 4×4. The locksmith, she realized, and suddenly she wished she'd allowed Emma to persuade her to leave without witnessing this.

Gesh said, 'Mrs Watts, if you're unable to move your furniture out today we'll be forced to lock it inside the house, and it will be up to you to contact the landlord to arrange access and storage charges.'

Angie swallowed dryly. At least they weren't going to try and dump it in the garden – she'd read somewhere that that could happen whether it was legal for them to do so or not – and she could only feel thankful that this man didn't seem to realize that Agi and Roland Shalik would far rather that he did.

The next minutes passed in a blur that seemed timeless and surreal as the locksmith went about the task of making sure she couldn't get into her beloved house again. Meanwhile Melvin escorted the bailiffs from room to room, monitoring their search for anyone who might be hiding in an attempt to stay put.

Emma slipped an arm round Angie's shoulders and rested her head on hers. There were no words to make this any easier; all she could do was let Angie know she was there.

Angie opened the text and passed over her phone.

As she read it, Emma's eyes widened in shock.

'It came about an hour ago,' Angie said. 'I've no idea who sent it. I don't even know whether to believe it, but God knows I want to.'

'I think we should,' Emma told her. 'I mean, why would anyone say it if it wasn't true?'

'But why just sign themselves off as a friend? They'd surely know I'd want to be in touch to find out more.'

Having no answer for that, Emma simply gave the phone back and went to find out how things were progressing downstairs.

CHAPTER SIXTEEN

It was just after three thirty when the bailiffs finally encouraged everyone to leave the property – property? as though it had lost its identity – through the open front door. The new locks had been fitted and the locksmith had left. Angie was already wearing her coat, her bag was on her shoulder, so she forced herself to move one foot in front of the other, feeling as though the house itself was trying to pull her back inside.

When she reached the van it felt odd to see it looking as it always did; the houses around her and the green with its trees and stream hadn't changed either. The ground was solid under her feet, the clouds above were holding on to the rain, the familiar sound of seagulls ripped and trilled through the air.

Life went on even as worlds fell apart.

She turned back and saw the bailiffs locking the front door and nailing something across the letter box.

'You should go now,' Melvin told her gently. 'I'll stay and make sure they leave the place intact.'

Taking the van keys, Emma eased Angie into the passenger seat and closed the door. After speaking with Melvin for a moment, she got into the driver's side and started the engine. That was when Angie spotted Agi parked further down the street, watching through the shadow-dappled windscreen of his Toyota. Though a blind rage tried to seize her, a cold and powerful calm suppressed it. 'Do you see him?' she asked Emma as they drove towards him.

'I do,' Emma confirmed. 'Ignore him.'

Angie wanted to, she really did, but there was nothing in her that would allow him the satisfaction of thinking that she'd left with her head down. So she stared at him, eyes cold, mouth curved in a smile that suggested she knew something he didn't. Or she hoped that was how he'd interpret it. He'd find out soon enough that for the time being at least his boss had to store and take care of her furniture, so good luck selling the house while it was in its current state.

Ten minutes later Angie and Emma were at each end of the sofa in Emma's sitting room, legs curled under them as they drank tea and watched raindrops meandering down the windowpane. The reality of being this side of the eviction process was still trying to establish itself; it had actually happened, the house was no longer Angie's and never would be again.

To calm herself Angie kept focusing on the text about Liam. It was easier than trying to face the enormity of the situation. That was soon going to close around her like a folding umbrella; the words about Liam were like faint glints of sunlight on the darkest day.

She asked herself again and again who could have sent it, and why today? Was Liam really safe, or was it one of Grace's Facebook friends making mischief?

She looked up as Emma's phone rang.

Seeing a number she didn't recognize Emma was about to ignore it when she remembered she'd given Melvin her number.

'They've gone,' he told her when she answered. 'Someone else turned up after you'd driven away, I'm guessing he was the landlord or someone working for him, but he didn't introduce himself.'

'It was someone called Agi,' Emma said, putting the call on speaker. 'One of the landlord's thugs. Did he speak to you?'

'Only to ask who I was and what I was doing there. I told him I was a neighbour; I won't go into what he said in return. It wasn't helpful or particularly polite.'

Emma's lip curled. 'I'm sorry you had to meet him. I'm sorry you got dragged into this at all, but at the same time thank you...'

'I didn't get dragged in,' he corrected her, 'I volunteered, and I'm glad I was of some help. If you can text me your email address I'll send you my contribution to the inventory photos.'

'Of course. I'll do it right away.'

After she'd rung off, Emma did as he'd asked and sat staring down at the phone saying nothing for a while, until she remarked idly, 'He reminds me a bit of Matt Damon, does he you?' When Angie didn't answer she glanced up and seeing how lost and shattered her sister looked she moved over to hug her.

'It's funny, isn't it,' Emma said after a while, 'how strangers can come out of nowhere and end up making all the difference.'

Angie understood what she was saying – their mother used to call such people angels sent by the Universe – and it was true Melvin had been kind today, more than kind, but as for making all the difference... Even the mysterious text hadn't done that because she was homeless now, had no bathroom or kitchen to call her own, no back garden for the children to play in, or rooms for them to retreat to, or familiar place for them to chat as a family. The loss of 14 Willow Close was so enormous that she still couldn't give it a proper perspective; couldn't quite make herself accept that she'd never drive down that street again, or walk through that front door, or climb those stairs. When she pictured it, just the other side of the footbridge from where she was now, she could almost feel it waiting for her, expecting her to come back, to be its beating heart and living soul the way she always had.

She wasn't going to allow herself to think of who might live there next, whether they'd cherish the place as dearly as she and Steve had, or change it in ways to suit their own tastes. It wouldn't help to torment herself like that; she had no control over it, so for her own sake, and the children's, she must try to force herself to let go.

'Here they are,' Emma said, as a car drew up outside and the children got out. 'I'll go and thank Rachel for bringing them.'

Happy not to see or speak to anyone apart from her family right now, Angie went through to the kitchen to take out the after-school snacks she'd bought specially for today. Cheesy Wotsits for the boys, a banana and date bar for Grace, and a bottle of cloudy lemonade for them to share. She and Emma would stick with tea, though they'd have no trouble seeing off an entire bottle of wine right now, and probably more, if they had some.

Alcohol wasn't the answer. She must keep remembering that as the temptation grew stronger, and not let herself go near it while things were so bad. She'd seen too much evidence of what that slippery slope could lead to, and she was in a terrible enough place already.

'Mum?'

She turned to find Grace and Zac at the door, pale-faced and watching her with a mix of hope and dread in their eyes.

They knew it had happened, of course they did, they wouldn't be here at Emma's if it hadn't, but she could see how desperately they wanted her to tell them that it had all been a dreadful mistake and everything was OK.

Opening her arms, she caught them to her, and pressed kisses to their hair as they hugged her back.

'Was it terrible?' Grace asked, searching her mother's face with red-rimmed eyes.

Angie attempted a smile. 'There was no fuss,' she assured her. 'They were quite polite, actually, and Melvin, the new neighbour, came in to lend some support.'

'His twins are in my class,' Zac told her.

Angie gazed lovingly down at him. 'How was your day at school?' she asked.

His lower lip trembled. 'I couldn't wait to get home,' he confessed.

'Nor me,' Grace said. 'It was hard to think about anything else.'

'I kept wanting to cry,' Zac admitted, 'but I was afraid someone would see and tease me.'

'I'd have whacked them if they did,' Jack informed him, playing the older cousin as he came into the kitchen. His eyes lit up when he saw the snacks. 'Are they for us?' he asked excitedly.

'For you all to share,' Angie told him.

Harry came skidding through the door. 'I'm starving,' he cried, and seeing the Cheesy Wotsits he gave a whoop of joy.

Angie watched her nephews dive in, and tried nudging Zac to join them, but it seemed neither of her children was hungry today.

Taking out her phone, Angie showed Grace the text about Liam. 'Do you think one of your friends might have sent it?' she asked. 'As some kind of joke?'

Grace was astonished and perplexed as she shook her head. 'I don't see why they would,' she replied. 'I mean, it's not horrible or anything, and why send it to you, not to me, if it's my posts they saw? How would they even know your number?'

It was a good question that no one had an answer for, so Angie put the phone away and hugged Grace to her.

'I want to believe it,' Grace whispered.

'Me too,' Angie whispered back, picturing her beautiful boy looking healthy and strong, a long way away from the gangs where they could never find him.

Dream on, Angie.

Later, as they set the table for supper, Grace said to her mother, 'Are you sleeping here tonight?'

Aware of Emma listening, Angie was about to answer when Zac said, 'Can I sleep with you? I don't mind if it's on the sofa.'

Angie quickly put on a smile as she turned to pass around the glasses. 'I've arranged to stay at Brenda Crompton's,' she told them. 'You know, the lady from the food bank.'

The children didn't know Brenda, but Emma did, and since Brenda was the kind of person to help during a crisis it was likely Emma believed her. But Angie wasn't the kind of person to ask such a favour when she knew how disruptive it could be to take in a homeless person, what a burden they could turn into, and she didn't want Brenda to fear that from her. So her arrangements for tonight, and for all the nights that followed until she and the children were given a place together, were not what she was telling her family.

CHAPTER SEVENTEEN

Later, after a supper of sausage and mash followed by a game of Monopoly – the irony of a property game in which she ended up with the 'go straight to jail' card twice wasn't lost on Angie – she put on her best comforting smile as she prepared to say goodnight to the children. She was sure they couldn't see how sick and anxious she was feeling inside, or how desperately she wanted to cling to them, but she knew that like her, they were thinking of their empty home all in darkness across the footbridge.

'I'll be here when you get up in the morning,' she promised, hugging them hard, 'and it'll seem like I was always here.'

Zac was crying, and with a terrible wrench in her heart she saw that Grace's eyes were full of tears too. They were afraid and confused, their world was in turmoil, and they had no idea what to expect from the days and weeks to come, what other shocks and traumatic upsets might be waiting for them. Still, at least they knew they were remaining with Auntie Em in the short term – that was familiar and safe – while their mother went to stay with a woman from the Salvation Army.

'She's a very nice lady,' Emma assured them as Angie put on her coat. 'She's really kind and she'll take good care of Mum, so don't you go worrying yourselves now.'

'But why can't you stay here?' Zac pleaded with Angie. 'I don't want you to go.'

'I know,' she murmured, ruffling his hair, 'but we've been through this, sweetheart. We don't want Auntie Em being forced out of her house for overcrowding, and if I'm here…'

'But how will anyone know?' he protested. 'If we turn the lights off and pretend there's no one at home then no one will see us.'

If it could only be so easy, Angie was thinking as she kissed him and looked over his head to Emma. There was every chance Amy Cutler was hiding behind her curtains right now watching Angie's van, waiting for it to leave – and if it didn't she'd be straight on the phone to Shalik.

Seeing the strain in Emma's face, she felt a deepening guilt tighten her heart as she damned herself and Amy Cutler for bringing them to this.

'Just take care of yourself,' Emma murmured as they hugged goodnight at the door. 'They'll be fine with me, you know that.'

Of course Angie knew it, but she also knew that Emma was as worried as she was that Shalik might kick up about the children and threaten eviction. The house belonged to him and if he wanted Emma out she'd have to go.

As Angie drove away in torrential rain, waving to the children who were watching from the window, and blowing kisses in return for theirs, she felt the break in contact as she lost sight of the house as though it were a physical splintering in her heart.

She turned out of the Fairweather estate and headed for town. With each minute that passed her anxiety about the night ahead was growing to a pitch that made it difficult to focus on the road. She forced herself to breathe steadily, to count to ten, to think of Grace and Zac, Em and her nephews, her precious family who were safe tonight.

It was all that mattered; she only had to get through the next eight hours and in the morning she would see them again.

As she reached town, her small van passing under gleaming streetlights, one unassuming vehicle amongst many others, she headed for the seafront, certain it would be busy at this hour, in spite of the weather. She wasn't wrong. It was Friday, so youngsters were out in numbers, swarming in and out of rowdy bars that lined the Promenade, mixing their cocktails, smoking, guffawing, the girls staggering on impossible heels and seeming not to notice the cold rain soaking into the gooseflesh of bare white thighs.

Circling at the end of the Promenade she passed the red-carpeted steps of the Royal Hotel where a uniformed doorman stood on duty, and joined the traffic crawling along the west bank of the grassy island that ran parallel to the shops and bars on the other side.

Finding an empty parking spot almost opposite the Seafront Café, closed now, she turned off the engine and sat staring at the exquisite Victorian beach shelter a few feet away. With its dark red pillars, grey tiled roof and ornate filigree benches it offered scant protection from the elements, but emaciated and shivering human bodies were already scrunched down in sleeping bags for the night, or buried under cardboard, or wrapped in sheets of tinfoil. Later, Angie knew, it was possible they'd find themselves being urinated over, kicked, dragged out of their flimsy shells and mocked by drunken louts looking for sport, or maybe to impress a bunch of equally drunk girls.

She wasn't planning to join the street sleepers; her only reason for choosing this spot was because she could stay for a while, blending in as if she were a mother come to drive a revelling teenager home.

Would she see Liam? What would she do if she did?

Thought you'd like to know Liam is safe.

Time ticked on, and as she grew colder and sadder, more desperate for her children and Steve, she saw more than any mother would ever want to see. Projectile vomiting over pavements and shopfronts; girls humped against walls or cars with a drink in one hand, brushing strands of hair from a bemused face with the other. She spotted dealers lurking on corners, saw how much business they were doing, and watched them melt like shadows into darkness each time blue flashing lights changed the tenor of the night.

Finally, around 2 a.m., lights began going off in the bars and clubs, slowly turning a kaleidoscopic façade of stately Victorian properties to a still and soundless terrace. Stragglers pitched in all directions, then zero-hour workers, exhausted and desperate for their beds, began trickling on to the street.

A transit van drew up outside one of the seamier clubs and a group of young girls in microscopic skirts and faux-fur jackets got in. Suddenly one of them broke free and started to run. A heavy man bolted after her, caught her by the hair and dragged her back to the van. No one emerged from a police car parked nearby though they must surely have seen it. Moments later it was as if the brief drama had never happened, and as Angie stared at the emptiness she felt certain the girls had been trafficked here and were now kept in virtual slavery. There was always someone, she thought bleakly, who was worse off, and God knew they were.

She couldn't stay here any longer. She was under a lamp post, might already have been noticed without realizing it and she was afraid that someone desperate for cover might try to force their way into the van.

Her fingers were stiff as she restarted the engine; not even her thick down coat and woollen gloves were enough to keep out the bitter cold tonight. Her feet were numb, and almost slipped off the pedals as she started to pull away.

Just a few more hours and she'd be able to return to Em's.

Wishing she could afford the petrol to drive around for all that time with the heater going and the van keeping her safe and dry, she turned back along the Promenade towards the Royal Hotel. It was laughable to imagine she could book in there for the night – she couldn't spare the money for even the cheapest B & B when she needed every last penny for the children – but it was a pleasant fantasy for a moment as she passed.

The red-brick building of the station soon loomed up in front of her, familiar turrets and grey slate roofs, yet it seemed eerily different with no lights on inside. Opposite the locked, arched doors of the entrance, next to the beach, a kids' carousel was bundled up inside thick tarpaulins; close to it was Merry Mick's hot-dog stall shuttered up against the wind. Litter skidded across the pavement towards the wet sand; against a front wall a lone rough sleeper was tucked in under a bench where an iron grille presumably leaked a residue of warmth from the waiting room the other side; it was a shapeless, hopeless bundle of rags that made her heart twist with pity and fear.

Going past the station, she turned into the car park behind it. Five vehicles were sitting motionless in the dim glow of a single lamp post, waiting, presumably, for their owners to return. Whether these were people overnighting in other cities, or in one of the B & Bs close by, was impossible to tell. She only knew that their cars were going to keep her company for the next few hours while she waited out the night, and maybe even attempted to sleep.

After reversing the van into a space at the back of the car park, manoeuvring it so she was facing the ticket office across the black expanse of tarmac, she closed her fingers round the ignition keys, not quite able to turn the engine off. The rear-view mirror was an oblong of black, but she knew that a high, thorny hedge was behind her, creating a barrier between her and a sprawling scrapyard of decrepit caravans and rusting fairground rides. She was partly in light, but mostly in shadow, and hopefully in view of a CCTV camera that was keeping watch on proceedings, presuming it was working.

When she finally turned off the engine she felt an unnerving silence creeping in through the clicks of cooling metal and seeming to bind her more tightly in this frightening nether world. There was no sign of anyone; nothing moved apart from skittering rubbish and stray dead leaves picked up by swirls of wind from the sea. When she'd come here two days ago to assess this spot as a possible place to hide away during the early hours, she'd had no idea it would feel so lonely or sinister in the dead of night.

After making doubly sure the driver's and passenger doors were locked, she removed her seat belt and reached for the pillow she'd stored behind her seat. She'd also brought a duvet, a holdall full of clean clothes to change into, a bottle of tap water and a toilet roll, but she couldn't find the she-pee Steve had bought her a few years ago at the Glastonbury festival. She could do with using it now, but she was too afraid someone would notice the van moving if she climbed into the back. She couldn't even summon the nerve to lie across the front seats; she would feel so vulnerable and exposed if she did; faces could loom up to the windows looking in…

She sat silently, rigidly, staring out at the night, heart

thudding erratically as she gave up all hope of sleep; it would never be possible while she was so taut with fear. Not for a single moment had she considered how terrifying it might be to spend a night in the van, and realizing how much worse it must be with no shelter at all wasn't helping her to feel any better.

Her mind wandered back across town to Emma and the children, and how she was going to explain asking to use the shower in the morning. Emma would know that Brenda Crompton would never deny her such a basic need, but maybe she could say that she hadn't wanted to use up Brenda's hot water. She couldn't use up Emma's either, not when her sister was already on a plan with British Gas to help meet her bills. This left Angie with the problem of where to shower, where even to clean her teeth – and what was she going to do in the coming days when she needed to wash her hair? She couldn't do it in the public toilets next to the beach, it was banned, or in the ladies' room of a department store, it was banned there too. She thought of the day shelter over on City Walk; it had a female-only space providing hot showers, a change of clothes, even a launderette and nourishing meals – but it was for women at risk of being forced into sex work or trying to escape domestic abuse. She hardly qualified on either count, but even if she did she'd almost certainly know one of the support workers there and she simply couldn't bear for anyone to find out just how bad things had got for her.

She was so caught up in the horror of her future that it took a moment for the sound of footsteps crunching on the gravel outside to reach her. She tensed so tightly it hurt, and pushed herself so hard into the seat she felt she might disappear right through it. A man laughed, and she almost whimpered, as though he was laughing at her. Then she heard the electronic beep of a car unlocking. A few minutes later a middle-aged, well-dressed couple drove off in an Audi, leaving her looking after the tail lights and feeling more alone and more wretched than she would have believed possible.

Eventually, telling herself she might feel safer if she weren't visible to any chance passer-by, she climbed over the seat into the back of the van, moving slowly in an effort not to rock it. After scrambling through the bags she had stored there, she covered herself with the small duvet and used her holdall as a pillow while clutching the real thing to her chest for extra warmth. She had no idea what time it was now, or if she'd be able to catch an hour or two of sleep, she only knew that if she thought about Steve it seemed to calm her.

After a while it began to feel as though he wasn't just with her, but that he was holding her close, breathing warmth and comfort into the icy air. She kept her eyes closed, not moving a muscle in case it made him go away. But he stayed and she could feel his arms around her, his body melding into hers as though they were becoming one. Dimly she was aware of the need to pee increasing, until it grew so intense that she had to find the she-pee. She scrabbled around for it, feeling sure she'd brought it. She found the toaster and vacuum cleaner, a pair of Steve's shoes and oddly a birthday card for Zac with a unicorn on the front. Her bladder felt as though it was ready to burst. She had no choice but to sneak out of the back of the van and hide under the hedge while she relieved herself.

It wasn't easy when she was wearing a thick coat with several layers underneath; it was soon a frustrating pantomime of tugging and pushing, with her woollen hat becoming entangled in spiked branches and her bare skin flinching at the cold as she was finally able to let go.

She was still going when she realized that the van was

rocking. She could hear voices and saw dark figures crawling in through the open back doors. She was too terrified even to breathe; what if they found her with her jeans around her ankles, what would they do?

They were taking her purse and her phone; her sleeping bag; her van keys – and as the driver's door was wrenched open she tried to scream. No sound came out. She tried again and again, until finally she woke, trembling and sobbing and unable to stop even when she realized it was a dream.

CHAPTER EIGHTEEN

'Angie? Could I have a word?'

Turning from the boisterous game that was rolling up and down the football pitch with small-boy exuberance making up for skill, Angie felt herself blanch even as she smiled. It was Bob Collins, the neighbour who'd taken over Steve's role as Santa last year, and who'd also stepped in to coach the Fairweather under-eights football team – a job Steve had loved with a passion. She'd always liked Bob, so had Steve; certainly she'd never detected any harm in him, and she was trying not to now, but it was proving hard.

She'd brought Zac here this morning, to the playing fields above Kesterly, to take up his usual right-wing position for a match against the West Common under-eights – always a big event in the local fixture list. On arriving they'd been informed that Zac had been relegated to the subs' bench today, in spite of being the team's highest scorer. His mates even called him the Egyptian King, after Mohamed Salah, his favourite Liverpool player. She'd told herself it was probably tiredness and the after-effects of such a stressful first night without a home that were making her want to recoil from Bob Collins now, or even punch him for doing this to Zac…

'I hope you don't mind me asking,' Bob said, a gentle hand on her elbow as he turned her away from the other spectators, walking her into the wind that scudded across the open fields, 'if everything's all right with you?'

Certain she could hear whispering coming from the other parents, those who'd no doubt sucked up Amy Cutler's gossip and were eager to find out more, Angie said, too brightly, 'Of course it is. Why do you ask?'

Bob gave a curious little grimace that came with a shrug. 'It's just that someone mentioned you moved out of number fourteen yesterday, and when Candy and I went over to check up on you we saw that the letter box had been sealed up.'

'We did that,' Angie said hastily, 'because the landlord asked us to. He wants to make sure no one, no hooligans I mean, can post anything through while the place is empty.'

Though Bob clearly didn't believe her, his tone remained gentle as he said, 'So you have moved out? I wish you'd said something, we'd have given you a hand.'

'That's very kind of you, thank you.'

'So where are you living now?'

'We're… The kids are staying with Emma, and I'm with a friend until our new place is ready. We're getting it fixed up a little before we move in.' She smiled again, and wondered where the lies were coming from. She'd had no idea they were even there, yet apparently they were having no problem spilling out of her.

With a glimmer of relief showing through his concern, Bob said, 'We're going to miss you on Willow Close. It won't be the same without you guys. I do hope you'll let us have your new address before you disappear altogether.'

Certain he must know her departure was an eviction, she said, 'Of course,' and they both turned around as a raucous cheer went up. Bob ran to the touchline to congratulate his boys, who'd just equalized. Angie looked across to Zac and saw that he was on his feet, waving his arms and yelling 'brilliant', 'nice one' to the scorer, which was so typical of her boy; no one would know how crushed he was not to be on the field.

He was so like Liam in that aspect of his personality.

Earlier, at Emma's, when she'd woken Zac with a kiss, he'd come alive so suddenly when he'd realized it was her that he'd rolled them both off his mattress on to the floor with the joy of his embrace. He'd been so relieved to see her that he'd clasped her with his arms and legs, and not even when she'd whispered, 'OK, I submit,' would he let her go.

'Football today, you need to get ready,' she'd reminded him, hands pinned to the floor either side of her head as he grinned triumphantly down at her.

He looked instantly worried. 'Did we remember to bring my kit and boots?' he asked.

'Of course. I've just checked your bag and they're definitely there.'

He grinned all over his dear freckled face. 'I'm going to score ten million goals today,' he'd told her, 'and if a scout is watching he'll sign me up and make me a professional, then I'll be able to buy our house.'

When they'd arrived for the game and he'd found out he wasn't on the first team today he'd said, 'Sorry, Mum,' as if it were his fault and he was letting her down, 'but they might put me on at half-time and if they do I'll definitely score.'

Now, as Bob Collins jogged back to her, flushed and

windswept, she wanted to turn away, put a stop to where this little chat was going, but there was no escaping him.

'Angie, I'm really sorry about this,' he began awkwardly, 'but I've got to mention Zac's football dues. As you know, Amy Cutler does the accounts, and she's mentioned they're quite behind… You know how everyone wants their boy on the first team, and there's a tournament coming up that we'd love Zac to play in, but if you're finding it difficult…'

'It's OK,' she said shortly, 'you'll get the outstanding dues, *and* his fee for the tournament by the end of the week.' Her smile was glacial as violence burned in her heart. *Is that what you were hoping to hear? Or were you waiting for me to confirm what Amy Cutler's already told you, that we've got nowhere to live, no money in our pockets and sod all hope for the future?*

His eyes were still on hers. 'Marvellous,' he said, seeming lost for any other word. 'Marvellous.'

Glancing back to the subs' bench, she said, 'So now, does Zac get to play today?'

Zac did play and he scored a goal, and his teammates were clearly so thrilled to have him on the pitch that they kept hugging him, even when he didn't hit the back of the net. By the time they came off it was hard to recognize one player from the next, they were so caked in mud, but Angie soon found her boy, happier and dirtier than everyone else, and after wrapping him in the old towels she kept in the van for this very purpose she plonked him into the passenger seat to take him back to Emma's.

That was how she managed to get a bath that day, quickly slipping into the murky water after she'd hauled him out of it and sent him off in a big blue towel to dry down.

Not long after Angie had wiped the muddy water from

herself Emma returned from dropping her boys at their dad's for the weekend, and setting a large white box in the middle of the kitchen table she busied herself with the kettle.

Recognizing the box as one of Fliss's from the Seafront Café, Angie regarded it curiously. 'Can I ask what's inside?' she ventured, not wanting to remove the neatly tied blue ribbon to take a look for herself.

Emma flushed slightly as she said, 'I thought I'd take something over to Melvin's to say thank you for yesterday, and given that he has kids a cake seemed like a good idea.'

Wishing she could have done this herself, Angie fought her helplessness and said, 'It's a lovely thought. Would you mind saying it's from both of us?'

Surprised, Emma said, 'Of course it's from both of us... Oh Angie,' she murmured, going to wrap her sister in her arms. 'I'm sorry, if I'd known it would upset you...'

'It's not the cake,' Angie wept. 'It's everything, but it's OK, I'll be fine in a minute.' Ripping off a sheet of kitchen roll, she dabbed her eyes and allowed Emma to push her into a chair.

'Here we are,' Emma said a few minutes later, as she brought mugs of tea and a couple of biscuits to the table. 'This should cheer you up a bit.'

Angie tried not to grab one of the Hobnobs; she didn't want Emma to suspect this might be the first thing she'd had to eat since last night.

Emma apparently did suspect it. 'So what did Brenda give you for breakfast?' she asked, as she sipped her tea.

Angie grimaced. 'I left so early that I didn't want to bother her,' she replied.

'And did you get a hot dog after football?'

'Yes, of course we did,' Angie lied. 'What is this? Do I look hungry, or something?'

Emma regarded her carefully. 'I think you probably do,' she

admitted. 'And it's my guess that you bought a hot dog for Zac, but didn't have one yourself. Am I right?'

Angie gave an exasperated sigh. 'I honestly didn't fancy one,' another lie, for the way her mouth had watered when Zac had bitten into his had been nothing short of painful. 'So I'm a bit peckish now...'

'How much money do you have in your purse?' Emma asked bluntly.

Angie shook her head. 'I'm not sure, but if you need more for the kids...'

'That's not what I mean, you've given me plenty for them, it's you I'm worried about. You can't go starving yourself, Angie...'

'How can you say that after the slap-up meal you served us last night? In case you didn't notice, there wasn't a scrap left on my plate.'

'I did notice, and I think it was probably the first food you'd had all day, and now I'm wondering what you ate the day before.'

Angie's eyes closed as she let her head fall back, trying to sink the tears before Emma spotted them. 'With all that's been going on,' she said, 'I haven't had much of an appetite.'

Emma continued to watch her. 'You still haven't told me how much you have in your purse,' she prompted.

'I have enough.'

'Enough for what?'

Angie put out a hand, palm forward. 'Will you stop with the mothering,' she scolded. 'I'm fine, honestly, well, not fine, obviously, but it'll be OK.' *Please don't ask how,* she silently willed. She had less than ten pounds in her purse, no cash due from covering various shifts and nothing left on her credit card to last the rest of the month. This meant she'd have to be sparing with the near-full tank of petrol she had, so tomorrow morning she'd leave it in the station car park and get the bus back here. God bless the old mayor who'd brought in the one-pound fare... Thoughts of the old mayor took her straight to Martin, and how his playful text the other day had lifted her spirits. Just a few short words that had probably meant nothing to him, but she'd read them again a few times since, and each time they made her smile.

Where was he now? What was he doing on this wintry Saturday afternoon? It was impossible to imagine what his life was like when she'd never mixed in his sort of world, much less lived in it.

'Would you like me to go through everything with you?' Emma offered. 'Maybe I can help out in some way...'

Coming back to earth, Angie sighed. 'You're already doing enough,' and turning as Zac came into the kitchen she scooped him up on her lap.

'Where are Harry and Jack?' he asked his aunt, helping himself to a biscuit.

'They've gone to their dad's until tomorrow,' Emma reminded him.

'Oh yes, I forgot.'

He seemed so forlorn, so unbearably lonely without his cousins and a dad of his own, that Angie couldn't stop more tears welling in her eyes.

'They said they'll be on the PlayStation,' Emma told him encouragingly.

Zac brightened a little. His cousins had another PlayStation at their dad's, so it would almost be like they were here. 'We're in the middle of a game with these players from Denmark,' he explained as he slid off Angie's lap, 'and we were winning last night. I'll go and see if anyone's logged in.'

After he'd gone Emma said quietly, 'So what about those accounts?'

Knowing she couldn't bear even her sister to realize how bad things actually were, Angie said, 'Let me go through it on my own first then we can talk. Now tell me about Grace. Did she say where she was going today?'

'To swim club with Lois.'

'Of course. How did she seem?'

'Hard to tell really, she must have been late because she went off in a bit of a rush.'

Glad to think Grace was carrying on as normal, Angie sighed shakily and began clearing up the kitchen. The last thing she wanted was Grace taking on some misguided sense of responsibility. She was her father's daughter in that respect, always feeling she had to fix problems, even when it was completely beyond her to know how.

Grace and Lois were searching for a table in the café at Kesterly indoor pool, their hair still wet following the afternoon swim club, their appetites raging after so much exertion.

'I promise I'll pay you back,' Grace insisted as they squeezed into a small corner between the window and a vending machine.

'Don't worry about it,' Lois told her. 'It's just one session.'

'Plus a doughnut and hot chocolate…'

'… and when you're earning I know you'll make good. Now, come on, show me the message. I've been dying to read it. When did it come?'

'Just after I woke up,' Grace replied, starting to grin, for she already knew how her BFF was going to respond.

'And you didn't send it straight to me,' Lois cried, snatching the phone from Grace's hand. She began reading aloud. There was so much noise echoing around the swimming baths that even Grace missed most of it, but it didn't matter, she could more or less remember what it said. *Hi Grace, like I promised I've been giving your situation a lot of thought and doing some research on how best I can help. From your YouTube and Facebook posts it's clear you're into acting – you have a real talent by the way – so I've been in touch with some contacts of mine and several have already come back to say how impressed they are by what they've seen. They're all agreed that you could make some serious money if you were cast in the right productions. Would you be interested in pursuing this further? If not, no worries, I'm sure I can come up with something else. Anya ☺*

Lois's eyes were as round as her specs as she looked at Grace. 'TFA,' she murmured, shorthand for totally effing awesome.

Grace was still grinning as she bit into her doughnut. 'I wonder what sort of parts she's talking about,' she mused, thinking of the many she'd like to play such as Arya Stark in *Game of Thrones*, or Luce Price in *The Fallen* or Miss Adelaide in *Guys and Dolls*. She'd played Miss Adelaide in the Fairweather Players' production last year and everyone had said it was amazing that someone as young as her could sing and dance and act so well.

'You need to ask her,' Lois declared, waving to their coach as he came into the café. 'Is she thinking screen or stage? You can do both, no problem, and we'll have to prepare you for auditions. I'm definitely up for that. OMG this is totally, totally lit.'

Grace put her phone away just in case the coach came to join them. Since receiving the message she'd been lurching between excitement, nerves and then guilt for not worrying more about her mum. But she was doing this for her so that should make everything all right, shouldn't it?

She did her best to join in the chit-chat when the coach plonked himself and a burger down on the windowsill next to their table, but her mind was all caught up with other things and her eyes kept drifting to the street below. Today was one of the many times she'd wondered what she'd do if she saw

Liam on his way somewhere, or just hanging around, and now her mum had received that text it was seeming more possible that she might. There was no sign of him today, not that she'd really expected there to be, but it didn't stop her hoping. She'd found nothing on any of her social media pages to give her a clue as to who might have sent the text, but whoever it was had definitely looked at her posts because they'd said so, and now she was wondering if it might have been Liam himself or maybe it was Anya. If she was a friend of her dad's then it was possible she had her mum's mobile number.

'Why don't you ask Anya if she sent the text about Liam?' Lois suggested after they'd said goodbye to the coach and taken themselves outside to wait for Lois's mum to come and pick them up.

'I think I will, when I answer her message.'

'Which you're going to do today? I'd definitely be finding out more about that if I was you.'

'Don't worry, I'm going to,' Grace assured her. 'I've just got to work out what to say.'

'We can do that together… Are you coming back to mine? Yes, you have to. Oh God, this is totally amazing. I can't wait to get on it.'

It was just after five that evening when Emma returned from delivering the cake to Melvin and his family. As she let herself in the front door she called out to Angie that they had a visitor, and realizing it was her cue to cover up the paperwork spread over the kitchen table, Angie went about it quickly, trying to steady her erratic heartbeat.

Her first thought, when she heard a male voice, was that Emma had brought Melvin back with her. Maybe he'd come to thank them for the cake they'd given him to say thank you. That could almost be funny.

Please, please, don't let it be Agi come to cut up rough about the furniture.

To her surprise it turned out to be Bob Collins, looking slightly embarrassed, but sounding forthright enough as he greeted Angie with a warmth she couldn't quite return.

'I hope I'm not interrupting,' he said, glancing between the sisters, 'and I promise I don't mean to... Well, I could have got this all wrong, and if I have, I'm sorry, but I wanted you to know that we... that's me and some of the other parents of Zac's football team, we've had a bit of a whip-round, and I thought I should let you know that the dues are taken care of and we'd love Zac to play in the tournament.'

As a lump formed in Angie's throat she hardly knew what to say. She'd thought so ill of this man earlier, and the other parents, and now here they were showing her more kindness than she could ever deserve.

'That's really lovely of you, Bob,' Emma told him gently. 'It's just been a bit of a difficult time lately, and...'

'Don't feel you have to explain,' he interrupted. 'I understand that things can get the better of you sometimes. I just want you to know, Angie, that we're here for you, all of us on Willow Close and here on The Beeches... I guess it's difficult to ask for help, but if you need anything...'

Angie tried to speak, but only a sob came out.

Going to put an arm around her, Emma thanked Bob again. 'Will you stay for a cup of tea?' she offered.

He was already backing away. 'I have to run,' he replied, 'we're taking the kids to the pictures tonight.' A thought suddenly occurred to him. 'Do you think Zac might like to come with us? I mean, if he's not doing anything else.'

Zac did want to go, and because she couldn't allow Bob and Candy Collins to pay for everything, Angie pressed two one-pound coins into his little fist as he was leaving. It wouldn't get him much, maybe a small bucket of popcorn, but at least he'd have something to share, and she knew that would mean a lot to him.

'So,' she said to Emma, returning to the kitchen after seeing Zac off, 'how did you get on at Melvin's? Was his wife there?'

Emma frowned slightly. 'She answered the door. She's quite odd, isn't she?'

Angie shook her head. 'I've never met her. Why do you say that?'

Emma shrugged. 'Well, she wasn't rude, exactly, but when I told her why I was there she didn't invite me in. She just took the cake and said that she'd make sure Melvin got it.'

'Was he there?'

'Yes, because he came out before I could get to the footbridge and called me back to apologize for not asking me in. He said the cake was a lovely gesture, but we shouldn't have.'

'And you said?'

Emma's eyebrows arched comically. 'I told him he was our hero and that we really couldn't have managed without him yesterday, which we couldn't, and you'll never guess what, he blushed. Isn't that cute? How many men do you know who are even capable of blushing?' She sighed theatrically. 'Such a shame he's married,' she commented, glancing at her nails, 'because I think he likes me.'

Amused, Angie said, 'What makes you say that?'

'It must have been when he asked if a shag was out of the question that gave him away. Of course, I had to tell him I'm busy tonight, but…'

'You are such a wind-up,' Angie groaned, going to put the kettle on.

'I prefer to call myself a dreamer,' Emma sighed, sinking down at the table. 'Anyway, he was obviously embarrassed about the way his wife had behaved and he said if we need help with anything else we know where to find him. I thanked him and made it clear that there won't always be a cake at the end of it, and that made him laugh. It's lovely when you make someone laugh, isn't it? Not as good as a blush, or maybe it's better.'

Thinking of how much Steve had made her laugh, and of the short text from Martin that had pleased her so much, Angie circled her arms round Emma's neck and dropped a kiss on the top of her head. It was important to make the most of these light-hearted moments when so much was going wrong in her world, and when even more could be awaiting her.

They spent the next hour or so carrying out an Internet search for jobs that Angie could fit around Bridging the Gap – or something that would pay her well enough to start a whole new career. Not that they hadn't done this before, many times, but things could change by the day, and maybe the answer to everything was no more than a few clicks away.

'Here's one,' Emma said after a while, turning her screen so Angie could see it. 'You can work your own hours from home as a customer-service agent.'

Angie's eyes were tired as she looked at it. 'I've seen it before,' she said, 'and it isn't real. Agencies post things like that just to get you to sign up with them, then they keep offering you something completely different, and pressure you to take it.'

Emma pointed out another. 'How about becoming a carer? They're looking for someone to do night shifts at Greensleeves, where Craig's the resident entertainer.'

With a small nod, Angie said, 'I could give them a call, but if it's more than three nights a week…' She shook her head irritably. 'I'm being too picky, I know. Actually, I'm starting to wonder if I might be better off not having a job at all. My credits would probably increase, and I'd have all the time in the world to spend with the children…'

'You'd also have the jobcentre breathing down your neck every five minutes, trying to force you to take any old thing, and docking your allowance if you don't.'

Knowing how true that was, Angie made a note to contact Greensleeves on Monday, and a local agency that specialized in 'temporary' and 'home work', and shut down her computer.

It was past nine by the time Grace messaged to let them know she was staying at Lois's, and just after that Zac came back dying to tell them all about the movie he'd seen, how much he'd had to eat and drink at Pizza Hut afterwards, and how someone had almost run in front of the car. Though he was doing a valiant job of hiding his tiredness Angie could see it, so she sent him to get ready for bed, and by the time she went to tuck him in he was already asleep.

'I shouldn't be too late for Brenda,' she said to Emma, trying to hide her misery as she reached for her coat. 'It wouldn't be fair.'

'No of course not,' Emma agreed, coming with her to the door.

As Angie stepped outside the night air enveloped her in its icy grip, and after giving her sister a hug she set off to spend another night in the van.

CHAPTER NINETEEN

On Monday morning, after spending a third torturous night in the van, Angie arrived at the church office to collect the keys for Bridging the Gap, and found the place deserted. She called out, expecting Rosa, the vicar's wife, or Ivan, the parish manager, to appear at any minute, but no one did.

Her heart started to pound. She had to seize this opportunity – it was God given and would harm no one, she reminded herself – and allowing herself no more time to think she moved swiftly across the room to the cabinet where the keys were kept. Finding the one to BtG in its usual place, she unhooked it, helped herself to the one next to it as well and stuffed both into her pocket.

Despite the sub-zero temperature it was a bright morning with a heavy frost sparkling on the brown beech hedge that ran alongside the road, making the cobwebs glisten like crystals as she passed along the scattered stone path to her own office. She was warmer now than when she'd got to Emma's earlier, but not much, for it felt as though the freezing cold of the past three nights had seeped right into her bones.

Once again she'd been at Emma's before the children had woken, and after making breakfast for all four of them and quickly cleaning her teeth while Emma sorted out sports kits and book bags, she'd ironed Grace's white shirt, then driven them all to school. Emma stayed behind to clear up and wait for a plumber to come and sort out the washing machine. Of all the times for it to break down there could hardly be a worse one, when it was required to take twice as many loads.

Letting herself into the BtG office, Angie closed the glass-panelled door behind her, dropped her bag on her desk, piled her coat on top of it and went through to the washroom. It had only a tiny handbasin the size of a fruit bowl, a low loo with an old-fashioned pull-chain cistern and a steel box on the wall for paper towels. There was no heating, no mat on the floor or lock on the door, but at least there was a half-decent mirror, and the hot tap eventually produced a flow of warm water.

She washed herself quickly, teeth chattering with cold as she peeled away her clothes, elbows and back bumping the chilly brick walls as she contorted herself into useful positions. To her frustration she'd forgotten to bring a towel and deodorant from the van. At least she'd remembered clean underwear, and managed to step into it without too many staggers before tugging her jeans back on. Her thermal vest was fresh on today – she'd changed in the van this morning while it was still dark, skin prickling with the fear of someone arriving early at the station and spotting her. She'd also brushed her hair before going to see the children; Grace would have noticed right away if she hadn't.

Feeling marginally better after her attempted freshen-up, she returned to the office, put her coat back on, picked up her bag and left.

Twenty minutes later she was at Timpson's in midtown, waiting for a copy of the borrowed key to be made. She felt terrible doing this, as though she were a criminal, and maybe she was, but she'd rather be arrested and thrown into a police cell for the night than face another in the van. She knew she was lucky to have a vehicle, that dozens of others in this very town had no roof at all unless they were fortunate enough to make it into one of the shelters. She simply couldn't handle the cold any longer, much less the terror of being so alone and such easy prey to any madman or gang that might stumble upon her. She'd hardly slept since losing her home, and when she had she was so tormented by fears of attack or worse that on waking it was virtually impossible to know where her nightmares began and ended.

Taking the new and old key from a greasy-haired youth, she pulled a five-pound note from her purse and received change of forty-five pence. Now, for the princely sum of four pounds fifty-five, she should be under cover until the local authority could find a proper home for her and the children.

A proper home. Who was she kidding? She knew very well that council-allocated properties almost never fitted the description of 'proper' and though the worst ones were usually described as temporary, plenty of people were still in them several years later.

However, she had to try and stay upbeat, somehow make herself believe that a decent place might come up earlier than expected. Easier was to switch her mind to the day ahead and all she needed to get through. It couldn't be all about her and her predicament, she had other responsibilities, not least to her residents.

Following two back-to-back meetings with potential new

sponsors she returned to the van and made a call to Greensleeves Care Home to enquire about the position of carer.

The job was still available, but they had a long list of people to interview and as she had no experience in the field... Blah, blah, everything she'd expected, but at least they were polite.

She made several more calls, most ending more or less the same way, and trying not to become any more despondent than she already was, she started the engine and headed for the church. It was the lunch hour by now, so probably a good time to return the 'borrowed' key to the office. If anyone was there she'd say she'd picked it up by mistake, but no one was, so she was soon at her desk checking emails.

There wasn't a single one offering a shred of hope that her life was about to change for the better, not even a spam message inviting her to ring a number to claim thousands she hadn't won. Nor were there any replies from the supply agencies she'd submitted applications to the day before, but it wasn't realistic to expect anything more than an automated response so soon.

It wasn't realistic to expect a message from Martin Stone either, but to her amazement one arrived in the middle of the afternoon, stunning and thrilling her all in one go.

Hi Angie, thought you'd be interested to know that Yeddon Farm is starting up a new training scheme for cider-makers. Any use for your guys? M

It was a great opportunity, there was no doubt about that, but right now all the residents were gainfully employed. She gave herself a moment to think before replying, aware of how good it felt to know she'd been in his mind, even for such a prosaic reason. She laughed out loud when she imagined what Emma would say if she knew what she was thinking.

She texted back: *Thanks very much. Really kind of you to remember us. We're all taken care of for the moment, largely thanks to you, but I'll give the farm a call anyway to ask them to think of us in the future.* She paused, trying to summon something witty to say at the end, until she realized she was trying to engage him in something more personal, so she simply tapped in her name, pressed send and put the phone down again.

Moments later another message arrived. *Understood. Don't forget to be in touch if there's anything else I can do for your guys. How's everything with you?*

Her heart gave a jolt of surprise that turned rapidly to concern. Surely he didn't know what was happening to her? Was this his discreet way of trying to find out if it was true? How was she going to reply? She'd almost rather die than let him know she was homeless. Worse would be to tell him, if he didn't already know.

Realizing she was going into this far too deeply, she sent a brief text back saying, *Everything's good, thank you. Hope it is with you too.*

Several minutes ticked by with no response so reminding herself that she hadn't actually asked a question, she put her phone aside again and went back to what she was doing.

With her mind still so full of him it was hard to concentrate, but eventually she forced herself to let go, and just as she did he texted again.

Everything good here. Working too hard as usual, but off for a break with the family tomorrow. Looking forward to getting out of this weather.

She stared at the words, feeling their casual warmth and friendship fading into the cracks of her sadness, and she couldn't help wondering about his family, what his wife was like, how old his children might be, where they lived. She thought back to the first time she'd met him, at his father's funeral when most of the town had come to pay their respects. She was sure she could remember a dark-haired woman in the family party, and two teenagers, a boy and a girl, but there had been so many people there it wasn't possible to know who was related to whom. She read his message again and considered asking about his children, in a chatty way, but decided not to. She needed to get a grip on herself now and return to her own world.

Hope you have a lovely time, she texted back briefly, and turning her phone off she resisted entering his name into Google to find out more about him and instead opened up a new email that had just arrived from a supply agency.

Apparently an Airbnb cleaning service was increasing its staff by four to work on zero-hour contracts. Her housework skills were required to be of a very high standard, she would have to go in at an hour's notice if needed, and in all cases she would need to recycle the rubbish after the guests left, and take the linens to the laundry.

She wondered what Martin's wife did for a living, and guessed it probably wasn't cleaning for Airbnb.

Deciding she had to give the job a go even though she already knew she couldn't be that flexible, she arranged to meet the company manager on Wednesday, noted down the time and location and clicked through to start updating the BtG accounts.

An hour later the sound of Emma's voice outside woke her with a start. She had no idea how long she'd been asleep, she only knew that her neck was stiff and she was so hungry she was ready to eat her laptop.

'Are you still here?' Emma asked, coming in the door. 'I thought you were viewing a studio flat for Alexei at three?'

Seeing it was already ten to, Angie shot to her feet. 'Is the washing machine fixed?' she asked, reaching for her coat.

Emma grimaced. 'For now, but he reckons I need a new one, and guess what, he can do me one for under three hundred quid. I think I'll wait for the old one to break down again, and I'll try to get at least half out of Ben. Is Grace with us for tea later? She said something about going to Lois's again tonight, but I haven't heard from her.'

'Me neither. I'll find out and let you know. You're picking the boys up from after-school club?'

'Yes, at five. I promised to pay today, is that going to be OK for you?'

Swallowing anxiously, Angie said, 'How much do I owe?'

Emma consulted her phone. 'We're a bit behind,' she admitted, 'so it's twenty-five for me and forty-five for you.' Her eyes went to Angie's, and seeing the look on her face, she said, 'I'll see if I can put it off until your benefits come in.'

Relieved and mortified, Angie said, 'Thanks. They're due at the end of the month so not long now.' And as soon as they were paid into her bank account they'd sink into her overdraft like raindrops into an ocean.

'By the way,' Emma said as Angie turned to the door, 'I had a text from Melvin today saying the cake was delicious, thank you very much.'

Angie turned, eyebrows raised. 'So you messaged back to ask if he saved you a piece?' she teased.

Emma blinked in surprise. 'As a matter of fact I did, as a joke, and now I see you're taking the whatsit, so ha ha and off you go. I'll see you at home around six.'

Angie was ten minutes late for the viewing and could have wept when she was told that the studio she'd hoped to reserve for Alexei had already gone. She was falling down on her duties, and her residents who were working so hard to improve their lives deserved far better.

'Oh, is not-not a problem,' Alexei stammered when she stopped by Hill Lodge to break the news. 'I am happy here with my father,' and Angie had to laugh at the wicked grin he gave Hamish and Hamish's roll of the eyes in response.

'How come you're not at work today?' she asked Alexei, sipping from the tea Hamish had handed her as soon as she'd come in. She'd called ahead to let them know she was on her way, and clearly Hamish had immediately put the kettle on.

'Sunday and Monday my days off,' Alexei reminded her. 'It is a very g-good job. I am liking very much to be with John Lewis. A better class of person, but-but not everyone polite.' He shrugged, showing that bad manners didn't particularly upset him. 'I have promise of more eggs next time I deliver to farm, so I shall sh-share with Hope House if enough.'

'That's very kind of you,' Angie smiled. Aware of the rumble in her tummy, she added, 'Maybe you'll invite me for an omelette.'

Both men lit up at the prospect of having her as a guest and immediately Hamish was suggesting all sorts of fillings, sending her hunger pangs into a frenzy and practically making her drool when he promised home-cooked chips as an accompaniment. 'None of your frozen nonsense,' he added with scorn.

Reminding herself that she was getting one good meal a day with Emma, and these men weren't much better off than she was, she said, 'I wasn't being serious, but it's lovely of you to offer.' Changing the subject, she asked, 'So how's Craig getting on entertaining the folks at the care home?'

Hamish chuckled fondly. 'I think he finds it hard to tear himself away. You should have heard him this morning, he left here at ten on the dot singing "Blue Suede Shoes" like he was Elvis himself.' He grimaced. 'OK, that's overstating it, but it wasn't half bad, for him. He's like a sponge where songs are concerned; he only has to hear the lyrics once and it's like he's always known them. Pity he doesn't always get them in tune.'

Smiling, Angie finished her tea and said, 'No more hallucinations?'

Hamish shook his head. 'Everything seems fine, although

he says he's writing a song for Sasha, so real or not she's apparently back on the scene.'

Since Hamish didn't seem concerned about that she decided not to be either, and moving on she asked how Mark Fields and Dougie were getting on at the building site.

Hamish shrugged. 'I'm guessing no news is good news,' he replied. He gave a short sigh and began clearing the table. 'You know I don't like telling tales out of school,' he continued, running the hot water and waiting for the boiler to ignite, 'but Fields brought a woman back here on Saturday night. I didn't see her, but I heard her...'

'I see her,' Alexei interrupted, 'she was, y-you know.' He drew big balloons in front of his chest.

Hamish said, 'I'm not against anyone having a sex life, good luck to him if he can get it, but we have rules here about bringing women in...'

'We do,' Angie confirmed, 'so I'll talk to him.'

'While you're at it you might remind him he has duties around here too,' Hamish added. 'He's not the most hygienic person we've ever had, far from it in fact, and no way do the rest of us want to clean up after him.'

Angie's heart sank as she sensed an eviction warning looming. She'd never liked that part of her job, no matter how bad someone's behaviour might be, for she knew very well that an actual eviction could very easily put them back on the streets. Their struggle to reclaim a decent life would be doubly difficult a second time around.

As soon as she got to the van she made a quick check of her emails. Please *please* let there be some good news from the housing office. Even if there wasn't a place for her and the children to go to this week, next week would do, or even the week after, just as long as there was somewhere.

There was nothing from them, or from potential employers,

but the message she'd been dreading since Friday had finally arrived.

Taking a breath, she forced herself to click it open.

Please contact this office to discuss payment of outstanding rent and the removal of items remaining at 14 Willow Close. Ashley, PA to Roland Shalik.

Closing the screen down, Angie started the engine and headed off along the street towards town, doing her best not to torment herself with where this was all going to end.

Grace and Lois pushed open the door to Mrs Hedges's classroom and made their way to the back, where they slipped behind two desks set slightly apart from the others. Several of their year group were already seated, unpacking books or madly finishing text messages before they were told to put away their phones.

'If I don't hear back from her today,' Grace said miserably as she checked her WhatsApp for the umpteenth time that day, 'it'll be too late. My contract runs out tomorrow…'

'But you told her that in the message you sent on Saturday,' Lois pointed out, 'and if you give her the number of your new Sim she'll be able to text.'

Grace nodded and Lois couldn't have looked more sympathetic. This was the worst thing that had happened to Grace so far, after losing her house, obvs, but at least she'd still be able to make calls and send texts. Being without the Internet though, no Instagram or Facebook, no YouTube, no apps at all… It was going to be a total nightmare.

'Let me see the message you sent again,' she said, holding out her hand.

Grace turned her phone round so they could read it together.

Hi Anya, thanks for the lovely things you said. I would like to help my mum and if you think it's possible for me to be an actress – I mean one that gets paid – please can you tell me how to go about it? Thank you, Grace Watts. PS I can only text and phone after Monday because my contract is due to expire then.

She ended with the number for her new Sim card.

Though she knew instinctively that her mum would go mental if she had any idea about this, even if Anya did know her dad, she quickly reminded herself that her mum wasn't really in a position to be overly cautious about anything right now.

As though picking up on her doubts Lois said quietly, 'Listen, I've been thinking, and I know it would be great and everything if this Anya is genuine – and if she is I'm totally with you, like one hundred per cent – but what if, like you said before, she turns out to be some sleazeball bloke using a female profile to get to schoolgirls?'

Grace's face paled. She wasn't stupid, she'd known all along there was a risk, but Anya looked really nice. Lois had said so herself enough times, so why was Lois trying to spoil it all now?

'Don't be upset with me,' Lois urged. 'I'm only trying to look out for you, and honest to God, I think she's for real. I'm just saying, that's all. If you like, I'll come with you if you decide to meet her.'

Grace looked up as a burst of laughter erupted over the other side of the room, and felt her cheeks begin to burn. It was obvious the Northsider gang – kids from the Temple Fields estate and surrounding areas – were laughing at her. There were only five of them in this class, but there were a hundred or more of them spread all over the years like a nasty disease. This wasn't the first time they'd mocked Grace, they often made her the butt of their jokes, though luckily they'd never gone as far as to smack her around or try to force her to buy drugs the way they did with some of the younger kids.

The way they had with Liam.

'Hey Gracie, found anywhere to live yet?' Cortnie Jenkins sang out, her coarse, nasal voice dripping with sarcasm, her smile shot through with meanness.

'You should be over here with us,' Jordan Bates informed her, her thickly made-up face peering out from behind a hand mirror. 'I mean, you're going to be living up our way soon enough, so why not start hanging with us now? We could all do with someone to take on our homework.'

'Especially Darren,' Mason O'Farrell jeered, cuffing the flaxen-haired boy next to him, who immediately twisted O'Farrell's arm in a brutal grip. 'Got the real hots for you, has Darren,' Mason told her, laughing as his friend swore viciously into his face.

'Heard from your brother Liam lately?' Cortnie asked, tearing open a bag of crisps.

Although Grace flinched, this wasn't the first time they'd mentioned Liam, they did it quite often, and she knew better than to rise to it, for she was well aware that Jordan Bates's cousin, Moggie Merino, was one of the guilty five serving a life sentence for murdering her father.

Her father. Thinking about him was suddenly making her want to cry.

'We can tell you where your brother is if you like,' Jordan offered with a smirk.

'Keep ignoring them,' Lois whispered.

Grace delved into her bag and took out the books she needed for this lesson, wishing it could be a gun so she could make them all shut the fuck up.

Mrs Hedges entered and wished the class good morning. Grace liked her a lot. She'd become something of a hero around the school – apart from with the Northsiders – after one of their mothers decided to sock her in the face for telling her daughter she dressed and behaved like a slut. Mrs Hedges always did tell it like it was, and clearly not even physical intimidation was going to change her. 'OK,' she continued breezily, '"Dulce et Decorum Est" by Wilfred Owen. I hope you all read it over the weekend and have something intelligent to say about it by now. Who's going to start? Jordan, how about you?'

'Oh Miss,' Jordan complained. 'I hate reading poetry, it's like total BS to me.'

Moving on, Mrs Hedges invited George Trevors to share his insights into the poem.

Used to the way this particular teacher never tried to persuade the Northsiders to engage, preferring to focus on those who wanted to learn, Grace opened her notebook and did her best to look as though she was paying attention. She'd learned the poem by heart and could discuss it if Mrs Hedges asked her to, she'd even worked out what the similes were, one of the teacher's favourite challenges, but right now she was transfixed by the message she'd just received from Anya.

Holding the phone in her lap, she nudged Lois and turned it so she could see the two short lines displayed on the screen.

You shouldn't be without your phone. If you let me have the name of your service provider I'll take care of the contract for you. A ☺ PS Stand by for some very good news.

CHAPTER TWENTY

Angie left the warmth and family cheer of Emma's just after nine, and drove through mizzling rain and a thickening ground fog to her new refuge for the night.

It wasn't so bad really, she told herself as she headed to the outskirts of town. She'd just had a lovely meal – though strangely had been unable to eat much in spite of her hunger – and she'd been able to spend a few hours with her children before it came time for her to go back out into the night. Some people had no family at all, and no shelter either.

It almost made her smile now to think of how much she'd enjoyed working through a pile of ironing while listening to the boys thumping around upstairs and Grace, seated at the kitchen table in front of her, memorizing a monologue that she and Lois were planning to post on YouTube. She'd always detested ironing before, but now she was just glad to be warm and fed and feeling as though she was helping Emma to cope with the increased burden of two more children, as well as the worry about Angie's situation.

'Mum, are you listening?' Grace asked without looking up.

'Mm, sorry,' Angie replied, folding a pair of football shorts and adding them to the pile. 'What were you saying?'

'I asked if you know someone called Anya?'

Angie wrinkled her nose. 'I don't think so. Why?'

Grace simply shrugged and carried on with what she was doing. A while later she said, 'She knew Dad.'

Angie stifled a yawn. 'Dad knew a lot of people,' she replied, and unplugging the iron she set it to cool on a worktop. 'So what are you doing?' she asked, glancing over Grace's shoulder as a burst of laughter erupted from the screen.

'It's a student performing a Caryl Churchill monologue,' Grace told her. 'She's really good and it's dead funny. Lois wants me to learn it because she thinks it's where we need to go next.'

Impressed, Angie nodded and went to pack away the ironing board.

Grace said, 'Wouldn't it be great if I could get a job as an actress? I mean one that pays megabucks.'

Angie had to smile, all too familiar with Grace's dream. 'It would indeed,' she agreed, 'and I'm sure one of these days you will, because you're beautiful and talented and you deserve to be recognized…'

'It could make us really rich,' Grace enthused, 'I mean if I got some good parts, and then we wouldn't have to worry about anything ever again.'

Wouldn't have to worry about anything ever again, Angie was thinking as she parked the van in a residential street close to the church. How wonderful that would be, and she so badly wanted to believe that day would come that she decided she would. It was better than scaring herself to death with the alternative.

Hearing her phone buzz with a text, she let it wait as she dragged her holdall from the back of the van, and tightening the strings of her hood set off past the 1950s semis with small gardens, brick porches and neat bay windows. Every now and again she caught a glimpse of those inside and couldn't help wondering if they knew how lucky they were, slumped cosily in front of their TVs, or tucking into cartons of Chinese takeaways. They probably wouldn't be sparing a thought for anyone without a home tonight, any more than they'd suspect it of her if they happened to see her go by.

When she reached the church boundary she forced down her fears about being here after dark and when no one else was around, and squeezed through a gap in the beech hedge next to the locked gate. Then, not daring to use the torch on her phone in case someone spotted the beam, she made her way carefully through the foggy darkness to the BtG courtyard. It would be bad enough if Ivan or the vicar alerted the police to an intruder; worse would be when they discovered it was her.

She crept quietly past her office to the charity store next door, and propped her bag between her knee and the wall to search for the key she'd had cut this morning. She was suddenly sick with dread that it might not work. She should have checked earlier, not left it to chance like this.

Her hand shaking, as much with anxiety as cold, she inserted the key in the lock and tried to turn it. It wouldn't move. She couldn't believe it. She tried again, but it still wouldn't turn.

No, no, no, this couldn't be happening.

With a horrible panic building she tried again, and again, wiggling, pushing, pulling, bruising her fingers and chafing her hands as she pushed uselessly at the wooden door. She couldn't spend another night in the van, she just couldn't.

There was always the office, she reminded herself, but Ivan

often patrolled the place at night, and if he shone his torch in through the window he'd see her, huddled like a tramp on the floor.

Blinded by tears, she gave it one last go.

The lock turned and the door creaked open in a manner that seemed almost wearied by its decision to give in.

Soaked through and stiff with cold, she bundled herself and her bag into the store and locked the door behind her. She couldn't worry now about how she'd get out if the key didn't work again, she was just so glad to be inside where it was damp rather than wet, a degree warmer, and out of the fog.

It took a moment for her to adjust to the darkness. She didn't move, simply waited, remembering from some random school lesson that night vision had something to do with rods in the eyes that acted as light detectors. Finally hers worked and she was able to see a small, smeary glass panel near the ceiling, and the shelves of clutter that lined the walls. The fusty stench of used and discarded clothing was stifling, the air was clogged by it, as if old earth and ash had been mixed with sweat and worse.

After hanging her coat on the corner of a shelf in an attempt to dry it out she began layering second-hand clothes on the floor, creating a kind of mattress for her sleeping bag, and when eventually she slipped inside it, using the pillow she'd brought to support her head, she was almost snug. The air didn't seem to stink quite so much any more, and the cold brick walls were starting to feel more like friend than foe.

She lay quietly listening to the rain, and faint scuttling and scratching noises that she hoped were outside. She wasn't afraid of rats or mice, but she didn't like them either, and she certainly didn't want them running over her in the night. She quickly switched her mind to other places, other times, and found it helped to pretend she was camping in the Ardèche with Steve and the children. She imagined them inside their tent, the others fast asleep already as she looked forward to kayaking the next day, or paddleboarding, or fishing. Steve was right next to her. If she put out a hand she'd be able to touch him, and if he turned on to his back he'd probably start to snore. She wanted to wake him up, to feel him pulling her against him, to hear him laugh and groan as one of the children tried to snuggle in between them.

Suddenly remembering she'd received a text, she scrabbled for her phone, irrationally certain it was going to be from the person who'd told her Liam was safe. She hadn't heard anything since, but they surely weren't going to leave it there.

The message was from Grace.

TOM. Had to borrow £4 from Auntie Em.

TOM was time of the month, and though Grace still wasn't regular Angie couldn't detest herself more for not even thinking of it.

Deciding it was too late to send a message back in case it woke Grace up, she put the phone down again and tried to go back to the French campsite. Instead all she could connect with was a terrible build-up of despair. Somehow she must keep it in, force herself to pull away from the demons of self-pity and despondency that were threatening to engulf her.

Where are you going on holiday? she texted Martin in her mind.

To Switzerland, skiing. Do you want to come?

I'd love to, but I can't leave the children behind.

Bring them too. Mine will be there, and I know you'll get along famously with my wife.

She slept fitfully, the hours moving with cruel slowness, each fifteen minutes marked by the gloomy bongs of the church clock. By the time her alarm went off at five thirty she'd been fully awake for a while, too afraid of oversleeping and someone finding her here to relax into the early-morning embrace of unconsciousness.

It was still dark, but there was no patter of rain on the roof or sound of wind gusting in from the estuary. The cold was like real ice on her skin as she used the she-pee and thanked God that she hadn't needed it through the night. She poured water from a bottle on to a wad of toilet roll and wiped it over her face and hands; then digging a hairbrush from her bag, she tugged it through her greasy hair. She could hardly stand the feel of it on her scalp, and it hadn't even been a week since she'd last washed it. She imagined it stringy and lifeless, clinging to her face, even crawling with lice. She'd have to wash it at Emma's later. She'd try turning it into an event by asking Grace to blow-dry it for her and maybe French-plait it again.

The prospect of the closeness and cleanliness buoyed her through the scramble to find fresh underwear in her holdall, and once she'd put it on she dressed herself again in the clothes she'd worn the day before and had kept on all night. If Emma's washing machine gave out again she'd offer to go to the Laundromat since a hand wash would be no good in this weather, they'd never get anything dry.

Sending a silent plea to the lock to turn, she slid in the key and to her relief the door opened as though there had never been a problem. She stepped out into veils of clammy fog drifting in from the countryside like ghouls on their way to the graveyard. Locking the door, she pocketed the key and stole quickly through the darkness to the van. The streets were so quiet and still she could almost hear her heart beating. She felt achingly alone being out at this hour with no one else around. It was as if some kind of apocalyptic event had occurred and everyone had disappeared.

For one terrible, terrifying moment she thought the van had gone, but then she spotted it further down the street, right where she'd left it.

Hi Grace, phone contract taken care of and paid in full for next six months. A ☺

Grace was in the sports changing room, staring at her phone and feeling all kinds of weird as she read and reread the message. She wasn't sure if she'd really expected Anya to do it, but she obviously had, because Grace was still able to go online with her phone and use her apps. And six months were paid up front!

What was she going to tell her mum? Maybe she didn't have to tell her anything. They'd already got the new phone – a burner phone as the drug dealers called it – so from now on her mum would text and call on that. It would mean carrying two phones, but that was OK, she'd just have to make sure her mum didn't see that she still had the other one.

For now she needed to thank Anya.

It's really kind of you to do that. Thank you.

She was dying to ask Anya about the good news she was on standby for, but afraid it might seem pushy, she simply forwarded both messages to Lois who was at the dentist this afternoon and got changed for PE.

Angie was back at Emma's for the evening, and in spite of her tiredness and mounting frustration that none of her efforts to improve her situation had worked today, she was blinking at her sister in disbelief, fully engaged with what she'd just said. 'You're going out with *who*?' she demanded, planting her hands on her hips.

'Sssh,' Emma cautioned, nodding towards the sitting room

where Zac and Harry were engrossed on the PlayStation. 'I don't want the children to hear.'

'Who are you going out with, Mum?' Harry shouted, his gaze never wavering from the screen.

Emma sighed and rolled her eyes.

'She's got a date,' Jack called from upstairs.

'What are you going to wear?' Grace wanted to know, walking into the midst of it all and shrugging off her coat to hang it on the stair post at the end of the hall.

Emma treated Angie to a narrow-eyed glare.

'What's his name?' Zac demanded, keeping focus on the game.

'Never you mind,' Emma scolded, and closing the sitting-room door she waited for Grace to do the same with the other door, and was about to speak again when Angie said to Grace, 'Is something wrong?'

Grace simply slumped down at the table, phone clasped between both hands.

This meant there was.

'We won't be able to help unless you tell us what it is,' Emma prompted.

Grace scowled. 'I'm fine, OK?'

Emma held up her hands. 'Just asking.'

Grace's head went down again, and Angie trailed her fingers over her wavy hair. It was the time of the month, of course, but she could sense that something else was going on. Now clearly wasn't the time to ask.

'OK,' Emma said, drawing it out, 'if there's nothing wrong with you, can we go back to talking about *me*?'

To Angie's relief Grace laughed. To her aunt, she said, eyes wide with interest, 'So who's the date with?'

'Wait till you hear,' Angie cautioned.

Keeping her voice low, Emma said, 'If you have a problem with me going on a date...'

'Don't be ridiculous,' Angie scolded. 'It's not the date I have a problem with, it's who it's with. He's married, Emma.'

Grace's eyes rounded. 'Who are we talking about?'

'Melvin,' her mother replied. 'The man who lives two doors down from number fourteen. What are you thinking?' she hissed at Emma. 'How can you...?'

'If you'd let me get a word in,' Emma hissed back, 'I could tell you that his wife has left him.'

Angie's eyebrows rose in shock that quickly turned to suspicion.

Emma mirrored the look. 'Apparently it's been on the cards for a while, and after she took off this morning he texted to ask if I'd like to go for a drink on Saturday night.'

'Blimey, he didn't hang around,' Grace commented archly. 'Must be keen.'

Emma shrugged. 'Well, we can't blame him for that, can we?'

Though Angie laughed, she was still concerned. 'So *she* moved out, not him?' she asked.

'That's what he said.'

'So where are you going for your date?' Grace wanted to know as she checked her phone.

Emma was about to reply when Angie received a text. 'I haven't finished yet,' Emma cried, as Grace gave a gasp and dashed out of the room. She turned back to Angie and realized from the look on her sister's face that her limelight was lost.

'Take a look at this,' Angie said, handing over her phone.

Emma scanned the message and gave a groan of anger as she sank down in a chair. 'The bastard,' she murmured through clenched teeth. 'What I wouldn't do to that man, given an axe.'

SHALIK HOLDINGS
Re: 14 Willow Close
To: Angie Watts Cc: Ashley Jonuzi
Dear Angie, As a gesture of goodwill I will arrange for your belongings to be removed from 14 Willow Close, free of charge, and taken to your chosen storage facility. If you are unable to meet the cost of storage I'm assured help can be obtained from social services. Please send details of the facility as soon as you have them as there is someone interested in buying the property and I wish to press ahead.
Roland Shalik

Angie was still reeling at the last sentence and how inevitable, irreversible everything was becoming, and in such a short space of time.

'That scumbag sends you a message like that less than four days after you move out!' Emma spat in disgust. '*And* in the middle of the evening. I mean, no time would be good, but why now? And if he's so eager to sell it makes you wonder if he's got his own problems with money,' she added tartly.

'Delete it,' Angie instructed. 'I'm not responding to it, so you might as well.'

Emma looked pleased and wasting no more time she hit the dustbin icon, saying, 'Dear Roland Shalik, *Bugger off*.'

Angie had to smile, despite the clenching of her nerves. He wasn't going to go away, obviously, but she definitely wasn't inclined to make things any easier for him. She was even considering breaking into the house on Willow Close to retake possession of it rather than remain homeless for one more night. Squatter's rights? She might actually do it, were she not so afraid of the tactics Shalik would employ to remove her.

After going upstairs to say goodnight to the children, she returned to the kitchen to find Emma speaking to someone on the phone.

Melvin, Emma mouthed, pointing at the receiver.

Angie smiled. She was glad to think Emma's life was moving in a positive direction, even if her own wasn't – provided Melvin was on the level, of course.

Leaving her to it, she picked up her bag, blew Emma a kiss and went to put on her coat.

Time to return to the Hotel Storeroom.

Grace was under the covers, texting so furiously with Lois that she didn't hear her mother leave. *Anya wants to chat on WhatsApp tomorrow at four. We'll go straight to yours from school, yes? OMG, what shall I say? What shall I wear? We haven't even recorded the* Top Girls *monologue yet. She's got to be genuine if she wants to chat, don't you think?*

CHAPTER TWENTY-ONE

Angie was inside the Citizen Service office behind the main council building, having turned up at nine on the dot in the hope of persuading someone in this department to speak to someone in housing about her urgent need for somewhere to live.

Was anyone listening? It never seemed as though they were, but she had to keep trying.

Since all twenty of the seats in the waiting room were taken, she stood against the wall and let her eyes fall shut as she tried to gather some strength into her thoughts as well as her body. It felt so long since she'd had a good night's sleep, safe and warm in a bed, her children close by and a proper bathroom next door. The loss of her cherished home was crushing her both emotionally and physically, not to mention the debt that continued to rise, and Shalik's email informing her that he was intending to remove her belongings was making everything worse.

She had to find storage somewhere, but first she needed to be sure that social services would cover the cost.

There were so many people waiting, and the sense of hardship and incipient despair filling the air was almost palpable. She could feel herself being sucked into it, yet another helpless victim of the austerity that had created a different class – the working poor, with jobs but no homes, always in debt.

She was one of the people she used to watch on TV and feel desperately sorry for.

Just before eleven she left the building, having spoken to no one. She had an interview with the Airbnb turnaround company on Heath Street at eleven fifteen and she didn't want to miss it.

By midday she knew she might just as well have carried on waiting, for exactly as she'd suspected it was minimum wage, zero hours and she was unable to meet the demands of the job alongside her commitment to BtG.

As she returned to the van Emma rang. 'Hey, where are you?'

'Just about to go to Hill Lodge. Where are you?'

'At the office. Have you spoken to Grace this morning?'

Angie immediately tensed. 'No. Why? Is she all right?'

'Yes, she's fine. I just wondered if she'd told you that she babysat for an hour last night while I popped over to see Melvin.'

Angie took out her keys and got into the driver's seat. 'So after I left last night, you went on a date?' she asked, not sure whether she was cross about it or not. *More likely jealous,* she told herself, thinking of the hours she'd spent trying to imagine she was in some secret hideaway with Steve.

'It wasn't a date,' Emma protested. 'We just had a drink and a chat, you know, like you do when you're getting to know someone.'

'And?' Angie prompted, sensing there was more.

'Well, we got along so famously I could have been tempted

to break my rule of "never on the first night" but you'll be happy to hear I didn't. We did kiss though, and it was pretty amazing.'

'Are you sure about his marriage breaking up? I mean, it's a permanent thing, is it? You don't want to get involved if it's just a trial separation.'

'Apparently they've already tried that, and moving here was an attempt to get things back on track, but it hasn't worked out. Anyway, I hope you don't mind, but I told him about you having to find somewhere to store your furniture and, wait for this, he rang me just now to say that he should be able to find some space for you to use, free of charge. He runs a kitchen company over on the business park,' Emma explained. 'Apparently the warehouse is huge, and as soon as the latest orders have gone out, which is due to be the end of next week, he'll be able to move your things in.'

Pushing past a swell of emotion, Angie said, 'That's so kind of him…'

'You have to email Shalik right away,' Emma told her, 'and if he has a problem with waiting, or thinks you're just stalling, Melvin says he'll contact him direct to assure him he's got everything in hand. Can't see Shalik playing the bully with another man, can you?'

No, Angie couldn't. After asking Emma to thank Melvin for her, she tapped out a quick email to Shalik on her phone and sent it on its way.

Anya turned out to be really nice, all friendly eyes and neat blonde hair and a smile that made her look more like Rita Ora than Lady Gaga, Grace thought. She was enchanted, especially after all the lovely things Anya had said at the start of their video call about the work her dad had done on Anya's house in the Garden District – a really posh area of town, so

Anya must be minted. She'd asked how her mum was, too. Grace had told her that they still hadn't been given anywhere else to live yet.

'Oh no, I'm really sorry to hear that,' Anya said gently. 'It must be so hard for you all.'

'Yes, it is,' Grace admitted, wondering if Anya might have a house they could rent at a price they could afford. She glanced at Lois, who was next to her, but out of shot so Anya wouldn't see her, and received an encouraging thumbs up.

'Well,' Anya said with a smile, 'I know how much you want to help her, and I'm pretty sure I've come up with a way for you to make a lot of money doing the thing you love most.'

Grace was so excited she could hardly breathe.

'One of the friends I contacted about you has confirmed to me that he's going to be shooting a short movie in the area in the next few weeks – *and* he's so impressed by your videos on YouTube that he wants to meet you.'

Grace's hands flew to her face as she gasped with joy, while beside her Lois punched the air.

Anya smiled. 'I'll be in touch with a time for you to meet once I've spoken to him. Now, before you go, let me have your bank details… Do you have a bank account?'

Grace blinked in surprise. 'It's a savings account, but there's nothing in it.'

Looking sorry about that, Anya said, 'Well there will be by tomorrow, if you message me the details. I'll send over fifty pounds as an advance. You can treat yourself to something nice to wear.'

Grace's heart had begun racing at the mention of fifty pounds. It felt like more than she'd ever had in her account in her life, although it wasn't, it was simply that it had been empty for so long that it seemed that way. Next to her Lois pressed down hard on her thigh in barely suppressed excitement.

Anya said, 'I have to go now, but you can get hold of me any time this way, I've always got my phone with me.'

'Thanks,' Grace whispered.

Anya smiled again. 'I'm glad to do this for you and your family. Your dad was a good person.'

Grace swallowed noisily. 'Can I… Should I tell my mum that you're trying to help us?' she asked.

After some thought, Anya replied, 'It's probably best you don't for the moment. Let's make sure we can really get things going and then we'll surprise her. How does that sound?'

Grace nodded. 'It sounds good,' she agreed.

Moments later the screen cleared and Lois, overcome with elation, flopped back on the bed and kicked her legs up and down in glee. 'Fifty quid!' she exclaimed. 'Grace you've found your fairy godmother, no doubt about it.'

Angie was at Hill Lodge when she received a message from Shalik saying *Two weeks, not a day more.*

Though the leniency surprised her, she wasn't sure about trusting it; however, for now she'd take it at face value and forward it to Emma, with an additional thank-you to Melvin.

After pressing send she exhaled loudly, as though she'd been holding her breath for days.

'Everything all right?' Hamish asked, looking up from the plaster samples of Georgian and Regency cornices that he'd spread out on the kitchen table for her to admire, along with various magazines showing how impressive they were *in situ*. She was always moved by the pride he took in this house, and perhaps most of all by the fact that he paid for small renovations and even some repairs out of his own pocket.

She smiled. 'Yes, fine,' she assured him, and reaching for her cup she grimaced when she found the tea had gone cold.

Getting up to put the kettle on, he said, 'You know, as a

rule I'm not someone to pry, but I am a good listener, and I can tell something's on your mind. Has been for a while.'

Angie's eyes flicked to his dear face and went back to her cup as she started to put him off, but all that came out was a ragged sort of sigh. 'I'll be fine,' she assured him. 'Just a few things to sort out.'

'Are the children OK?'

She nodded. 'Yes, they seem to be.'

'Money issues?'

Managing a wryness she didn't feel, she said, 'Same as everyone, these days. But don't worry, we'll survive.'

Matching her tone he said, 'You know what you need, don't you? You need an Angie in your life. It worked for me, and it's working for Craig and the others. Even our friend Mark Fields admits he's living a better life than he was, thanks to the chance you gave him to come here.'

Finding herself alarmingly close to tears, Angie got to her feet to stretch her legs. 'So it's working out for him at the building site?' she said, thinking of Martin, and the holiday he was no doubt already enjoying with his family on ski slopes or in sunny climes.

'As far as I know,' Hamish replied.

'And Craig's OK?' she asked. 'How's the songwriting going?'

Hamish smiled fondly. 'Better than you might think – and here's something else to surprise you: Sasha, his "girlfriend", is real.'

Angie's eyes widened with interest. 'Does that mean you've met her?'

'Only briefly. She waited outside the other evening while Craig came in to fetch something, so I went out to say hello.'

Like a good father would, Angie smiled to herself. 'And?'

'She seems a nice enough girl. About his age I'd say, foreign, maybe Polish or Romanian, of course I didn't ask. I didn't really get a chance to talk to her, because Craig came out and off they went to watch a band in some pub, apparently, and I didn't see him again until the next morning.'

'So he stayed with her?'

'I guess so.'

Wondering where that might have been, Angie glanced down at her phone as it started to ring, and seeing it was Emma she clicked on.

'Great news from Shalik,' Emma declared.

Deciding everything was relative Angie said, 'Indeed. Did you thank Melvin for me?'

'Not yet, but I will. Now, are you planning on coming back to the office today?'

'I will if you need me to.'

'I think you should.'

Frowning, Angie said, 'Is everything OK?'

'There's a policeman here. He wants to talk to you – and before you start panicking, it's not about Liam.'

'So what is it about?'

'I don't know, but I guess we'll find out when you get here.'

CHAPTER TWENTY-TWO

As Angie entered the office her eyes darted anxiously between the grey-suited man getting up from her chair, and Emma who was at her desk looking both baffled and vaguely defensive.

'DC Leo Johnson,' the detective reminded her. 'We've met before.'

Angie nodded, taking the hand he was offering. 'What can I do for you?' she asked.

'Actually, it's more what you can do for us,' he replied with the ghost of a smile. 'There was a mugging during the early hours of Monday morning, close to the station…'

Angie froze.

'… and CCTV footage shows your van in the station car park around the time it happened.'

Angie's mouth dried as Emma looked at her in confusion. Brenda Crompton's place was the other side of town.

'So I'm here,' Johnson continued, 'to ask if you saw anything that might help us.'

Angie could feel a painful heat spreading over her cheeks. 'I-I don't think so,' she stammered. 'W-what time did it happen?'

'Around 3 a.m. The videotape shows you parking the van just after ten thirty and…'

Realizing he was about to say that it didn't show her getting out of it, or driving off, any time before the mugging, Angie jumped in quickly. 'I can promise you I didn't see anything or anyone suspicious.'

Apparently surprised by the speed of her response, Johnson frowned.

Flustered, Angie looked from him to Emma and back again.

'She wouldn't have been there then,' Emma told him. 'Not if you say it happened at three o'clock.'

Realizing from the change in Emma's tone that she'd guessed more than Angie wanted her to, Angie kept her eyes fixed on Johnson as she said, 'I'm sorry, I wish I could help, but there was no one around when I parked.' That at least was the truth.

Emma said, 'I hope you're not thinking it has anything to do with my nephew, Liam.'

As Angie started, Johnson said, 'He's not who we're looking for,' and reaching into his pocket he pulled out a card and put it on the desk. 'If anything comes to mind,' he said, 'you can reach me on either of these numbers.'

Emma waited only until the door had closed behind him before rounding on Angie. 'What the heck's going on?' she demanded angrily. 'Why was the van in the station car park at any time, never mind at 3 a.m.? Brenda Crompton lives at least an hour's walk from there, and as far as I'm aware there's on-street parking outside her house.'

Angie swallowed dryly.

Emma stared at her hard challenging her to answer, until with an agonized groan she clasped her hands to her head. 'Please tell me you're not sleeping in the van,' she implored. 'Please, please.'

'I'm not,' Angie assured her.

Emma lowered her hands.

'Not any more,' Angie added.

As Emma's eyes closed she said, 'I knew something wasn't right. I could tell… I should have… For God's sake, *why* didn't you go to Brenda's?'

'Because she doesn't have room, and anyway I didn't want her to know my problems.'

Emma threw out her hands in exasperation and disbelief. 'She's a kind woman, Angie, she'd have…'

'Gossiped, you know that. She always does. OK, perhaps not maliciously, but she can't keep things to herself.'

'Then why not ask someone else? There are plenty of people who'd take you in. Good God, if I'd known you were in the van I'd have made you stay at mine and to hell with Amy Cutler.'

Angie simply looked at her; her actions could only be justified by misery and pride, and she didn't want to admit either.

'Where are you staying now?' Emma wanted to know. 'You implied you're not in the van any more. So where?'

After a beat, Angie's eyes slid towards the wall that divided them from the storeroom.

It took only a moment for Emma to catch on. She started to speak, but lost her words.

'It's dry, more or less, and safe,' Angie explained, 'and it won't be for much longer. I'm sure they'll give me a place soon, and please, whatever you do, don't tell the children.'

Emma snapped, 'Of course I won't tell them, but you can't go on sleeping there, I hope you realize that. I have to ask because you've clearly lost your mind.'

Inwardly wincing, Angie said, 'I can't risk coming to yours…'

'You'll have to…'

'I won't, but if you don't mind me having a bath or shower every couple of days… Oh Em, please don't cry. Please. It's not so bad, really…'

Emma shouted, 'Yes it *is* bad, Angie. It's about as bad as it gets and I'm trying to think of how to get you out of it, but I can't and I feel so useless, and when I see what happens to people in your position, those that sleep rough…'

'Stop,' Angie begged. 'Please just stop. We're going to work this out, Em, I promise you.'

'But *how*?'

'OK, we can't see the answers right now, but that's because we're in the middle of it. Once I get my own place, and find a way to make more money, it'll all start coming good again.' There was no point telling Emma that she couldn't see a way of ever paying off the amount she owed, that it was only going to get worse; it would get them nowhere, at least not today.

In the end Emma said, 'OK, if you won't stay with me and you feel you have to sleep in *there*,' she didn't even glance towards the storeroom, 'then we have to make sure you're comfortable and that you've got everything you need.'

Touched by how hard she was struggling to do her best, Angie said, 'I've already taken care of it. I've got a sleeping bag and a small duvet, the she-pee Steve gave me…'

Emma flinched. 'For God's sake…'

Angie put up a hand. 'It's fine, it's just the showering and keeping warm that's a problem, but there's an electric heater in there that might work if we can find a plug. And if you're happy for me to use your bathroom, I'll pay you for the hot water and…'

Emma exploded, 'It's not about money anymore,' she cried furiously. 'It's about you and what's happening to you and that bloody son of yours, because if it weren't for him Steve would still be alive and you wouldn't be in this horrendous position.'

Silence ticked on as the truth of Emma's words weighted the air between them, and filled them both with a grief that was too raw and painful to touch with any more words.

In the end Emma said hoarsely, 'I'm sorry. That was mean and unhelpful and the last thing you needed.'

Angie didn't deny it, just glanced at her phone as it rang and let the call go to messages.

'I don't suppose you've had any more texts about him?' Emma asked. 'No, you'd have told me if you had.'

'This isn't about Liam,' Angie said quietly. 'It's about how truly sorry I am for what all this is doing to you, because I know how much you care and you don't deserve all the stress…'

'I'm not the one we need to worry about,' Emma broke in quickly. 'It's you we have to take care of, but I can't bear to think of you in that awful storeroom.'

'It's better than the van, and maybe I can come to stay with you at the weekend. There's nothing to say you're not allowed visitors, and if Amy Cutler decides to make a fuss we'll just tell her I'm babysitting while…'

'We'll tell her to sod off, is what we'll do.'

'… you're out on your date with Melvin, but of course we won't tell her that bit.'

Emma wasn't distracted. 'We've got to find a way out of this,' she stated forcefully, as if a way really could be found. 'I know you're trying, and I know you're going to say that it's still early days in comparison to what some people go through, but we can't let this go on happening to you, Angie. I'm sorry, but we really can't.'

* * *

Hi Grace, Still waiting to hear back from the director, he's always very busy, but meantime, I'm sure you know that all actors have portfolios. I thought we should get one together so I'm sending some links to the kind of shots I think would work for you.

Grace clicked on the first one, teeth chattering from the cold as she and Lois, tucked in behind the sports hall, watched the small screen revealing the kind of fashion shots they were used to seeing in their teen magazines. Grace's heart turned over with excitement. There was a girl with perfect make-up, hands either side of her face, eyes closed and amazing red lips pouting towards the lens. Another showed a girl with a radical blonde boy cut glancing back over her shoulder, a mischievous look in her eyes as if daring someone to follow her. A third was a seriously skinny girl leaning against a wall, hair in pigtails, school uniform dishevelled as she scowled down at her phone. The fourth showed two girls in floaty dresses seeming to dance on a beach.

Grace felt a dizzy sort of thrill as she imagined having a portfolio and an Instagram page showing herself like any one of these.

Don't worry about clothes or make-up at this stage, just see if you can strike some of the expressions and poses. Practise in front of a mirror, and if you can, take some shots and send them over. Did you receive the money transfer? A ☺

Grace had received it, she'd checked using her app during morning break. It had made her feel all weird again, as if this was happening to someone else and she was just watching.

Lois was still flicking through the links. 'I bet these girls were paid a fortune,' she murmured. 'Look, that one's from *Bella* and the one on the beach is only from a movie poster.' She peered closer. 'Must not have been released here,' she commented, 'because I've never heard of it, but it looks cool. *Beach Babes II*. We'll have to Google it.'

'I love those dresses,' Grace said wistfully, imagining herself in the pale blue one. A thought suddenly struck her, making her feel light-headed. 'What if they want to fly me to a beach somewhere?' she asked. 'What would I tell my mum?'

Lois snorted. 'At your age she'd have to go with you as a chaperone, and I can't see her minding that too much.'

Grace grinned. 'No, she'd love it. It's been ages since we had a holiday.' Her heart twisted as she recalled the amazing time they'd had camping in the Cotswolds Water Park for her eleventh birthday, when her mum and dad had taken them rowing and waterskiing and she had met her first boyfriend, Max.

Since fifty quid wasn't anywhere near enough to help them afford a holiday again, much less get their house back she was seized by a sudden urgency to add as much to it as she could as soon as she could.

Thanks for the links and the money, she messaged back, *will take some shots. Please let me know when I can meet the director*. She showed it to Lois.

'Send it,' Lois instructed, 'then please can we go in? I'm freezing my whatsits off here.'

'We'll take some shots tonight though, won't we?' Grace urged, going after her.

'No problem. We are going to totally blow them away. Just you wait and see.'

CHAPTER TWENTY-THREE

'Oh, Angie, I'm glad I caught you.'

Angie turned back from leaving the church office to see Ivan entering from one of the prayer rooms. He looked smart this morning in a navy pinstriped suit and crisp white shirt, so he was presumably going into town on parish business.

'This came for you,' he said, and going to his desk he picked up a small pile of envelopes and handed it to her.

The bottom fell from her stomach as she realized what it was – her forwarded mail, mostly fairly obvious final demands, or letters with a government seal. She felt a fiery flush heat her chest and her cheeks as she said, 'Thank you,' and made to leave.

'Is everything all right?' he asked before she could reach the door.

She stopped, thinking fast. 'Yes, fine,' she tried to assure him, forcing a smile as she turned around. 'I'm… We're moving house and it… I thought it would make more sense for everything to come here until we're properly settled. That way nothing would get lost.'

His lofty brow wrinkled with a curiosity that seemed to border on suspicion. 'I hadn't realized you were moving,' he commented carefully.

To her relief his phone rang then, but as she made to go and join Emma in the BtG office, he said, 'Hang on, there's something else. I'll just take this,' and clicking on his mobile he announced his full name to the caller.

As she waited Angie tried to stop her heart from racing and her thoughts crashing into each other. She'd been homeless for ten days now and it seemed to be throwing her perspective on everything, for sometimes she couldn't even remember what day of the week it was, or what she was supposed to be doing in the next hour. She'd been on edge all this past weekend, had barely slept in spite of being at Emma's and had felt close to panic when she'd had to return to the storeroom last night. She might not have gone had they not spotted Amy Cutler out in the street, making a pantomime of clocking the van.

'She's asking for it,' Emma had growled, clenching her fists. 'Why does she have to be such a bitch?'

Angie had replied dolefully, 'Let's forget about her. I'll go when I'm ready, now carry on telling me about Melvin.'

Now, as Angie stood waiting for Ivan, she couldn't recall what Emma had told her, although she was sure the first proper date had gone well. Her mind moved to Grace and Lois, who'd seemed so proud of some shots Lois had taken of Grace, but she could barely picture them now. Had she given the right response? They'd mentioned something about a portfolio, which would be the sort of project they'd get involved in. She was certain Zac had scored at football yesterday morning, but for the moment she'd lost track of how many times and whether she'd remembered to cheer.

She glanced down at her phone as a text arrived.

It was from Hamish.

Mark Fields has been fired from his job. Apparently he called the site manager the C word. Can't see any going back from that. H.

She looked up as Ivan finished his call. 'I have to run,' he said, 'but I wanted to let you know that someone will be coming later to change the lock on the storeroom door.'

Angie could only stare at him.

'We've had reports, *sightings*, of someone coming and going at night,' he continued, 'which suggests that it's being used by a rough sleeper. I don't know how they managed to get a key, but there are people in and out of here all the time. Of course, we're all about helping these people, but we don't want anywhere on church premises being turned into a squat or a drug den. I don't suppose you or Emma have seen anyone suspicious loitering about?'

Angie swallowed dryly. Her heart was thudding too hard. 'No,' she replied, 'but we'll keep an eye out.'

He smiled, and wiping a gnarled hand over the small amount of hair on his scalp, he gestured for her to go ahead and followed her out into the blustery morning.

Hi Grace, the shots you sent were perfect, every one of them. You are a truly beautiful girl. I am hoping to have some very good news for you by the end of the day. A ☺

Grace turned her eyes to Lois and as they grinned they smacked each other's hands in a triumphant high five.

'Melvin just rang,' Emma announced as Angie came into the office. 'He says he can let us use one of his vans to move the furniture to his warehouse on Friday. It's much bigger than yours so we won't have to do as many trips.'

Angie took a moment to adjust to the good news that was actually terrible news, but before she could speak Emma's hand went up to stop her.

'You had a visitor earlier,' she said, her tone making it clear it wasn't a welcome one. 'Thankfully Ivan and Rosa weren't around, because he turned out to be a debt collector.'

Angie paled.

Emma looked both hurt and angry as she pointed at Angie's desk. 'I've spent the last half an hour going through all the final demands and multiple fines you've got hidden away in there,' she stated, 'and don't start kicking off about me invading your privacy. You know you'd have done the same in my shoes. So, were you ever planning to tell me how bad it really is?'

As Angie drew breath to answer Emma continued.

'It has to be dealt with,' she snapped. 'This denial that you seem to be in has got to end or we really will go under.'

It was the *we* that hit the hardest.

'Do you realize,' Emma ranted on, 'that if you ignore a summons to court you could be arrested and even end up in prison?'

Yes, Angie did realize that, but, as with all the other dreadful possibilities on her horizon, she'd been telling herself 'it just wouldn't happen.'

'When you go to court,' Emma continued, 'and I hope you know you'll have to, you need to be able to tell the judge that you're working to pay off your debts. That's going to mean having more than this job. OK, I know you've tried to find others to fit in with it, and you're doing all sorts of temporary cover. Cash in hand isn't exactly above board, though, so you need to… No, we *both* need to find something that pays more than this.'

'No!' Angie cried heatedly. 'It's not your responsibility to sort out my problems…'

'I'm your sister, for God's sake...'

'Emma, listen to me. You know very well that I can only get another job, or jobs, if you help with the children. This one suits you, so you need to stay here and I give you my absolute word, on Mum's grave, that I will find myself more work *tomorrow*.'

Emma stared at her and Angie stared back, holding her sister's big, frightened eyes and willing her to trust that she would do as she'd promised, because she would, and when she did, everything would be all right. She didn't believe it herself, not for a minute – in fact the very mention of prison had all but felled her – but somehow she had to make Emma believe it or they really would both go under, and if they did all four of their children could very well end up in care.

A few minutes later Angie was outside on the footpath to the church, trying to clear her head with some fresh air. The exchange with Emma was still burning inside her, with its terrifying warning of all that could lie ahead if she didn't get a grip. Her thoughts were a chaotic jumble as they raced from the housing office (she hadn't called them yet today, but she must); the lunchtime shift she'd agreed to cover at the Half Moon; there were more forms to fill in to keep her benefits coming; she'd promised to do a supermarket collection for the food bank... She hadn't told Emma yet about the storeroom lock. If she did she knew her sister would insist on her sleeping at the house again tonight, and every other night, until something was sorted. But after Amy Cutler had been so blatant about spying on them... Then she remembered the news about Mark Fields. Damn him for letting her down, and letting himself down too. What was she going to say to Martin? Why was she even asking herself that? Why would Martin care? He was on holiday with his family... She rested against a tree and took in deep breaths of cold air. She was going to be all right, she told herself. She wasn't going to panic. She couldn't allow herself to do that.

Grace gasped in astonishment, clasped her hands to her face, turned to Lois and back to the screen of her phone where Anya was watching her. This was totally amazing. Absolutely, completely *lit*. Excitement was rushing all over her, making her heart beat fast and her breath catch in her throat. They were going to be shooting a new teen movie very close to Kesterly, and the director who'd seen her YouTube videos and had said he wanted to meet her was now saying that he wanted her to audition for a part.

Anya's friendly eyes shone as Grace took in the news.

'When is it?' Grace asked breathlessly, suddenly fearful she wouldn't be good enough to impress the director. 'Will I have much to learn? How many others are up for the part?'

'The director and his team are going to be here tomorrow,' Anya replied. 'They'll be interviewing for most of the day because there are lots of roles to cast. The one you're up for isn't a lead, but it's a crucial part and he's already told me it's yours if you can pull off a good audition when he sees you.'

Grace's head started spinning. She could feel Lois's fingers digging into her leg, and hear the track 'Breathin' from Ariana Grande's *Sweetener* album playing in the background to drown out the sound of her talking to Anya. She must keep *breathin and breathin*...

'I expect you'd like to hear more about the film and exactly why the director feels you're so right for it?' Anya prompted, a gentle tease in her voice.

Grace nodded. 'Yes, yes, definitely,' she replied, sitting to attention to show how ready she was to listen.

'Well, the shots you sent for your portfolio,' Anya began,

'caused quite a sensation. There's so much we can do with them, and because they're so good the director has decided that you could be just who he's looking for to play the female lead's younger sister in his new film. He's asked the actress who's already been cast as the lead to be there for your audition, so he can assess the likeness between you.'

Grace nodded, taking it in, already seeing herself interacting with a girl she hadn't met, playing out a story she didn't know. She could do this, she really could – that was what her acting coach at Fairweather Players always said, and he was usually right.

'She's older than you,' Anya continued, 'sixteen, and in the story she uses you to stand in for her when she'd rather be other places. It gets you both into a lot of trouble, and when she disappears no one will believe you when you say you don't know where she is. I'm probably not telling this too well… The script is still being finalized, but apparently there'll be a couple of key scenes ready for you to audition with.'

Grace said, 'Can I see them before, so I can learn them?'

Anya smiled. 'I'm sure that'll be possible. Don't worry about what to wear; if you're coming straight from school your uniform will be fine, and if the director decides you need make-up someone will be on hand to sort it out.'

Grace was trying hard to think what else to ask. She looked down as Lois rapidly tapped a question into her phone to prompt her. Turning back to Anya she said, 'Where do I have to go for the audition?'

'I believe they've rented some space in the studios at WCA – West Centre for Creative Arts. Do you know it?'

Grace was mega-impressed. It was where scenes from some major movies had been shot, and where some top-selling albums had been recorded. 'Shouldn't my mum be there,' she asked, wanting to demonstrate that she knew about these things, 'you know, with me still only being thirteen?'

'Technically, yes,' Anya agreed, 'but she's got so much going on right now and I'm very happy to be your chaperone. Are you OK with that?'

Was she? 'Yes, of course,' she said. 'Thank you.'

Anya smiled again. 'I have to go now, but I'm really pleased about this and hope you are too… Oh, hang on, what am I thinking, I haven't told you the best news of all yet. If you get the part, and I'm pretty sure you will, the fee is ten thousand pounds plus royalties, with five thousand payable upfront.'

Grace was so stunned she couldn't speak. Next to her Lois mock-fainted on to the bed.

'So in next to no time,' Anya said happily, 'you could be in a very good position to start solving some of your family difficulties.' She added gently, 'I know that's what really matters to you, and it's what would make your dad very proud of you.'

CHAPTER TWENTY-FOUR

Today was the day.

Angie was going to prove to herself, and to Emma, that she was still capable of turning everything around and getting herself out of the unholy mess she was in. Since she couldn't face spending any more nights in the van, and the storeroom was no longer an option, she'd agreed to stay at Emma's for now, but was determined it couldn't be for long. So she'd started the day with her usual call to the housing office, forcing an appointment out of them for the day after tomorrow, then she'd spent the next two hours ringing employment agencies, practically begging them to find her something, *anything* that she could add to the hours she already had. Otherwise, she'd give up BtG and commit herself to a position that would provide her with a good income and full-time working status, if there was such an opening.

So far the only job she'd been offered was a 7 p.m.-to-midnight shift sorting waste at a recycling plant ten miles outside of Kesterly – protective cap, mask and gloves provided by the company. She'd have to work for an entire month before she was paid, and the agency would take their cut before transferring the rest to her bank account, where it would be swallowed up by her overdraft. However, she had to show the court proof of her finances increasing when she appeared for non-payment of her TV licence.

Now she was in the process of going door to door in Kesterly, hoping a more personal approach might produce some positive results.

'Oh gosh, I'm sorry, we don't have anything to offer you at the moment,' the kindly woman who owned the smart hairdresser's on the seafront said, seeming genuinely to mean it. Angie knew little about her, apart from the fact that her name was Gina and her twenty-eight-year-old daughter had died quite recently, so life probably wasn't very easy for her right now either. 'Have you tried next door at the gift shop?' Gina asked.

Angie nodded; yes, she'd tried the gift shop and had been told that there were no vacancies there.

Thanking Gina with her friendliest smile Angie turned to leave, pulling her padded coat more tightly around her as she trudged on through the bleak, wintry day. Staying on the Promenade for now she called into a newsagent-cum-post office, Gigi shoes, a B & B, and an old-fashioned haberdasher with a surf shop attached. Apparently no one needed extra help for cleaning, or serving, or stacking shelves, or anything at all. So how, she was asking herself, was she going to pay the road-tax bill that had managed to reach her this morning, or the MOT that would have to be carried out before paying the tax? And what if the van needed work?

Stiff with dread she pressed on with her job search, reminding herself not to look desperate, for it would only put people off, and might even scare them. As she passed the Seafront Café she resisted the temptation to try and throw herself on Fliss's mercy again; she already knew there were no vacancies there at present.

On reaching the quaint Dickensian-style front window of Glory Days on the corner of Prince's Arcade, she went to push open the door and found herself confronted by a *Closed* sign. This was one of her, Grace and Emma's favourite boutiques, with its art deco jewellery, feathered hats, flapper dresses and fur-trimmed capes. Entering it was like being transported into another era, or a land of make-believe, and the two women who ran it were always friendly and helpful.

Hoping the closure was simply seasonal and not a result of hard times, Angie walked on past the teddy bear shop (closed until May), the fragrance boutique (also closed until May), and after trying the estate agent where she was told they were fully staffed, thank you, she went on into the Inner Courtyard. Its central fountain and uneven cobbles seemed forlorn today, but maybe that was her mood, not helped by the fact that most of the shops and businesses looked deserted. However, there was a light on in Ogilvy Antiques on the opposite side of the square, so doing her best to pluck up her spirits she went to try it.

The man seated at a large oak desk to one side of the cluttered shop, with a laptop open in front of him and an assortment of mosaics beside it, regarded her regretfully as she explained why she was there. She was becoming depressingly used to that expression.

'We're not actually open at the moment,' he told her. 'I'm normally out back in the workshop restoring and repairing. I'm only sitting here because the Wi-Fi connection's better.'

She suddenly realized this was Blake Leonard, who'd been in the papers a couple of years back when his teenage daughter had gone missing. They'd found her in the end, but not alive. Angie's heart went out to him as she wondered if he was even close to getting over it; she knew she would find it impossible.

She thanked him as graciously as she could and left, still hearing the tinkle of the bell over the door after it closed.

As she turned back to the Promenade she could feel a horrible agitation starting to build inside her. She wanted to cry and beg someone, anyone, to tell her what to do. She looked up at the sky, shouting inside, *Steve, please help me to get through this because I don't think I can do it on my own.*

She waited for an answer, watching the clouds, silently imploring them, barely aware of the rain that was coming down soundlessly in an icy soft veil that soaked her face and hair and trickled inside her collar. She thought she could hear him, she was sure she could, but she couldn't make out what he was saying.

In the end, feeling more wretched than ever, she began retracing her steps along the Promenade. She was telling herself that she wouldn't give up, she'd never do that; she just didn't know what to do next.

As she reached the Seafront Café a small group of women rushed past her and in through the door, shaking out umbrellas and laughing at their luck in escaping the worst of it. She reflected on how wonderful it would be to go in with them, to sit around a table drinking hot coffee, or chocolate, order one of Fliss's delicious specials and spoil herself with a dessert, maybe even a glass of wine…

Realizing her mouth was watering she started to turn away, but paused as her eye was caught by a man sitting in a window booth. Though the glass was steamy on the inside and spattered with rain on the outside, she recognized him right away. Her eyes moved to the person opposite him. She was young and blonde, talking animatedly and making him laugh.

Angie barely knew what she was doing or even thinking as she started for the door. Pushing it open she made her way through the crowded tables right up to the booth, where she came to a stop without even knowing what she was going to say.

Martin Stone looked up in surprise. 'Can I help?' he said, frowning.

'I-I'm sorry to interrupt your lunch,' Angie stammered. 'I know this is… It's just…'

His frown deepened as he regarded her more closely. 'Angie?' he said uncertainly. 'Yes, it is you. You're soaked through. For heaven's sake, come and sit down.'

'No, I just, I'm sorry to do this but I…' She had to say this, she just had to get it out. 'I need a job,' she blurted, 'and I was…' Tears suddenly fell out of her eyes, unstoppable and huge and drowning her voice into humiliating silence.

He got quickly to his feet, held her steady as awful sobs shook her, and easing her gently into the booth next to the blonde, he called out to Fliss to bring a hot chocolate.

'No really,' Angie protested, rigid with embarrassment.

'Yes, really,' he insisted.

'You should take off your coat, it's soaked,' the blonde told her.

'This is my daughter, Alayna,' Martin explained. 'Alayna, this is Mrs Watts. You might remember her husband, Steve. Yes, help her take off her coat.'

Angie tried to protest again, but the girl was already unwinding her sodden scarf, and it was as though her strength and so much else was unravelling with it. 'I-I'm sorry,' she stammered, 'I didn't mean to interrupt your lunch…'

'It's OK, we've finished,' he told her, and taking the scarf from his daughter he waited for the saturated coat and said, 'These need to be dried off somewhere.' Holding them up he looked around, and as if by magic a server appeared to take them from him.

'One hot chocolate,' Fliss announced, placing a large steaming mug on the table. 'Oh, Angie, love, look at you. You're chilled to the bone. Get that down you now and there's plenty more if you want it.'

Realizing the time for pride was long past, Angie said, 'I can't pay, Fliss. I don't have any money, so you'd better take it away.'

'Leave it right there,' Martin instructed as Fliss planted her hands on her hips.

'You're not leaving here until I've seen you drink every last drop,' Fliss informed her bossily.

Angie started to speak, but only a sob came out. 'Please don't be kind to me,' she tried to laugh. 'It's making me cry and I've already made a big enough fool of myself.'

'Bloody nonsense,' Fliss snorted. 'Now drink, and I'll be keeping an eye on you to make sure you do.'

As she turned to carry on dealing with the lunch-hour crush, Alayna said quietly, 'Dad, I have to go.'

Angie immediately started to get up. 'I'm sorry, I've...'

Putting a hand out to stop her, Martin spoke to his daughter. 'Yes, of course. Call me when you get there.'

With a smile, Alayna said, 'I need to get out.'

Martin let go of Angie's arm and stood up too as Alayna slipped out of the booth.

'I have to catch a train,' she explained to Angie, 'but it was lovely meeting you.' She embraced her father, whispered something in his ear, and reaching for her bag she made her way to the coat racks. Angie stared after her, admiring how polite and poised she was. Grace would do well to turn out like her, she thought.

'Please don't let the chocolate go cold,' Martin warned, 'or Fliss will find a way to blame me.'

Aware of what a dreadful mess her face and hair must be, Angie dipped her head and sat down again.

She felt him watching her as she cupped her hands round the white china mug, allowing the heat to sink into her icy skin. His scrutiny felt unsettling, but oddly comforting too, as if someone was looking out for her, at least for these few short minutes.

She lifted the mug and treated herself to a deliciously warming swallow and when her eyes finally went to his she felt a flush of colour rise in her cheeks. She'd made such a fool of herself, pleading for a job, crying, *sobbing* like a child… 'I'm sorry, I…'

'No more,' he said, putting up a hand. 'You don't have anything to be sorry for.'

She looked at the hand, large and masculine, like Steve's and yet not like his because this one wasn't stained with paint or dusty; it was clean and tanned and strong. His face was tanned too, evidence of his recent holiday. It made his thick fair hair seem lighter and his penetrating eyes even bluer.

'So what's this about needing a job?' he asked, as a fresh mug of coffee was set down in front of him.

She felt embarrassment threaten to overwhelm her again, but she pushed herself past it; it really had no place in her world any more. 'I realize I can't work as a labourer, or anything else on a building site,' she said, 'but maybe you could use a cleaner, or a delivery person, or…' she couldn't think of anything else, not while his study of her was so intense.

'What happened to the charity?' he asked. 'Bridging the Gap, isn't it?'

She nodded. 'I'm still there, but I… I'm just not earning enough. I need to find another job to work around it, or some night shifts, although that's not great for the children, obviously. Your daughter is beautiful, by the way. How old is she?'

His eyes sparkled with the ironic pride of a father. 'Twenty-two. She graduated from Bristol last summer with a degree in Theatre and Performance Studies. She's now taking a year off to decide what she really wants to do.'

Angie had to smile.

'Actually, she's off to London today. She has an interview at the Royal Court in the morning.'

Angie was thinking how entranced Grace would be to meet someone like Alayna. 'Is she an only child?' she asked, feeling more comfortable now she wasn't talking about herself.

'No, I also have a son. Luke. He's twenty-three and committed to protecting wildlife in Africa.'

Angie's eyes widened. How could she not be impressed by that? If only Liam had been left alone to choose a similar path…

'What?' Martin prompted, as though sensing he'd triggered something in her.

She shook her head. 'Nothing. I was just… So does your son live in Africa?'

Martin nodded, with a rueful smile. 'He certainly does and he hardly ever comes home, so we have to go there to see him. We couldn't stay long this time, but frankly I think we were lucky he could fit us in at all.' The intensity of his gaze deepened. 'But we're not here to talk about me,' he reminded her gently, 'and can you drink some more chocolate please?'

Obediently she took another generous mouthful – not as hot as the first, but delicious nonetheless.

'I'm guessing,' he said, 'that things have been tough since you lost your husband.'

She took a breath and lost it in a surge of emotion.

'It's OK,' he murmured, covering one of her hands with his, 'with the way things are these days a lot of people are finding it hard, and being a single mum, trying to do the best for your family…'

'You have to stop,' she told him, 'I already warned you, being kind will make me cry.'

He smiled and she felt almost dizzied by it, as if it were sweeping her away from the deadening horrors of her world.

'Tell me about it,' he said gently. 'Tell me what's really happening, and then I'll be in a better position to know how I can help.'

To Angie's surprise, once she got started, she found it easier to open up to him than she'd have imagined. He was a good listener who showed no signs of shock or judgement, even at the worst parts; he seemed only to give her his full attention, as though nothing else in the world mattered beyond what she was telling him. He didn't ask many questions either, just nodded now and again, or frowned as though going deeper into a thought, apparently immersing himself in every part of her wretched tale.

When she got to the part about losing her home, his eyes closed as if he was feeling the horror of it himself. 'And Hari Shalik's son is your landlord?' he already seemed to know the answer to this.

'Was,' she corrected. 'That's the only good part of it, I suppose, that I don't have to deal with him any more. Or I wouldn't if I didn't still owe him so much rent. He's informed me that I have to move my furniture out or he'll do it for me. Luckily a friend of my sister's has somewhere for me to store it.'

He nodded thoughtfully, and asked her to continue.

'There isn't much more to tell,' she said. 'I've lost my home, I've run up a crippling amount of debt, and next week I'm due to appear in court for non-payment of my TV licence.'

She swallowed hard on her dread and embarrassment. 'I'm sure it'll be the first of many summonses, and I'll be fined for non-payment of them too, which is a bit crazy when the whole reason I'm there is because I can't afford to pay in the first place. Anyway, it's why I'm so desperate to find a job, or jobs, to add to the one I already have, so that I can at least show the court that I'm making an effort to sort things out.'

Clearly understanding that, he said, 'So are you living with your sister now?'

She stiffened; this was one truth she really couldn't bring herself to admit to. 'The children are,' she replied. 'I... stay there at weekends. During the week I... I stay in various places.'

He frowned, and his eyes became so penetrating that she felt sure he was actually reading her thoughts.

Quite suddenly he said, 'Have you eaten today?'

She started, not having expected the question, but when she began to say that she had, other words came out. 'No, not really, but I'm not hungry.'

Raising a hand, he called out to Fliss. 'Can we have a fish-finger sandwich over here? And another hot chocolate, please.'

'Coming up,' Fliss called back.

Angie said, 'You don't need...'

'I take it you like fish-finger sandwiches,' he interrupted, 'or am I inflicting one of my favourites on you?'

She had to smile at that. 'It was one of Steve's favourites too,' she told him. 'And yes, I'm a fan, but I can't let you...' She stopped as his mobile rang, and watched him check who it was.

'I can always ring back,' he said, letting the call go to messages. 'Now tell me more about Shalik. Did he go through all the proper channels to get you out?'

'Yes, he did, unfortunately, and that's why I can't forgive myself, because I knew it was coming, but I buried my head in the sand and told myself it would work out somehow.' She closed her eyes, wishing it was all just a bad dream and that where she was now, with him, feeling safe and less panicked than she had in so long, was the only reality.

'Shall I tell you what my daughter whispered to me before she left?' he said. 'She said, whatever's wrong, Dad, you have to help her, OK?'

Angie smiled at the generous heart, just like Grace's, while inside she felt ashamed of having appeared so wretchedly needy.

'We're going to sort this out,' he told her, clearly having come to a decision. 'We'll start with a job. It's in my office – my PA needs help and we'll be glad of whatever hours you can give us.'

Angie started to protest, but she seemed to have stopped breathing.

'I'll pay you fifteen pounds an hour in whatever form you like, to make sure it doesn't get soaked up by the bank to clear the overdraft. Perhaps your sister can receive it and give you the cash?'

Before she could answer he was saying, 'The debt needs sorting out, obviously, but there are experts who can advise you on that far better than I. I'll put you on to someone as soon as I've made a few calls. Next, you can stay at my place until the council can come up with something suitable.' He laughed, 'Don't look like that. I won't be there. I'll move in with my mother. And no need to worry, she's used to it, and so am I. There's always someone in town who needs a flat for the duration, and it's usually mine that gets taken over. Luckily, no one's using it right now, apart from me, and as I said, I can stay at home.'

Angie was overwhelmed and confused. 'But what about your wife?'

For a fleeting moment the light seemed to dim in his eyes,

and she detected a different sort of tension in his frown as he said, 'Ex-wife.' It was apparent that he regretted this, and Angie wasn't sure what to say.

'Actually, she's someone else I think you should meet,' he told her. 'She has a lot of contacts in the police, so maybe she can help to find Liam.'

Angie's heart skipped a beat. This was beyond anything she could have hoped for.

'Do you still have the text telling you he's safe?' he asked.

She nodded.

'Good. You can show it to her when you see her. She's just back from a long trip to New Zealand, but I think she should be over the jet lag by now.' He returned to the main issue. 'I know people at the council,' he informed her, 'so I'll see if we can move things along on the housing front. I've no idea if they have anything on the Fairweather estate, but if they do it's probably already taken. Still, no reason not to try and push for it. What you need is a three-bed place, am I right, and hopefully somewhere close enough to the schools so your children don't have to change.'

He looked up as a waiter delivered a chunky fish-finger sandwich oozing melted butter from its crusty sides and accompanied by a small pot of thick, creamy ketchup with a tiny marble spoon.

'OK, I'm going to leave you to eat that in peace,' he said, 'while I go over there and talk to the bloke in the corner.'

Angie glanced in the direction he indicated.

'He's a site engineer,' he explained. 'I'm hoping to recruit him for a project we're looking at starting next year. I'll be right back, and then we'll go and meet Martha. My PA. It might help to know that she's not exactly like other people, but don't worry, I think you'll like her.'

* * *

Half an hour later Angie was walking along the Promenade beside Martin, feeling as though she was in a dream as they headed in the direction of the marina and she tried to stay under the vast golfing umbrella he'd borrowed from Fliss to keep them both dry. As they passed the early-Georgian terraces that housed many flats, hotels and businesses she kept expecting them to turn into one, but it wasn't until they reached an imposing Regency mansion standing on its own at the back of a small car park that they'd apparently arrived. It was a three-storey red-brick building, with a black front door between crescent-shaped bay windows each side of the ground level, and tall, white-framed sash windows on the upper floors. Wide marble steps led up to the entrance, an elegant handrail either side and two small olive trees at the top that Angie realized must be fake, for live plants wouldn't flourish at this time of year.

'There's a separate doorway at the side,' he told her, 'which takes you to the flat on the first floor, so not much of a climb. The second floor is home to an old friend of mine who's away for the next couple of months, so you don't need to worry about him.'

As he folded down the umbrella he gave the glossy black door a shove. It opened easily to display a classic Georgian-style hallway with a black and white tiled floor, a grand dark wood staircase with intricately carved rails, and two sets of double doors that presumably opened into opposite wings of the house.

It was magnificent, Angie was thinking as she took it all in, from the watercolours on the walls, to the scuffs on the paintwork, to the alluring woodland scent emanating from the diffusers dotted around the place. She was just beginning to imagine what it must have been like at the time it was a family home when Martin tapped on a door to the right and called out, 'Martha? Are you decent?'

The mischievous look in his eyes made Angie laugh.

'Oh no, not that old chestnut,' a weary Scottish-sounding voice called back. 'I take it you've got someone with you you're trying to impress.'

Martin grinned and pushed open the door. 'Good you've got your clothes on,' he declared, 'and very lovely you look too.' He held out a hand to Angie and drew her into the room, which was crammed with books, papers, files, boxes, three desks, half a dozen computers and a large TV screen on one wall.

'Martha, let me introduce you to your new assistant,' he announced dramatically.

Martha's eyes rounded in amazement. She was a short, stocky woman of around sixty with wavy salt and pepper hair, a small round face, blue-framed glasses, and such a fierce demeanour that Angie almost took a step back.

'Since when do you choose my assistants?' she enquired loftily of Martin.

'Since today,' he replied. 'I had to snatch Angie up quick before someone else got her. She's highly sought after...'

'Cut the blather,' she scolded, and returning her flinty eyes to Angie she gave her such a frank up-and-down that it was all Angie could do not to squirm. 'So you're Angie, are you?' she said finally. 'Do you have a surname?'

Before Angie could reply Martin said, 'She's Steve Watts's wife.'

Martha's rapid thaw was so visible it was almost comical. 'You're Watty's wife,' she said, in a tone that suggested this changed everything. 'Then come in my dear, take off that wet coat for heaven's sake and let's talk about your duties. Can you use a computer?'

As Angie confirmed that she could, she glanced at Martin and found him grinning like Lewis Carroll's satisfied cat.

'What are you waiting for?' Martha asked him. 'You know where the kettle is. Angie, do you prefer tea or coffee?'

'Uh, tea,' Angie replied, feeling as though she'd walked into some kind of theatrical scene where all roles were reversed and she was yet to find out what hers was.

'Same for me,' Martha told Martin, 'and put the milk in a jug and sugar in a bowl. We want Angie to think well of us before she finds out what we're really like.' Turning to Angie she said, 'You haven't taken that coat off yet, so come along, let's be having it. How long can you spare today? I'm not expecting you to do any work, it'll just be good for us to have a little chat about the kind of things I'll be asking of you. Mostly filing and answering phones and trying to tidy this place up a bit. There you are now, sit yourself down at that desk. It'll be yours when you're here. The office over the other side of the hall is our lord and master's when he's here, and don't be afraid to go in when he is, he's usually on his own because he doesn't have any friends.'

'I heard that,' Martin shouted out from the adjacent kitchen.

'He was supposed to,' she told Angie. 'Now, when can you start?'

CHAPTER TWENTY-FIVE

Emma stared at Angie in stunned amazement, her mouth opening, closing, and opening again until she finally cried, 'You are kidding me. Martin Stone – *the* Martin Stone – has given you a job *and* a place to live?'

'To stay,' Angie corrected with a smile. 'It's only temporary, and you're talking about him as if he's a celebrity or some kind of royalty…'

'Around here he practically is.' Emma threw out her hands, dumbstruck again until she broke into gales of laughter. 'Only you, Angie Cross,' she declared, using their maiden name, 'could go out in the morning practically destitute and end up in a whole new world belonging to one of the richest and fittest blokes in town.' She laughed again with pride and delight. 'Yes, only you, my wonderful star-crossed sister, could pull off something like this.'

Angie wrinkled her nose. 'I'm not sure "pulling off" is the right way to put it,' she objected. 'It makes it sound as though

I went into town with the intention of forcing myself on him – that wasn't a good turn of phrase either. Anyway, what really matters is that I'm going to be paid fifteen quid an hour for twenty hours spread over five days, and before I left he told his PA to give me a hundred pounds as an advance.'

Emma almost fainted. 'A hundred quid,' she echoed incredulously. '*A hundred.* My God, someone's looking out for you somewhere. Well, we know his name's Martin Stone, but I can hardly get my head round it. We don't even know him, so why should he…'

'He knew Steve,' Angie said, 'I'm pretty sure he's doing it for him, and, well… I know this is going to sound weird, but it was like Steve took me to him today. I think Steve knew he would help.'

Emma shook her head, not so much in disbelief as in wonder.

Angie started to speak again but found herself suddenly overwhelmed by tears. She had no idea if it was relief making her emotional, or the fear that it would all somehow go up in smoke and she'd end up worse off than before, or if she was simply exhausted. She swallowed hard and took a shaky breath. 'You know that warning,' she said. 'If it looks too good to be true then it is too good to be true.'

'I always hated that saying,' Emma stated dismissively. 'Now tell me about the flat.' She grinned at her sister. 'My God, I still can't believe it. You're only going to be living – *staying* – in a fancy pad overlooking the bay. Will you be allowed visitors?'

Angie choked on a laugh. 'I'm sure I'll be very happy to entertain you as soon as I'm in residence,' she teased grandly.

'Just listen to her,' Emma chuckled. 'So will you be there tonight?'

'I've got the keys, but he wants me to wait until tomorrow so he'll have time to pack some things and the cleaning lady can go in to change the sheets.' It was still making her light-headed simply to think of someone going to so much trouble for her. It was embarrassing her too, worrying her even, for she should be doing the cleaning and sorting things out, not having it done for her.

Emma's eyes were sparkling. 'Cleaning lady, linens… Next thing we know you'll have a chauffeur. So have you actually *seen* the flat yet?'

'No, there wasn't time, I had to get back here to the office, but if the downstairs rooms are anything to go by I think it's probably quite large. You'll know the building, it's the big Georgian house at the end of the Promenade, close to the marina.'

'Oh my God, of course I do. It's amazing. I didn't know it was offices though, I thought it was all flats. Is there enough room for the kids?'

'To be honest I didn't like to ask. He was already being so generous. I mean, it could be that he's assuming they'll be with me. I'll have a better idea, I guess, when I find out how many bedrooms there are.'

'Just as long as you know it's fine for them to carry on staying with me – not that I see much of Grace, she's been spending most nights at Lois's lately. Actually, I think we should drop over a bag of fancy groceries to Lois's mother now you're in the money, because she's been feeding Grace pretty regularly. You know, some artisan bread, marinated olives, sun-dried tomatoes, bottle of wine, that sort of thing.'

'That was one of my first thoughts when Martha gave me the advance,' Angie said. 'They've been so good to her, it's hard to think of a way to thank them enough.'

'Well, they'll be pretty certain that you'd do the same for Lois if anything ever happened to them, so don't worry yourself too much on that score. Now, back to the job, exactly what will you be doing?'

Still faintly dazed by it, Angie said, 'I'll be the general office assistant working for Martha, the PA. She's a scream, by the way, wait till you meet her, you'll love her. Anyway, I'll be filing, answering the phones and general emails, sorting out the thousands of box files she's got piled up everywhere. Apparently there are other offices belonging to the company over in the business district where accountants, planners, architects, all sorts of other staff are based, so I'll be ferrying stuff between the two when needed, and out to various construction sites. Martin's based at the house, as they call it, but apparently he's not there much, because he's pretty hands-on with the projects, to quote Martha.'

Emma gazed at her with more thrilled incredulity. 'Seems your husband's ability to make friends and influence people is turning out to be as good as an insurance policy,' she commented fondly.

'Almost,' Angie agreed, 'but we're still technically homeless, and I've still got a mountain of debt to clear. Actually, Martin's going to put me in touch with a lawyer so I'll have someone to come to court with me next week.' She was ludicrously close to tears again, and all because someone was actually going to be there to help her through that horrible ordeal. It was almost inconceivable after she'd felt so alone.

'Oh Angie,' Emma murmured, going to embrace her. 'It's beyond wonderful, what's happened today, and you totally deserve a break, but I can see it's a lot to take in.'

Angie sniffed away the tears. 'I'm an emotional wreck,' she groaned, her voice muffled by her sleeve. She was aware of how her thoughts kept going back to the moment when, standing in the rain, she'd asked Steve to tell her what to do. It seemed crazy to think he'd been watching and listening and then guiding her footsteps to where she'd needed to go, but it really was how it felt. So if her husband was near, was it any wonder she felt emotional?

Dabbing her eyes, she said, 'Let's take a detour to Waitrose on the way home. We can pick up some lovely things there for Becky, Lois's mum, and we'll also get something scrumptious for our tea – on me.'

'It's a deal, just as long as you keep back at least fifty quid, so you don't end up with nothing any sooner than you have to.'

Angie was reaching for her phone. 'I'll text Grace and tell her I'll definitely be at yours tonight. I should also email the ghastly Shalik to confirm that my furniture will be gone on Friday. Is it still OK with Melvin?' she added worriedly.

'Of course. He's going to ask a couple of the warehouse guys to come and help us, so it should be done quite quickly.'

Angie's smile of gratitude was weak; although the tide might be turning on her luck in some ways, the thought of moving everything out of Willow Close still felt as though she was turning away from Steve...

'Oh, hello, I'm glad you're both here.'

It was Ivan coming through the door in his smart grey overcoat, collar up to his ears and a tartan cap keeping his balding head dry.

Emma quickly removed their bags from the only comfy chair, while throwing a glance at Angie underlining what a rare honour this was.

'Oh, no, thanks,' Ivan replied when Emma offered him some tea. 'I know you'll be wanting to get off soon so I'll try not to keep you.' He removed his cap and clasped it between both hands as he perched on the edge of the armchair.

'Is everything all right?' Angie asked, getting a coldly distinct feeling that it wasn't. Surely he hadn't found out that she was the rough sleeper in the storeroom?

'I'm afraid not,' he admitted gravely. 'We had some very sad news today. Our benefactress, Mrs Masters – Carlene Masters – passed away last night.'

Angie and Emma looked at each other, their minds leaping to what this might mean for them and the residences.

'Was it sudden?' Emma thought to ask.

'I'm not sure of the details yet,' he replied, 'but as you know, she was quite elderly. The vicar is in touch with her family. She has two nieces who live in London.'

Angie recalled the vicar's wife once telling her how the nieces never went to visit the old lady, apparently a source of great sadness for their aunt.

Emma asked bluntly, 'Is this going to affect Bridging the Gap?'

Ivan sighed. 'I'm afraid I'm not sure about that either, but of course we're hoping it won't, at least not in a negative way. It's my understanding – the vicar's too – that the properties are bequeathed to St Mary's, and if that proves the case the church will naturally want to keep them going.' His eyes drifted off to the middle distance, as though he was still trying to process the news himself.

'Are you OK?' Angie asked. 'Are you sure we can't get you something?'

'I'm fine, I'm fine,' he assured them. He attempted a smile. 'I knew her, a long time ago… She was a special lady.'

Having no problem believing that, considering her generosity, Angie put a comforting hand on his arm.

Collecting himself, he said, 'This means, of course, that we probably shouldn't bring anyone else into the houses for the time being, not until we're clearer about the way things are going. It would be awful, wouldn't it, to offer some poor chap a place only to have to tell him… Well, I'm sure it won't come to that.'

As the door closed behind him Emma said, 'I haven't had chance to tell you yet, but I spoke to Hamish earlier and apparently Mark Fields has done a moonlight.'

Angie wasn't sure whether to be relieved or concerned.

'He cleaned out the food cupboards before he left,' Emma continued, 'and poor Hamish had only just done a shop.'

Making a mental note to replace the groceries from BtG funds, Angie said, 'If those houses don't end up belonging to the church then I'm already worrying about what will happen to Hamish. The others are young enough, strong enough... He doesn't have anyone. No family at all to take him in, and we know he can't work...'

'Stop,' Emma interrupted firmly, 'let's worry about it when we know we have to, because we probably won't. What you need to do now is focus on the good fortune that's come your way today.'

'That's just it though, isn't it,' Angie sighed. 'As one person is saved another goes under, and actually far more go under than ever get...'

'Angie,' Emma cut in darkly. 'Right now, tonight, you, Hamish and all the other residents have roofs over your heads, and you will for the foreseeable future. So I say it's time to get ourselves to the supermarket and then we can go home and really whoop it up as we sort out what needs to be taken to the launderette tomorrow, because the washing machine has broken down again.'

Angie had to smile. Of course Emma was right – scaring herself over things that might never happen wasn't only ludicrous, it was a waste of energy. She needed to be positive and thankful and to find a way of texting Martin without gushing.

In the end she said, *It's hard to find the words to thank you without going too far and embarrassing us both, but I'm sure you know how much your help means to me and my family. Angie*

His answer came back a few minutes later. *Glad to be of help. Hope you'll be able to cope with Martha. :D*

CHAPTER TWENTY-SIX

'There it is, over there,' Grace said, looking up from iMaps on her phone to a small rank of shops on the other side of the street. Just past it on the right was a large gateway with a sign over it welcoming visitors to WCA – WEST CENTRE FOR CREATIVE ARTS.

They'd cut school early and caught the number 46 bus here from the centre of town, just as Anya had instructed, and even though they'd visited the centre before on a school trip it was quite a while ago, so they'd looked up the address and post-code in case they got lost.

As they turned in through the gates, apprehensive and not a little overawed by the size of the place, they took in the vast grey stone building spread grandly across the back of a large car park, with a huge sign across the front advertising office and studio space for rent. They knew it had been a factory years ago, but with its tall barred windows and yellow iron staircases on the outside it looked more like a prison.

'There don't seem to be many people here,' Lois remarked as they passed a handful of cars looking vaguely abandoned in a space that could have accommodated hundreds of vehicles.

Grace pointed to a truck close to the entrance; on its side were emblazoned the words TRC Film and TV Lighting Hire.

They giggled as they collided with one another in the revolving entrance doors, and half stepped, half spilled into a high-ceilinged lobby with red plush bench seats, low-hanging lamps suspended over black wood tables and a large, semicircular reception desk at the centre of the back wall. A security guard was behind it talking on the phone, and barely looked up as they approached.

'Oh my God,' Lois muttered.

Grace followed her eyes to the felt board displaying names of the companies that were based here. Although Grace didn't recognize any of them, she was just as impressed, for in spite of the missing letters in some cases they were clearly all film companies, or photographic studios, or music-recording suites.

'Can I help you?' the security guard asked gruffly as he ended his call.

'We're here to see Anya,' Grace informed him, realizing too late that they should have found out her surname.

Before he could respond lift doors opened in an alcove to the left, and a blonde woman dressed in a tight black skirt and high-heeled ankle boots stepped out. It took Grace a moment to realize it was Anya, for she looked different to the way she did on WhatsApp, not as sparkly-eyed, nor as tall as she'd imagined her to be. Her hair was kind of stringy and her complexion badly pocked, and in spite of her smile she wasn't giving off the same sort of friendly vibe.

'Grace,' she pronounced, taking Grace's hands and holding

them out to get a good look at her. 'Lovely. He'll be pleased,' and turning an arch gaze on Lois she drawled, 'And who do we have here?'

'Lois is my best friend,' Grace told her. 'She's been helping me to learn the scenes you sent.'

Lois said, 'Acting's not really my thing. I want to get into the production side, if I can.'

Anya looked her up and down, and her manner was far from welcoming. 'OK, follow me,' she said, and turning back to the lift she ushered them in ahead of her.

As they rose to the second floor Grace and Lois exchanged anxious glances. This definitely wasn't starting off the way they'd expected it to. Why was Anya behaving so strangely? She'd been so lovely in the message she'd sent earlier: *Really looking forward to meeting you. I have a feeling things will go very well. A*☺ Now she wasn't saying anything at all, in fact she seemed a bit cross.

Following her out of the lift and along a quiet corridor, Grace felt Lois move in close to her as though she was about to whisper something, but then Anya was opening a door and gesturing for them to go in ahead of her. They found themselves in a small, dimly lit room with plush seats in cosy nests of four either side of a reception desk, and an enormous soda machine in one corner.

'Chose whatever you want to drink,' Anya told Lois, waving her to the machine. 'Just press the buttons, everything's free.' She turned to Grace. 'Are you ready?'

Startled by the abruptness, Grace couldn't think what to say. She found herself nodding and glancing at Lois as she allowed Anya to steer her through a heavy studded door. Anya turned and said to Lois, 'It's a closed set, so you'll have to wait here.'

'Cool,' Lois replied faintly, looking worried.

The door closed with an airy clunk and Grace blinked at

the bright lights, so dazzling that it wasn't possible to make out what sort of room she was in, though she assumed it must be a studio. She took a glass that was being thrust into her hand.

'Iced lemonade,' Anya told her. 'It's so hot in here you'll need it.'

She was right; the heat was overwhelming, and it was so stuffy it wasn't easy to breathe.

Grace drained the glass, and because it was so refreshing she was happy to take another.

'Is that Grace?' a male voice enquired. It was deep and gravelly, the kind of voice her dad used to put on when he was playing a monster.

'She's here,' Anya announced. She gently nudged Grace forward and Grace felt her nerves fray as an enormous man with a balding head and goatee beard stepped into the light. He had a piercing in one nostril and in both ears, and his smile showed the glint of something, maybe another piercing, in his tongue. She couldn't see his eyes because he was wearing dark glasses, but his skin was the same colour as the shadows behind him. A girl seemed to float out from nowhere and she was so white by contrast, hair, skin, dress, that she almost seemed translucent.

'Hello Grace,' she murmured, giving her a little wave, but she wasn't looking at Grace, she didn't seem to be looking at anything at all.

'Grace brought a friend with her,' Anya stated loudly.

At first the man said nothing and it was impossible to know where he was staring as his eyes were concealed, but Grace felt sure it was at her. 'Why did you bring a friend, Grace?' he asked smoothly.

She opened her mouth to answer, but nothing came out. She was feeling woozy, she realized, and it wasn't easy to stay standing.

Dimly she wondered if there had been alcohol in the lemonade, but she didn't like to ask.

She watched the girl drape herself over a wide chaise longue, and was aware of being steered towards it. As she sat she felt her head loll forward and struggled to keep it up. She put out a hand to steady herself but then someone was lifting her feet, helping her to lie down. She tried again to speak, but her tongue felt so heavy and it was impossible to keep her eyes open. She sensed rather than saw the man come to kneel beside her. 'You shouldn't have brought your friend,' he whispered in her ear. 'It's not what you were told to do.'

Lois's house was in darkness when the car pulled up outside to let her and Grace out into the damp, blustery night. This wasn't unusual, for the TV room and her parents' bedroom both overlooked the back garden, but it was so late it was most likely that everyone was already in bed.

Fingers crossed.

'Are you OK?' Lois asked Grace, putting an arm around her as the car drove off, red tail lights glowing as it paused before turning left out of the street.

Grace nodded. 'I think so,' she croaked. Her throat was so parched she could hardly get the words out, and her head throbbed so badly she was only just managing to register where they were.

'Come on,' Lois said, 'we need to go in, but we have to be quiet in case anyone hears us.'

Understanding, Grace allowed her to lead the way, keeping close behind and tiptoeing through the front door once Lois had managed to open it.

They got as far as the first landing before the lights suddenly went on and Becky, Lois's mother, was standing in her bedroom doorway glaring at them so fiercely that Lois half slid behind Grace.

'What the hell time do you call this?' Becky demanded, her elfin face white with anger. 'I've been calling you for hours. Your mother has been here looking for you, Grace. She's out of her mind with worry. So where the hell have you been?'

Lois swallowed hard and glanced at Grace as she said, 'We – we went to a party after dance class. I'm sorry, we should have rung to let you know...'

'You're damned right you should have, and what are you doing going to parties on a school night? Where was it?'

'It... um, it was at someone's house over... by the garden district.'

Becky peered more closely at Grace. 'Have you been drinking?' she wanted to know. 'Yes, of course you have. Look at the state she's in. Get her up to bed now and I'll text her mother to let her know she's all right. It's lucky for you, Lois Holbrook, that your father's away working this week or there would be hell to pay, staying out till gone eleven on a week night and not asking permission – or getting in touch to let anyone know where you were.'

Bundling Grace to the narrow staircase leading to the loft, Lois said quickly to her mother, 'Please don't tell Angie about her being drunk. Just say we got carried away dancing or something and didn't notice the time.'

Becky scowled at her hard. 'If Angie didn't already have enough on her plate I wouldn't lie for you,' she stated. She inhaled crossly. 'And Grace had better be OK for school in the morning, because I'm not going to lie for you twice. Once you've got her upstairs make sure there's something next to the bed in case she's sick. If she is and it goes all over the place *you* will be the ones cleaning it up.' She was going back into her room when she stopped and turned round, brow furrowed with confusion. 'How come she's drunk and you aren't?'

'I just... I didn't really have anything. I mean, she didn't either, but what she did have went straight to her head.'

Becky frowned suspiciously and with another meaningful look at them both she closed the door behind her.

Minutes later Grace was sprawled on the small guest bed next to Lois's larger one, feeling as though she was drifting and pitching. Lois sat cross-legged beside her, checking Grace's mobile. 'Shit, there are a ton of calls and texts from your mum,' she warned. 'Do you want to let her know you're all right?'

Grace nodded, but when she tried to reach for the phone her hand simply fell back on the bed.

'Don't worry, I'll do it,' Lois said. Speaking aloud as she typed, she texted, 'Mum, I'm really, really sorry. Didn't mean to worry you, but I'm fine. Just didn't hear the phone because the music was so loud.' She stopped and scrolled back through Angie's messages. 'Better check to see if there's anything you should be responding to,' she explained. She stopped at the earliest text. 'She's saying here that she's got some good news and she wants you to go to your Auntie Em's for tea so she can tell you.'

Grace groaned and tried to take the phone again.

Lois moved it away and carried on typing. 'Can't wait to hear your good news. Too late to call now, but will try you on way to school in the morning. Sorry again. Love you.' As she put the phone down she looked at Grace helplessly, uncomprehendingly, not sure what to do next. 'Are you all right?' she asked. 'Do you need to be sick?'

Grace shook her head and fleetingly opened her eyes.

'So what the hell happened?' Lois whispered urgently. 'I thought you were never going to come out of there. I was dead scared. Do you realize I was locked in that bloody room? I don't know if someone did it on purpose, but no one answered when I shouted and knocked on the door. Then I couldn't get a signal on my phone...' She broke off as a tear rolled from the corner of Grace's eye. 'Oh Grace,' she whispered frantically, 'what is it? Tell me what happened.'

'I don't know,' Grace sobbed. 'I can't remember anything.'

'But you must remember something. You have to.'

Grace shook her head. Everything was blank, and her head hurt so much.

'When you went in,' Lois prompted, 'what happened then? Who else was there?'

Grace tried to make herself think. The memory was fuzzy, but after a moment she said, 'There was a man and a girl in white... I... They gave me a drink and after that...'

Lois's eyes rounded with horror. 'Oh God, oh God,' she muttered, not wanting any of this to be real. 'Grace, tell me, do you think...? Listen, you've heard about those date-rape drugs, they go on about it in school, so is it possible someone might have... you know... spiked your drink and had sex with you?'

Grace moaned in despair. 'I don't know,' she choked.

'How can you not know?'

'Because I can't remember.'

Lois hardly knew what to do or say, but somehow she forced herself to think rationally. 'All right, all right,' she said, as much to calm herself down as Grace. 'How do you feel down there?' she urged. 'If someone raped you you'd be able to feel it. Does it hurt?'

Grace wriggled a little and shook her head.

'Are you sure?'

'Definitely.'

'OK, that's good. Do you hurt anywhere?'

'Just my head… Oh God, I'm scared, Lois. You won't tell my mum, will you? You won't ever tell anyone…'

'Cross my heart and hope to die.'

Grace sobbed into her hands. 'They could have done anything to me, Lois…'

'Ssh, ssh, as long as you're not hurting down there we know you weren't raped, and that's what really matters. OK?'

Grace tried to nod.

Lois went into the bathroom, filled a glass with water, grabbed some wet wipes and the plastic waste bin and went back to Grace's bed. 'You know what I reckon,' she said, gently cleansing Grace's face, 'I reckon Anya's the front person for some paedo ring, and me turning up with you ruined everything. You could see how pissed off she was about it… Oh God, Grace, anything could have happened to you.'

CHAPTER TWENTY-SEVEN

As Angie indicated to turn out of Emma's street her mobile was resting on the front passenger seat of the van, switched to speaker, her version of hands-free. 'Well as long as you're all right,' she said to Grace, raising her voice to be heard. 'You had us all in a terrible state last night worrying about you. It's not like you, and it's not like Lois either. So are you sure you're telling us the whole story?'

Grace's voice was slightly muffled as she said, 'Definitely.'

Sceptical, but not wanting to pick a fight on the phone, Angie said, 'You sound tired, which is hardly surprising given the time Becky says you got in.'

'I'm fine,' Grace assured her. 'Just kind of, you know.'

With a roll of her eyes, Angie said, 'I'm sure I don't know. I want you to come home tonight. Something's happened, something good and I want to share it with you.'

'Can't you tell me what it is now?'

Should she? It would deprive her of seeing Grace's face light up when she explained about the flat, but she sounded pretty low this morning – ashamed of having caused all that fuss last night most likely – so she could probably do with some cheering up. 'I've got a place to stay,' she announced, experiencing a heady rush of euphoria simply to say the words. 'And it's not just any place, it's lovely. I should be able to move in later today.'

Grace's tone was still flat as she said, 'Where is it?'

'Would you believe, on the Promenade? It actually overlooks the sea. Well, I think it does, I haven't been in it yet…'

'Are you saying the council gave you a place on the Promenade?'

Angie laughed. 'I wish. No, it belongs to a friend. Well, he's a friend of Dad's actually, who's offered to let me stay there until the council can come up with something permanent.'

Grace was silent.

'Are you still there?' Angie asked.

'I don't think you should take it,' Grace snapped.

Angie blinked in astonishment. 'What are you talking about? It's a very generous offer and…'

'OK, so what's his name, this friend of Dad's?'

Angie was about to tell her, but instead she said, 'Why? What difference does it make?'

'None. I'm just asking. Is it someone we know?'

'Kind of. His name's Martin Stone. You might have seen signs on building sites for Stone Construction. He and Dad knew each other quite well.'

'So he's a builder?'

'A bit more than that, but essentially yes.'

'OKaaaay.' She was sounding slightly less hostile now. 'So how come he's letting you have this house?'

'Flat, and it's bit of a long story, so I'll tell you tonight. Are you at school now?'

'We've just got here. Becky dropped us off.'

'Good. I hope you apologized properly for all the upset you caused last night.'

'Yes, of course. Can we forget it now?'

With a sigh, Angie said, 'Just as long as it doesn't happen again. You know how I worry if I can't get hold of you.' She didn't add that it reminded her too much of how it had been with Liam, Grace would know that anyway. 'I'll send you a text as soon as I know what's happening later.'

'OK. Love you.'

'Love you too.'

As she rang off Angie pulled up at traffic lights and quickly checked the texts that had come bundling in while she was on the phone. There was one from an outreach worker asking if she could fill in for her on Saturday night serving drinks at the bingo; and another from one of the volunteers at the women's shelter hoping Angie could cover her pizza-delivery shift on Friday. They were both offering to pay her in cash, and ordinarily she'd have jumped at it, but now she had to consider her new position with Stone Construction. It was possible she'd be required to work late one or two evenings a week, and there were also the deliveries she was expected to make between the house, the main offices and the several building sites, plus, of course, her duties at BtG.

To her great relief, she'd been able to cancel her job at the recycling plant. It might not have been as bad as she feared, but on the other hand it might have, and anyway, she really, really didn't want to sort through other people's rubbish.

The third text was from Hamish letting her know that there was a leak in the bathroom at Hill Lodge, but not to worry, he'd fix it himself. *Don't want to be running up bills where we don't have to,* he added. She quickly messaged back to thank him and clicked on to the final text. It was from Martha, containing the name and number of a debt consolidation adviser whose services were apparently free of charge.

Feeling a surge of gratitude all mixed up in fear and humiliation, Angie put the van into gear and drove on along the coast road. Martha – and Martin – must surely wonder why she hadn't found this information out for herself by now, but she had known these debt services existed. She just hadn't been able to face the shame of confessing what a terrible mess she was in. She didn't want to now, she was going to hate every minute of it, but she'd come to accept in the last twenty-four hours that she couldn't expect others to help her like this if she wasn't prepared to help herself.

Right now she was on her way to meet with the lawyer Martha had texted her about at eight this morning – she was an early bird. Apparently he was going to talk to her about her court appearance next week.

An actual lawyer was going to help her with a hearing for non-payment of a TV licence. It felt like a fantasy.

Martha had texted: *Himself says not to worry about how much it's going to cost because the lawyer owes him plenty of favours.*

They really did come from different worlds, Angie thought, and how lucky she was to have been invited into his, at least for a while. 'Thanks, Steve,' she whispered, 'because I know it's you making this happen.'

Later in the day Angie called Hamish from the BtG office to check everything was OK at Hill House.

'Leaky bathroom sorted,' he told her in a brief but satisfied way. 'Just needed a new washer. The bloke at B & Q was very helpful, explained what I had to do. I didn't tell him I already knew – it would have spoiled the fun of showing off for him.'

Angie had to smile; Hamish was nothing if not generous.

'No word from Mark Fields,' he went on, 'not that I expected any, but I've had quite a long chat with Craig's girlfriend, Sasha. She's Romanian, by the way, and it turns out she's managed to escape from a very unfortunate situation over on the Temple Fields estate where she was being held against her will and forced to do things… Well, I'm sure you're following me. We all know what goes on in certain *properties* over there. Poor thing's terrified of them finding her again and she's got no money to go back to her country or papers which might qualify her for aid. She holing up in one of the scrap caravans on the dumping ground behind the station, and that's where Craig stays when he's not here. So, I hope you don't mind, but I've told her she can come here for something to eat and to get warm now and again. She seems like a good girl and the others know not to act up around her, or they'll have you to answer to.'

Angie smiled, even as she felt deep pity for the girl. Thank goodness Sasha had Hamish and Craig for the moment. Just like she had Martin. 'It's good you've done that,' she told Hamish. 'She needs to feel safe, so we'll see if we can think of somewhere a bit more comfortable for her to stay for a while.'

Sounding pleased, he said, 'I won't say anything to her yet, but I think she'll be glad to know we care. Now, did I tell you I found more cornicing at the reclamation yard? Loads of the stuff, and I got it for next to nothing because of the state it's in. With any luck this should have all of the downstairs done by Easter.'

Feeling a churn of dismay, as the future ownership of the properties was still unknown, Angie said, 'I know you love doing it, and you do a fantastic job, but please make sure you don't end up out of pocket.'

'No fear of that,' he assured her. 'Now I can hear another phone your end, so I'll let you go and answer it.'

As she rang off Angie reached for her mobile, and seeing it was Martin she felt a fluttering inside turn into a tightening of unease. *Please don't let him be saying he's changed his mind about the flat.*

'Hi,' he said, his voice echoey as if he might be driving. 'Is this a good time?'

'Yes, it's fine,' she assured him. 'How are you?'

'I'm good. I was wondering how you got on with the lawyer today?'

Allowing her spirits to lift a little, she said, 'He was incredibly helpful. Thanks so much for putting me on to him. He's going to work with the debt consolidation adviser as soon as I've had the meeting, to prepare something to impress the court.' She didn't add that she'd been told she must find the money for the licence fee somehow, so the lawyer could present it with his request for no fine. She didn't want Martin thinking she was hinting for him to help. She'd take on the bingo and pizza-delivery shifts and anything else she could find.

'Excellent,' he declared. 'So when do you see the adviser?'

'I've made an appointment for tomorrow at three.'

'Great. Don't forget he or she will need to know everything, so don't hold back. And keep in mind that however bad you think your situation is, they will have heard worse. Really. Now, about the flat. I've taken everything I need and it's being cleaned as we speak, so it should be ready for you to move into around five. Martha's going to stay on to help you, so give her a call to let her know what sort of time to expect you.'

She smiled. 'I don't know how to thank you. What you're doing…'

'Just make yourself at home, and don't let Minerva

McGonagall bully you – although I think it's only me she enjoys exercising her fiendish powers over.'

Angie laughed at the reference to the headmistress of Hogwarts and looked up as Emma came in.

'OK, I have to go,' he said. 'I'm going to be in London for the next couple of days but Martha should be able to handle any issues if they crop up tonight… Hang on, I'm forgetting the most important part. I've spoken to Andee, my ex, and she'll be happy to meet with you one day next week to talk about Liam. She used to be a detective, by the way, so she has all the right contacts. Martha will give you a number so you can arrange it. OK, that's me gone, call if you need to, otherwise I'll be in touch soon.'

As the line went dead Angie clicked off at her end and looked at Emma.

'Whoever that was,' Emma commented, starting to unpack her bag, 'they've put some colour in your cheeks, so I'm going to guess it was your new boss and landlord.'

Angie didn't bother denying it. 'I can move in tonight,' she declared joyfully.

She took out her phone to text Grace, letting her know she'd pick her up from school if she was happy to skip dance class tonight.

'If you're still OK to collect the boys from gymnastics,' she said to Emma, 'why don't you bring them to the flat after so they can see it, and then you can leave Zac with me for the night?'

'No problem,' Emma replied, breaking into a grin. 'I'm looking forward to this. Talk about from rags to riches…'

'OK, don't let's get carried away. It's only temporary and I haven't told you about the rest of my day yet. With the lawyer? And the debt adviser?' Angie clarified when Emma looked blank. 'Well, I haven't actually met the debt adviser yet, but I will tomorrow, and Martin's just told me that his wife – ex-wife – is willing to meet with me next week to see if she can help to find Liam. She used to be a detective apparently.'

Emma punched the air. 'Your luck is definitely changing,' she dared to say.

'Don't, you'll jinx it,' Angie protested.

'Sorry, sorry, your luck's still in the toilet.'

'You're definitely going to think so when I tell you I have to come up with a hundred and fifty quid for the TV licence by next Wednesday.'

Emma baulked.

'I think I can raise about a hundred if I take on the couple of jobs I was asked to cover today, and I've still got forty left from the advance Martha gave me. That leaves me short…'

'I can do the rest.'

'But it's also going to leave me with nothing to live on until I – or you – get my wages from Martin at the end of next week.'

'It's OK, Ben's maintenance payment is due the day after tomorrow, that should see us through. At least we'll manage to eat and give the kids their lunch money.'

Angie's eyes softened. 'I'll pay you back one day, I hope you realize that.'

'Don't worry, I'm counting on it!'

CHAPTER TWENTY-EIGHT

'So you're Grace, are you?' Martha asked, holding a hand out to shake as if she were meeting a visiting dignitary. 'Your mother tells me you're thirteen, but I expect you'd like me to say you look older, so shall we say sixteen?' Her forbidding scowl transformed itself into a winning smile. 'I knew your daddy,' she said, slipping an arm round Grace's shoulder to steer her around to the side of the big Georgian house. 'We had a great fondness for him, you know, and something tells me we'll have the same for you. Are you keeping up?' she asked Angie, casting a quick glance over her shoulder.

'I'm right here,' Angie assured her, loving the way the older lady was making Grace feel so welcome, although only just able to hear her above the roar of the tide across the street.

'You go first,' Martha instructed, standing back so Grace could lead the way up the outside steps to a green front door.

At the top Grace waited for Martha to open up, but she stood aside for Angie to use her key.

'I have a spare for emergencies,' Martha informed them, 'but this is your home for the duration, so it's only right for you to let us in.'

Obediently Angie unlocked the door, aware of how hard her heart was beating, and winking as she caught Grace's eye. Though she was relieved to see her looking better than she'd sounded on the phone this morning, it was clear she still wasn't on great form.

As they stepped into the entry hall Angie immediately felt the warmth embracing them. Martha quickly reached in to turn on the lights, and as Angie looked around at the pale grey walls, vibrant art and half-open doors, she became aware of the pleasing scent of citrus mingled with something decidedly more masculine. It was as if, she thought, Martin had just slipped out and left the scent of himself behind to greet them.

'Shall we start through there?' Martha suggested, pointing them to a set of double doors.

Grace went first, pushing the right-hand one wide and gasping in awe as she took in the sitting room, twice the size of the one in Willow Close. 'Oh Mum, this is amazing,' she murmured, turning to Angie.

Angie had to agree. With the enormous corner sofa piled with downy cushions, non-matching love seat, assortment of other armchairs, exquisite pale green silk wallpaper and towering sash windows that overlooked the bay, she might have thought they'd stepped into the pages of a glossy magazine if the room didn't feel so comfortably lived in.

'Oh wow, look at this,' Grace marvelled, going to inspect the intricately carved marble fireplace that occupied the lower half of an end wall, 'and the mirror is totally awesome.' It rose up over the chimney breast almost to the ceiling, framed in silver filigree and creating a reflection so large it was as though another room was beyond it.

'Even more awesome,' Martha declared with a twinkle in her eyes, 'is this.' Picking up a remote control she pressed a button, and a watercolour of Kesterly Bay transformed itself into a giant TV screen. 'Boys' toys,' she commented to Angie. 'His daughter, Alayna, did the painting, and Luke, his son, had the idea of using it as camouflage. And this lovely wallpaper,' she said to Grace, 'can you guess who put it up?'

Grace's eyes shone. 'Was it my dad?' she asked, flushing with the hope of it.

'It was indeed. So we know it won't fall down any time soon.' Pointing to the old-fashioned steamer trunk that was doubling as a coffee table in front of the sofa, she said, 'All the remotes are in there for the TV and whatever shenanigans it performs, for the music system, the lights… There might even be one for the carpets to whisk you off to Aladdin's cave, who knows? Now, I expect you'd like to see the rest of the place.'

Angie and Grace followed her past a large oak dining table with eight matching chairs to a partially open door at the far end of the sitting room, and into a wide galley-style kitchen with a bar and three stools in front of the arched window and two long walls of flat-fronted white units. Martha pressed various doors and as they swung open she introduced them to ovens, a microwave, a pull-out larder, a fridge-freezer, a recycling unit, a coffee machine, even a warming drawer. The double sink had a tap that produced instant boiling water, she explained.

'The door at the end,' Martha told them, 'leads into a utility room, but you might like to check it out later because I think we have visitors.'

Grace ran to let Emma and the boys in, excited to begin her own guided tour. She ushered them straight into the sitting room and as her brother and cousins gaped open-mouthed at the mega-TV Emma faked a swoon.

'Oh wow, there's a treasure chest,' Jack cried, spotting the steamer trunk with its brass hinges and handles. 'Is there anything in it?' he asked, looking hopefully at Martha.

'Just remote controls, magazines and books, I think,' she replied, 'but you never know with these things. You might have to find out for yourselves what's buried at the bottom because there might be a map to some secret hideaway, but not now,' she said to Angie, 'because himself has instructed me to order in fish and chips for your supper. Is everyone OK with that?'

The boys gazed at her as if she were some sort of Nanny McPhee.

'Who's himself?' Zac whispered to his mother.

'He's the wizard who owns this place,' Martha informed him, 'but don't worry, he's a dud because he can't do any magic.'

Thinking that was exactly what he had done, Angie said, 'We'd all love fish and chips, thank you, but we must pay for it.'

Martha's eyebrows arched as she turned away as if to say, *Nice try, but not happening*. 'It should be here in about twenty minutes,' she announced, glancing at her watch, 'so I'm going to pop down to the office for a while, and I'll bring it up when it arrives.'

As the front door closed behind her Emma turned to Angie, too dumbfounded and entertained to do anything more than laugh. 'She is adorable,' she declared. 'I love her already, and this place… My God, it's like you've suddenly morphed into Julia Roberts and any minute now Richard Gere's going to come through the door calling himself Martin…'

Angie's eyes shot a warning.

'Who's Richard Gere?' Zac asked. 'Is he someone else Dad knows?'

'I've seen that film,' Grace piped up, 'but I can't think what it's called.'

'It doesn't matter,' Angie replied, giving Emma another look.

'Do you think there's a PlayStation?' Jack demanded, pressing a remote control. 'Oh my God! Look at this,' he cried, and everyone laughed as a padded footrest slid out from under the sofa.

'I want to live here,' Harry stated. 'It's totally awesome.'

'We all want to live here,' Emma informed him, 'but I'm afraid you're stuck with the place you've got.'

'Are you going to be living here?' Harry asked Zac.

Zac looked at his mother.

'He'll be staying here, sometimes,' she explained. 'And the rest of the time he'll be with you until we get a place of our own.'

'Can't we have this one?' Grace asked only half mischievously.

Angie's eyebrows rose. 'In our dreams,' she replied. 'Besides, it already belongs to someone, and lovely as it is when we all snuggle up together, we'd soon get fed up of sharing a bed if we had to do it every night.'

'How big is the bed?' Emma wanted to know.

'No idea, we haven't been in there yet. I'm not even sure which door it is. Let's look.'

Back in the hall Angie stumbled first into a cupboard, then a cloakroom with loo and hand basin, before finally pushing open the door to a bedroom that was probably half the size of the sitting room, but presumably every bit as light during the day with its tall sash windows, and seeming, in spite of how neat it was, just as lived in. It was only as Angie looked at the bed with all its masculine yet tasteful blue-grey linens and giant upholstered headboard, that it fully hit her: this was Martin Stone's apartment, his bed, the one he usually slept in and that she would be in tonight…

She felt herself growing hot as she watched Emma flop out like a starfish on the bed, seeming as though she'd happily drown in its sumptuousness, while Grace went to inspect the closets and declared there was plenty of space and hangers for her ballgowns.

This got a laugh from both Angie and Emma, and when they found the en suite bathroom there was even more excitement. It was entirely black apart from the white claw-foot bathtub that was big enough for two, and the oval basins on top of the vanity unit whose mirror lights were so flattering they were managing to make even Angie look beautiful, in spite of how bedraggled she felt.

'Mum! Mum!' Zac cried, rushing in to find her. 'I just took my shoes off and the ground is really warm.'

'We should all have taken our shoes off before we set foot in the place,' Angie stated, 'but it's not too late. Come on, back to the front door everyone.' She needed to get out of this bedroom and give herself a chance to breathe before she ventured in again.

It was past nine o'clock by the time Emma and her boys tore themselves away to go home and Zac changed into his pyjamas before dragging his sleeping bag to the sofa, where he fell asleep almost instantly. Grace went into the bedroom to finish some homework, while Angie cleared up the kitchen. They'd had a riotous fish-and-chip feast with Martha, who had nothing short of a miraculous gift with children. After the boys had got over being completely overawed by her, which had taken all of five minutes, they'd been utterly blown away by her, mostly because of the way she bossed Angie and Emma around. They'd found it hilarious and even tried it themselves, unabashedly egged on by Professor McGonagall, as they now called Martha. Or Prof for short.

It turned out she had three children of her own, and five grandchildren, most of them within a thirty-mile radius of

Kesterly so they were always under her feet, but she was doing her best to talk them into emigrating to America or New Zealand so she'd have somewhere lovely to go for holidays. If she managed it, she would consider taking these three boys on as surrogate grandchildren, and Grace could be her best friend and fashion adviser. Apparently Mr Prof was alive and well, but she was working on a spell to turn him into a younger man.

Now everything was quiet in the apartment, and as Angie stood gazing out at the night, the sea swallowed by darkness, her eyes followed the sweep of the Promenade lights as far as she could see. Her emotions were so high and so mixed she hardly knew what she was thinking or feeling, apart from an overwhelming relief to be here with her two younger children. She wondered about Liam and where he was tonight, if he really was safe.

Would that person ever text again?

She felt an inescapable guilt for having the good fortune to be helped by Martin when not half a mile away there were sad and sorry souls shuffled under benches and in doorways, trying to stay warm for the night. She couldn't see the station, it was too far from here, but in her mind she held the image of herself in the back of the van, parked behind it, never dreaming for a second while she was there that she'd ever set foot in a flat like this, much less be offered it as a refuge.

Her eyes returned to the dense black of the bay with just a pinprick of light on the horizon as a ship slipped away to the open sea. She was sure Steve was watching and telling her to relax. She was trying to, and at some point she was sure she would, but right now she couldn't just forget about the rough sleepers practically on her doorstep, or those in panic about where their lives were going, or the desperate people who didn't even dare to dream anymore. Would they ever be blessed with this sort of good luck? What had she done that they hadn't to deserve it?

Martin had texted during the evening to say he hoped they were settling in and that Martha had told them where to find the wine. How was she ever going to thank him for his kindness? How could she sleep in his bed without constantly thinking about him?

In the bedroom Grace was sitting cross-legged on the floor private-messaging with Lois.

LOIS: *Have you heard anything from A?*

GRACE: *Still nothing.*

LOIS: *Good.*

GRACE: *I feel a bit scared.*

LOIS: *I know what you mean. Did your mum ask you any more about last night?*

GRACE: *No, not yet.*

LOIS: *That's good. Nor mine. Has your memory come back?*

GRACE: *Not really.*

LOIS: *Shame. Or maybe not. If A gets in touch ignore it.*

GRACE: *Don't worry, I will.*

LOIS: *OK. Better go. See you tomorrow.*

It was all right, Grace tried telling herself as she put her phone down and turned to bury her face in the downy quilt with its lovely scent of fresh laundry. No one knew what had happened, not even her, so there wasn't anything to worry about. She just needed to chill and forget all about it.

CHAPTER TWENTY-NINE

Angie found the first week of staying at Martin's flat surreal and crazy on just about every level. There was the bewildering paradox of living in a place of such luxury while undergoing her first brutal sessions with a debt adviser. There was also the sheer awfulness of returning to Willow Close to watch her furniture being carted out, looking as helpless as she'd felt to stop it from happening. It was the worst kind of grounding experience after the headiness of the past few days, a stark reminder of how desperate her financial situation remained.

True to his word Melvin oversaw the removal, making sure everything was carefully handled and stored in a secure area of his company's warehouse. He even encouraged Angie to go and see it for herself, so she'd know exactly where it was and that it was being well looked after. She might have gone had she not had to rush off in Emma's car to spend the evening delivering pizzas dressed as a bloody panda.

What the hell did pandas have to do with pizzas? she'd like to know. *Just please God don't let Martin or Martha call in with an order.* He was back now so it could happen, and she knew she'd simply die if it did.

Fortunately it didn't, but she wasn't so lucky with Amy Cutler, who was amazed and thrilled when Angie Watts turned up at her door looking like Po Ping's girlfriend. Satisfaction didn't even begin to cover it.

'I'm sure I have some bamboo around here somewhere,' she'd said, glancing behind her as if there really might be the odd stalk or two, 'if you don't mind waiting.'

'I'm good, thanks,' Angie said tersely. 'Fifteen pounds will do just fine.'

'Oh, is that how much I owe? No problem,' and delving into her purse she handed over a twenty-pound note. 'Keep the change,' she smiled.

Angie was tempted to slap the five-pound note back at her, but decided it was better in Zac's pocket than in that appalling woman's, so she kept it.

'By the way,' Amy said, as Angie turned to go. 'I thought I should tell you before anyone else does that my friends, Phil Cotter and his wife Jenny, have had their offer accepted on your old house. I'm sure you remember them. They own the dry cleaner's on Manor Road. They're cash buyers, so they'll be able to move in as soon as everything goes through.'

Angie's heart had hit the floor. Yes, she knew the Cotters; they'd stiffed Steve once over a payment of hundreds of pounds, and now they were going to get his house. Where was the justice in that? However, she wasn't going to give Amy Cutler the gratification of a response so she simply walked away, desperately wishing Emma was there to give the woman a thump in the face. Emma wouldn't worry about the consequences the way Angie did.

Knowing that Shalik had already more or less sold the house affected Angie deeply throughout the weekend. She struggled hard to put it out of her mind, to focus only on the many ways in which her life was improving, or was perhaps about to improve, but it seemed her attachment to number 14 had no intention of letting go any time soon. Thinking back over the years she and Steve had spent there with the children, she wondered if she would ever hear any more from the mysterious 'friend' who'd texted assuring her that Liam was safe.

Fortunately, on Monday her double duties at BtG and Stone Construction began in earnest, and kept her so busy that she had little time to think of much else. She already loved working with Martha, learning all about the company and how Martin liked things to be done. She hadn't seen him since his return from London, but when he called in briefly that afternoon he took the time to ask how she was and if everything was OK with the flat.

'We need a catch-up,' he told her as he was leaving. 'Can you look at my diary and schedule yourself in one evening this week that suits you? Say around six? I'll meet you here, if that's OK.'

Without waiting for a reply he ran down the front steps, answering his mobile as he went, and moments later he was driving away in his black BMW.

'Thursday,' Martha announced as Angie walked back into their office. 'He's got something on every night this week, but he's not due at a dinner until eight on Thursday.'

'Is he always so busy?' Angie asked, going to pack up the documents she was about to ferry over to the retirement-village building site. It made her think of Mark Fields, which inevitably took her mind to Hamish and the fact that he'd probably start wondering soon why no one was moving into Hill House to take Fields's place. She and Emma needed answers about the will, so they could plan for the future of the men who didn't even know their home was in jeopardy.

'Yes, he's always busy,' Martha was saying, 'but he likes it that way, keeps him out of trouble, he says. Did he happen to mention that he's spoken to the housing officer on your behalf?'

Angie's eyes rounded as her insides lurched. 'No, he didn't. When?'

'I believe he called last Thursday while he was still in London. He won't have heard back yet because Ronald Cousins, the head honcho, is away until next Monday, but being who he is himself usually gets a pretty quick response. And I believe you're getting together with Andee tomorrow, is that correct?'

Angie nodded, nervous and excited about that too. Someone was finally going to try and help her to find Liam, and not just anyone for it was Martin's ex-wife who she had to admit she was intrigued to meet.

Martha's smile filled with affection. 'She's a lovely woman. You'll like her. Everyone does.'

Though Angie longed to ask why her marriage to Martin had broken up, of course she didn't. It was hardly any of her business, and she'd rather dance naked round Asda than have either Martha or Martin think she was prying into his private affairs.

Now, here she was on Wednesday afternoon at the Seafront Café, sitting opposite Andee Lawrence in the very same booth where she'd sat with Martin only a week ago. It seemed longer, although in other ways it still felt like a dream. As did the surprise of finding out that his ex-wife was none other than the kind woman she'd seen in the supermarket all those weeks ago filling the foodbank box. The woman she'd thought about several times since. She was beautiful, almost mesmerizing, with her soft dark curls, luminous aquamarine eyes and exquisitely shaped face.

After she'd ordered tea from a server she turned to Angie, and Angie felt a pleasing lift inside. She liked this woman instinctively, and could already feel her hopes rising.

'I was really sorry to hear about your difficulties,' Andee said softly. 'I hope you don't mind that Martin told me. I think he wanted me to understand why it's important to try and help you.'

'No, I don't mind,' Angie replied, knowing that she did, but she was hardly in a position to object. 'It's very kind of you to meet me.'

Andee smiled, and Angie couldn't help wondering what on earth had gone wrong between her and Martin. How could he have left this woman when she seemed so perfect? Or perhaps it was the other way round, and she'd left him.

'He knew,' Andee continued, gesturing for the young waiter to set down their tea tray, 'that as soon as he told me you'd lost track of your son I'd want to help. You see, finding missing people was… Well, let's say it was kind of my thing when I was a detective.'

Angie said wryly, 'I hope you don't mind me saying, but you don't look like a detective, or not how I imagine one to look anyway.'

Andee was clearly amused. 'It's been said before,' she replied, 'and I try to take it as a compliment.'

'Oh it is,' Angie assured her, and before she made a fool of herself by trying to tell Andee how she actually did look, she picked up one of the small teapots and filled her cup with the same mixed-berry infusion that Andee had ordered. She'd never had it before, but she liked the smell already. 'I'm guessing he told you who my son is,' she said, bringing them to the sobering reality of why they were there, 'and what happened to his father?'

Andee nodded slowly. 'Yes, he did. Actually, I should probably tell you that I remember your husband quite well. He did some work for me when I first started as an interior designer, and I hired him again when I took on the flats over at the marina. Sadly, he didn't finish them…' She paused as the reason he hadn't came into focus. Her eyes were tender as she said, 'I can't begin to imagine how hard it was for you, or what you've been through since, but as a mother myself I can imagine how desperate you are to find your son.' She didn't add *no matter what he's done or who he is now,* but Angie heard the words anyway.

'Thank you,' she said softly. 'There are some who'd say I'm lucky to be rid of him after what happened, so thank you for not being one of them.'

Andee took a sip of her tea. 'People often make judgements that are best left unspoken,' she replied in a tone that suggested she'd come across it often. She put her cup down. 'Martin mentioned a text.'

Angie took out her phone, called up the message and passed it over.

After reading it Andee checked the sender details and found, as Angie had, that they'd been withheld. 'Do you have *any* idea who might have sent it?' she asked.

Angie shook her head. 'I don't even know if it's genuine. I mean does someone really want me to know he's safe, or are they just trying to mess with my head?'

Andee passed the phone back. 'Don't delete it,' she advised, 'but for the moment there's not much I can do with it. Even if I was still on the force I probably wouldn't get the go-ahead to try and trace it, because it's not threatening or attached to a crime.' Apparently sensing Angie's disappointment, she added, 'In my experience people don't send messages like this if they're trying to mess with your head, or certainly not just the one, so I see no reason not to hope that he really is safe.'

Grateful for the reassurance, Angie held on to it, and said, 'I probably drove the police mad during the months after he vanished. I kept going to the station begging them to try and find out where he was, or who he was with, but they had him down as a gang member, and he was seventeen, so he was never going to be a priority.'

'No, he wouldn't be,' Andee admitted. 'Am I correct in thinking that he was arrested for the attack on his father, but never charged?'

'That's right.'

'But those who were sent down were known to be friends of his? Or fellow gang members?'

Angie couldn't deny it, much as she wanted to. 'They're all local, but we – Steve and I – had read a lot about county lines by then, you know, urban gangs who use local gangs to target vulnerable kids in rural areas… After Liam was released, I guess it's possible those criminals moved him to another area to make him work for them there. Or maybe he's hiding from them somewhere as well as from me.'

Andee said, 'Why would he hide from you?'

Angie's voice faltered as she explained how she'd told her semi-delinquent son that he was dead to her. 'He'd lost his father,' she said wretchedly. 'It's possible he even witnessed what happened and there was nothing he could do to stop it. I don't know if that's true, but it's what I keep telling myself, so when he came home that day he might have been even more traumatized than the rest of us… And I – I didn't even let him in the house.' She turned to stare blindly out of the window, seeing Liam's haggard and frightened face as he'd watched her yelling at him, saying and doing nothing, until he'd finally turned away. 'I was out of my mind back then,' she said quietly. 'I couldn't think straight… I wanted to blame someone…' She swallowed and turned back to Andee. 'Not long before it happened he told my daughter, Grace, that he had to stay working for the gangs in order to protect us. Apparently they threaten people's families if they don't do as they're told.'

'Yes, it's how they operate, I'm afraid.' Andee refilled their cups and held hers in both hands as she thought. 'I have to tell you,' she said, 'that it's unlikely a county line gang is directly responsible for your husband's death. It happened too spontaneously for that, which would be why the police didn't look any further than the members of the estate gang who were arrested the same day. However, I think it's a reasonable concern that after Liam left you that day he was sucked back into the network and sent to work elsewhere. What I need to ask you now is that if we discover he is still involved with them, voluntarily, are you sure you still want to see him?'

Angie stared into Andee's watchful eyes, knowing it was a fair question, an obvious one even, but it wasn't easy to answer when she had Grace and Zac to consider. 'If he is still with them,' she said in the end, 'I really don't believe it would be voluntarily. He has mild mental health issues that make him easy to take advantage of, and it could be that he still thinks he's keeping the rest of us safe.'

Andee nodded her understanding. 'OK,' she said slowly. 'Now, before I talk to the Kesterly police, can you remember who you were dealing with at the time of Liam's arrest?'

Angie shook her head. 'It's all a bit of a blur, I'm afraid, but I'm sure I can find out.'

'It's OK, I can do that.'

'Actually, there is someone,' Angie said, producing her purse. 'It's a detective I saw recently. He wanted Liam's DNA in connection with a crime that had taken place in Bristol. It turned out that he had nothing to do with it…' She handed over the card she'd brought just in case.

Andee smiled. 'Leo Johnson. I know him well. He used to be one of my DCs. I'm sure he'll be willing to help us. To begin with, he'll be able to search the national database to see if Liam's name crops up anywhere else in the country. Of course there's a chance he's changed it, which'll make everything more difficult, but let's cross that bridge when – if – we come to it.' She glanced at her watch. 'You said you had to be somewhere by four?'

Startled by how quickly the time had gone, Angie said, 'Oh yes, I'm picking my youngest son and nephews up from school.' She dug into her purse for some cash to pay and pulled out a ten-pound note. 'I can't thank you enough for seeing me,' she said, putting the money on the table. 'You and Martin have both been so kind... I hardly know...'

'Don't worry about the thanks, or this,' Andee smiled, pushing the money back to her. 'We're both happy to help in any way we can. I'll be in touch as soon as I have some news.'

CHAPTER THIRTY

'Angie? It's Martin. Is this a good time?'

Smiling, because he invariably started a call that way, she said, 'It's fine. How are you?'

'I'm good. I believe we're getting together tomorrow evening, so I was wondering, instead of meeting at the office or the flat, how about a bite to eat?'

Experiencing a jolt of surprise, she paused at the gate to Hill Lodge to take it in. 'I'd love to,' she heard herself say as breezily as if she went out for bites to eat with him all the time. 'I'll just make sure it's OK for both children to stay at Emma's for the night. Actually, you have to be somewhere by eight, don't you? They'll be fine on their own until then.'

'My dinner's been cancelled so I'm free all evening, but if you want to be back by eight…'

'No, I'm sure it'll be OK with Emma.'

'Great. I can fit in with whatever time works for you. Is there anywhere in particular you fancy going?'

'Uh – um...' What sort of place would he like? She mustn't make it too expensive, or too downmarket. Italian? Indian? A pub? 'Why don't you choose?' she said, happily passing it back.

'Sure, I'll give it some thought. Text and let me know when and where to pick you up. You're at Bridging the Gap today, aren't you?'

'Only this morning. I'm with Martha this afternoon and most of tomorrow.'

His tone was droll as he said, 'Good luck with that,' and a moment later he was gone.

Angie remained where she was for a moment longer, absorbing the fact that he'd just invited her out for a meal. It didn't mean anything of course, she realized that, although uppermost in her mind right now was the fact that she hadn't been out with a man since Steve had taken her to the Luttrell Arms in Dunster just before the attack. But it obviously wasn't going to be that sort of occasion, nothing at all to do with romance and grabbing some time together away from kids and the pressures of the day. Martin most likely wanted to know all about her chat with Andee, and how things were going with the lawyer and debt adviser. After the meetings and phone calls she'd had over the past few days she had plenty to tell him on every front, but she must remember not to make it all about her. Good manners alone dictated the need to ask about his business at least, and it would be interesting to know more about his children...

For now, though, she must focus on why she was at Hill Lodge.

Closing the gate behind her, she went to rap on the front door before using her own key to let herself in. Her worry over the details of Carlene Masters' will hadn't gone away, but at least Ivan was in Spain now, attending the funeral, and by the time he came back at the weekend he'd hopefully have some news to put everyone's minds at rest.

'Ah, there you are,' Hamish stated as she entered the lovely warm kitchen to the mouth-watering aroma of something baking. 'Kettle's just about boiled and here's our new friend Sasha, who's very keen to meet you.'

A pale, almost emaciated girl in her early twenties with delicate features and wispy brown hair held out a hand to shake. Angie put real warmth into her smile. 'Hello Sasha,' she said, taking the slender hand, 'I've heard a lot about you.'

Sasha's answering smile showed white, healthy teeth, although a bottom one was missing. 'Hamish and Craig tell me a lot about you too,' she said, in a softly accented voice.

Craig came forward. 'We've made biscuits,' he informed her. He looked prideful, almost confident, something Angie hadn't seen in him before. 'We found the recipe on the back of a cereal box.'

'They're very good,' Hamish declared, sliding them on to a plate ready to bring to the table. 'I've already had two.'

Craig promptly picked up his guitar, strummed a few chords and sang something about special days and breakfast, or that was how it sounded. Angie noticed the shine in his eyes as he watched Sasha busying herself with cups and milk and sugar, while Hamish filled the big red teapot with boiling water.

Was it her imagination, or was Hamish avoiding her eyes?

'Sit down, sit down,' he urged, waving her to the table. 'Like I said in my text we have something to tell you, and I think you might need to be off your feet when you hear it.'

Surprised, and not a little perturbed, Angie pulled out a chair and glanced over to the sitting room. 'Are Lenny and Alexei at work?' she asked.

'Both up and out at the crack of eggs,' Hamish replied, setting the teapot on its cast-iron stand and tapping Craig on the shoulder. This was apparently Craig's cue to put down his guitar and pay attention.

Angie watched as Hamish filled each mug and Sasha did the honours with milk and sugar. Craig helped himself to a biscuit, and earned a scolding from Sasha for forgetting his manners. He immediately offered the biscuit to Angie minus a small bite at the top.

With a fond roll of her eyes, Sasha pushed down his hand and held out the plate of cornflake cookies.

'So,' Angie said once everyone was seated around the table and, oddly, looking at her as though she was supposed to get things started, 'I can't wait to hear what this is all about.'

Hamish looked at no one as he said, 'Actually it's Craig and Sasha who have some news.'

Angie immediately flashed on pregnancy and almost lost her smile.

'Craig,' Sasha prompted gently. 'You say you want to tell her.'

Craig looked at Angie and took a deep breath as if he were about to sing again. 'We are going to live in Hartcliffe,' he announced in a rush. Then, more slowly, 'Me and Sash are going to live in Hartcliffe.'

Angie's eyes moved from him to Sasha and on to Hamish who was staring down at his tea. 'Where's Hartcliffe?' she asked carefully.

'Is Bristol,' Sasha replied. 'I have friend there who offer us place to live and job for me in factory where she also work.'

Already seeing at least some of the problems this presented, Angie said to Craig, 'Do you want to move to Bristol?'

He gave a definite nod.

'But what about your job at the care home?'

Sasha said, 'My friend say he can play guitar in band that looks for someone like him.'

Angie's heart sank. That couldn't possibly be true, but she could hardly say so in front of Craig. She fixed Sasha with a look she hoped would transmit the doubt without Craig picking up on it.

'The band watch him on YouTube,' Sasha explained. 'They like his old music that Hamish teach him.'

Wishing she knew how worried to be, apart from very, Angie let her gaze return to Hamish. 'What do you think?' she asked him.

He cleared his throat and picked up his tea. 'I say it's wrong to stand in the way of young people and their dreams,' he replied in a tone that told Angie he didn't mean it. 'Good opportunities don't come along very often, so we have to take them when they do.'

Realizing how upset he was, Angie turned back to Sasha. 'Is this *really* a good opportunity?' she asked bluntly.

Sasha's tone was sanguine. 'We hope so,' she answered. 'Is hard to know for certain until we get there, but we think, me and Craig, is worth the risk.'

Craig said, 'It isn't good for Sasha to stay here. Bad people are out to get her.'

Angie looked at Sasha.

'I was sex worker,' the girl said frankly, 'and I run away, but first time they find me and make me go back. They grab me in front of Craig and he think is his fault. But is not his fault.' She glanced down at her clenched hands with their silver rings and chipped nails. 'I escape again after,' she said quietly, 'that is how I am here, but they still look for me.' She swallowed and added hoarsely, 'They make me do terrible things.'

Angie could imagine what sort of things, and felt as sickened by them as if they'd happened to her. How close had she really come to taking Shalik's route out of her misery? She wondered if he was the monster behind Sasha's exploitation, and felt almost certain that he was involved in some way.

Wishing she could ask what Craig and Sasha's relationship really was, like siblings, lovers, just friends, she said to Sasha, 'He'll need help registering for benefits when you get there, and you know about his episodes. He needs special care...'

'He will have me,' Sasha declared, putting a hand on Craig's and squeezing it tightly.

Angie waited for Craig to withdraw, but to her surprise he didn't. If anything he seemed happy about the physical contact, in fact about everything that was happening, and since he was free to come and go as he pleased, all she could think of to say next was, 'When are you planning to make the move?'

Craig said, 'We are going today.'

Stunned, Angie looked at Hamish and her heart turned over to see how bereft he was already feeling. He'd come to think of this young lad as the son he'd never had, and he clearly didn't want him to go. However, it didn't seem he was going to try and stand in his way.

Sasha said softly, 'I promise I will take good care of him. He very special to me, and I know he to you, so I not let anything bad happen to him.'

'And I will take care of Sasha,' Craig informed them.

Hardly knowing what else to say, Angie went for the simplest option. 'How are you getting to Bristol?'

'On coach,' Sasha told her. 'Is cheaper than train.'

Hamish suddenly said, 'In case you hadn't noticed, time's getting on. I thought you said the bus goes at midday.'

Giving Hamish a sorrowful look, Sasha got to her feet. 'I understand is hard to say goodbye to someone you love...'

'Do you want a hand down with your things?' Hamish asked Craig.

Ten tense minutes later Craig and Sasha were on their way

out of the door with brief hugs and promises to stay in touch, even to come back and visit. Angie stood watching them struggle to the gate with Craig's three boxes and guitar. She wondered if she should offer to take them to town in the van, but decided that Hamish was her priority right now.

Going back to the kitchen she found him clearing the table, his head down and seeming slightly shaky. She wanted to comfort him, but hugging him would embarrass them both, so she simply said, 'Can I give you a hand?'

'He'll be fine,' he responded stiffly, as though it was what she'd asked.

'Yes,' she agreed, because she had to.

He glanced at the Mickey Mouse clock he'd repaired and hung on the wall after Craig had found it somewhere and wanted to make it work. 'He forgot that,' he said, 'and look at the time. I've a lot to be getting on with and I expect you have too.'

Understanding that he wanted to be alone, Angie picked up her bag and said, 'Don't forget to call if you need anything.'

He nodded awkwardly, and realizing he was in a hurry for her to go now, she went to let herself out.

Grace and Lois were at the back of the school canteen huddled over Grace's mobile, hardly daring to breathe as they opened a message that had arrived during double History. This had been their first opportunity to read it.

The instant Grace saw what came on to the screen she let out a cry of horror and slammed the phone to her chest.

Having seen enough to utter a gasp of her own, Lois muttered, 'What the fuck?' She'd turned almost as pale as Grace and looked just as frightened.

Grace tried to swallow. The roar and clatter in the room was suddenly deafening, the heat unbearable. The image on her phone screen was still burning her eyes. She wanted to scream and cry, to curl up in a ball and die.

Lois quickly said, 'Come on, we need to get out of here.'

Minutes later, having fled along the hall and down two sets of stairs, they were in the library with the glass doors closed and a book lodged between the handles to stop anyone else coming in.

Lois looked at the phone still pressed to Grace's chest. 'Is there a message with it?' she asked frantically.

Grace couldn't bear to look. If she did she'd have to see herself again, with nothing on. *Oh God, oh God, oh God!*

'Shall I check?' Lois offered.

Finally, because she had to, Grace peeled the phone away from herself and snatched another quick glance at the screen. It had faded to black, so she pressed the home button and looked again. It was still there, that terrible, shocking picture that *she* was in…

'Hang on,' Lois cried, grabbing the phone from her, 'that's not you. I mean it's your face, it's one of your portfolio shots, but look at the size of those boobs. They're not yours. Someone's Photoshopped this.'

Grace looked at it in horror. Lois was right, they weren't her boobs, hers were less than half the size, but it was definitely her face and if anyone saw it they'd think it was her.

'Scroll down,' Lois insisted, doing her best to stay calm.

Grace did as she was told, and found another shot even worse than the first, with legs open and back arched, her face attached. 'Oh God, I can't,' she choked, passing the phone to Lois. 'You do it.'

After three more equally explicit shots, stuff that belonged on the dark web, Lois thought, she finally came to a message and as she read it her eyes bulged in horror.

Grace pressed her face into her hands. 'What does it say?' she groaned desperately.

Even though they were alone in the room, Lois read in a whisper:

Congratulations Grace, you've passed the audition and here are some lovely shots for your portfolio. There are others, but we thought these were the best so we've shared them with our backers and everyone is keen to see much more of you.

You will receive a text in the morning with an address of where to report for your first day of shoot. I know you won't let us down or tell anyone else about this. If you do I'm sure you can work out what will happen. Please give my best to your mum, A ☺ #SAVINGGRACE

Grace's eyes were burning with terror as she and Lois looked at one another. They had no idea what to do.

'You can't go,' Lois told her.

Grace shook her head.

'I mean, you really can't.'

'No,' Grace said hoarsely. 'But what if…'

'She's bluffing.'

Grace didn't understand.

'She won't post those shots for everyone to see. Apart from anything else *it's not you*, and she's the one who'd get into trouble for posting them, not you.'

'But how would they find her?'

Lois struggled for an answer. 'They won't have to,' she declared, 'because she won't do anything.'

Grace took the phone and turned it off, as though this could in some way erase what was on it.

They both jumped as someone tried to open the door. To Grace's horror it was at least four of the Northsider gang, laughing and bobbing up and down and pointing at her as if…

'Oh my God,' she cried, seizing Lois's hand, 'do you think they've seen them?'

'No! No, they can't have,' Lois insisted only marginally less panicked. 'She said she won't post anything if you go tomorrow, and it's still today.'

The bullies moved away, and Grace turned her tormented eyes back to Lois. 'I'll have to go,' she said shakily. 'If I don't...'

'You can't. Think what might happen...'

'What else can I do?' Grace shouted. 'If anyone sees those pictures, if my mum does, it'll totally do her head in and with everything else she's got going on...'

'Stop!' Lois cried urgently. She was thinking fast. 'We know they drugged you last time, so what if they do it again?'

'Thanks for that,' Grace cried in a fury.

Lois raised her hands to calm her down. 'Sorry, I was just saying... But don't worry, we'll think of something.'

'Like what?'

'I don't know yet, but cross my heart, hope to die, we definitely will.'

CHAPTER THIRTY-ONE

Angie was worrying about so much as she turned into the small car park in front of Martin's office – Grace and how distracted she'd seemed this morning on the way to school, Hamish and how he was coping with Craig's departure, the extremely alarming call she'd just received from the debt adviser – that she almost drove straight into Martin's BMW on its way out. Quickly hitting her brakes she began reversing into the traffic, only stopping when he tooted his horn and waved her in.

She did as instructed, and pulled up next to Martha's Golf as he gave another friendly toot before zooming off to whatever meeting or inspection or evaluation was next on his schedule.

Or maybe, given the time of day and the person in the BMW's passenger seat, he was on his way to a more social event. The woman, although glimpsed only briefly, was blonde and beautiful and had appeared very comfortable with where she was, next to Martin.

Maybe that was who the toiletries belonged to in his bathroom, and if it was she wondered how long they'd been together, how serious it was, if she could ask Martha about her without making it seem she was more interested than she was. The trouble with Martha was that almost nothing got past her, and even if Angie wanted to deny she felt attracted to Martin – who wouldn't be? – she knew Martha would tune in right away.

So she wouldn't ask, because it was none of her business, and she had far too much on her mind already. Wasting her time on the blonde in the car would do absolutely nothing to sort out the terrible shock she'd just had about her council-tax debt.

Checking her phone as she went into the office she found a text from Grace letting her know that she'd be staying at Lois's. She quickly forwarded it to Emma so she wouldn't expect her niece for tea, and looked around for Martha.

'In here,' Martha called out from Martin's office, as though she had eyes that could see through walls. 'There's a set of drawings on your desk to go over to the retirement village, but have yourself a cup of tea first.'

Shrugging off her coat while composing replies to various emails in her head, Angie took herself into the kitchen and began rinsing out the mugs in the sink. Noticing a faint lipstick mark on one that presumably belonged to the blonde in Martin's car, she wondered if she should wear lipstick when she met him later. The idea caused a tightening of nerves to shoot through her like a firework. She didn't want to send any wrong signals and make herself look foolish, but on the other hand she ought to make a bit of an effort. She'd already planned to pop over to Emma's later to drag a box of clothes from the attic in search of a decent top or dress, and hopefully she'd have time to wash and blow-dry her hair before he picked her up.

'Did you see Martin on your way in?' Martha asked, back at her desk now.

'I almost drove into him,' Angie confessed.

Martha's tone was wry as she said, 'That would have been awkward.'

Angie chuckled. 'Tea or coffee?'

'Tea, thanks. He's booked a table at Luca's over at the marina for seven, but it can easily be changed if the time doesn't work for you.'

'That fine,' Angie replied, more than a little relieved to know the evening was still as planned. 'I'll be at the flat so I can meet him here.'

'You need to tell him that, not me. Have you seen my glasses? I've put them down somewhere…'

'On your head.'

Martha felt for them and broke into a laugh. 'First signs,' she declared cheerily. 'Now, I've got a – ah, here it is.' She held up a small brown envelope. 'Fifty pounds petrol money. Can't have you out of pocket with all the running around you're doing. If you need more, just holler.'

Carrying over the tea, Angie thanked her and picked up the envelope. It was far more welcome than Martha could have known, for she'd been planning to take the bus to the retirement village, then another to Emma's for a dress and yet another back into town. This would save her at least an hour and a half, so barring mishaps or emergencies she should be able to make herself nice and presentable for a meal at Luca's.

First, though, she'd better text Martin to confirm the time. As the marina was so close she would suggest she walked over and met him there.

His message came back an hour later. *Great idea to walk. We'll go together and I'll leave my car at the office.*

* * *

Angie was ready and waiting by a quarter to seven, having changed in and out of all four dresses she'd brought from Emma's at least a dozen times, unable to decide which one was right. Too short, too frumpy, too daring, too old… In the end she'd decided on a black silk-blend shift with a discreet crystal neck chain and her kitten-heel ankle boots. Steve had always insisted she had great legs – not long, but perfectly shaped, he'd said – though she was sure he'd pronounce them too skinny now. He also used to tease her that her bottom was irresistible, and that actually she was even more beautiful out of clothes than in, so perhaps she ought to give them up – at least when it was just the two of them at home.

She smiled to herself as the memories came up to make her feel happy and sad, and perhaps a little more confused about this evening than was good for her. However, the upside of holding on to thoughts of Steve was the way it made her feel more confident in her appearance than she had for a very long time. Though her hair was its usual tumble of soft red curls, this evening instead of scraping them back in a messy ponytail she was allowing them to fall loosely around her face and shoulders, with a glittery clip holding them back to one side. She'd have asked Grace to come and style it for her if it hadn't meant Grace would end up spending the evening here in the flat alone. She'd have more fun at Lois's.

Feeling a twist of nerves as a text jingled into her mobile she saw it was from Hamish and opened it. *Craig and Sasha have arrived safely in Bristol. Better late than never.* This last comment told her, as if she didn't already know, that he'd been waiting for the message like an anxious parent needing to have his mind put at rest.

Thanks for letting me know, she texted back, and she'd have tried to think of more to say if Martin hadn't just driven into the forecourt below.

Her nerves were still annoyingly jumpy as she quickly put on the only coat she had and raised the hood before making her way down the outside steps to meet him.

'Hey,' he said, coming to shield her with an enormous umbrella. 'Maybe we should go by car?'

'But the rain's not heavy,' she pointed out, 'and it'll only take us a few minutes to get there.'

'OK, you're the boss,' and holding out an arm for her to take, he tucked hers in closely and set off in the direction of the marina.

It did indeed take only a few minutes to reach Luca's – a cosy trattoria overlooking the south side of the marina where most of the leisure boats were moored – and for just about every step of it he was on the phone. Angie didn't mind, conversation at this point would have been difficult against the roar of the waves and speeding traffic, and she was quite enjoying holding his arm and listening to him giving instructions or opinions to the person – it sounded like an architect – at the other end.

'Sorry about that,' he said, ending the call as they arrived under the restaurant awning. 'I'll turn it off now, and I've asked Luca to give us a table where we're less likely to be interrupted. I'm afraid it's one of the drawbacks of being out with me, I never seem able to go anywhere without running into at least half a dozen people I know.'

Finding that easy to believe, Angie assured him she didn't mind and watched with amusement as the instant they stepped inside the restaurant he was greeted like a long-lost brother by a short, portly and very effusive Italian.

'Luca, this is my friend Angie,' Martin told him. 'Angie, this is Luca. Try not to mind if he flirts with you, he can't help himself.'

'For the ladies it is necessary,' Luca assured him, and taking Angie's hand he treated it to a flamboyant kiss.

The place already seemed full to bursting – how different it was at this end of the Promenade to the station end, Angie couldn't help thinking – but after their coats were taken Luca himself showed them to a beautifully laid table set into a niche towards the back of the noisy room. No sooner had their candle been lit and menus produced than Martin's phone rang.

'Sorry, I thought it was off,' he grimaced, and without checking who it was he kept his promise and closed it down.

Feeling she should do the same, she was taking hers from her bag when a server came to speak quietly into Martin's ear, and Martin immediately looked out across the restaurant.

'My ex-mother-in-law,' he explained to Angie, 'I ought to go and say hello. I'll be right back.'

Realizing it must be Andee's mother, Angie tried to get a glimpse of the woman, but Martin's retreating back was blocking the way. However she did see how warmly he greeted her and the man she was with.

Deciding to use these few minutes to text goodnight to the children, Angie pressed the home button on her phone and noticed that Grace had tried to call about fifteen minutes ago. It would have been while she was walking here so she wouldn't have heard it ring in her bag, and now wasn't a good time to call back unless there was a message requesting this. There wasn't, so she sent texts to both children telling them she loved them and wishing them goodnight. To Grace she added, *I should be home by ten, if you're still awake call me then.*

Nightmare! Nightmare! Nightmare!

Lois was standing in the doorway of her parents' sitting room, phone in hand as she watched the *Corrie* credits roll. There was no point trying to talk to her mother while the programme was on, but now it had ended Becky turned to offer her full attention.

'Are you OK?' she asked. 'You look like you've seen a ghost.'

Lois's hand tightened on her phone as she said, 'I can't get hold of Grace. She's not answering my messages or my calls.'

Puzzled, Becky said, 'Have you two had a falling-out?'

Lois shook her head impatiently.

'Maybe she's out somewhere with her mum?'

Becky looked down at her phone and taking a deep breath, she said, 'I don't think so. I mean…' Her eyes came up, bright with fear. 'Mum, there's something I have to tell you…'

Angie was telling Martin about her meetings with the debt adviser, Rudi Granger, trying hard not to feel embarrassed by her misery, but feeling it anyway. 'He has everything now,' she said, 'but I have to see him again to go through something that came to light today.'

Martin cocked an interested eyebrow, but she waved a dismissive hand. She wasn't going to mention the horrific increase in her council-tax debt; she wasn't even going to think about it, at least not tonight.

'OK,' he said, 'I'm glad he's turning out to be helpful,' and seeming still to be mulling it he picked up his wine. It was white and came from the same region of Italy as Luca – Timorasso, Angie thought he'd said, but he might have been referring to the name of the grape rather than the place. It was delicious, anyway; she just had to make sure she didn't have too much and end up saying more than she should.

'And Jerome's going to appear in court for you?' he prompted.

Angie tried not to wince. 'He says I don't need to be there. He's going to pay the outstanding bill – I've already given him the money – and then he'll explain my situation in the hope of reducing the fine.'

Martin's intense eyes were studying her closely, seeming to see, she felt, more than she wanted him to. It wasn't making her uncomfortable exactly, but she'd very much like to start steering the subject away from the mess she was in. Before she could attempt it, he said, 'Tell me more about Roland Shalik and the eviction.'

Smarting, she tried to work out how to voice the worst of her humiliations without sounding bitter or pathetic, but before she could begin he told her, 'I knew Hari, his father, pretty well. He was a good man, tough but fair, and I know how fond he was of Steve. Everyone did, including Roland, so I wouldn't be surprised if there was some jealousy there.'

Though Angie had long suspected this herself, she still had to say, 'Whatever nastiness Shalik has going on in his head, and I know there's plenty of it, I can't get away from the fact that I fell behind with the rent. And everything he's done to get me out has been above board; he gave me all the proper notices, he even offered to lend me money or find me somewhere else to live.'

Martin's expression showed what he thought of that. 'I can guess which properties he had in mind,' he said, 'and most would be on the north side of the Temple Fields estate, so you were right to turn them down. Please tell me you didn't accept a loan from him.'

'I didn't,' she confirmed, 'but I came very close. I even…' She faltered, realizing she was about to go a step too far with her admissions. He didn't need to know that things had got so bad she'd actually considered working for Shalik – and as recently as the morning she'd ambushed him, Martin, at the Seafront Café.

Seeming to suspect at least something of what she'd been about to say, Martin shook his head as if further condemning Shalik. 'It beats me how someone like Hari could have had such a thoroughly unpleasant son,' he commented. 'Nothing I ever hear about him is good, that's for sure, and plenty of it is downright despicable.'

Angie was on the point of telling him about Sasha, but since she didn't actually know if Shalik had been the one to exploit her she decided to let it go; the last thing she wanted this evening was to start discussing Shalik's involvement in vice.

After the waiter had ground pepper over their starters, Martin asked, 'Do you still have all the paperwork leading up to the eviction?'

Trying not to wince at the second use of the word, she said a simple 'Yes', while thinking if they had to keep talking about Shalik she was going to lose her appetite.

'I'd like to see it,' he explained. 'Can you bring it to the office?'

Knowing she didn't want anyone to see it, least of all him, she said, 'The lawyer has it right now, so if you're thinking there might be something I missed I'm sure he'd have picked it up.'

He didn't disagree. 'OK, I'll give him a call. Is your furniture still in the house, by the way?'

She shook her head. 'We moved it out last Friday. A friend of my sister's has it stored in his warehouse. He sells kitchens…'

'What's his name?'

'Melvin Humphries. He lives…'

'I know Melvin. We're about to award him a big contract to fit out the apartments in the new retirement village.'

Angie felt a beat of pleasure for Melvin, and relief that she hadn't had to try and put in a good word for him – Emma's last instruction before they'd parted company earlier. Emma had also behaved as if Angie were going on a date tonight, which had ended up making Angie lose her temper.

'Just stop!' Angie had snapped at her. 'It's not a joke and if you liken me to Eliza Doolittle or Cinderella or some other absurd fairy-tale airhead again, I'll whack you.'

Emma had laughed. 'Why don't you just loosen up and make up your mind to enjoy yourself? He's an attractive man who's taking an interest in you...'

'It's not that sort of interest, and the reason he's helping me is because of Steve.'

'OK, because of Steve, but he doesn't have to take you to dinner to find out how his rescue mission is going, does he?'

Though Angie had bristled at *rescue mission* she'd forced herself to let it go, because Emma was right of course. He didn't have to take her to dinner, in fact he didn't have to do anything for her at all, but she was beginning to understand just how unconventional and generous and unselfconsciously charming Martin was. He would take her, a virtual stranger, to dinner just as he would take one of his children, or a client, or anyone else if it was that time of day and he was hungry.

'I'm hoping to hear back from the chief housing officer next week,' Martin was saying, 'but I'm already reliably informed that there are only half a dozen council-owned properties on the Fairweather estate, which was where I was hoping to swing it. They're all occupied at the moment, and I'm not being led to believe that one will come free any time soon. Having said that, until I hear from them we won't know what is, or isn't, possible. I just want you to be prepared for the likelihood that you will have to leave the estate.'

Angie's heart clenched as she attempted a smile. 'I've been trying to prepare myself for that for a while,' she assured him, 'but I don't think it'll really sink in until I actually know where we're going.'

'Well, wherever it is we'll make sure it's not a temporary B & B, because we all know that temporary in those circumstances can mean two years or more with no kitchen and shared facilities.'

Feeling embarrassed and anxious again, Angie was grateful for the interruption of their plates being cleared to make room for the main course. She couldn't stop thinking of how beholden she was to this man, of how few people were swept clear of the gutter, as she had been, just as they were falling into it. How was she ever going to repay him? How long would his patience and generosity last?

'Have I upset you?' he asked softly.

She looked up in surprise, and seeing he meant it she smiled. 'Not at all,' she replied. 'I was just wallowing in the shame of what I've brought on myself, and how fortunate I am to be where I am… I don't mean here, in this restaurant, well I do, of course, because it's lovely, but I'm thinking of the flat, the job with Martha and how much you're paying me… There are so many people out there right now, this minute, in far worse situations than I even want to imagine, and I keep wondering who's helping them. The answer is no one, of course, or certainly no one like you.'

Though his eyes were gentle, they were starting to dance. 'So is this you asking me to rescue the whole town?' he asked.

She smiled again. 'Sorry, I just couldn't help thinking that way.'

'It's OK, I understand, and it's not that they don't matter, because of course they do, but just for now can you try to look a little less glum or people will think I'm boring you.'

She had to laugh, and as the moments of sad reflection receded she picked up her glass to drink more wine.

'Now I'm going to ask about Andee,' he told her. 'I find that's always a good way to go when things get awkward.' She wasn't sure whether he meant that, or was being ironic. 'She filled me in on your meeting after it happened,' he said, 'but have you heard anything from her since?'

Angie shook her head. 'Before I left she said it would probably take a while, so I'm not expecting anything yet.'

Apparently unsurprised by this, he sat back in his chair as their mains arrived – for her a pine-nut-crusted sea bass, for him a succulent *tagliata* (one of Steve's favourites).

'I was wondering,' she said, picking up her fork, 'how much your mother is enjoying having you around?'

Clearly amused by the question, he said, 'She took off for Majorca the weekend after I moved in, so she's not getting the real benefit of it. Anyway, it's her grandchildren she really loves having under her feet. Luckily my sister's kids are not far away, so she gets to see them more regularly than my two.' He went on, more gently, 'Do your children have grandparents?'

She shook her head. 'My mum would have adored them, and Steve's mum definitely did, but she passed away five years ago. It was awful, we were all very close to her, but at least she didn't see how bad things got with Liam, or what happened to her son.' Before he could respond in any way, she said, 'We can't keep talking about me; apart from it being all doom and gloom I really don't want people to think I'm boring you. So please can we talk about something else for a while?'

Grinning, he said, 'Sure. Do you have anything in mind or shall we just see where things go?'

She shrugged, a show of nonchalance that she didn't actually feel. 'Why don't you tell me more about you and your family?' she suggested. 'I know your dad was one of the most popular mayors we've had in Kesterly, so do you ever think about following in his footsteps?'

He gave a cry of laughter. 'Good God no. Unlike him I can't stand politics, so believe me, the town is safer if I stick with building up his business.'

'Did you always work for him?'

'No, in fact I never did. It passed to me when he died and

because I knew it was what he and my mother wanted – and because Andee and the children were here in Kesterly – I decided to move back and do the right thing.'

Puzzled, she said, 'So where were you before that?'

Sighing, he picked up his wine and studied it for a while. 'I guess you could say I was out there screwing up my life.' He smiled ruefully and drank. 'Of course I didn't see it that way at the time,' he continued. 'I thought I was… Hell, I don't know what I thought I was, apart from pretty damned clever and living the life I'd always wanted, regardless of what it was doing to anyone else.'

'And it wasn't the life you'd always wanted?' she ventured.

He shook his head and shrugged. 'I guess I did for a while, or at least I thought I did. Andee and I met at sixth-form college, here in Kesterly. We moved to London together, started a family, and when she set her heart on becoming a detective – following in her father's footsteps – I decided to sort myself out with a job working from home so I could take care of the kids. It all went along fairly well for a good many years, but over time I got to hate being a house husband. I might well have had to lump it if I hadn't made a success of an Internet security system I created while waiting for the kids to come home, but I did make a success of it, and when I was bought out by an American company it kind of went to my head. Not in a good way, I hasten to add. I decided I'd had enough of living with a woman who was married to her job, and kids who were teens by then and hardly ever at home. It was time for me, I told myself, and so off I went into the big wide world to get a taste of what freedom felt like.'

Quietly stunned by this, Angie said, 'So you just upped and left your family?'

He nodded. 'That's what I did, and now it's hard to put into words just how ashamed I am of it, and how much I regret it.'

'So how did Andee manage after you left?'

'With difficulty for the first year or so. She had money, I made sure of that, but it's not everything, in fact it doesn't even come close when you're feeling betrayed, abandoned, furious, trapped… She felt a lot of things that weren't good, especially towards me, and who can blame her? Then she got herself transferred from the Met to Kesterly CID and things slowly started to get easier for her. Her father had already passed away by then, but her mother was here, my parents too, of course, so they helped with the children while I carried on swanning around the globe on my freedom trip. Then my father died and when I came back to sort out the funeral I saw Andee and I realized straight away what a terrible mistake I'd made. I still loved her – actually I kind of knew that all along – and I'd missed out on so much of the children's lives that I knew even then that I'd never forgive myself. I thought they'd never forgive me either, any of them, but luckily for me they did.' His eyes had lost focus as he gazed at his memories and Angie could sense the remorse in him almost as deeply as she felt her own for sending Liam away.

'I wish,' he went on sombrely, 'that I could tell you it wasn't too late, that when Andee agreed to marry me after all those years of living together followed by a pointless separation we went on to live happily ever after, but I'm afraid it didn't work out like that. Oh, she married me, but only because it was what everyone wanted. You could say she sacrificed her own happiness for the sake of mine and the children's and our families', and I let her, even though I knew she didn't love me any more, or certainly not in the way she once had, or in the way I loved her. Added to that was the fact that she'd met someone else. She gave him up when I asked her to marry me, but her feelings for him…' He took a breath as he raised his eyes back to hers. 'He's a good guy, and frankly he deserves her far more than I do, because I can't see him walking out on her the way I did, or letting her put his happiness before her own.'

Thinking of how no one, no matter who they were, escaped mistakes, or pain, or betrayal, even tragedy, Angie said softly, 'Are they married now?'

He shook his head. 'They live together, in the garden district, and they're kind of in business together as well. He used to be an antique dealer until his partner took over that side of things; now he's a full-time property developer. She does most of the interior design for his projects, and now and again, usually when the project is something big like the marina, or the retirement village, Stone Construction is his go-to builder.'

'So you have a good relationship with him?'

'Sure. I like him and I've got a lot of time for his ideas as well as his business sense. Besides, in a town as small as this it would make for very uncomfortable living if we didn't get along, and I wouldn't want to inflict that on Andee, or my kids, or their grandmothers.'

Wishing there was a way to erase the sadness from his eyes, Angie dared to say, 'And all would be fine if you didn't still love her?'

There was a moment of stillness before he replied, and she was afraid she'd gone too far. Then he raised his glass and saluted her, as though congratulating her on her insight.

'What about you?' she asked after a while. 'Have you met someone else since?'

He cocked a lazy eyebrow. 'I did when I was travelling,' he said, 'but since I've been back, or I should say since Andee and I broke up…' His eyes rolled self-mockingly. 'I won't say there's never been anyone, because that wouldn't be true, but…'

When he let the sentence hang, Angie prompted him, 'But they're not Andee?'

He didn't deny it. 'Actually what I was going to say is that I don't think I'm much of a catch when I'm clearly still carrying a torch for my ex, which I suppose is the same thing.'

She thought it probably was, and deciding to go further, she said, 'I saw you with someone earlier, in your car?'

He frowned as he thought, then laughed. 'Oh, you mean Bel. Apart from being married to a good friend of mine, she's making a name for herself converting old farm buildings into desirable residences. We get together every now and again so she can run ideas past me. Today was one of those days.' He nodded towards her plate. 'Are you going to finish that?' he asked.

She looked down and smiled. There wasn't even a single crumb of crust left.

'Hello, I'm sorry if I'm interrupting.'

Angie looked up to see an elegant older woman with well-styled salt and pepper hair standing by them, smiling.

'I'm Maureen, Andee's mother,' she introduced herself. 'And you're Angie Watts?'

'That's right,' Angie replied, almost toppling the table as she tried to stand. 'It's lovely to meet you.'

'Oh no, don't get up. I hope you don't mind but Andee told me about your meeting, so I wanted to come and tell you that I hope you find your son.'

Touched and surprised, since this woman must surely know the circumstances of Liam's disappearance, Angie said, 'Thank you. That's really kind of you.'

Maureen patted her arm, and blowing a kiss Martin's way she went to put on the coat Luca was holding out for her.

Martin said, 'Her daughter, Andee's sister, disappeared when she was fourteen, so Maureen knows how it feels to lose a child that way.'

Angie's heart immediately went out to Maureen Lawrence. 'Did they ever find her?' she asked.

He nodded. 'It's a long story, probably for another time, but yes, they found her.'

'Not…?'

'No, not dead, far from it, but… Well, let's just say she was a very different person. Now please tell me you're going to eat a lovely big dessert, so I won't feel guilty if I do.'

It wasn't until they were outside the restaurant, walking back towards the Promenade, that Martin turned his phone on again to call a taxi to take him home. As he ordered it Angie switched her own on, not expecting any messages, but when she saw all the missed calls from Emma she came to a dead stop. 'Something's happened,' she said shakily, and quickly swiped to ring Emma back. 'Oh hell, my battery's gone.'

'What's her number?' Martin asked, opening up the numerical screen on his phone.

Angie told him and took his mobile as the call connected. 'It's me,' she told Emma. 'What's happened?'

'I'm not sure,' Emma replied, but the tone of her voice sent Angie's nerves spiralling. 'Just tell me, have you heard from Grace this evening?'

'No. I mean, yes, earlier, but… She's with Lois tonight.'

'Lois doesn't know where she is. She came over when Grace didn't answer her phone.'

'What do you mean? What the hell's going on?'

'That's what we're trying to find out. Things have been happening that we didn't know about, but right now we need to know if she's at the flat. Are you there?'

'No, but I'm only a few minutes away.'

'Go and check. If she is, great, if she isn't, you need to come here.'

Angie was running even before she rang off.

'What is it?' Martin asked, keeping pace.

'They don't know where Grace is,' she told him, her heart

fracturing around the words. 'She's supposed to be with her friend... Oh God, there are no lights on. I don't think she's there.'

'Go up and check,' he instructed. 'I'll wait here for the taxi. We've both had too much to drink to drive.'

Angie raced up to the front door, dropped the keys, fumbled them into the lock and was already yelling for Grace as she stepped inside. Every room was in darkness, and turning on all the lights didn't make a difference.

She wasn't there.

CHAPTER THIRTY-TWO

Angie was in the taxi beside Martin and somehow made herself let go of his phone as he put it on to speaker to take over the call to Emma.

'So when did anyone last see her?' he asked, his firm tone helping Angie to feel a little calmer.

'Apparently she went to Lois's after school,' Emma replied, 'but then she left, telling Lois she was sleeping here tonight.'

'Did she come to yours?' Angie asked, as if it could make a difference now.

'If she did I wasn't here. The first I knew of anything being wrong was when Lois called me about eight o'clock to say she was worried that Grace wasn't answering her phone. When I couldn't get an answer either I rang Lois back and...'

'Is Lois there?' Martin interrupted. 'Can you put her on?'

'Melvin's taken her and her mother to the police station so she can tell them what she knows.'

Angie's head spun. *They were talking to the police? This*

was a nightmare that had to end now. 'And what *does* she know?' she cried, feeling Martin's hand steadying hers.

Before Emma could answer Martin, mindful of the driver, said, 'We're less than two minutes away. Let's talk when we get there.'

As he ended the call, Angie said, 'Maybe we should be going to the police station. If Lois is there…'

'Let's see Emma first,' he advised. 'We need as clear a picture on this as we can get to be able to make the right decisions.'

Moments later Angie was running up to Emma's house, leaving Martin to pay for the taxi as she unlocked the front door. 'I'm here,' she called going into the sitting room.

Emma came out of the kitchen, white-faced and starey-eyed. 'Ssh,' she cautioned, folding Angie into an embrace. 'The boys are asleep. We don't want to wake them. Is Martin coming in?'

Angie looked over her shoulder and saw the taxi turning around to drive away. A moment later Martin came through the door, and Angie quickly introduced them.

'I've made some tea,' Emma told them. 'Let's go into the kitchen.'

Doing her best to stay sane, Angie said, 'Have you heard from Lois or Melvin? Why have they gone to the police?'

'They had to,' Emma replied wretchedly. 'Things have been happening… Oh God, there's no easy way to say this… Grace has been contacted by someone online and that's where they think she's gone.'

Angie reeled. This was even worse than she'd thought, so much worse that she could feel her control slipping. Shalik had got to Grace. 'Who is it?' she demanded. 'If that evil man has…'

Emma said, 'Apparently it's someone called Anya.' Angie stiffened. Hadn't Grace asked her about someone called Anya? 'She told Grace she could earn some money by acting,' Emma continued, 'and Grace went along with it, because this woman said she was a friend of Steve's.'

Angie's anguish twisted the very core of her. She hadn't been paying attention. This was her fault. 'Is she connected to Shalik?' she made herself ask again.

'All I can tell you,' Emma replied, 'is that she, whoever she is, set up an audition for Grace saying she could earn lots of money if she got the part… They took over her phone contract, even paid fifty quid into her account.'

Angie stared at her in disbelief.

'So she's gone for the audition?' Martin prompted.

Emma said shakily, 'She went the night she and Lois stayed late at some party, except there wasn't a party. Apparently there was a studio, but Lois didn't see it because she was locked in some kind of waiting room. She couldn't go anywhere or ring anyone until they eventually let Grace out.'

Angie was so tense, so terrified she could hardly speak. 'What did they do to her?' she asked hoarsely.

'All the girls knew at the time was that Grace had been given some sort of drug, we're guessing Rohypnol, but they were certain she hadn't been molested. Later, Grace received photos that she and Lois had taken, they thought for a portfolio, but they'd been mocked up with some other woman's naked body to make it look like it was hers. This Anya said it would be posted online if she didn't show up tonight.'

Angie was so appalled, so afraid that she couldn't make herself think.

'Does Lois know where Grace was supposed to go?' Martin asked.

Emma shook her head. 'She only knows where they went the last time, which is why we called the police. It's the old WCA studios on Hereford Road, but that place went out of business over a year ago.'

'We need to go there,' Angie cried, spinning round to Martin.

Holding her with one hand, he took out his phone with the other and made a call. After explaining who he was to the person at the other end, he asked to be put through to the officers dealing with Lois... 'What's Lois's surname?' he asked Angie.

'Holbrook,' she told him.

He repeated it, and was quickly put through to someone else. 'Barry? Yes, it's Martin. I'm with Grace Watts's mother. Can you give me an update?' He listened, eyes on Angie, until he said, 'OK, thanks. Call me as soon as there's any news.' After ringing off he said, 'Units have already been despatched to the WCA centre and Lois and her mother are still talking to detectives.'

'So we don't know yet,' Angie said raggedly, 'if that's where she went tonight?'

He shook his head. 'Barry, who I just spoke to, is an old school-friend. He'll keep us up to date with everything and let us know what we should do. For the moment he's recommending we stay put here in case she comes back or tries to call... You need to charge your phone,' he reminded Angie.

Scrabbling for it, she plugged it into Emma's charger on the worktop and prayed with all her heart there would be a message from Grace when it fired up.

There wasn't, and her heart clenched in horror as her imagination took hold. 'I can't just sit here doing nothing,' she pleaded with Martin. 'What if they've taken her somewhere else?' She'd heard about how young girls were trafficked between gangs, plied with drugs to make them compliant... The very thought of her baby at the mercy of such evil, being abused by sadists until they'd ruined her for ever...

'I know this is Shalik,' she said through gritted teeth. 'We have to find him,' she told Martin, shaking with the need to act.

Emma snatched up her mobile as it rang and put it on speaker. 'Melvin, what's happening?' she demanded.

'I'm bringing Lois and her mother back with me,' he replied. 'She's told them everything she can for tonight.'

For tonight? They thought this was going to go on...

'What about Grace?' Emma asked.

'No news yet.'

Angie's fist was pressed so tight to her mouth her teeth were puncturing her lips. She jumped as Martin's phone rang and watched as he quickly clicked on.

'Barry,' he said shortly. As he listened the intensity of his eyes deepened and his free hand tightened into a fist.

'What is it?' Angie cried.

'The Centre is deserted,' he replied. 'No sign of her.'

'They need to find Shalik,' she shouted. 'Please tell them...'

Martin's hand went up as he registered what else was being said. 'They heard you,' he told her as he rang off. 'Apparently someone's already been to his house, but no one's at home.'

Grabbing her phone, Angie scrolled to Shalik's number. 'I know you have her,' she yelled at the voicemail. 'You won't get away with it, you vile, sick bastard. Bring her back right now or I swear on her life I will find you and kill you.' Ringing off, she quickly connected to Craig.

'Who are you calling?' Emma asked.

'I have to speak to Sasha,' Angie explained. To Martin, she said, 'She's a girl I think might have worked for Shalik.' She listened to the ringtone pulsing its way towards voicemail. Before it got there, Craig's voice came down the line.

'Craig, it's Angie. I need to speak to Sasha. Is she with you?'

He didn't answer, but a moment later she heard Sasha's sleepy voice. 'Angie? Is everything all right?'

'No, it isn't. My daughter Grace has disappeared and we

think… I need you to tell me where we can find the people who held you. Do you have an address, or any kind of location?'

Sounding more awake now, Sasha said, 'All I can tell you is where I left last time. Is old bingo hall. I not know exact address, but is looking deserted from outside with boards on windows and there is small church next door.'

'Thank you,' Angie gasped. 'I'll pass this to the police. Can they call you?'

'No, no, please. I not want anyone to know where I am.'

Now wasn't the time to argue, so Angie thanked her again and rang off.

Martin was already connecting to his contact at the station, ready to hand the phone to Angie. Before she could take it, a small voice came from the doorway.

'Mum?'

Angie spun round, and seeing Zac she quickly went to scoop him up. 'What are you doing out of bed?' she asked, doing her best to sound calm.

'I heard lots of noise,' he said sleepily. He rubbed his eyes and pressed his hands to her cheeks. 'Why are you looking for Grace?' he asked.

Angie struggled for an answer.

'I know where she is,' he told her.

Her heart skipped a beat. 'What do you mean?'

'I can take you there if you like.'

Afraid he thought this was a game, she said, 'Just tell me where she is, sweetheart.'

Straightening his legs, he slid down to the floor and ran along the hall to get his coat. 'I'll take you,' he insisted, and digging bare feet into the nearest boots he opened the front door. 'Come on,' he urged.

Obediently, and wildly hoping that he really did know, Angie went after him, grabbing her own coat and aware of Martin and Emma following. Outside the door Zac caught hold of her hand and half led, half dragged her down the garden path. At the end he turned towards the footbridge. 'It's cold,' he said, starting to shiver.

'Zac, where are we going?' she almost shouted as they reached the green.

'To find Grace,' he reminded her.

At their old house he tugged her round to the side gate, opened it as if it had never been locked, and ran on ahead into the back garden. He began jumping up and down, waving his arms, until the motion sensors responded and flooded the area with light.

Angie watched, dumbfounded, as he ran over to the chill-out shed and wrenched open the door. 'Here she is,' he called from inside.

Staggering with disbelief, Angie raced across the grass and into the shed.

'I told you,' Zac said. He was standing beside his sister who was huddled under an old blanket, clutching her head.

'Oh my God, my God,' Angie sobbed, sinking down beside her daughter and pulling her in tight.

Grace shoved her away. 'I told you to get lost,' she snapped at Zac. 'You weren't supposed to say anything…'

Looking up at him, Angie said, 'Go back with Auntie Em. I'll bring Grace home in a minute.'

'No you won't,' Grace raged, 'because we don't have a home.'

'Go on,' Angie whispered to Zac.

When he'd gone she turned back to Grace.

'Don't,' Grace cried savagely as Angie tried to hold her again. 'I want to be with Daddy, not with you.'

'Oh Grace, don't say that. Please…'

'Why not, it's true? I'd rather be dead with him…'

'Listen, I know I've messed up badly and I'm really sorry, sorrier than you'll ever know, but we've got the flat for now, you like it there, and soon we'll have somewhere else…'

'But you still owe tons of money and I wanted to help… She told me… I thought…'

'Ssh,' Angie soothed, as Grace broke into sobs. She kissed her ice-cold forehead and pulled the blanket tightly around her. 'Lois told Emma everything,' she whispered, 'and you mustn't be angry with her for that, because if she hadn't… This woman who contacted you online, she's no friend of Dad's, she's…'

Grace pressed her face into her mother's shoulder and started to cry with wretched despair. 'I miss him, Mum, I miss him so much. It's not fair that he had to die.'

Crying herself, Angie murmured, 'I know, sweetheart, I know. I wish he was still here too, but we know what he'd say if he was, don't we?'

Grace waited, hardly breathing as though half expecting to hear her dad's voice speak.

'He'd say, what are my two favourite girls doing out here in the freezing cold at this time of night? Get yourselves indoors now or I'll cancel Christmas.'

Grace choked on a sob. 'He would say something dumb like that,' she sniffed. 'He was always making us laugh with his silly dad jokes.'

Smiling through her own tears, Angie stood up and pulled Grace shivering and shaking to her feet. 'Can you walk?' she asked. 'I'm afraid you're too big for me to carry.'

Grace nodded. 'I expect if Dad was here, he'd carry me.'

'Oh, I've no doubt of it.'

As they stepped out on to the dewy grass Angie saw a figure getting up from the swing. She heard Grace gasp and knew that she too, for one awful, wonderful moment, thought it was Steve.

Martin was holding a duvet that Emma must have given him. 'Here we are,' he said, coming to wrap it around Grace.

'This is Martin,' Angie said softly. 'It's his flat we're staying in.'

Grace nodded, but she was too cold and weak to say more, as folding her more tightly into the quilt, Martin scooped her gently into his arms.

He carried her all the way back to Emma's where Melvin, Lois and her mother were waiting, and as he laid her down on the sofa Zac climbed on top to snuggle into her.

'How did you know where she was?' Angie asked him.

'I saw her go over there,' he replied. 'I was watching from the window when she went over the footbridge, so I followed her. She told me to get lost, and that she'd kill me if I told anyone where she was.'

'You never do as you're told,' Grace murmured.

'I know,' he said cheerily. As everyone smiled with relief, he added, 'It's my turn to hide next.'

Angie didn't see Martin leave, she only knew he'd gone when she came back from the kitchen with a trayful of cocoa and Becky said quietly, 'He called a taxi before he went over to wait for you and Grace. I don't think he wanted to make a fuss about going.'

CHAPTER THIRTY-THREE

After spending most of the next day at the police station, Angie and Grace returned to the flat exhausted from all the questions and waiting around. It had been a gruelling five hours in spite of how kind everyone was, so finding that Martha had left a shepherd's pie for them to heat up made them want to hug her.

After turning on the oven Angie went back to the sitting room to find Grace slumped on the sofa, her eyes closed and a clump of damp tissue in one hand, nothing in the other where her phone usually was. Angie now knew all about the contract that had been renewed for Grace, and how it had been used to intimidate and terrorize her. The police had taken the phone hoping it would help them to trace this Anya character, although they were certain it wasn't her real name. No connection to Shalik had been established, nor had the ownership of the old bingo hall Sasha had told them about. Though the property had been quickly traced, it had been found empty, although with plenty of evidence of the repurposing of its function and signs of a hasty departure.

It made Angie sick to her stomach to think that Grace could have been one of the helpless girls who'd probably been bundled into vans and driven away at speed last night to God only knew where. The sheer horror of it threatened to overwhelm her; Grace so easily could have shared their fate.

Thank God a thousand times and more that she hadn't followed the instructions she'd been sent last night. Instead, terror-stricken and filled with dread, she'd thought of her dad and taken herself to the chill-out shed.

Was that Steve looking out for them again?

Attempting to sidestep what felt like a juggernaut of what-ifs coming right at her, Angie forced herself to focus on the here and now. The oven was on, they had food, and Grace was safe.

One step at a time.

Going to sit next to her daughter, she took her hand and entwined their fingers. Grace's eyes flickered open. The fear was still there, bright flecks in the clouds of exhaustion. She'd done well with the police, had answered their questions as clearly and honestly as she was able, and had gone through so many photographs of men and women that it had been hard to distinguish one from another in the end. She hadn't picked any out, not even Shalik when his face had come up, but as far as Angie knew Grace had never actually seen him.

'But you're going to question him?' she'd persisted when Grace had left the room with a WPC. 'I'm telling you, he's behind this.'

'We're following several lines of inquiry,' she was told in a manner that made her certain they were holding something back.

Surely to God they weren't as corrupt as Shalik.

Grace said, 'Did you tell anyone at school why I wasn't in today?'

Angie shook her head. 'I just said you were coming down with something.'

Grace studied her mother's face as if she was trying to figure something out. After a while she sat up and put her arms around her. 'I'm sorry for causing so much trouble,' she murmured.

'It's OK,' Angie said, hugging her back. 'The main thing is that you're here now and nothing bad happened to you.' There was no point admitting that she was still ricocheting through the horrors that had been so narrowly escaped. It was as though she was compelled in some appalling, relentless way to see the near-disaster through to all possible ends, each one worse than the last.

'Mum, you're shaking,' Grace said, pulling back to look at her.

'Am I? Probably just tired and hungry. Would you like to have a bath before we eat?'

Grace nodded. 'If you think it's OK to use the hot water again. I already had a shower this morning.'

'I'm sure it'll be fine,' Angie replied, certain Martin would say it was. She hadn't seen or spoken to him today – she'd hardly seen or spoken to anyone, having been so long with the police – but at some point she must thank him for all that he'd done last night. It seemed she was constantly thanking him, becoming more and more indebted to him, and it was starting to make her uneasy.

As she watched Grace pad through to the bedroom she went to answer a ring on the doorbell, expecting to see Emma, or maybe Martha. To her surprise it was Andee, holding up a bottle of wine, as if they were friends who often dropped in on each other.

'Thought this might be welcome,' Andee smiled, 'but if I'm interrupting I can come back another time.'

As Angie stood aside to let her in, she was trying in her exhausted state to brace herself for bad news. 'If it's about Liam,' she said, 'I don't think I can take…'

'It's not about him,' Andee interrupted gently, and went through to the sitting room. 'Is your daughter here?' she asked as Angie came in after her.

'She's in the bathroom,' Angie replied. She wondered if Andee had been to this flat before, and felt certain she must have with her and Martin being on such good terms. Was she aware that he still loved her and wanted her back? Was it ever likely to happen? Did she really need to think about this now? 'Shall I open that?' she offered, nodding towards the wine.

As they went into the kitchen Andee said, 'I've just come from the police station, so I've got a fair idea of what happened last night. I'm glad it ended the way it did.'

Feeling a heady rerun of relief drag her from the juggernaut's path, Angie said, 'Thank you, so am I.' She watched Andee take two glasses from a cupboard, and realized she was glad to have her here. She reached into a drawer for the corkscrew. This was someone she could talk to who understood police procedure, and who would know what she should do next.

When the wine was poured Andee raised her glass and touched it to Angie's. 'It's not easy being a parent,' she said kindly, 'especially a single parent who's no doubt still grieving for a much-loved husband.'

Angie swallowed hard. 'Please don't make me cry,' she whispered shakily.

Andee sipped her wine and waited for Angie to struggle back her tears and do the same. 'So, the real reason I'm here,' she began, putting down her glass. 'I can speak frankly with you?'

Angie nodded. 'Please do.'

'OK, at this moment in time there are certain things the Dean Valley force are not at liberty to share with you. However, they feel it would be good for you to know at least some of them, but in the strictest confidence.'

Angie regarded her carefully, unable to imagine what might be coming next.

'Apparently the National Crime Agency has been aware of this Anya for some time, although she uses several names. They call her the *Regrut,* which is Croatian for recruiter, because she's hired by traffickers – people, arms, drugs – to trawl the Internet looking for vulnerable kids. She studies their profiles, watches what they post, how they react to other posts, until she's told to start hooking them in. This makes her, of course, one of the very worst kinds of human being, but sadly there are a lot out there like her.'

Angie shuddered as she recalled how unguarded Grace had been on social media about losing her father. It had come out today, while they were with the police, that she'd even posted information – feelings – about how difficult her mother was finding it all, how they'd lost their house and how much she wanted to help...

'Grace wouldn't have had any idea that someone like that was watching her,' Andee said gently, 'kids rarely do, and some of these victims are way older and more sophisticated than her.'

'Do you know yet if this woman is connected to Roland Shalik?' Angie asked.

Andee shook her head. 'I haven't heard that specifically, but apparently he is a person of interest to the NCA, which is why you're not getting as much information as you might like about what's happened. Their focus will be on a much bigger, long-term investigation and they won't want local police getting in the way with a lesser case – this is how they will see Grace's, I'm afraid – especially if they're close to a breakthrough.'

Feeling a tightness in her head, Angie said, 'But what happened to Grace was an attempted abduction.'

Andee didn't deny it.

Imagining Grace walking into the lion's den of her own free will, Angie had to take a breath to steady herself. 'And are they?' she managed to ask. 'Close to a breakthrough?'

Andee shook her head. 'I don't know, but what I can tell you is how important it is for things to go ahead without Grace being involved in any way. Should it get out that she might have identified someone in one of the gangs there could be reprisals, and that's not what any of us want.'

Knowing exactly what the reprisals could be, Angie felt even more horror burning inside her as she recalled yelling into Shalik's voicemail that she knew he had Grace. Dully she said, 'You live your life trying to do your best, to be a decent citizen and all the time these dark forces, truly evil people… You don't even know they're there until you're suddenly sucked into their world, and we've already been there once, for God's sake.'

Andee's eyes softened with empathy. 'Everyone's doing their best to protect Grace,' she said. 'I'm told that last night's events have already been struck from the database and the search for Anya, the *Regrut,* as it relates to Grace, has gone away. We must let the NCA do the job their way.' Digging into her pocket, she pulled out a mobile phone and handed it over. 'Grace's,' she said.

Angie looked at it. She knew now that the contract had been extended to maintain contact with Grace, and it had been done in her name, another twist of the knife she'd like to stick in the woman who'd preyed on her daughter. Putting it down, she said, 'With all that's happened, all you've just told me… I can hardly believe how lucky I am to have got her back.'

'You're lucky she didn't go,' Andee corrected. 'And the reason she didn't is because she knew, in her heart, it wasn't the right thing to do. She might have told herself she'd do anything to help her mum, to save you all from the difficulties you're experiencing, but she knew, because her mother had taught her right from wrong, that what she was about to do wasn't the answer.'

Angie could sense the juggernaut again, and took another sip of wine as if this might stop it.

'It can be very hard for children Grace's age,' Andee continued, 'to understand fully what needs to be done to solve problems.' Her expression turned wry. 'Of course none of us would be so foolish as to tell them this, because we're aware that they know best.'

At last Angie managed a smile. 'She's usually such a sensible girl,' she said, 'and I guess in the end she was, but she still went to that studio…' She took a breath as the truth of that hit her again. 'I'll thank God, the stars, the entire universe until my dying day that they didn't keep her then. Do you know why they didn't?'

'The most probable answer is that Lois upset their plans. Having two teenagers go missing at the same time would have created a media frenzy they really wouldn't have welcomed. But don't torment yourself trying to get inside the heads of the Shaliks of this world. They don't think like us, much less behave like us.'

Accepting the truth of that, Angie only wished she knew how to handle this better, as more awful thoughts crowded in on her. 'Do you believe,' she said hoarsely, 'that Shalik was behind this?'

Andee took a breath and let it go slowly. 'I'd say it's possible,' she replied, 'even probable, but there's no evidence I know of at this stage to support it.'

Angie slumped back against the cupboards and let her head fall forward. 'He's out to get us,' she muttered shakily. 'My whole family, because I'm sure he was involved in grooming and corrupting Liam. I can't prove that either, but I just know that he was the puppetmaster making everything happen. And what about Steve?' Her head came up. 'Was Shalik behind that too? Did he order those thugs to do what they did?'

'I'm afraid it's the same answer,' Andee replied. 'It's possible, but with no evidence to link him to it, and no one coming forward to provide any…'

Angie sighed heavily. 'It's about his father,' she said quietly. 'He's getting back at us for the way Hari treated Steve like a son.' Her eyes closed as she wondered how much more of this she could take. 'Can you imagine being so full of hate that you'd destroy someone's life and then continue trying to destroy his family after he'd gone?'

Apparently sensing her fatigue, Andee said, 'Come on, let's go and sit down.'

Following her into the sitting room, Angie sank on to the sofa and watched as Andee refilled their glasses.

'How does Grace seem to be coping?' Andee asked, taking the love seat.

Angie pushed a hand through her hair. 'It's hard to tell when she's so tired – neither of us got much sleep last night – but what concerns me most is how this is going to affect her future. I've been advised to get her some help, especially for her grief, but advice is one thing, making it happen is another altogether.'

Andee nodded. 'I expect you're worried about how under-resourced the mental health services are, and of course they are, but there are other good organizations you can turn to. Winston's Wish is one; its whole *raison d'etre* is to help bereaved children. I'll find out more about them if you like, and send you some links.'

Angie's smile was weak as she nodded. Of course she'd have found the charities herself once she'd started looking. Nevertheless it was good of Andee to take an interest in a family she didn't really know. It had the vague effect of making Angie feel less afraid, less isolated than if she and Emma were trying to cope with this alone.

Andee said, 'I'm going to Sellybrook Prison at the end of next week to talk to one of Steve's killers. I'm not sure how much I'll get out of him, or if he has any idea where Liam is now, but the fact that he's agreed to see me suggests he might know something.'

'Which one is it?' Angie asked hoarsely.

'Sean Prince.'

Angie flinched.

'You know him?'

Angie shook her head. 'Only the name…' She took a breath as the horrific memories came flooding back.

'Sorry,' Andee said, 'maybe tonight wasn't the best time to mention it.'

'It's fine,' Angie told her. 'I just… There's so much to take in.' *And none of it, not even the fact that the NCA has their sights on Shalik, gets us away from how much debt I'm in.* That still had to be resolved, and though perspective was helpful in its way, for of course Grace and the safety of her children came first, it had no practical use when it came to getting their lives back on track.

Rising to her feet, Andee said, 'I should go, but I'll be in touch as soon as I have some news, and if you want to call me at any time you have my number.'

After she'd gone Angie stood staring at the glasses they'd drunk from, aware that the wine had done nothing to relax her; if anything she was feeling worse now than she had before.

Tiredness, she reminded herself. She needed to sleep, or at least find a better way to switch off for a while.

She also needed to eat.

Going to the oven where the shepherd's pie was now keeping warm on a lower setting, she left it where it was and went to check on Grace. She wasn't surprised to find her curled up under the sumptuous duvet on Martin's bed, fast asleep with her face cupped in both hands the way she'd always slept as a child, so she tucked her in tighter and pressed a gentle kiss to her forehead.

Nothing about their lives made sense any more, she was thinking as she returned to the kitchen and picked up her phone. What were they doing here in this wonderful apartment surrounded by expensive furniture and gadgets that weren't their own? Where were they going to end up? How the hell was she going to sort out Grace's wellbeing and somewhere to live, never mind what she owed now that the council tax arrears had soared to an amount she'd never be able to earn if she worked 24/7 for the rest of her life?

Scrolling through her photos, she eventually found a favourite one of Steve with his typical mischievous smile that seemed to say, *I've been here all the time, what took you so long?*

She tapped it to fill the screen and as her emotions engaged around the memories of how readily she'd depended on him, almost taking his strength for granted when times were hard, and how unflappable he'd always been, until the last, tears burned her eyes. 'Are you really watching over us?' she whispered hoarsely. 'Was it you who stopped Grace from going last night and took her to the shed instead? I keep thinking that it was, but is that because I want to believe it, or because it's real?' She attempted a smile. 'I can hear you telling me it doesn't matter, because all that does is the fact that she's safe. You're right, of course.'

Taking the phone to one of the kitchen bar stools, she perched on it and looked at her husband's smiling face again. 'Martin, Martha, Andee, they're wonderful people,' she told him, 'but you already know that, don't you? It's why you brought me here. I can see you fitting in really well with them, decorating this place, in and out of the office downstairs, going over colour palettes with Martin, teasing Martha… You never had a problem fitting in with anyone, and I didn't think I did either, but I'm worried about being here. I could get really comfortable, actually we already are, but… I can't keep taking from them like this. OK, I don't have much choice right now because I don't want to go back to where I was before they kind of took over things, but how am I ever going to repay them?'

His answer was so clear in her head that he might actually have spoken the words aloud. 'Stop this inferiority nonsense, Angie, and let them help. And keep in mind that you never know what the future holds, I might have that elusive lottery win lined up for you next, then you can pay them back with knobs on.'

'Mum?'

Angie started.

'I thought I heard you talking to someone,' Grace said, looking around in puzzlement.

'Andee was here,' Angie replied, discreetly pressing the home button on her phone to close down the screen. 'Are you ready for something to eat?'

Grace yawned as she nodded. Tousle-haired and sleepy-eyed

though she was, the short nap had already brought some colour back to her cheeks.

As Angie began to serve up, Grace said, 'That was Martin who carried me back to Auntie Em's last night, wasn't it?'

'That's right,' Angie confirmed.

'Mm, it's funny, but I keep thinking in my head that it was Dad.'

Angie smiled. 'We both thought it was him for a moment,' she admitted, 'but no, it was Martin.'

Taking out plates and cutlery, Grace went into the sitting room to lay the table. 'So what was he doing there?' she asked when she came back.

Angie's tone was light as she said, 'I had a meal with him last night, so I was with him when Auntie Em rang to say no one could find you.' Was it really only twenty-four hours ago? It felt like a lifetime.

Grace's head tilted to one side with interest. 'So was it like, a date?' she asked.

'No, it wasn't a date.'

Still looking curious, Grace reached for her mother's phone as it started to ring. 'It's him,' she declared, and looked up with a teasing sort of smile.

Angie took the mobile and waved for Grace to disappear.

Grace stayed where she was. 'Please tell him thank you from me for last night,' she said, 'and you probably ought to say the same, unless you didn't enjoy the *date*.'

Slanting her a meaningful look, Angie said, 'Hi, how are you?'

'I think I'm the one who should be asking you that,' he replied.

'I'm fine, we both are, and we want to thank you for...'

'Have you eaten?' he interrupted.

'Martha brought us a shepherd's pie. Actually, where are you? Would you like to come and help us eat it?'

'Well, as it happens, I'm downstairs finishing up in the office, and if you mean it...'

'Of course I do. You'd be very welcome.' Why wouldn't Grace stop looking at her like that? She was supposed to be traumatized, for heaven's sake; talk about a child's resilience.

'I'll be right there,' Martin told her.

As Angie rang off Grace said, 'So not a date, huh?' and taking out more cutlery and a plate she went to set the table for three.

'Please don't embarrass me when he gets here,' Angie implored, going after her. 'He's a lovely man, he really is, but I promise you it's not what you're thinking. For one thing he's still in love with his wife, for another he's my boss, and for another I'm hardly in his league.'

'Oh God, inferiority complex,' Grace retorted in a near-echo of what Angie had imagined Steve saying only minutes ago.

'And FYI,' Grace continued, 'you don't know what I'm thinking.'

Wasn't that the truth? 'Grace, this isn't a joke...'

'I never said it was...'

'... but if you're going to turn it into one I'll ask him not to come.'

'Too late, he's already here,' and in spite of how tired she looked she took herself off to answer the door, leaving Angie to wonder how soon she could persuade her to go back to bed.

CHAPTER THIRTY-FOUR

Almost three weeks had passed since the night of the juggernauts, as Angie often thought of it, and in that time Grace had settled back into school showing no signs – at least not yet – of the trauma she'd experienced. If anything she seemed brighter in her spirits than she had for a while, something Angie put down to her new job clearing tables and washing up on weekend mornings at the Seafront Café. If she wanted to help so badly then best to let her do it in plain sight, with Fliss watching over her.

They'd heard no more from the police since that dreadful night; like Andee had told her, it was as if, at least in the official world, it had never happened. Though Angie remained convinced that Roland Shalik had been in some way involved she was left to hope that some kind of net was closing in on him, and that when it did it would come so fast and so hard that it would shatter his world completely, the way he'd tried to shatter hers. It might not help her with her debt, or with somewhere to live, but it would please her greatly to know that he was being taken to a place where he could inflict no more harm on gullible and vulnerable young girls.

On the whole though, she didn't spend much time thinking about him, it did her no good. She needed all the presence of mind and mettle she could summon to face up to the devastating reality of how much she actually owed. She'd thought it was around fifteen thousand pounds – an amount that had made her a nervous wreck – but apparently it had escalated to a staggering thirty thousand. It was the local authority's efforts to collect the council tax that had caused the massive increase, so now she didn't only owe two full years' worth of tax payable immediately with interest, she'd also incurred a whole slew of other fees for searches and collection that made her head spin when the adviser, Rudi, had tried to explain them to her.

Words like trustees, insolvency practitioners, bailiffs, liquidators, estimates, creditors, had come at her like physical blows, every one of them dealt by a system she didn't even begin to understand. The words she wasn't hearing enough of but clung to desperately every time she did, were debt forgiveness and payment plan. Apparently it was possible for some arrears to be written off completely, while others could be paid over a longer period of time than the original agreement. The adviser was working with the creditors to sort this out as best he could, but the council tax bill and all the ruinous fees that had been added to it, thanks to a bankruptcy petition, were a liability he'd so far failed to reduce in any way.

She'd admitted this to no one yet, not even Emma, and she'd made Rudi swear not to tell Martin. She couldn't be sure whether this was because she was afraid he'd think she was asking for yet more help, or because he might offer it anyway and let her work out a repayment plan with him. Either way she simply wouldn't be able to bear it. It was bad enough that she was still in his flat all these weeks after he'd offered it and he hadn't asked for a penny in rent. Not that she had anything to offer; with her BtG income and benefits still being swallowed up by her overdraft and credit cards, she was left only with the wages Emma collected on her behalf each week and the cash Martha occasionally pressed into her hand.

She was beginning to understand now why people were driven to suicide over debt, for she was coming to realize just how brutally the system worked against them. It used to be credit cards and banks that ran people into trouble, the adviser had told her, but these days it was more often the local authority. There had been so many cuts to their funding that they'd become ruthless in their pursuance of outstanding bills, using every method possible to get the money, and making collection institutions rich off the back of it. Clamping down like this on people already suffering hardship made no sense to her, but she was in no position to fight it. All she could do was accept that suicide would never be an option for her, with Grace and Zac to think of – Emma too since she'd have to pick up the pieces. So one way or another, in spite of the night terrors and pleadings with God that went ignored, she was going to have to find a way of sorting this out.

One brighter light on the horizon was the fact that the council now had a place for her with three bedrooms, a shower room and a small garden. It was part of a terrace set back from a busy road only a mile from the Fairweather estate, and apparently it was in good repair. She hadn't seen it yet because she'd only been told about it yesterday – apparently Martin had vetted two other possibles that had come up first and had told the housing department to go away and think again.

Such power that people in her position could only dream about.

However, if he thought this one was acceptable then she wasn't only going to keep an open mind, she was going to make herself believe in it even before she got there.

She was also going to block all thoughts of Amy Cutler's friends, the Cotters, moving into 14 Willow Close this afternoon.

What she needed to focus on, as she drove away from the retirement village heading back to town, was the phone call she'd just received from Emma. They'd been expecting to hear more from Ivan ever since he'd returned from Carlene Masters' funeral and delivered the disappointing news that the nieces, not the church, had inherited the properties. No one had known until a few minutes ago what the nieces intended to do with their generous bequest.

Apparently they intended to sell.

Not only was this going to mean the end of Bridging the Gap, it would also make the residents homeless, unless she and Emma could find independent living arrangements for them before the houses went on the market.

'They say we don't have to rush,' Emma had told her, 'the nieces, who never went to visit their aunt once, but don't get me started on that, are happy to wait a month before contacting an estate agent.'

'A month?' Angie repeated in shock. 'And they think that gives us enough time? They have no idea, have they, and I don't suppose they care.'

'No, I don't suppose they do, but at least Lennie and Alexei stand a chance of getting somewhere, and somehow I'll sort out my guys too, I just don't know what we're going to do about Hamish.'

Even as Emma spoke, Angie's head filled with worry. In spite of everything she was going through in her own life, she hadn't once forgotten about Hamish and how it might affect him if Hill Lodge could no longer be his home. She'd even considered taking him to live with them if she was given a place big enough, but by the sound of it, the new house was only just going to fit the three of them.

The phone on her passenger seat rang and she clicked on saying, 'Hi, I was just thinking about you.' It wasn't true, but it could have been, for she spent quite a lot of time thinking about Martin these days. Moreover, she was confident enough to tell him so in a jokey manner.

'And there was me thinking about you,' he countered. 'Where are you?'

'Just coming past the garden centre on Radley Corner. Is there somewhere you need me to go?'

'I'd like you to come here, to the office. There's something I need to discuss with you.' He added quickly, 'It's nothing bad.'

Thankful for the last-minute reassurance, she said, 'I should be there in about twenty minutes. I was going to see the house on the way, but I think I'll wait until the children have finished school so they can come with me.'

'Good call,' he told her, and a moment later he was gone.

As she drove on she tried not to second-guess what it was about, for she'd only tie herself up in unnecessary knots, so she focused on Andee's visit to the prison instead. The first one she'd arranged had been cancelled due to an 'incident' Sean Prince had been involved in, so she was going tomorrow and would report back to Angie as soon as she left.

'Just don't get your hopes too high,' Andee had cautioned when they'd spoken earlier. 'It's possible Prince is going to give me the runaround just for the hell of it – it's the kind of thing individuals like him do in order to get a visit – but if I think he might have information on where to find Liam I'll give him five minutes with the benefit of the doubt.'

Andee was someone else who'd become a friend this past

month – well, that might be overstating it, but they'd spent a couple more occasions since the first one, sharing a bottle of wine and chatting, mostly about their children.

She was as easy-going as Martin, and possessed a similar knack for making someone feel as though they mattered. To Angie's mind, they seemed perfectly suited. However, she was coming to realize that Andee was as committed to her relationship with Graeme Ogilvy as she was to the decision she'd made a few years back to give up being a detective. It was still hard to think of her in that role, although there was no doubting her ties to Kesterly CID, most particularly to her old team headed by DCI Gould.

'Hey,' Martin said, looking up as Angie put her head round his office door. 'Come in. I've got some news – not bad – but I think you'll want to sit down for it.'

Unable to imagine what it might be Angie pulled out a chair and faced him across the clutter of architect's drawings and supplier quotations filling up his desk. His expression wasn't giving much away, but at least he'd said it wasn't bad – twice – and she trusted him, so there wasn't any reason for her heart to be thudding like it was.

He picked up a large buff envelope. 'Everything I'm about to tell you is in here,' he said, 'but there's a lot to take in, so I thought I'd give you the salient points before you read through it yourself.'

Confused, she took the envelope, glanced at it, then back to him.

'As you probably know,' he began, 'Jerome, who's been helping you with various legal issues, works for a firm that is headed by Helen Hall, the town's leading criminal lawyer. She's a good friend of Andee's, and it was Andee's idea that I should get her involved in this, so I contacted her a few weeks ago and what you have there, in that envelope, are the results of her team's investigations. I'm sorry I didn't tell you anything about it before, but to be honest I was acting on a hunch and if it hadn't paid off it would have raised your hopes unnecessarily.'

Not entirely sure she was following this, Angie tilted her head, waiting for him to explain.

He smiled. 'What you have there,' he said, pointing to the envelope, 'amongst other things, is a copy of Hari Shalik's will, and on page four you will see that he has named Steve as one of his beneficiaries.'

Angie went very still.

'I'm going to say,' Martin continued, 'that this was Hari's way of thanking Steve for everything he'd done for him, but that's me putting my words on it. What's not in question is that Hari wanted Steve to have 14 Willow Close, which means,' his eyes started to twinkle, 'that you, as Steve's widow, are the legal owner of that property.'

Angie stared at him in shock.

He hadn't finished. 'You are also,' he told her, 'the owner of two adjacent semis on The Beeches, one of which is where your sister lives.'

Angie's head started to spin, so fast she could hardly catch a thought to make sense of it. Her house, Emma's, even Amy Cutler's were *hers*? It was too much to take in. She was surely dreaming, and yet Martin's expression was telling her she wasn't – and if she wasn't then it would mean that all this time when she'd been struggling to pay the rent, when she'd failed to meet it and Roland Shalik had enforced her eviction, he'd been cheating her of what was rightfully hers. She struggled to draw breath.

Martin said, 'Unsurprisingly we've discovered that Roland Shalik's lawyer is as corrupt as he is, so it's lucky we explored this when we did or it could have got a whole lot more complicated.'

Angie turned round as Martha came in carrying a bottle of champagne and three glasses.

'Congratulations, Mrs Property Mogul,' she teased, setting it all down on a corner of Martin's desk.

Angie started to speak, but hot, bewildered tears suddenly fell from her eyes. They wouldn't lie to her, she knew that, not over something like this, nor would they have told her about it unless they were certain it was true. But she couldn't take it in, couldn't even begin to assimilate what it was going to mean…

'Here, drink this, pet,' Martha encouraged, passing her a glass, 'it's the best medicine for shock.'

Taking a glass too, Martin said, 'The people who're supposed to be moving into the house today were informed last night that it can't happen, and Melvin's been keeping a watch on the place this morning ready to turn back any removal vans.'

Angie finally managed to say, 'Does Shalik know that you have the will? How did you even get it?'

'It was simpler than you might think,' Martin replied. 'One of the legal team approached his estranged wife, Sarina, and she was extremely helpful. Apparently Hari changed his will just after he was told his cancer was terminal. Roland and his lawyer believed they'd destroyed all evidence of it, but Sarina not only knew about it, she managed to get hold of her own copy. Her purpose was to make sure she got everything Hari had promised her, because she didn't trust Roland to carry out his father's wishes. As it turned out Roland did give her what was rightfully hers, so she had no reason to challenge the will because she thought her husband was acting on the correct one. She had no idea until the legal team approached her that Roland had cheated you and Steve out of what should have been yours. As soon as she was told she handed over her copy for scrutiny. And to answer the other question, yes, Shalik knows we have it. As soon as he found out, which was a couple of weeks ago, he offered to refund all the rent you've paid since his father's death – he has to do that anyway – along with a large cash payment as recompense. Or you could call it a bribe not to take matters further. The legal team turned this down on your behalf. I hope that was the right decision?'

Angie managed a nod, feeling sure she'd agree once she had a proper handle on it.

Martin continued, 'He was arrested two days ago, charged and released on bail pending further investigations into "other matters". If you're worried he might try to contact you, I think you can rest easy. The further investigations kind of dwarf what he's done to you, so he's got plenty else to be thinking about.'

Martha said, 'He's a liar and a cheat who deserves to go to prison for this.'

'He will, and not only for this,' Martin assured her.

Angie looked at them, wishing she could feel something more than incredulity, or find the right questions to ask, but for the moment all she could say was, 'What about his wife? Is she safe? I should thank her…'

'Apparently she's already returned to her family in Pakistan,' Martin replied, 'but I'm sure we can get an address if you want to write to her.'

Angie nodded. Yes, she did want to write to her, but not today. Today, in this moment, she was aware of a strange, numbing exhaustion starting to spread through her as if trying to shut her down.

Martha eased her into a chair and gently massaged her temples. 'Shock's definitely got a hold of you,' she declared, 'but not to worry, it'll pass.'

Martin's eyes were gently smiling as he watched her.

'You'll be glad to have your flat back,' she tried to joke.

He shrugged.

Martha said, 'We need to contact the debt adviser and make sure Angie's outstanding rent is removed from what she owes. I know we've already had a cash refund of rent paid… Is it in the envelope?' she asked Martin.

He nodded.

Angie looked at the envelope that apparently contained more cash than she'd ever held in her life. She pressed her hands to her cheeks. They were burning hot and she was shaking. It still felt like a dream, and for some bizarre reason she thought she was going to throw up. She took a breath to steady herself and felt Martha's comforting hand on her shoulder again. She couldn't tell them what was in her mind now, it wouldn't make sense to them, or it would make her seem ungrateful, or… She had no idea how they would take it, but she couldn't stop herself thinking of all the other people who'd lost their homes through the roll-out of universal credit, the build-up of debt, the actions of unscrupulous landlords… Yes, she'd been cheated out of hers so she deserved to get it back, but if these past months had taught her anything, it was that everyone deserved somewhere to live.

On the other hand it cheered her to know that there was one person she could help now, and that was Hamish. If she couldn't find a suitable place for him by the time Hill Lodge and Hope House were sold, he could come and stay with them at Willow Close.

CHAPTER THIRTY-FIVE

Andee had been through the necessary undignified security checks and was now seated at a small square table in the prison's visitors' area. It was as gloomy as a medieval dungeon with its high, church-like windows and dark stone walls, and as malodorous as a bunch of unwashed men could make it, with a heavy dose of bleach trying to cover it up. The noise of children shrieking rose in peaks from the low burble of adult voices, while burly, belligerent guards kept watch from a wooden dais next to the security doors. Everything was just as she remembered from a previous visit, when she'd been helping a friend with a case of wrongful imprisonment.

She kept her eyes averted, unwilling to engage with anyone else in the room. Prince hadn't made it through from his cell yet, but she had no reason to believe he wouldn't show.

'He'll enjoy a bit of grandstanding,' her old friend and ex-boss, DCI Gould had commented, when she'd told him where she was going today and why. 'He's an arsehole of the first order. The very definition of scum. You'll see what I mean.'

She recognized Prince the instant he came into the room, from the shots Gould had shown her. He was scraggier now, and taller than she'd imagined, but it was the same tattooed neck, scarred cheeks and mean little eyes that had made viewing the photographs so unpleasant. His mouth, she noticed as he came closer, was a home for open sores, and if they weren't puncture wounds and track marks in the creases of his elbows she had no idea what else they could be.

'Well look at you,' he drawled, sitting in the chair that was bolted to the floor and folding his tatooed arms. His unfortunate smile showed chipped, nicotine-stained teeth, and his voice was the rough croak of a heavy smoker overlaid with arrogance and menace. 'Didn't realize you were going to be a shot of eye candy. You might not be no spring chicken, but reckon you're upping my cred around here, so thanks for that.'

Having no intention of engaging with that, Andee came straight to the point. 'Do you know where Liam Watts is?'

Prince regarded her in mock astonishment. 'What, no Hi Sean, thanks for seeing me, Sean? Where's your manners, Mrs Ex-detective?'

She wasn't surprised he'd looked her up; in fact she'd expected it. 'Am I wasting my time?' she asked shortly.

His grin widened. 'No, I wouldn't say that, but I want to know what's in it for me?'

'I haven't brought cigarettes or drugs and I'm not giving you money, so looks like it's time for me to go.'

'Hang on, hang on,' he raised a hand to stop her. 'There are other ways of making it worth my while.'

She guessed from the leer what was coming next.

'How about a quick hand job under the table?' he suggested.

Her answering stare was one of such withering pity that it brought colour to his unshaven face.

He ran a thick hand over his chin and after a moment he said, 'There's got to be something in this for me, or why the fuck would I bother?'

Andee said, 'I don't think you know where he is. You're just bored, you wanted a visit to break up the monotony of your pointless days, that's why you agreed to see me.'

He cackled, apparently enjoying the mindread.

Deciding to take a different tack for a moment, she said, 'Did someone order you to attack Steve Watts that day?'

His eyes narrowed as he looked back at her.

She waited, doubting he'd answer, but still willing to give him the chance.

He hawked loudly but mercifully didn't spit. 'There's certain people out there,' he said, swallowing the phlegm, 'who might suffer if I answered that, so think what you like.'

Guessing there was a threat hanging over his family to force him to maintain silence, she said, 'Did you mean to kill him?'

He shrugged, and she realized he didn't care one way or the other.

'Was Liam with you?'

His beady eyes bored into hers. 'Yeah, he was there.'

'Did he try to stop you?'

He gave an incredulous snort. 'Lady, Liam Watts doesn't have it in him to stop picking his nose, so no way was he going to mess with us.'

So, if this lowlife was to be believed, Liam *had* witnessed his father's murder. 'Were you acting under instructions from one of the London gangs,' she asked, trying again, 'or was it someone local?'

His eyebrows pulled together. 'Who the fuck are you talking about?' he sneered. 'I don't know no London gangs.'

'No, of course you don't,' she said sarcastically. 'But you do know who runs the streets on the estate.'

He leaned in a few inches and it was all she could do to stop herself backing away from his foul breath. 'Lady, you don't want to go poking about in this shit, not if you want to stay breathing, know what I mean?

'Is that a threat?'

'Take it any way you like.' He sat back again, puffing out his scrawny chest as though it was something to be proud of.

'Is Liam still being controlled?'

He snorted a laugh. 'Now how the hell am I supposed to know that, being stuck in here?'

She sat staring at him, aware that being incarcerated did nothing to stop the flow of information.

In the end he surprised her when he said, 'The answer to your question is I don't know where he is.'

At that she picked up her bag and rose to her feet. 'I know you don't care that he has a mother who's been going out of her mind trying to find him,' she said, 'but if you have any humanity in you at all you might give it some thought.'

'Ho, ho, ho,' he guffawed, but as she turned away he said, 'Try talking to Moggie Merino's sister. That silly bitch always had a soft spot for your boy, she might know where he is, if she knows anything at all, but chances are her brain's all messed up by now.' He grinned and mimicked shooting into a vein. 'Know what I mean?'

Andee left, ignoring the wolf whistles and crude gestures that accompanied her across the room, relieved when she was back out into the fresh air.

Minutes later as she headed back to town she was connecting to Angie on the hands-free.

* * *

Angie was in the bedroom of Martin's flat, packing up her and the children's belongings, when the call came from Andee.

'It was much as I expected,' Andee told her. 'He doesn't know where Liam is, but he did suggest I talk to Maurice – Moggie – Merino's sister.'

Angie's mouth turned dry. The mere mention of the attackers' names could make her feel nauseous as, like a grisly conjuring trick, it brought back memories of that terrible time.

Andee continued, 'Apparently the girl had a soft spot for Liam, so it's possible she sent the text telling you he was safe, but we won't know that for certain until we talk to her. I'm guessing she's still on the estate, but those particular streets aren't somewhere I can go unaccompanied so I'll see if I can get someone from the station to come with me. First though, do you know anything about her? Is she someone Liam mentioned or ever brought home with him?'

Sitting stiffly on the edge of the bed, Angie said, 'He never introduced his so-called friends, but some of them were girls. Do you know the sister's name?'

'No, but it'll be easy enough to find out. I just want you to be aware that there's a chance Sean Prince is setting me up as sport for his old chums on the outside.'

Angie's eyes closed. 'What kind of people are they?' she muttered.

'I think we already know that,' Andee replied soberly. 'Incidentally, Prince didn't admit that the gang was instructed to attack Steve, but he didn't deny it either.'

Angie's heart turned over. 'So it's possible Roland Shalik was behind it?'

'If he was I don't think we'll ever get anyone to admit it. Apparently their families – those who are on the outside – are being used as insurance.'

Understanding what that meant, Angie put a hand to her

head. 'He can't get away with it,' she muttered. 'He just can't.'

'One step at a time,' Andee cautioned. 'Let's put him aside and focus on finding Liam for now. I'll give the station a call today, but we all know how overworked and under-resourced they are, so I've no idea yet when I'll be able to talk to Merino's sister. As soon as I do I'll let you know.'

After the call ended Angie remained sitting on the bed, phone clutched between both hands, as she replayed the conversation and Andee's advice to forget Shalik for now and focus on Liam. It made sense, of course, and actually it wasn't difficult, because much as she wanted to know if Shalik had been involved in Steve's killing it would never bring Steve back, so finding her son was what really mattered.

'Hey, you're slacking,' Emma declared, coming into the room. 'One more trip down to the van should just about do it. I bet you didn't realize you'd brought so much stuff with you.'

It was true, Angie hadn't, nor had she imagined that she'd find leaving the flat such a wrench, especially when she was returning to Willow Close. Not that she wanted to stay, she really didn't, but everything seemed to be happening so fast that she wasn't sure she had a proper grip on it all.

'Melvin rang a couple of minutes go,' Emma told her, sealing up another box, 'the furniture's arrived and they're starting to unload, so if you want to make sure everything goes in the right place we need to get a move on.'

Pulling herself together, Angie quickly shook out fresh sheets for the bed and began to make it. A laundry service, sent by Martha, had come to collect the used ones this morning and apparently the cleaner was due at four.

'There's no need for you to do anything,' Martin had told her when he'd called first thing, 'just concentrate on getting yourself settled back in at home.'

Despite his words, she couldn't just leave without at least tidying the place and making sure all the dishes were washed and put away where they belonged. She'd sorted out the remote controls, making sure none were missing, and she'd done her best to replace everything they'd used from the fridge. He'd told her not to, of course, but she'd wanted to, if only to show him that she didn't take anything for granted.

'Hey,' Emma said from the bedroom door, 'leave that for the cleaner. We need to get going.'

Angie quickly finished the bed, carefully arranged the pillows and smoothed out the cover. She wondered if Martin would be sleeping here again as soon as tonight, and realized she probably ought not to dwell on that.

Picking up her phone and bag, she hefted a holdall on to her shoulder and made her way to the door. This was no time to start feeling nostalgic about a flat that wasn't even hers, she told herself as she locked up, although she knew she'd always have a deep attachment to the place for the sanctuary that it, and its owner, had provided at one of the worst times of her life. Now she was returning to Willow Close where she and the children belonged, and where they would carry on with their lives able to feel safe and secure in their own home.

As Emma drove them away in the van, Angie said, 'Have you had any luck finding a suitable place for Hamish?'

'No, nothing yet,' Emma replied, 'but we've still got a few weeks – in fact, it could take months for those houses to sell given the state they're in, maybe longer, so I'm sure we'll come up with something by then.'

Although Angie nodded agreement she knew that Hamish wouldn't do well living alone, and that there was virtually no chance of finding him another place like Hill Lodge, where he was head of the house with his surrogate family around him. 'I still don't think we should tell him anything yet,' she said. 'It'll only worry him, and who knows, the buyers, when they come along, might want to keep the houses running as they are.'

Emma cast her a sceptical look. 'We both know that's not very likely,' she commented, 'but I agree with the part about not saying anything for now. Of course he'll wonder why we're not filling the vacant place, but it won't be the first time we've had a little hiatus so hopefully he won't think too much of it.'

After a while Angie said, 'I'm considering inviting him to live with us, if we can't find the right place for him.'

'Yes, I know you are,' Emma replied, 'but you're assuming he'll want to be your lodger, and I'm not sure that he will.'

Since Angie wasn't sure of it either, she let the subject go and checked who was calling her mobile. 'It's Martin,' she said. 'He'll probably want to know if we've left yet.'

'Tell me,' Emma challenged, as Angie clicked on, 'is this the second or third time he's called today?'

Angie held up four fingers and said into the phone, 'Hi, we're on our way to Willow Close now.'

'Great. Anything I can do?'

Wanting to say yes, just so she could see him, she said, 'I think we're fine for now, but thanks for asking.' He was busy and just being kind, the way he always was.

'OK, well you know where Martha is if you need anything.' As she laughed he added, 'Me too,' and already picking up another call he rang off.

CHAPTER THIRTY-SIX

The first week back at Willow Close was a hectic and even stressful time thanks to all the bureaucracy involved in making the house theirs again, but the joy of being there, of waking up in their own beds, of cooking in their memory-filled kitchen and being able to take baths and showers in their familiar bathroom was the very best feeling in the world.

One of the first things Angie had done with the thousands of pounds she'd received in refunded rent was rush to the pawnbrokers to redeem her wedding ring and Steve's mother's necklace. In a rash moment while there she'd redeemed other items too, all of them belonging to strangers, and had trusted the broker to make sure they were returned to their owners – or hocked again if it was what they wanted. She only wished she could have bought back Steve's piano and the treasured rocking horse, and the many other precious items the children had given up when times had been really tough, but she had to accept that they'd all gone now. This was a new start, she reminded herself, and what really mattered was the fact that they were together and safe in the house that Steve's friendship and loyalty to Hari had earned for them.

Of course her debts hadn't gone anywhere yet, but thankfully the total had almost halved once the outstanding rent had been removed. So she now owed just over fifteen and a half thousand pounds to various creditors, with eleven thousand of it due to the local authority for council tax arrears and 'other agency' fees. She'd heard on the radio, only a few days ago, about a man who'd ended up taking his life as a way out of the same situation. It had just about broken her heart to listen to his family explaining how impossible it had been for him to meet this debt; it had to be paid because there was absolutely no forgiveness from the local authority or from the recovery organizations it employed.

Dealing with creditors was very different for Angie now that she had proof of property ownership to show to the bank, backed up with an estate agent's contract to market Amy Cutler's house.

'You're kidding me?' Amy Cutler had snarled when Angie had broken the news of their new relationship. 'I'd have thought, after what happened to you, the last thing you'd want is to make someone homeless.'

'If I can find an investor who's happy for you to stay,' Angie replied coolly, 'I'll be fine with it. If I can't, you'll still have plenty of time to sort out somewhere else to live.'

The hatred that blazed from Amy Cutler's fierce little eyes might have felt more alarming if Angie hadn't been enjoying her satisfaction so much. Shallow, she knew, but hey, the woman had been an absolute bitch to her, and there really wasn't any chance of her being homeless when she had a good job and plenty of family in town.

'And as soon as you get the proceeds from Amy's house,'

Emma had declared later, randomly throwing a bundle of twenties in the air like it was confetti, 'you'll be free and clear of all that wretched debt *and* you'll have the rental income from mine to live on.'

'I'm not charging you rent,' Angie protested hotly. 'You're my sister.'

'Ben pays it,' Emma reminded her, 'and think of it this way, it might make up for the loss of wages if there's no more BtG.'

This was true, it would, but Angie wasn't going to get worked up about BtG and the uncertainty there until she had to, which would be when the houses went on the market, and that still hadn't happened yet.

It was during their second week back at the house, with all the boxes mostly unpacked by now, that Grace had the brilliant idea of celebrating their return with a party. Almost immediately they set about inviting everyone they needed to thank for helping them during their difficult time, up to fifty people, and later they drove over to M&S to order the food. Feeling uncomfortable about buying so much when there were so many who were barely able to afford a sandwich, never mind a feast, she'd ordered a dozen platters to be sent to the night shelter, and a large box of tinned and dried goods for the food bank.

Martha was the first to RSVP on behalf of Martin.

My dear, the whole family is going to a wedding on Saturday – Andee included. Martin's nephew is getting married in the church at Westleigh. I'm just off to collect Alayna from the station because himself is tied up this morning. However, Darth and I would love to come.

Darth was what she called her husband after Darth Vader – his name was Derek – and Angie had to admit she was looking forward to meeting him. At the same time she was beyond disappointed that Andee couldn't make it, which was nothing to how crushed she felt that Martin couldn't either. Still, at least it spared them the awkwardness of having to turn her down if they'd wanted to, for they had the perfect excuse.

When the day came the house filled up so quickly that Angie could hardly keep track of who was coming and going, but to her delight the lawyer and the debt adviser who'd helped her so much these past weeks both turned up along with their partners, as did the team who'd uncovered Roland Shalik's fraud. Everyone who'd asked her to cover shifts for them was there, most of the neighbours, colleagues from the shelters in town, the food bank and of course from BtG. Sadly Hamish couldn't make it, he'd gone down with flu. However, he'd caught the bus over yesterday to help with the heavy work, until Melvin had driven him back with strict instructions from Angie to make sure he went straight to bed. It was the first time a resident had been to her home, but she saw no reason to continue adhering to the petty rule of no socializing when, to her mind, it treated them as lesser people.

The biggest hits of the day were, without a doubt, Martha who breezed in dressed as Professor McGonagall, and her husband, who made a very convincing Dumbledore. The kids – and there were at least twenty of them – went wild, especially when they were each presented with a wizard's wand from Martha's magic bag.

'There's one for you, Grace,' Martha told her, digging out the last two, 'and for your friend here.'

'Awesome,' Lois beamed, taking hers. 'I have so many spells I need to make happen, I can't wait to get started.'

Martha looked interested.

'They're teenagers,' Dumbledore reminded her. 'They don't divulge secrets to oldies like you.'

Accepting this, Martha trotted back outside to where Lois's

mother was plying the kids with squash, while Emma circled the adults topping up glasses with the wine Martin had sent over as his contribution to a party he couldn't attend. Andee had texted her regrets the day before and wished everyone a lovely time, with a PS that said: *We've located Merino's sister and hope to see her sometime next week. Will let you know when it happens.*

'Mum! Mum!' Zac cried, zooming into the kitchen with his wizard's wand and almost colliding with her. 'Say a wish and I bet I can make it come true.'

Angie laughed. 'I think I've had enough wishes coming true lately,' she protested.

'No, no, you've got to do it,' he insisted.

Obediently, Angie closed her eyes, made a wish and opened them again.

'What was it?' he demanded.

'I'm not telling you.'

'But I can't make it come true if I don't know what it is.'

Grace said, 'I bet I know what it is.'

Angie regarded her suspiciously. 'Bet you don't,' she countered.

'If I whisper it, will you tell me if I'm right?'

Angie considered this. 'No,' she decided. And to Zac, 'If you're a real wizard you'll be able to read my mind and make it come true anyway.'

'I'll tell you my wish,' Emma offered.

Delighted, Zac spun round, wand at the ready.

'I wish I had a million quid.'

Zac waved and chanted, waved again and ended with a 'Pzzazz!'

Emma looked up and around.

'It doesn't happen straight away,' he told her, 'you have to wait.'

'OK, just let me know when to expect it. I'm available any time.'

Off he zoomed again. Apparently it was time for a game of quidditch over on the green – and exactly how Martha and her husband were going to pull this off, everyone had to see.

It turned out to be an actual game – no broomsticks required – although to lend some authenticity they'd brought along a quaffle, two bludgers, some hoops and a snitch in a sock. It was hilarious, especially when two teams formed, Muggles vs Wizards, and as everyone ran and dodged, swooped and screamed, Angie could almost feel Steve smiling down on them.

This was very definitely his kind of party.

It was almost ten o'clock by the time Emma and Melvin, the last to leave, took their kids in separate directions – he a couple of doors down to number 18, Emma over the footbridge back to her semi. Zac had already crashed out on his bed, wizard wand still gripped in his fist, chocolate cake smeared in his hair.

As she gazed down at him, Angie knew that the headiness she was feeling had as much to do with knowing she didn't have to worry about whether they could afford to run a bath in the morning as it did with the wine. She had enough credit on her meter card now to last at least until the end of the week, and then she'd just top it up again. Her thoughts went, as they always did when she was reflecting on how lucky she was, to the thousands of people out there who remained trapped in the awful spiral of debt and poverty that she'd managed to escape. She could feel their angst and despair as if it were still her own. Who was there to help them? Not the government, she knew that much, for they were all about enforcing cuts that made struggling people's lives worse.

She was going to try and do something about it. As yet she had no idea what, but there was simply no way she could carry on now as if her experiences with austerity, eviction and debt escalation hadn't happened. She needed to put them to good use, and she would.

'I don't think I told you earlier,' Grace said, putting away clean glasses as Angie returned to the kitchen, 'but you look amazing in that dress. It really suits you.'

Angie smiled with pleasure. 'Thank you,' she said, glancing down at what she could see of it under her apron. It was made from royal blue stretch lace with a deep V back and close-fitting sleeves, and she had to admit she'd felt good when she'd put it on. She wondered if she should tell Grace that the only other time she'd worn it was when she and Steve had been invited to a cocktail party at a boutique hotel he'd worked on, but before she could come to a decision Grace was heading back into the sitting room to see if there was any more to wash up.

A moment or two later Grace called out, 'Mum? Someone's just pulled up outside in one of those little Audis and I think she's… It looks like she's coming in here.'

Puzzled, Angie removed her hands from the washing up, grabbed a towel and went to investigate.

There was indeed a young, willowy blonde at the end of the path, and a man was walking round the car to join her.

'Oh my God, it's Martin,' Grace declared, excitedly.

To Angie's astonishment it actually was.

Grace turned to look at her. 'Did you know he was coming?' she whispered, as if they might be overheard.

'No.'

'But it was your wish, right?'

Angie's eyes widened. 'Is that what your guess was?' she countered.

'No, not this exactly, but I reckoned it had something to do with him. Who's that with him?'

Angie started as the doorbell chimed, and quickly whipping off her pinny and shoving it and the towel at Grace she went to answer the door.

'Hi,' the blonde said with a sunny smile. 'Are we too late? We are, aren't we?'

Recognizing Alayna, Martin's daughter, Angie said, 'No, no, of course not.' She pulled the door wider. 'There's still plenty to eat and drink...'

'Oh, I swear we had enough at the wedding, but we thought we'd just drop in on our way back into town to see if the party was still going.'

'My designated driver,' Martin announced, following his daughter inside, white shirt open at the throat, black bow tie hanging loosely from the collar. 'We're too late,' he told her. 'I said we would be.'

'No Dad,' she corrected, 'you said it would still be happening.'

Martin glanced at Angie and shrugged helplessly.

Laughing, Angie said, 'Grace, this is Alayna, Martin's daughter.'

Grace's eyes were already alight, as if she'd just come face to face with an actual celebrity, maybe even a goddess. 'I recognize you from the photos in your dad's flat,' she told Alayna.

Tucking an arm through Grace's as if they'd known each other for ever, Alayna walked her through to the kitchen saying, 'I expect Dad will have a glass of red wine, if there is any. I'll have a Coke, and if you'd like us to leave after that we will.'

Angie didn't hear Grace's response, she only heard herself laugh as Martin sighed with exasperation. 'I told her about Grace,' he confessed, 'I mean, only about her love of acting and theatre, which is right up Alayna's street, of course.'

Angie smiled as she gestured for him to sit down. 'I think Grace just experienced a crush at first sight, so I hope they don't forget our drinks.'

He looked around at the after-party debris scattered over the coffee table, in the fireplace and even over the floor. 'We really are too late,' he insisted, 'but it looks as though everyone had a good time.'

'Mostly thanks to Martha and Darth – do you actually call him that?'

He laughed. 'When she's there I do, and I think he kind of likes it. Did they come in fancy dress?'

'They did,' she confirmed, watching him settle into the armchair Steve used to favour for reading the paper. It seemed strange and yet OK to see Martin there instead.

'They always do if they know there are going to be kids. I'm sure if mine didn't love their real grandparents so much they'd have traded them in years ago for Martha and Derek.'

Angie smiled, and looked up as Grace and Alayna came in, each carrying a large glass of red wine.

'Grace is going to show me her room,' Alayna announced, handing a glass to her father. 'No rush about leaving, your chauffeur is sober even if you aren't.'

Martin cast a pained look Angie's way as Grace gave her a glass almost without looking, she was so entranced by Alayna.

When they'd gone Angie said, 'So how was the wedding?'

Martin waved a hand. 'All the usual stuff, beautiful bride, handsome couple, speeches too long, dad dancing best entertainment, granny love over the top – we're big on that in our family, because they only have grannies these days, no grandpas.'

'I'm not getting a great sense of romance here,' Angie informed him drily.

He laughed. 'That's because I'm telling the story. If you asked Alayna or Andee, or the groom's mother, my sister, they'd probably do a much better job of describing it. But it was a lovely day and I'm very fond of my nephew so I'm happy to see him jetting off into the sunset with the girl of his dreams.'

'Does that mean they've already left on honeymoon?'

'About an hour ago, which is why we felt OK about leaving when we did. The disco had just got going and, according to Alayna, I'd already embarrassed myself – and her – enough for one day, so it was time for us to leave. The truth of the matter is she was being pestered by some guy she wasn't interested in, so being the great dad I am I suggested we should pretend I was drunk so she had to take me home – and then we could drop in on you on the way. And here we are. So that's my day. Tell me about yours. Who came and did you have a good time? I mean *you*, not everyone else, because I'm sure we can take that as a given.'

Enjoying how relaxed he seemed as much as the fact that he'd thought to drop in, Angie reflected a moment on the day and said, 'The best part of it was being here in this house, obviously. In some ways it was almost like we'd never left, but I think it'll take a while for us to recover from the last couple of months.' She brightened her smile. 'It was a party Steve would have loved, so I feel we did him proud.'

Martin nodded. 'I'm sure you did.' He took a sip of his wine and put the glass down on the small table beside him. 'I can see why you feel so attached to the place,' he remarked, looking around, 'it's got a great feel to it.'

Pleased he thought so, she said, 'We loved it right from the start – actually we're the only ones to have lived in it.' Her eyes twinkled. 'I expect it's a little different to your family home.'

He tilted his head to one side. 'You might be surprised,' he countered, 'we didn't move to where my mother is now until my sister and I were in our teens. Before that we were in a place quite similar to this, over in Northfields.'

Since Northfields was no grander a suburb than the one she'd grown up in, Angie felt glad to know that their backgrounds weren't so very different after all. However, she couldn't help wondering what his family home was like these days, up there on Westleigh Heights. 'Are you pleased to be back in the flat?' she asked, sipping her wine.

He shrugged. 'Alayna's taken it over for the next couple of weeks. She loves it there because it's in town, Luke too when he's around, but for me, it's not ideal living over the office. It means I spend too much time at work and while I don't have a problem with that, my family are always on my case about it. Now, tell me who else came today, apart from the obvious suspects.'

Glad to be able to say that virtually all the people he'd put her in touch with had made it, she then ran through a list of friends, neighbours and colleagues, ending with the BtG residents. 'It was a real shame Hamish, our oldest guy, couldn't make it,' she sighed. 'He doesn't socialize much, but I think he was really looking forward to it – he even came to help with the preparations yesterday, but we could see then that he wasn't well. I'll probably drive over there tomorrow to check up on him.'

'This is the Hamish you've been telling Martha about?' he asked, picking up his glass again. 'The one you have a particular soft spot for?'

Surprised that Martha had mentioned it, Angie said, 'That's him. Did she also tell you that the houses are going up for sale so we have to find alternative accommodation for the residents?'

'She did. And you're worried about Hamish because of his age.'

'And his health. He has a lung condition that makes it difficult for him to work, but try telling the employment people that. They're forever getting him assessed or cutting his benefits, or even coming up with jobs that are totally unsuitable. It's why he was made a permanent resident, so he wouldn't end up back on the streets thanks to all the lack of understanding – and he's taken such pride in Hill Lodge. He fixes everything he can, from plumbing to electrics to floorboards to actually restoring some of the original features. Finding somewhere else for him is going to be hard, because Hill Lodge really is his home.'

Martin was listening with his eyes down, and for a moment she thought he might have drifted off until he said, 'He's ex-armed forces, is that right?'

'Yes. He doesn't talk about it much, but he was in the first Iraq war and came out suffering with PTSD. It went undiagnosed for a long time, as did the problem with his lungs; by then he was in a sorry state. He even spent a period in prison, I think for drugs, but I'm not sure. When he was released he was right back on the streets until he was taken in by the men's shelter in town. Someone there saw to it that he received proper medical attention, and over time with the right care and encouragement he began to want to live again.'

'And his progress was good enough to get him a place with Bridging the Gap?'

She nodded, and paused for only a moment before deciding to go straight for it. 'I don't suppose you have any flats or studios that might be suitable for him?' she asked.

He sighed and shook his head. 'I don't have a huge portfolio of properties myself these days, and the places I do have are already rented on long-term contracts. But I'll ask around and give it some thought. I'm sure we'll be able to come up with something.'

Angie's eyes shone with hope. 'That would be wonderful,' she exclaimed. 'And if you know anyone who might want to buy the properties I'm sure a really good deal could be done on price, because they're not in a great state of repair and if they do want to carry out some work Hamish could help.'

He smiled. 'No promises,' and draining his glass he looked up at the ceiling. 'All seems to have gone quiet up there,' he commented. 'Do you think they've fallen asleep?'

Angie went to check and discovered that the girls were watching YouTube videos with the sound down low.

'Grace has been showing me some of the productions she's been in,' Alayna informed Angie. 'She's clearly very talented.'

Grace was glowing. 'Alayna's waiting to hear about a job at the Royal Court in London,' she told her mother, 'but while she's here she's going to take me to meet some of the people she knows at the theatre in Kesterly. Isn't that amazing?'

'It certainly is,' Angie agreed, wanting to hug Alayna for making this naïve, star-struck teenager feel special. To Alayna she said, 'I think your dad's ready to go home.'

Alayna nodded. 'Can we just watch to the end of this one? It's only a few more minutes and then I'll be down.'

Leaving them to it, Angie returned to the sitting room and found Martin standing in front of the hearth looking at the family photos. 'No news on Liam?' he said, putting down the framed shot of her and Steve proudly smiling at their firstborn when he was only hours old.

Realizing he'd guessed it was Liam because of how young she and Steve looked, she said, 'Andee's hoping to see someone this week that might be able to help. She's the sister of one of the attackers.'

'Then let's hope it comes good,' and his expression lightened as they heard footsteps on the stairs.

'It was great to see you again,' Alayna said, hugging Angie.

'I'm so glad things have worked out the way they have. You've got a lovely home.'

'Thank you,' Angie smiled, hugging her back. She wanted to tell her the turnaround in fortune was all down to her dad, but sensed he'd probably rather she didn't.

'I'll walk you to the car,' Grace offered, clearly not wanting to be parted from her new idol just yet.

As they started off down the path Angie was about to follow when Martin said, 'Do you know Leanne Delaney?'

Angie frowned as she thought. 'The name rings a bell…'

'She lives up at Ash Morley farm…'

'And has the vintage shop, Glory Days, in town. I know who you mean, but I don't actually know her.'

He shrugged. 'She's throwing a party for her mother's 70th next Saturday. I was wondering if you'd consider being my plus one?'

Angie's heart somersaulted. 'Uh, um yes, I'd love to,' she stammered. 'Thank you.'

'Good,' and tugging off his bow tie he followed his daughter out to the car.

After they'd gone and Grace had finished gushing about Alayna, Angie stood in the middle of the room smiling. He'd made the invitation seem so casual, and she felt sure it was, but she knew already that Grace and Emma would see it as nothing less than a date.

CHAPTER THIRTY-SEVEN

'So what did you make of that?' Andee asked Barry Britten, the off-duty PC who'd just accompanied her on an unedifying mission into the worst streets of the Temple Fields Estate.

'If you mean,' he said, indicating right as they approached the Tesco roundabout, 'did I believe the woman, then I honestly don't know. Did you?'

Andee sighed, and mulled over their short conversation with Alice Merino, Moggie's much older sister. She'd had such a severe case of the shakes, and was so preoccupied by some grievance with a fellow hooker, that most of what she'd said hadn't been worth listening to. However, she'd eventually admitted to knowing Liam, and she hadn't shrugged off the suggestion that she'd had a soft spot for him. But as for sending a text to his mother…

'Why would I do that?' she'd asked, eyes flicking up and down the empty street as she took a deep draw of her roll-up. 'I don't even know the woman.'

Sensing more disinterest than lies, Andee said, 'So can you tell us where Liam is?'

Alice coughed, and attempted incredulity. 'How should I know?' she wheezed, picking a strand of dyed blonde hair from her lower lip. 'It's been two years or more. He ain't sent no postcards or emails, if that's what you mean, and I don't do social media.' She took another drag on her roll-up. 'I never had nothing to do with what happened to his dad, so if that's what this is about...'

'It isn't,' Barry told her shortly. 'We're just trying to find him. So where did he go after his mother threw him out?'

Alice threw out her hands. 'Two years ago, man, how am I supposed to remember something like that?'

'Try,' Andee pressed.

After grinding her cigarette underfoot she said, 'He came here, to me, all right, but he didn't stay long and when he left he didn't tell me where he was going.'

'Are you sure?'

'Course I'm bloody sure.'

'Did he go with someone?'

'No idea, didn't see him go.'

'Can you make a guess as to where he might have gone?'

Jigging about on her heels and still shivering in her fake leather jacket and micro mini she glanced up and down the squalid street again, probably worried her pimp was watching, Andee realized. Quite suddenly she said, 'Can't talk to you,' and began walking away.

Andee said now, 'On the face of it I'd say we've just wasted our time, but she knows something, I'm certain of it. The question is, how to get it out of her?'

Barry cast her a sidelong glance, as though suspecting she might already have the answer to that.

Andee sighed and let her head fall back. 'We made a mistake

in approaching her here, on the estate,' she said. 'The handlers, and Shalik will be one of them, have eyes everywhere, and they won't like any of their girls talking to the police.'

'So do you want me to get her to meet us some place else?' Barry offered. 'Like cell number four at the station?'

'Bit extreme,' she replied, checking her phone as it rang. Seeing it was her old boss, DCI Gould, she clicked on.

'Are you still on the estate?' he asked curtly.

'Just leaving.'

'Did you get what you want?'

'No, but we're going to try again.'

'No. What you're going to do is stay clear of there for the next few days at least, and I mean well clear. Have you got that? Of course you have,' and the line went dead.

It was just after eight on Wednesday morning, while Angie was getting the children ready for school, that Martin rang. Surprised, not only because it was so early, but because as far as she knew he was in London all week, she left the children to continue their breakfasts, and took her mobile into the hall. 'Hi,' she said, with what she hoped was the right degree of warmth for a friend who was also her boss. *Please don't be calling to say you can't make it back in time for the party.*

'Sorry, can you hang on one sec?' he asked, 'I'm just about to go through an underpass and I'll...'

lose you? she added for him.

As she waited she went to check the contents of Zac's sports bag next to the front door, and wasn't in the least surprised to find a kit that needed washing. Tossing it under the stairs to add to the load Emma had brought over last night, her own machine still being on the blink, she made a mental note to use some of her cash to get Emma a new Whirlpool asap. She was also, now she was the landlord, going to send a handyman to fix all the other problems in Emma's house before he made a start on this place.

'Are you still there?' Martin asked, coming back on the line.

'I am,' she confirmed.

'Have you heard the news this morning?'

'No, I'm afraid in this house it's either video games, loud music or grumbling to get us going for the day. Why?'

'You need to put it on,' he instructed. 'Maybe not anywhere near Grace for the moment, but there have been a series of dawn raids across the country in something called Operation Springtime. Twenty arrests so far, apparently, and one of the mugshots they keep flashing up is this Anya – aka Besjana Ajeti from Albania.'

Turning cold at the thought of this evil woman, Angie said, 'Please tell me they've got her too.'

'It seems they have. The operation is being compared to the one in Rotherham, but that's the news channels; I don't know if the police consider it in the same light, because this one seems to have a more international reach. But what's important for you, for Grace and all the other kids who've been groomed by these bastards, is that the ring has been broken.'

Angie was sitting on the bottom stair by now, taking it in and already knowing what she was going to ask next.

As though reading her mind, he said, 'Yes, Shalik's properties were amongst those raided, and as far as I know he's in a police cell right now, facing serious charges such as trafficking, pimping, grooming, it goes on. And this in addition to the fraud he's already up for. I don't know if they'll ever be able to connect him to Steve's murder, but you can be sure that POS is going down for a very long time.'

Angie was waiting for the relief and satisfaction to sink in, to get a sense of justice taking its course, but right now all she seemed to be feeling was an overriding revulsion tinged with sadness, not only for the pointless loss of Steve's life, but for Hari. 'His father didn't deserve a son like that,' she said quietly.

'No, he didn't,' Martin agreed. 'If he'd known what was happening – and it must have been going on while Hari was alive – I'm sure he'd have disowned him, probably even shopped him.'

Suspecting he was right, Angie decided to move away from the subject for now. She needed to think it through later, while she was alone, and she didn't want Shalik swamping any more of this phone call. 'Grace is seeing Alayna after school,' she told him.

Going with it, Martin said, 'So I hear. I've warned my daughter not to be overwhelming, because she can be quite good at that.'

'Grace is already overwhelmed and loving every minute of it. Lois is going along too. You know, you have a very special daughter who definitely takes after her father, because she hasn't thought twice about taking a couple of wannabes under her wing and helping them to grow in confidence and feel OK about having dreams.'

There was only silence at the other end.

'Hello?' she said.

Nothing.

'Hello?' she said again. 'Are you there?'

Still nothing.

Realizing they'd lost the connection she clicked off, and was about to go and hurry the children along when he rang again.

'Sorry about that,' he said. 'I'm heading into an underground car park, but tell me first, has Andee managed to talk to the girl on the Temple Fields estate?'

Angie said, 'I haven't heard anything yet. Have you?'

'No, nothing, but with what's going on over there right now

I expect Andee's decided to stay well away for the time being. Next question, are we still on for Saturday?'

'Of course. I'm looking forward to it.'

'Me too. I'll call when I'm back and arrange a time to pick you up.'

Later in the day Angie was at Hill Lodge with Hamish struggling to keep her mind off Martin and Shalik and all that was going on in her world, while watching the videos Sasha had posted on YouTube of Craig playing in his new band.

'He's not bad, is he?' Hamish commented proudly. 'A lot better than he was a few months ago, anyway.'

This actually was true. 'There's obviously something about your favourite oldies that works for him,' Angie smiled, touched by how impassioned Craig looked as he performed. This was new too, for he'd rarely shown emotion before.

'It seems to be working out well for him up there in Bristol,' Hamish said, closing down his laptop, 'and that's what really counts.'

Sensing how much he was missing Craig, Angie wished she could tell him that she was bringing in another lonely and vulnerable young lad who needed a father figure. She was sure Hamish would willingly rise to it, but for the time being there wasn't anything she could say about newcomers.

'And what about you?' he asked suddenly, visibly brightening. 'If you don't mind me saying, you're looking very… sparkly.'

'Sparkly?' she laughed.

'In the eyes. I was getting quite worried about you for a while, you just didn't seem yourself. Not that it's any of my business, but I got a feeling that things had changed when you decided to have a party, and not only with the house. By the way, I wish you'd told me what you were going through, because I could have been a better friend.'

'You're always a good friend.'

Clearly pleased by that, he carried on as if she hadn't spoken. 'And now look at you today, pretty as a picture and mind not quite on what we're doing, so I've been trying to work out if you're in love, or maybe you've found that lad of yours?' His eyebrows raised expectantly, making Angie wonder if he was hoping Liam might one day be his next surrogate son.

Smiling, she said, 'Neither, but someone is trying to help with Liam, and I'm hoping to have some news soon.'

'That's good to hear. Very good. I know how much it's troubled you not knowing where he is.' He gave an affectionate sigh. 'You're a good mother, Angie. There are plenty out there who wouldn't care after what happened, but you're definitely not one of them.'

'And you're a good friend,' she told him again, really wanting him to believe it. 'To me, to Craig, to everyone who comes here. You've made a big difference in a lot of people's lives.'

He seemed touched by her words, but quickly moved on. 'I'll put the kettle on if you have time for a cuppa before you go. Did you bring the fundraising files with you? I've had some ideas I think might work.'

As Angie tried to conjure up an excuse for why she didn't have them, her phone jingled with a text.

You'll have heard by now about the NCA raids on the estate, but I've already spoken to Merino's sister and I'm sure she can help us. I'm hoping to speak to her again next week once all the chaos has died down.

See you at the party on Saturday. Andee x

Angie looked up to find Hamish regarding her, his smile full of fondness. 'Yes, definitely sparkly,' he told her with a little chuckle.

CHAPTER THIRTY-EIGHT

Martin arrived at eight on Saturday evening as promised, pulling up behind Angie's van in his smart BMW, on the phone as usual, although he'd rung off by the time she reached the end of the path to get in the car. She was wearing a black, figure-hugging, over-the-knee silk dress, the classiest (she hoped) and most expensive she'd ever owned, with matching three-inch-high sling-backs and a small silver cross-body bag. Grace and Emma had helped to style her, using Emma's credit card for now, trawling just about every online store there was and ordering practically everything they liked the look of, leaving her to return all the discards on Monday.

'Wow,' Martin murmured as she slipped in beside him. 'You look lovely.'

Glowing and tensed up with nerves, it only occurred to her then that maybe she should have invited him in for a drink. Too late, he was already turning around to drive back out of the street.

To her dismay she couldn't seem to think of a sensible word to say, so she embarrassed herself with, 'You look lovely too.'

His blue eyes shone with humour as he cast her a glance. 'How's everything at home?' he asked. 'Kids still settling in well?'

'It's almost like we never left,' she replied. 'For them, anyway, but I'm getting there. Did you have a good week in London?'

'Mm, not bad. It was worth going, which isn't always the case. Excuse me,' he said, as his phone rang and Alayna's name came up on the screen.

'Hey Dad, just wondering if you're coming back to the flat tonight or going to Grandma's?'

'I don't know. I haven't really thought about it. Why?'

'Because I'm inviting a couple of friends over later, and if you're not staying here they can.'

He shrugged. 'I guess that's my decision made, then. Say hi to Angie.'

'Oh, hi Angie. How are you?'

'I'm good, thanks. And you?'

'Yeah, cool. We had a great time at the theatre on Wednesday, did Grace tell you?'

Angie smiled. 'I haven't heard about anything else since. It was really kind of you to introduce her to so many people.'

'Oh, they loved her – and Lois. I think a few things could work out for them there. So where are you guys going?'

'I already told you,' Martin replied. 'To Wilkie's birthday party at Leanne's.'

'Oh yeah, amazing. She is so cool. Do you know Wilkie, Angie?'

'I've read about her in the papers from time to time,' Angie replied. 'She's a bit of an activist.'

Alayna laughed. 'That's one way of describing her; firebrand is another, adorable is another. Whatever, she's definitely a character and I'm sure you'll love her. Is Mum going, Dad?'

'I should think so. She and Leanne are good friends. If you're intending to raid my wine store tonight then make sure it's not the good stuff.'

'You are so mean. Hope you guys have a great time. Love to Mum if you see her. Love to Grace, Angie. Tell her I'll call her on Monday.'

No sooner had she rung off than Martin's phone rang again. This time it was someone called Carol.

'My mother,' he explained, and clicked on. 'I'm on my way,' he told her, clearly anticipating her question.

'Good, everyone's asking where you are. You're bringing Angie, aren't you?'

'Of course. I told you I was.'

'Excellent, we're all looking forward to meeting her, so hurry up and get here. I don't know why you always have to be late.'

As he rang off he cast a wry look Angie's way.

Feeling thrown by what she'd heard, Angie said, 'I didn't realize… I…' She'd been expecting to blend in with the throng, simply to watch everyone else and listen and make sure she didn't drink too much.

'I'm afraid the story of Roland Shalik trying to cheat you out of your house is out,' he confessed. 'Nothing to do with me,' he added hastily. 'Look no further than Martha.'

'Or,' Angie laughed, 'the *Kesterly Gazette*. A reporter called me soon after you did on Wednesday.'

'Did you speak to him?'

'I said that I don't wish my name to be associated with Shalik's and that I hope never to see him again in my life.'

He looked impressed. 'So you won't be going to court when the trial comes up?'

'I shouldn't think so, unless I have to give evidence, but my guess is the other charges will take precedence, and I definitely don't want anyone getting confused and thinking I had some involvement in that. Grace has been through enough, so have I; let him be jailed for the worst of his crimes and we'll get on with our lives. Now, I'm not going to let that loathsome man take up another second of this evening, so please can we change the subject?'

Smiling, he turned left at the top of the estate and crossed a cattle grid to head up a dirt-track drive towards a sprawl of old farm buildings, all of which had been converted into very smart dwellings. Apparently Wilkie lived alone in the farmhouse, her daughter Leanne and partner Tom were in the converted barn, and the lovely Polish girl, Klaudia, who worked at Glory Days, was in the stables with her children. Angie knew all this because Steve had freshened up these residences only a year before he died.

'Before we go in,' Martin said, bringing them to a stop behind a haphazard arrangement of cars, 'how's your guy Hamish? Over the flu?'

Surprised and touched that he'd ask, she said, 'He seems much better, thanks. When I spoke to him earlier he was in the middle of baking a cake, and that's always a good sign.'

Martin nodded. 'Glad to hear it,' and turning off the engine he said, 'OK, ready?'

'I guess so.' She smiled past a twist of nerves. 'Are you?'

He laughed. 'It's not me they want to see, it's you, but don't worry, if it starts to get too much I'll do my best to rescue you.'

It turned out to be one of the most exhilarating evenings Angie could remember in a long time, maybe since the surprise party Steve had thrown for her thirtieth at Crustacean, the best restaurant in town. Everyone was so welcoming and friendly and sorry about Steve, whom they all seemed to have known, and complimentary about her dress and her hair, which Grace had folded into a loose French plait. Andee seemed genuinely thrilled to see her, coming to embrace her like an old friend, and taking her aside for a quick moment to say, 'I've already spoken to Alice Merino. I'm not sure if she's giving me the runaround, but I'm going to follow up on what she told me just in case. The only thing is, Graeme and I are going to be in Stockholm for the early part of next week, so I won't be able to do it until we get back.'

'That's OK,' Angie assured her. 'I'm just grateful that you're doing it at all.'

Andee smiled, 'We'll get there,' she promised, 'now before someone else steals you, come and meet Graeme.'

He turned out to be an extremely distinguished-looking man, darker-haired than Martin, about the same height and age and slightly more serious-minded, Angie thought, but what did she know? This was their first meeting, and she didn't know Martin well enough to be making comparisons.

Next thing, she was being steered towards a magnificent raised stone fireplace at the far end of the barn to be introduced to the birthday girl.

'Wilkie,' Andee said, 'this is Angie Watts.'

The older lady's face lit up with so much girlish joy that Angie found herself laughing. 'Angie, my dear,' Wilkie cried, grabbing Angie's free hand – she was holding champagne in the other – 'I am so happy to meet you. I hope Martin told you how delighted I was when I heard you were coming. You know I was completely in love with your husband, we all were, and now I'm completely in love with your daughter. What a beautiful and talented young lady she is.'

Knowing that Grace had been swept off her feet by Wilkie when they'd met at the theatre with Alayna on Wednesday,

Angie smiled warmly as she said, 'Thank you. From the way she talked about you I can tell you the feeling is mutual.'

Wilkie beamed. 'We have a wonderful community programme going at our newly named Delaney Players. Grace and her friend Lois are going to be very welcome assets, that's for sure. Leanne, there you are. Have you met Angie yet?'

Angie turned to see a tall, shapely woman with enchanting pre-Raphaelite looks thrusting a tray of drinks at her mother so she could take over the hand Wilkie was holding. 'I'm so glad you made it,' she said kindly, 'and you look lovely. Did Gina at The Salon do your hair? If she did I must ask her to do the same with mine. She's around here somewhere.'

Angie said, 'Actually my daughter did it. I'll tell her what you said, she'll be so thrilled I won't hear the end of it.'

Laughing, Leanne said, 'It's Grace, isn't it? She's in the year below my daughter at school. We should have invited her too.'

'Oh, she's fine, she's gone to the cinema with her aunt and cousins this evening.'

'Leanne,' Martin said, coming up behind them. 'Always lovely to see you. Is Tom here?'

'He just popped over to the hotel to sort something out. He should be back any minute. Have you seen your mother? She was looking for you.'

'I'm right here,' a voice spoke up from behind Martin, and standing back he drew in a small, elegant lady with the same arresting blue eyes as his, and an irresistibly twinkly smile. 'Angie,' she said affectionately, 'I'm Carol. I feel I know you already, I've heard so much about you from Martha and Alayna. It's lovely that you're here.'

'Thank you,' Angie smiled. 'I'm glad I came.' She glanced quickly at Martin and had a horrible feeling she might have blushed. Worse, he might have noticed. 'When did you get back from Majorca?' she asked Carol politely.

'A couple of days ago. I wasn't going to miss Wilkie's birthday do, and there are a few things I need to catch up on here. Now, I'm not going to hog you this evening, but I'd love to talk to you at some point about all the wonderful work you do at your transition houses.'

'Of course,' Angie promised, and feeling Martin's hand on her arm she allowed herself to be led away so he could introduce her to more of his – or Wilkie's – friends.

Over the next couple of hours she was sure she met all of Kesterly's finest, from property developers, to surgeons, to lawyers, to antique dealers, to Detective Chief Inspector Gould, and Tom, Leanne's partner, who Martin informed her used to be a spy. She wasn't sure if he was serious or not, but she certainly liked the idea of it.

After meeting Tom she spent a while chatting with Gina, the charming hairdresser, and her husband Gil, who came up to express how outraged they'd felt when they'd heard about Shalik trying to cheat her out of her house, and how delighted they were that everything had worked out the right way in the end. Angie offered condolences for their recent loss – Gina's daughter had died not long after becoming a mother – and they did the same for Steve.

She wasn't entirely sure how much champagne she was drinking, she only knew that her glass was constantly being topped up and that every time she glanced surreptitiously around for Martin she felt even more bubbles of happiness simply to see him.

It was long after midnight by the time they left, having stayed with the diehards spread out around the fireplace on sofas and giant cushions exchanging views, laughing at outlandish stories and drinking more wine or coffee. Angie had loved every minute while sitting beside Martin, who hadn't had his arm around her exactly, but he had put it across the back of the sofa behind her. When he helped her to her feet she gave an embarrassing little stagger into him, but quickly righted herself. She wasn't drunk, she was certain of it, but she was definitely light-headed, and it wasn't entirely the fault of the wine.

The instant they stepped out into the chill night air she regretted not bringing her only coat, but it would have spoiled the look of her outfit, it was so shabby. She really must find the time to buy a new one.

'Here,' Martin said, slipping off his jacket and wrapping it around her. She felt his residual warmth sinking into her, and inhaled the male scent of him mixing with his aftershave. It felt even more intoxicating than the wine.

'So,' he said, once they were on their way home with the heater on full, 'you had a good time?'

'It was wonderful, thank you,' she murmured. 'Everyone was so friendly.'

He seemed pleased. 'They're a great bunch, that's for sure – and what's not to love about Wilkie?'

Angie chuckled at the way Wilkie had got so carried away while standing on a chair to thank everyone for coming, that she'd toppled off straight into Tom's arms. 'She's adorable,' she commented. 'Lucky Tom caught her.'

'Someone's always close by when she gets up on something to make a speech, because she works up such a passion she practically flings herself off.'

Laughing, Angie said, 'Your mother seems lovely too. She has a wicked sense of humour, especially where you're concerned.'

He sighed. 'I won't ask what she told you, I'll just feel thankful that she didn't bring the baby photos with her.'

Angie said, 'What makes you think she didn't?'

He glanced at her quickly, ready to protest until he realized she was teasing. 'OK, you got me,' he laughed, 'but I wouldn't have put it past her.'

Loving that anyone might think she'd be interested in his baby photos, she was about to ask more about his mother when he said, 'Did you manage to talk to Andee about the girl on the estate? Has she seen her yet?'

Sobering slightly, Angie said, 'Yes, she has, and apparently she has some sort of lead that she's going to check out when she gets back from Stockholm.'

He nodded, keeping his eyes straight ahead, and when he didn't comment further she wondered if it was the mention of Andee going away that had quietened him.

She wished she could take it back, or think of something else to distract him, but they were turning into Willow Close now and moments later he pulled up behind the van.

'Would you like to come in?' she offered, her heart in her mouth in case he said no – or yes.

'It's late,' he responded. 'Maybe another time?'

'Of course,' she smiled, clinging on to the last three words, and pushing open the door she stepped out before slipping off his jacket. 'Thanks for a lovely evening,' she said, laying it on the passenger seat. 'I really did have a wonderful time.'

'Thanks for coming,' he smiled, and after waiting until she was safely inside the front door, he turned the car around and drove off into the night.

CHAPTER THIRTY-NINE

Expect a message/call from Carol Stone. She's just contacted me for your number. Martha xx

Angie barely had time to feel surprised, or anything at all, before the next text came in.

Hello Angie, Carol Stone here, Martin's mother. I was wondering if you'd like to come and have tea with me here at the house on Thursday afternoon. If it's not convenient don't worry, we can always sort out another time. Very best ☺

Before messaging back Angie carried out a quick check of her calendar, and seeing she was due to be with Martha that day she decided it would probably be OK if she took a couple of hours off to have tea with the boss's mother. To make sure, she texted Martha and got an answer almost straight away.

Absolutely fine. I'll send you the address.

'So you think it's about BtG?' Emma asked when Angie told her about it later as they prepared an evening meal together.

'She mentioned it at the party, so I can't imagine it would be anything else,' Angie replied. 'If she wants to make a charitable donation I'll have to explain our position, if Martin hasn't already.'

'Will he be there?'

Angie frowned. 'Not that she mentioned.'

Emma removed a sizzling roast chicken from the oven and set it to rest on the counter top. 'Melvin likes a leg, if that's OK,' she said, peeling off the oven gloves. 'He should be here around six, he said.'

'Are you seeing him *every* night now?' Angie asked.

'More or less. He can't get enough of me, and I think we can understand that. The boys love him, in fact I think they might enjoy being with him more than with their dad, but don't quote me. Anyway, back to Martin, I can't believe you haven't heard from him since Saturday. And you haven't seen him either?'

'I haven't been in the office much this past couple of days, and when I am he's somewhere else. Oh God, do you think he might be avoiding me?'

Emma raised an eyebrow, not fully taken in by the mock paranoia. 'I just find it odd,' she said, 'that you go to a party together and have a fantastic time and now nothing.'

'I told you, I think he was a bit thrown when I mentioned Andee was going to Stockholm. He'll probably have guessed it was with Graeme, and I think he still finds it hard.'

Emma mulled that over for a moment. 'How long have they been apart now?'

'A couple of years, I think, but Steve's been gone for that long and there are times when I still miss him as much as I did at the beginning.'

Appearing to accept that, Emma picked up Angie's mobile as it started to ring. 'Ah, speak of the devil,' she commented.

She handed over the phone, and seeing who it was Angie turned her back as she answered. 'Hi, how are you?' she asked softly.

'I'm good,' Martin replied. 'Are you?'

'Yes, I'm fine. We're just making dinner. Emma and I.' How fascinated he must be to know that. Should she invite him?

'OK, I won't keep you, I was ringing to find out if you might be free sometime at the weekend for a lunch or dinner?'

Reining in a burst of happiness, she said, 'That would be lovely. I don't have any arrangements right now, so you choose.'

'OK. How about lunch at the Mermaid on Sunday? In fact, we could all go, Emma, Melvin, the kids, Alayna and my mother if they're back from Dorset.'

Although it was disappointing not to be just the two of them, she still loved the idea. 'I'm seeing your mother on Thursday,' she told him.

'So I hear. Alayna's driving her to Dorchester on Saturday to see an ageing cousin, I don't think they're planning to stay the night, but if they do they won't make the lunch.'

'Well, from our end I'm sure everyone will jump at it, we all love the Mermaid.'

'Great. I'll probably catch up with you at the office sometime between now and then, but if I don't I'll book for... How many are we?'

She quickly counted. 'Definitely eight, possibly ten.'

'Got it. Good to hear you,' and before she could say it was good to hear him too he rang off.

She turned back to Emma and tried to look nonchalant.

'OK, so you haven't learned the rules of hard to get yet,' Emma commented.

Angie slanted her a look. 'Let's not try to read too much into this,' she cautioned.

'Bollocks to that,' Emma declared and wrapped her in a

bruising hug. 'Now tell me everything he said, word for word, and did he mention me?'

Andee rang the following afternoon while Angie was waiting for Grace and Lois to come out of school so she could drive them to their dance class. 'Andee, are you back?' she asked after clicking on.

'Late last night,' Andee confirmed, 'and I've been busy this morning. Tell me, are you doing anything tomorrow afternoon?'

Angie said, 'I'm going to have tea with Martin's mother.' She winced, hoping that was OK. 'Why, do you want me to come somewhere with you?'

'No, but I think you should be at home. I'll talk to Carol and explain…'

'What do you mean?' Angie interrupted, her heart swelling with the crazy hope that this was going to be good news. 'Have you found Liam?'

'Yes, I have. I spoke to him earlier and I'm going to bring him to see you tomorrow.'

'Oh my God,' Angie gasped, putting a hand to her head as she tried to take it in. 'Is he all right? Is he there now?'

'He's fine. He's not here, but he really is safe. He wants to tell you everything himself.' There was a moment before she said, 'Angie?'

'Yes?'

'He's very glad I found him.'

By two the following afternoon Angie was in such a high state of nerves that she couldn't stop pacing, or wringing her hands, or checking the window every two minutes. She'd spent most of the morning cleaning Liam's room in case he wanted to stay; she'd made sure his cherished colouring books were where they'd always been in the drawer under his bed, his toothbrush was in the bathroom with the others and his dressing gown hung on the back of the door. She'd even tried to bake a cake, but she'd obviously forgotten a vital ingredient, and it had ended up in the bin.

Last night she'd spent a long time talking with Grace and Zac, explaining that it was possible their brother would be here when they got home from school the next day. They'd both appeared shocked and bemused, uncertain what to say, so she'd gone on to tell them about Andee's search, and had finished by assuring them that Auntie Em would pick them up unless something changed.

Before she'd left this morning, Grace had whispered, 'When you see him please tell him I can't wait to see him.'

The words had melted Angie's heart. 'Of course I will,' she'd promised, hugging her, 'and I expect he can't wait to see you either.'

Later, as she'd been trying to decide whether to go to the supermarket or not – as if she might miss him if she did – Carol Stone had texted to say how happy she was to have heard the news from Andee.

Martin called just after, to let her know he was thinking of her, and he was sure it was all going to be good. *Eleven for lunch on Sunday?* he messaged a few minutes later, turning Angie's heart inside out with the hope it actually might happen.

Then Martha was in touch with more words of support, followed by yet another bossy message from Emma telling her to calm down, take big breaths and if that didn't work, drink gin.

It was going to be fine. It really was. Andee had told her that he'd said he was glad she'd found him, so that must surely mean he wanted to see his mother. It couldn't be that he was going to seize this chance to wreak some awful revenge on them all for Angie throwing him out at the time of his dad's death, or that he was going to confess something terrible about Steve. He wasn't malicious or vindictive, not the Liam she knew, the Liam before the gangs had got to him.

It was just after three when Andee's Mercedes finally pulled up behind the van. Angie couldn't bring herself to go to the window so she stayed where she was in the middle of the room, having already opened the doors for them to come in. Her hands were clenched tightly at her sides, her heart was thudding so hard it was hurting her chest.

Was Steve watching? Did he know this was happening?

Andee came into the house first, turning as she reached the sitting-room door to encourage Liam to follow.

When he came forward, bigger than Angie remembered and different in other ways too – his skin was clear, his hair was shorter and he had a Prince Harry beard – Angie clasped her hands to her mouth as she howled with more love and relief than she'd ever felt in her life.

'Liam,' she gasped brokenly. 'Oh Liam,' and as she ran to him he dropped what he'd brought in with him and lifted her off the floor into a giant hug.

'Hello Mum,' he whispered into her hair.

They stood holding each other tight, the bond that they shared seeming to wrap itself around them more tightly than ever. He was her firstborn, Steve's precious boy come back to her.

She drew back to look at him, hands cupping his face as she searched his teary eyes, and when she found the boy she'd always loved and struggled to protect she began crying again. He was still there, the real Liam, the innocent who'd been stifled for a while, but thank God not destroyed.

'You look wonderful,' she sobbed, and he really did. Gone was the riot of greasy ginger curls that used to stick to his head with dirt and even blood. It was razor-cut now and tamed by gel. His skin practically glowed with health, no more sores or angry spots, just the cheeky designer stubble that suited him well. But it was his beautiful eyes that reached right into her heart, for they weren't just his father's, they were his own, young and uncertain and eager to be everyone's friend.

'I brought you something,' he told her, and stooping to pick up the paper bag he'd come in with, he took out an oblong wooden plaque and handed it to her. It was a house sign for 14 Willow Close with exquisite carvings of trees and wildlife around the borders and four neatly bored holes for hanging. 'I did it myself,' he announced. 'I'm a trainee carpenter.'

'Oh Liam,' she sobbed, knowing he couldn't possibly have made this overnight. So when had he started it? What had prompted him? She'd be able to ask soon enough, for now she didn't want to bombard him, only let him know that this would always be the most precious gift she'd ever received.

He smiled to see her pleasure, and though one of his front teeth was chipped it was the most beautiful smile in the world.

She hugged him again, feeling small in his big arms and enveloped by how happy he was making her. In her heart she knew a great deal of damage must have been done to him on many levels, and that he had probably changed considerably, but for now, today, he looked and sounded like the son, the young man, she'd always dreamed of him being one day, and that was enough.

Taking his hand she said, 'Let's go and make some tea. Andee, you'll stay, won't you? Please,' she added, when Andee seemed about to protest. 'Unless you need to rush off.'

'I'll stay for a while,' Andee smiled, and closing the doors that were still open she followed them into the kitchen.

After sitting him down and pressing a kiss to his lovely new hair, Angie filled the kettle and tried to sound chatty rather than demanding as she said over her shoulder, 'So how, where did Andee find you?'

Liam looked at Andee and giving him a smile she said, 'Have you heard of Deerwood Farm? It's about fifteen miles inland towards...'

'Yes, I've heard of it,' Angie said, looking from one to the other of them. 'It's where they help children who've just come out of care.'

'That's the Deerwood Project,' Liam told her. 'I didn't just come out of care, so I wasn't one of the residents, but Hanna, that's who runs it, let me stay anyway.'

'It was Hanna,' Andee said, 'who sent the text to tell you he was safe.'

'I didn't know she'd done that,' Liam admitted, 'but I'm glad she did now.'

'But why didn't she say who she was?' Angie asked.

'She needed Liam's permission to let you know where he was,' Andee explained, 'and he still thought you didn't want him.'

Appalled at the consequences of her furious words to him after Steve's death, Angie flung her arms around him again. 'I'm sorry, I'm sorry, I'm sorry,' she murmured. 'You must never think that again, because it wasn't true, not ever. Oh God, I've got so much to make up to you.'

'It's all right,' he told her earnestly, 'I'm glad I went to Deerwood. It's a great place.'

Wanting to know all about it, from how he'd got there, to why he'd been allowed to stay when the Deerwood management were so strict about who they took into their coveted spaces, Angie hardly knew what to ask first.

'Alice Merino told him about the project,' Andee began. 'She had no idea if it was where he'd gone, but she remembered it was one of the things she'd said to him before he disappeared from the estate.'

'I went to Alice when I left here,' Liam explained, 'because I couldn't think of anywhere else to go. She let me stay at hers and didn't tell anyone I was there because we didn't want them coming for me again. After what happened to Dad…' His breath caught, and as sobs heaved in his chest Angie clasped him again. 'Oh Mum, what they did to Dad… I tried to make them stop, but no one listened. I – I heard him scream out my name, and I screamed too, but they wouldn't *stop*.'

'Ssh, ssh,' Angie soothed, tears streaming down her cheeks as she tried not to picture the terrible scene, with Liam looking helplessly on. 'It's all right, I always knew you weren't to blame. I'm so sorry I sent you away, I wasn't thinking straight that day… I tried to find you…'

'Alice told me you'd feel like that, but you said I was dead to you…'

'Oh Liam, I should never have said that. I didn't mean it. I was just so upset about Dad and everything that… I swear I didn't mean it. I love you more than anything. You're my beautiful, beautiful son that I don't deserve, but I'm so happy you've come home.'

'I wanted to come home,' he told her, 'lots of times, but at first I was afraid someone might be watching, that they might do something to hurt you to make me go back with them. So I stayed with Alice, and when I got to Deerwood I changed my name so everyone over there calls me Robert. I work for Sam who does all the maintenance and building jobs. I'm training to be a carpenter, but I do painting and decorating sometimes, like Dad.'

Hoping with all her heart that Steve could hear him, Angie squeezed him again, and gave a splutter of laughter as Andee brought tea to the table.

'Sorry,' she said, 'that was supposed to be my job.'

'It's fine,' Andee told her. 'Now I think you two need

some time together, so I'm going to leave you.' She smiled fondly at Liam. 'Welcome home,' she said softly.

'Thank you,' he replied, surprising Angie as he stood up to shake hands. 'I'm glad you came to find me.' He turned anxious eyes back to his mother. 'I'll still be able to work at Deerwood, won't I?' he asked.

'Of course,' she promised. 'If that's what you want.'

How on earth they were going to get him out there and back each day was a problem for another time. For today, she just wanted to make the most of this homecoming, and when Emma arrived with Grace and Zac, which was due to happen at any minute, she could enjoy – she hoped – the long-awaited reunion of all three of her children.

Although it didn't get off to a promising start it could have been a lot worse, Angie decided, since her biggest dread was that Grace and Zac would be scared of their older brother. However, initially all three appeared more shy than nervous or hostile, seeming unsure what to say, and looking to their mother for guidance. Then quite suddenly Grace threw herself at him and cried, 'I'm so glad you're back. We've been really worried about you.'

Appearing both surprised and pleased, Liam returned her embrace, and laughed as she began jumping up and down with excitement.

Zac watched, apparently unsure what to do, until Liam held out his hand to him. 'Hey Zac,' he said gently, 'do you remember me?'

Zac nodded and seemed so small as he gazed up at his big brother, even taller now than his dad had been. 'You look different,' he told him.

'He looks fantastic,' Grace gushed, squeezing Liam's arm.

'Liam's been living out at Deerwood Farm,' Angie told them.

'He's got a job and he's... Well, he'll tell you all about it himself. For now, I think we should ask him if he can stay for a while before he has to go back?' She made it a question for Liam to answer, wanting him to know that there was no pressure. She was happy to play this however he wanted.

He said, 'Sam's given me the next three days off. He lives here in Kesterly with his wife and children, and he's going back to Deerwood on Monday morning so he said he can give me a lift.'

'That's lovely,' Angie smiled, thrilled that he appeared willing to stay all weekend, and already keen to meet Sam, and everyone else at Deerwood. 'So,' she said, looking to the others for support, 'maybe we can show you your old room?'

'I'll take him,' Zac offered. 'It's exactly the same,' he told Liam, grabbing his hand. 'When we came back we put everything where it used to be, didn't we, Mum?'

Clearly bemused, Liam said, 'Came back from where?'

'I'll tell you another time,' Angie promised.

'Come on,' Zac urged, tugging his brother to the door.

Angie watched them go, pride in them both turning into a sob in her throat.

Grace came to put an arm around her. 'He looks like Dad, doesn't he?' she said softly. 'Your hair, but everything else is Dad.'

Angie smiled through her tears and felt sure Steve was somewhere close by, feeling as much pride and love as she was.

'So this place he's been staying,' Grace said, 'it's good, is it?'

'From everything I hear about it, excellent. He seems to be happy there. He's training to be a carpenter.'

Grace looked impressed. 'Wow! But he always was good at making things.'

'He brought us a sign for the house,' Angie told her, and she had to swallow hard as she thought of all the work he'd put into it, and how awful it would have been if he'd come back to find they'd gone. 'It's on the sofa,' she said, 'go and take a look, it's beautiful, and I'll text Auntie Em. She's keen to see him, and shall we order in pizza for tea?'

Grace grinned at her. 'Isn't it amazing that we can do that now without worrying if we can afford it?'

'It really is,' Angie agreed, and picking up her phone she texted Emma to tell her to bring the boys over.

After that she felt positive enough to text Martin and say: *Eleven for lunch on Sunday.*

CHAPTER FORTY

By the time Sunday came Liam had slotted so well back into the family it was almost as though he'd never left, which was typical of him, Angie reflected emotionally, he'd always been far more forgiving and able to exist in the moment than the rest of them. She had to admit it was taking time for her to adjust to having such a large person around again, but she loved every minute of trying. He was an instant hit with Emma's boys, getting so involved with their and Zac's computer games that his shouts and cheers were a constant source of amusement for everyone. Although he was so much more grown up now, the child in him lived on in many ways, as touchingly and unselfconsciously as the smiles he kept giving her. She was impressed by his willingness to help out around the house, always making his own bed, cleaning the bathroom after himself and never failing to rinse the dishes before stacking them in the dishwasher. He'd learned how important it was to do this at Deerwood, he explained, where everyone had to pull their weight or they were out.

'It's an amazing place, Mum,' he told her proudly. 'I can't wait to take you there. You will come, won't you? They've already said they want to meet you.'

'Of course I'll come,' she assured him. 'You just tell me when and I'll make sure I get the time off.'

Seeming thrilled, he hugged her as if there had never been a bad day between them – and as happily as if he hadn't spent the past two nights sobbing in her arms when Grace and Zac were in bed. He was clearly still traumatized by what had happened to his father, although apparently he was undergoing counselling at Deerwood.

'They told me I should try to talk to you about it,' he'd sniffed last night, using a sleeve to wipe his eyes. 'They've wanted me to come and see you for a long time, but I was afraid to let them bring me.'

As Angie's heart folded around the words, he lifted her face so he could see into her eyes, the way he used to when he was a child. For one awful moment she flashed on the image of him snarling the foulest words at her, spitting them out like venom. Then it was gone and her real boy was back. She took a breath, bracing herself to explore where neither of them ever wanted to go again, but she knew it had to be done. 'The day it happened,' she said shakily, 'before... When Dad arrived on the estate... Did you know how far they were going to go when they attacked him?'

Liam looked perplexed and frightened, but she could see his effort to be strong and truthful. 'No,' he whispered. 'I just heard him shouting for me. They were all hanging about in the next street, and when they heard him they started to laugh. Then suddenly they started marching.'

Trying to push the horrendous images from her mind, she said, 'Did someone tell them to do that?'

His eyes went down. 'I think so. Before it happened Princey was on the phone. I don't know who to, but when he rang off I heard him give the order for everyone to follow him.'

Taking another deep breath, she said, 'Could he have been talking to Roland Shalik?'

Liam looked away. 'I don't know,' he mumbled. 'Sometimes he took orders from him, but I never knew what they were.'

'Did you ever speak to Shalik yourself?'

He swallowed noisily. 'Not really, only sometimes he'd tell me I was a good boy for doing as I was told, and everyone would be safe if I stayed that way.'

Biting down on her rabid hatred for the man, she said, 'Did you ever tell the police you thought he might have been involved in Dad's killing?'

He shook his head. 'I couldn't, I didn't know for certain and I was afraid of what would happen if I did. Anyway, it wasn't only him, there were other men too who used to come from London. I was scared of them all.'

Hardly able to imagine, much less understand the world her son had been sucked into, Angie was coming to realize from these first few steps towards bringing him back to his real world that she would never be able to pin Steve's killing on Shalik. Somehow she would have to force herself to accept retribution in the way it was happening now, as he was tried and imprisoned for other equally abominable crimes.

Maybe it was best that way, for they really didn't want him playing any kind of role in their future; they needed to be as free of him now as it was possible to be.

'I used to have dreams about Dad,' Liam said softly, 'nightmares really, but they don't happen so much any more. The trouble is, being back here, seeing everything the same, but not… I can't stand that he's not here.' He gulped, and sank into her arms again.

As she held him Angie knew that there was still a very long way to go, not only in coming to terms with how Steve had died, but for her to be able to completely forgive Liam, despite knowing he really couldn't be blamed for his involvement. She would deal with it though, and as she did she'd stay mindful of what really mattered, which was that they were going forward together into a far better life for him, and – this was harder to accept when she thought of Steve – for her too.

On Friday Liam had his first encounter with Martha and there was no doubt it was a big success, hardly surprising given Martha's natural affinity with the young. Then Angie took him to meet Hamish, which didn't go quite as well, mainly because Hamish wasn't feeling too good.

'We'll come again next Saturday,' Liam told him before they left. 'I'm going to be spending weekends at Mum's from now on. During the week I'm at work.'

Hamish's eyes softened with affection as he patted Liam's hand, and Angie felt sure he was thinking of Craig and how things were working out for him too. 'It's doing my heart good to see you,' Hamish smiled at him, 'and I can see it's doing the same for your mum.'

Liam looked thrilled and gave Hamish's hand a vigorous shake goodbye to show how pleased he was to have met him. 'He's nice, isn't he?' he remarked as he and Angie returned to the van.

'He really is,' Angie agreed, 'and provided he gets to stay in that house I think he'd value your help with some of the work he does there.' *And even if he doesn't get to stay, I think you two will be good for each other anyway.*

On Sunday they ended up being nine for lunch at the Mermaid, since Carol and Alayna had stayed on in Dorset for an extra few days. Their party was seated at a long window table overlooking the small beach belonging to the pub, Angie between Grace and Liam, who seemed a little shy at first, but began coming out of himself when Martin asked about his work at Deerwood. To his delight it turned out that Martin knew his boss, Sam Baker, and the farm's owner, Shelley Raynor.

'She doesn't get involved in The Project very much,' Liam told him, in case he didn't already know that. 'It's Hanna Coolidge, her daughter, who runs that side of things. The kids who come in after they leave care, they're usually being saved from the streets so they're glad to have somewhere to go, but if they take drugs or anything they're out.' He added with guileless solemnity, 'Sometimes we sit around talking about our time working for the gangs, it's a kind of group therapy thing.'

Before anyone could comment on that, his cheeriness returned and he said, 'The best part of it for me is learning to do woodwork. After I made Mum a sign for our house they got me to do all the signs for the farm, and now we're thinking about taking a few commissions from outside.'

'I'll be interested to see them,' Martin told him, nodding to the waiter to start clearing the table. 'My company has a lot of requirements for signs, so perhaps we can put some orders your way.'

Liam's eyes widened with delight, as though Martin were the answer to everything. 'If you mean it,' he said, 'I'll get Hanna to send you a link to the website we're creating. It's not ready yet, but it should be soon.'

'I'll contact her myself to make sure she has our details. Now, do you have enough room for dessert after that gigantic roast? I can highly recommend the spicy plum crumble.'

'That's what I'm having,' Zac called out to him.

'Me too,' Jack and Harry echoed.

'I'll have the chocolate brownie,' Grace decided, 'and I'm not sharing,' she told her aunt and mother. 'They always order extra spoons for themselves,' she explained to Martin, 'and end up eating most of it when it's supposed to be mine.'

Clearly amused, he said, 'Well, on this occasion I'm hoping to remove your mother from harm's way and take her for a little stroll on the beach.' To Angie he said, 'There's something I'd like to discuss with you.'

Aware of Emma whispering something to Melvin as she got up, Angie studiously ignored them, certain she'd rather not know what was being said, having seen the mischief in Emma's eyes.

As they went outside, pulling on their coats, Angie paused beside the shrine to Daisy Bright, a young girl who used to live at the pub with her parents and who'd been murdered at the age of eighteen. It was a tragic reminder of how vulnerable children could be; in Daisy's case it was a friend's jealousy that had brought her precious life to an end.

What family was without its share of tragedy?

'Did you know her?' Martin asked quietly.

Angie shook her head. 'Not really. I knew her parents of course, Jules and Kian. I expect you did too.'

'I think everyone did. It was a shame when they left, but it was hard to see how they could stay after what happened. Did you know,' he added wryly, 'that there used to be a ghost in the pub called Ruby, and she was so attached to them that when they moved to Ireland she apparently went with them.'

Angie smiled. 'I have heard something like that,' she said, and fastening the buttons of her smart new puffer jacket, she fell in beside him as they crossed the stony sand towards the water's edge. Though it wasn't an especially cold or windy day, only occasional bursts of sunlight were breaking through the low clouds and there was a light drift of rain in the air. Just enough to play havoc with her hair, but she was happy to suffer it to find out what was on his mind.

It seemed for the moment, though, that he wanted to talk about Liam, and she didn't mind as it gave her the opportunity to thank him for being so good with him today.

Martin laughed. 'Did you think I'd ignore him?' he teased.

'No, of course not, but what you said, about the signs… I expect you saw how much it meant to him.'

'I'm genuinely interested to see them,' he assured her. 'Those kids at Deerwood get some pretty good skills training, and I'm all for helping someone to get started in the wider world.'

Angie frowned. 'I'm not sure he's planning on joining the wider world,' she admitted. 'As he keeps telling me, he's not one of the residents. He works for Sam and he gets paid, so I don't see he has much incentive to leave.'

'Not yet, no, but things are always changing, and meantime Sam Baker is a great boss for him to have. He'll treat him fairly and teach him well. I think you're already seeing evidence of that.'

She smiled, because she certainly was.

'Have you talked about his father?' he asked gently.

'Yes, we have. Not in great depth yet, but I know now that he did witness what happened.'

He gave a murmur of sympathy. 'I imagine it's quite painful for you both,' he said.

'It is, but it has to be done and in the end it'll help us both to heal.'

He stopped and gazed out at the misty horizon, leaving her to wonder what he was thinking. Sometimes he was so easy to read, and other times, like now, he really wasn't.

In the end she said, 'I'm guessing you didn't really bring me out here to talk about Liam.'

His eyebrows arched as he said, 'Not strictly true, but you're right, there is something else.' Taking her hand he linked it through his arm, and began walking them on towards the cliffs where seagulls were swooping and shrieking around the waves that crashed and sprayed over the rocks. 'My mother wanted to have a chat with you herself, as you know,' he began, 'but she's not sure how long she's going to be in Dorset. Her cousin's pretty sick and his wife isn't coping well, so she feels she ought to be there.' He stooped to pick up a perfectly intact scallop shell and handed it to her. 'You'll remember,' he continued, 'that I said I'd give some thought to the fate of the BtG residences. Well, my mother is interested in buying them.'

Angie's eyebrows shot up with surprise.

'It's not generally known,' he went on, 'that she's part of an investment group that owns a few properties like it – one of the night shelters in town, for instance, a couple of refuges, the Crescent Moon rehabilitation centre. Actually, it was my father who started the group when he turned the old timber yard into a night shelter, and she's carried it on since he died. When I told her about Hope House and Hill Lodge I wasn't surprised that she wanted to know more. She still does, so she's asked if you can email her the last few years' accounts, the tax returns, the cost of the houses, their state of repair, that sort of thing.'

'Of course I can,' Angie exclaimed excitedly.

He smiled, and turning to gaze into her eyes, he said, 'If she goes through with it, there'll be no reason for you to try to find somewhere else for Hamish. And if she doesn't, she's mentioned a small cottage on our land where he can live rent-free in exchange for helping out around the place.'

* * *

Angie and Emma were so eager to share their news with Ivan the following morning that they drove to the church together, breaking several speed limits along the way as they tried to decide whether they'd now arrived at the right time to tell Hamish what was happening.

'Maybe we should get all the information to Carol first,' Angie said, checking her phone as a text came in from Liam. *Going to send Martin some samples of my signs. Sam says he's a good bloke.*

Feeling a surge of love tangling up with all sorts of other emotions, she sent a message back saying *Definitely think Martin is a good bloke. Can't wait to see you next weekend.*

'I know we can't act as brokers for the houses, as such,' Emma was saying as they turned into the church-office car park, 'but I think we can do our best to make sure Carol's investment group gets the properties at a knock-down price if they want them.'

'I'm sure we'll have Ivan onside for that,' Angie agreed, and clocking his car, she said, 'OK, let's go break the good news. How many Brownie points do you think we might earn for this?'

Laughing, Emma hauled her bag from the back seat, and was just catching up with Angie when Rosa, the vicar's wife, came out to meet them.

'I'm glad you're here, ladies,' she said, and Angie noticed right away how pinched and nervy she seemed.

'Is everything all right?' she asked. 'We have something to tell you that...'

'Come into the office,' Rosa interrupted. 'My husband's there. He and Ivan... Come in,' and turning around she went through the door first.

Confused, and concerned, Angie cast a glance at Emma as they followed. Rosa clearly wasn't herself, and it wasn't very often they saw the vicar at this time of day, so what was going on?

Inside, Ivan was at his desk, looking so shattered that he barely seemed able to hold himself up. The vicar was standing to the side of him, hands clutched behind his back, his normally cheery face more solemn than Angie had ever seen it.

'Come and sit down, ladies,' he said quietly. 'We have something to tell you.'

Rosa indicated two chairs for them to take in front of Ivan's desk.

Starting to get a horrible sixth sense about this, Angie sat down, and looked from Ivan, to Rosa, and back to the vicar. Something was very wrong here, very wrong indeed.

'I'm afraid,' the vicar began, and cleared his throat, 'that our dear friend Hamish...'

'What?' Angie prompted urgently. 'What about him?'

In a hoarse, faintly strangled voice the vicar said, 'I'm afraid he's taken his own life.'

Stunned, Angie shot to her feet. 'No,' she told him angrily. 'No, that's not... He wouldn't...'

Emma grabbed her arm, but Angie shook her off.

'Tell him he's wrong,' Angie instructed her. 'Hamish wouldn't do that... He *wouldn't*,' she told the vicar.

He regarded her with dull, tragic eyes, and as she looked back at him she felt her control slipping away. *Not Hamish. No, no, not Hamish. This couldn't be real.* 'What happened?' she demanded fiercely. 'Tell me what happened.'

'Lennie and Alexei found him this morning,' the vicar replied softly. 'The police and paramedics are there now, but there are no suspicious circumstances.'

Angie's hands flew out helplessly. 'Oh God, oh God,' she cried desperately. 'Hamish, you can't. I won't let this be true...'

'How exactly did he...?' Emma said.

'He hanged himself in his room, the vicar replied.'

Angie cried, 'Why? I don't understand. I know he was upset about Craig going...'

Ivan said brokenly, 'I'm afraid it was my fault. I told him the houses were for sale and that we were trying to find a new place for him to live.'

Angie gaped at him in disbelief. He'd *told* Hamish, frightened him when there had been no need to. 'I thought we agreed,' she raged. 'He didn't need to know until...'

'I went to see him,' Ivan explained, 'we got chatting and I thought... I thought he should know the truth so he could start to prepare himself.'

Angie glared at him, wanting to hit him right off his chair. 'When?' she demanded. 'When did you tell him?'

'About a week ago.'

She thought back over the past few days, flashing on images of Hamish showing her videos of Craig, making tea in his big red pot, seeming sad when Liam was there, but pleased to meet him... He'd known all that time that he was losing his home and he'd been waiting for her to tell him.

'Oh Hamish,' she sobbed wretchedly. 'I'm sorry. I'm so sorry.'

'It was my fault,' Ivan choked.

'Yes it was,' she agreed brutally. 'He needed you to protect him, not *prepare* him. He was a good person, one of the best people I've ever known. He deserved more, Ivan. We'd have found somewhere... We *have* found somewhere. He could have stayed where he was. We've found a buyer. OK, it's not definite yet...'

'His home aside,' Rosa said quietly, 'we have to remember that he was quite sick.'

'What difference does that make?' Angie shouted at her. 'He's always been sick, but he copes and the reason he copes is because we gave him a home, and it was *you* Ivan, who told him he could stay so he'd never have to worry again. Now you do *this*?'

'Angie,' the vicar said gently, 'I understand how upset you are, we all do, but when someone takes their own life it's their decision, their…'

'Don't lecture me,' Angie seethed. 'I don't want to hear about who is or isn't responsible, because we all are, me and Ivan most of all. He wouldn't have done it if you'd just waited, Ivan, and he wouldn't have done it if I'd been honest with him. Oh God,' she groaned, her eyes closing as she sank back into the chair. 'I can't bear it. I just can't.' It was the thought of the days, hours, minutes leading up to it, the preparations he must have made, and he'd been all alone…

'I have to get out of here,' she suddenly cried, and taking herself out to the car park she stood looking down over the cemetery to the roof of Hill Lodge at the bottom. 'Hamish!' she whispered brokenly, desperately. 'Oh Hamish! I'm sorry. I'm so, so sorry.'

'Hey,' Emma said softly, coming up behind her. 'You can't do this to yourself. He'd have known why you were holding back on him, he might even have been glad of it, so don't blame yourself. It's the last thing he'd want.'

Angie sucked in her trembling lips as tears flowed down her cheeks. 'He was more than a resident,' she said shakily, 'he was like family, and I should have told him that.'

'You did. OK, not in words, but in so many other ways,' and as Emma's tears fell too they clung to one another, so broken-hearted and lost in the shock of it all that it was a long time before they let go.

'I think we should go home,' Emma said, her voice still clogged with emotion. 'If anyone needs us they can call.'

Angie didn't argue, just followed Emma to the car, only turning round when Rosa came out of the office.

'He left this,' Rosa said, holding out an envelope. 'It's for you.'

Angie stared at it, understanding straight away what it was and trying to summon the courage to take it. 'Have you read it?' she asked, when she saw the seal had been broken.

Rosa shook her head. 'The police… They had to, in case…'

Angie nodded and mumbled a thank you before turning to get into Emma's car.

My Dear Angie,

We've come to know each other well over the time you've been with BtG so I think you might feel some sadness at my passing, but please try to reflect more on the good times we've shared. We've had some lovely chats on both sunny and wintry days, we've laughed a lot, cried some too, and we've always done our best for the luckless individuals who've come through the residences. There aren't many who care about old down-and-outs like me, most would rather not think about us at all, but no one could ever say that about you. You have the biggest heart I've ever known.

This seems a very poor way to thank you for making the past few years of my life the very best of my life. Knowing you, Angie, has made me see the world differently, not always as a place where men like me are despised or simply forgotten. You showed me so much kindness it was as though light shone out of you and into me. You are a very special person, my dear. It has been a true pleasure and honour to know you. If I'd ever had a daughter I'd have been so proud if she was just like you.

God Bless you Angie, my angel,
Your friend always,
Hamish

CHAPTER FORTY-ONE

One month later

It was a warm evening, as though summer had come early just to entice out the peonies and floribunda roses that Angie had planted one spring to mark seven years of being in the house. They came every April, shyly at first, but soon gathering confidence in the warmth, until their blooms were as welcome as their fragrance. The air was scented by them, along with candlewax and the delicious drift from the barbecue that Liam and Zac were manning between them.

Angie sat at the end of the crowded garden table watching them, a glass of wine in her hand, small flutters of emotion playing about her heart. As a mother it was impossible not to feel happy to see her sons together, taking over their father's role at the grill, while their sister and her friend went about the terrace lighting more candles as the sun slowly sank into the horizon. As a friend, a surrogate daughter even, she continued to feel the ache of Hamish's loss almost as keenly as she had on the day it had happened. She was dealing with the guilt slightly better now, but she knew in her heart it would never really go away.

She should have included him more, brought him here to meet the children, talked to him about Steve and Liam, told him about Martin – he'd have enjoyed what was happening there, she felt certain; he liked a good puzzle. Most of all though, she should have made sure that he knew without any doubt that she wouldn't have allowed him to go to a place where he'd have felt lonely or unwanted, with no one to care what happened to him.

If only she'd been in time to tell him that he actually had a choice – he could have remained in his beloved home at Hill Lodge, or he could have had a cottage to call his own on the Stone family estate.

There had been a quiet service at the church to say goodbye to him; the other residents, Craig and Sasha and several outreach workers had all been there. So had Martin, his mother and Alayna. Carol had said they wanted to show their respect for someone who clearly deserved it. His ill-treatment by the authorities and neglect by the armed forces made it all the more important for him to receive a proper send-off from those who'd known him – and those who were sorry that they hadn't had the pleasure.

Only Angie and Emma had joined the vicar and his wife a few days later for the scattering of his ashes in the small garden behind Hill Lodge. They'd all agreed that it was where he'd want them to go, and after the vicar and Rosa had left Angie and Emma had planted a rose bush just for him.

Later they'd driven to Carol's up on Westleigh Heights, to talk about the future of the houses and Bridging the Gap.

As sad as they'd been on that day, Emma's gush of expletives when the gates had swung open to let them into the grounds of the Stone family home had made Angie laugh. The drive was long and straight, edged by poplars, with gently sloping lawns spreading out each side to the nearby fields. The house itself was an old manor with russet-coloured walls, tall sash windows and a beautifully carved portico surrounding the front door.

The elegance of the interior was instantly apparent, with its circular entrance hall, wide sweeping staircase, and family portraits on the walls. Angie had quickly searched for one of Martin, but if it was there she hadn't spotted it by the time Carol, having greeted them, led them through to an informal summer room at the back of the house. It was clearly where the family spent most of their time, with a trio of slouchy sofas looking as comfortable as feather beds around a glass coffee table, a large TV in one corner and a cosy-looking wood burner in another.

'Please tell me if I'm wrong,' Carol said after she'd poured the tea, 'but I think Hamish would want you to carry on with Bridging the Gap. It does so much good, and with so many of these types of facilities closing down due to lack of funding, it would be a great pity for BtG to go the same way.'

Angie and Emma had already discussed how they saw their future now, and had decided they didn't have the heart to continue after Hamish, but when Carol put it like that...

'My small investment group is still interested in buying the houses,' she explained, 'and we're keen for you to run them. I've already discussed it with the vicar and he's very happy for things to stay the same, apart from the ownership of course, and we might need to do a little renovation here and there to make sure everything is safe and to code. But the important thing is that when I depart this world Martin and his sister will inherit my controlling share so I think we can be sure the properties will be transition facilities for some time to come.'

Angie and Emma hadn't needed much more persuading than that, though Angie knew that Hill Lodge would never be the same for her without Hamish. During the few visits she'd made since he'd gone it had felt empty, robbed of its soul, and full of her failings as a friend – but if his death, and her own recent experience with homelessness had taught her anything, it was how much even the small amount she contributed mattered to those who received it.

The other change that was happening at BtG – or more accurately the church – was the introduction of a new parish manager. Ivan had resigned even before Hamish's funeral, and although Angie had apologized for everything she'd said on that terrible day, he'd never be able to forgive himself, he'd said. It would be too hard for him to face her each day, knowing as he did how fond she'd been of their dearest resident.

She'd made up her mind to try talking to him again in a month or two. For now, though, she accepted that he needed time to recover, and the vicar and his wife were helping him with that. Suicide was an appallingly selfish act, but how could she not understand why Hamish had felt it to be his only choice? He'd believed he was about to be cast back on to society's scrap heap and having experienced it before he would have dreaded going there again. He knew better than most how little help there was for men in his position, old, infirm and with no family to call on. People might react to stabs of conscience with the toss of a few coins into a cap, or some sandwiches dropped next to a sleeping bag, but after that they found it easier to think of something else. Councillors, politicians, those with real power, regularly talked the talk when the news cameras were on them, making promises, setting targets, but little ever came of it.

Hamish had known all that better than anyone.

Angie felt more of a responsibility for those in need now than she ever had, and having been rescued from the fate most of the working poor and homeless would never escape she believed she had a duty to help them. She'd had plenty of ideas over the past weeks, some big, some small, only to find they were unworkable once she'd thought them through. She'd definitely come up with something, though; she'd create a project or find a way to start changing things, and spending time at Deerwood Farm with Liam was proving truly inspirational.

She'd visited several times now and had been blown away by just about everything. Liam had a small workspace of his own in one of the artisan sheds, where he could craft his signs when he wasn't helping Sam Baker with a building or maintenance project. He'd been given a private room in one of the residences with shared bathroom and kitchen, and he was clearly well liked by everyone. Though he hadn't met the project's criteria for intake – he was too old and had never been in care – the Raynor family and those who helped run the facility had taken him in anyway, and had brought out everything that was good in him while slowly and carefully doing their best to heal all that had gone wrong.

Angie was entranced by the place, and the family, but though she was happy to learn from them she knew she could never achieve anything as important as Deerwood, since she had neither the budget nor the land to enable this.

'But you do have the same sort of passion,' Martin had told her only last Sunday, when they'd dropped Liam off after a weekend at home. 'And remember, that place was the brainchild of Hanna Raynor – Coolidge as she is these days – when she was no more than a teen herself. It's taken time, and a lot of it, to get it to where it is now.'

'Meaning I'm thinking too big too soon?' Angie challenged.

'Something like that.'

Of course he was right, in fact he was usually right about everything which was both maddening and reassuring and could sometimes set her on another way of thinking, as it had that day. It wasn't only about ideas, land and money, it was also about power.

'No,' he said, before she could get her next words out.

'You don't even know what I'm going to say,' she protested.

'I do, and I'm not going to run for mayor, so let's leave it there and call Emma to find out where everyone is. If they want to join us for pizza, tell them we'll be at Sandro's in about half an hour.'

Sandro's, whose pizzas she'd once delivered dressed as a panda, and been royally humiliated by Amy Cutler. The very same Amy Cutler who was now her tenant in the semi next to Emma's, although a local businesswoman was due to close on the place soon to add to her small portfolio of buy-to-lets. So Amy was going to get a new landlord, which she'd be very happy about (until her rent was increased, which Angie was sure it would be). And Angie was going to be very happy too, for after the sale went through and the government had helped itself to its share of her inheritance she'd finally be able to pay off the outstanding council tax and colossal recovery fees.

She would also, she was thinking now, as she soaked up the peaceful evening air on the terrace while Martin poured more wine into her glass and Zac carried a plate of burgers to the table, be in a financial position to start something new, if she could only decide what it should be. She'd discuss it with Emma and Martin once she was certain about how much cash was available.

'Can you two just stop now, please?' Emma asked in weary exasperation. 'You've been talking kitchens ever since we sat down to eat. They're really not that fascinating, you know.'

Martin and Melvin regarded her in astonishment.

'Oh, but they are,' Melvin protested. 'If you saw the drawings...'

'No, no, please,' Emma cried, covering her eyes as he tried to pass her his phone.

'That's the trouble with you,' he told her, 'you don't appreciate art when it's staring you in the face.'

Angie caught Martin's eye and smiled at the humour in his. Something she was coming to learn about him was that he'd let anyone rattle on about anything for as long as they liked; if he found it boring he'd just switch his mind elsewhere until they were done. Not that Melvin was boring, far from it, and anyway this kitchen installation project was of interest to them both. But she'd seen Martin do it with others both at work and during the various social occasions they'd been at together, and she was also starting to detect the moments when he became aware that she'd clocked him. They were moments that invariably made them both smile, and set her mind off down avenues she'd decided were probably best not to explore too deeply.

They were good friends who were spending time together a couple of times a week, maybe grabbing an early bite to eat somewhere in town, or, if Grace was with Lois and Zac at Emma's, at a pub a little off the beaten track. They found it easy to talk about everything, apart from what might be happening between them, and maybe for him nothing was.

However, he seemed to like being here at the house, and whenever he sank into Steve's chair, inside or out here on the terrace, she would find herself thinking that if Steve could see him he'd feel proud to have Martin in his place. She sometimes wondered what Steve would make of the fact that the most physical contact she and Martin had had was when he'd tucked her arm through his that day at the beach – and when he'd comforted her at Hamish's funeral. It wasn't that she didn't want more, she did, very much, but she kept reminding herself that if he did too he'd surely make it clear.

'He knows it'll never work again with Andee,' she'd said to Emma only last night, 'but that doesn't mean he's over it.'

'I'm sure he is,' Emma had argued, 'given how much time he spends here.'

'OK, then maybe he's still not ready to move on.'

'Maybe he thinks you aren't,' Emma countered tartly.

Angie hadn't engaged with that, simply because she hadn't known what to say.

Now, getting up to go inside for the baked potatoes, she was aware of Martin's eyes following her, and wished she knew how to let him know her feelings without making him uncomfortable, or herself want to curl up and die if she'd got things wrong. She thought of Steve and what his advice might be, and almost groaned when she heard him say, 'He'd be lucky to have you.'

What would Hamish's advice be? She didn't know because she'd never allowed him to come that close, and she would never stop regretting that.

By the time she returned to the terrace everyone was on Martin's case again about running for mayor.

'Stop, stop,' he protested, raising his hands. 'I swear I'm rubbish at politics, but actually I do know someone who'd be quite good at it if she'd give herself a chance.'

Angie immediately thought of Andee, and was about to agree when she realized everyone was looking at her.

'Yay! Mum for mayor!' Zac cheered, waving his arms.

'Mum for MP,' Liam insisted. 'I'll be your campaign manager.'

'So will I,' Grace piped up. 'Lois and I can go door to door and we'll do all your research…'

Lois beamed loyally.

'I'll write your speeches,' Emma volunteered. 'You can vet them,' she added to Martin.

'I'll organize the kitchens,' Melvin put in, making them all laugh.

'OK, very funny,' Angie declared, scowling at Martin, who seemed to approve of everything that had been said.

'I happen to know that our local MP is looking for a researcher,' he told her. 'You feel passionately about the homeless, so who better to fight for them than someone who understands and genuinely cares?'

Clearly stirred by this, Emma said, 'Think about everything you've been through, Angie. You know more than most what it's like to have a child targeted by criminal gangs; you also know about Internet predators, and ruthless landlords. You've been the victim of debt build-up thanks to universal credit, and you've existed as one of the so-called working poor, so who is better placed to tackle what it's doing to terrified and neglected people than you? You know how you were treated by the system, so isn't it time to fight for those who are still trapped – who don't stand a chance of coming out of it the way you have?'

Knowing she couldn't even begin to argue with that, Angie turned to Melvin as he said, 'While you're at it, you could start a clean-up campaign for the Temple Fields estate. With Shalik and his thugs behind bars awaiting trial it should be better over there, but I'm told the north side is still infested with drugs and crime, and it's disgusting that nothing ever really gets done about it. Even the police won't go there unless they're armed, or at least in groups.'

Angie looked at Martin, and seeing the way his eyebrows were raised she realized that he was in full support of everything that had been said and was waiting for her to comment.

'I'm not having this conversation now,' she declared, reaching for her glass. 'I've had too much to drink, and clearly you all have too, so let's eat up and at least try to pretend we're sober.'

She needed more time to mull things over, to consider what

her role should actually be. She'd already been thinking that getting inside the system somehow, and rousing it into proper action, might be a good way to go. She just had to work out exactly how to get started, to focus herself in a way that really would make a difference.

It wasn't until much later, after everyone else had either gone, or disappeared off to bed, that Angie walked Martin out to the front door.

'You really should consider meeting Miles Granger,' he said, referring to their MP. 'Like Emma pointed out, you've been there. You can speak from the heart, and that'll go a long way with the electorate when it comes to the credentials of someone they're being asked to vote for.'

That felt a bit dizzying – *the electorate.*

'Keep it mind,' he said, 'and we can discuss it another time. Right now I have something else to say.'

Interested, she tilted her head for him to continue.

'After everything you've been through,' he began, 'it's my opinion that you could do with a break, so I was wondering how you might fancy somewhere like the Seychelles?'

Her eyes shot open as her heart did a triple somersault. 'You – you mean with you?' she asked stupidly.

He laughed. 'Well, you can go on your own if you like...'

'No, no, I didn't mean that. I just... Would we share a room?'

'Unless you'd rather sleep alone.'

'Oh no, I definitely want to sleep with you.' Hearing herself, she winced and groaned. 'Did I really just say that?'

Eyes full of laughter, he leaned forward and whispered, 'Be ready to go by next weekend,' and after touching a kiss gently to her mouth he walked to his car, leaving her in no doubt that at last they were both very much ready to move on.

ACKNOWLEDGEMENTS

My biggest thank you goes to Rachel Parfitt who contacted me out of the blue one day to share with me how much she'd enjoyed my book *Dance While You Can*. During our email exchanges I learned a little about Rachel's work with www.edgehousing.org which transitions homeless men from shelters to independent living. I asked if we could meet, and when I understood that her organisation provided homes and even a family for those who were trying to make their way back into the world, that was when this book was 'born'. Over time, Rachel shared many stories with me that were both shocking and heartbreaking – and I only wish I'd been able to do justice to the many brave and lonely people she told me about. We all know these people exist, but perhaps we don't often think about those who do so much to help them.

My next thank you goes to Mike and Sally Zamparelli who run Wick House, a sheltered accommodation facility in Bristol that provides vital support for homeless men. Seeing the work that's carried out there was extremely moving and I came away much wiser and sadder for realizing how hard it is for shelters like theirs to survive.

Lastly, but perhaps most importantly, my sincere thanks go to those who've asked to remain nameless, but who so bravely shared their own stories of how they exist on benefits, and how some of them have ended up losing their homes. Their experiences were truly shattering to hear about and I feel on one level that I've let them down with this book. There is no one there to make things all right for them, the way there is in these pages; their hardship and nightmares continue with no end in sight. However, this is a work of fiction and as such it can only highlight the misery and injustice many of our fellow citizens suffer at the hands of a system that is supposed to support them. Sadly, it cannot solve it.

No, I'm not forgetting my amazing publishing team at HarperCollins – I never could. Thank you so much to all of you, especially Kimberley Young, Kate Elton and Liz Stein for all the incredible energy and support you've put into this book. In steering me away from too much brutal reality I believe you've helped me to create a far more readable and hopeful story.